Beck
&
Call

EMMA HOLLY

OTHER TITLES BY EMMA HOLLY

The Prince With No Heart

The Assassins' Lover

Steaming Up Your Love Scenes (how-to)

The Billionaire Bad Boys Club

Tales of the Djinn: The Guardian

Tales of the Djinn: The Double

Beck & Call: The Billionaires

◆

Hidden Series

Hidden Talents

Hidden Depths

Date Night

Move Me

The Faerie's Honeymoon

Hidden Crimes

Winter's Tale

Hidden Dragons

Hidden Passions

BECK & CALL ...

The man everybody wants

Women can't keep their hands off billionaire Damien Call. The mysterious mogul has it all: fast cars, killer looks, and a brain that just might be his best asset.

The woman he can't resist

Mia Beck loves her job at a PI firm. Her coworker Jake stars in most of her daydreams, so seeing him everyday is no hardship.

The dom who masters both

Jake hasn't believed in human goodness since he worked black ops for the CIA. Romancing innocent Mia is unthinkable, no matter how enticingly submissive she seems to be. Then a case of corporate espionage forces them to pose as dom/sub duo, to catch the eye of accused wrongdoer Damien. No fantasy is off limits for this voyeur—until the attraction the pair exerts lures him to go hands on . . .

◆

A smile flirted around Damien's mouth. "Before we sign my proposed agreement, would you two consent to a test of your chemistry? I'd like to confirm that the electricity you generated at Audition wasn't a fluke."

"Here?" Mia asked, startled.

"We're private," Damien assured her.

"This is your workplace."

"So it is." Damien flashed a grin that made him look more like a pirate than a sober captain of industry. "I thought, perhaps, you'd like to turn the tables on your friend."

The CEO caught Jake unprepared. Lust streaked through his veins and heated his genitals. Damien wasn't the only one with a hard-on then.

Mia blushed and stammered. "I'm not . . . I don't . . ."

"We'll keep it simple," Damien soothed. "No whips. No chains. Just you in control of him. Do you think you'd enjoy that?"

CONTENTS

Chapter 1	1
Chapter 2	18
Chapter 3	31
Chapter 4	49
Chapter 5	69
Chapter 6	82
Chapter 7	90
Chapter 8	106
Chapter 9	116
Chapter 10	133
Chapter 11	148
Chapter 12	163
Chapter 13	171
Chapter 14	187
Chapter 15	200
Chapter 16	215
Chapter 17	225
Chapter 18	233
Chapter 19	242
About the Author	254

CHAPTER 1

WHO got the morning coffee for Discreet Investigations was never up for grabs. Twenty-two-year-old Mia Beck was the three-man office's secretary and bottle washer, so the task fell to her. Her degree from a fancy liberal arts college didn't matter. She was "it," rain or shine.

Today the forecast was rain, a steady, misty curtain that turned the buildings of Brooklyn's riverfront moody and romantic. Fog swallowed the bridge to Manhattan until it seemed more ghost than structure. As she juggled bags and shoved her key in their metal door, Mia indulged in one of her favorite daydreams: pretending she was a PI's dame from an old movie. Her Humphrey Bogart couldn't manage without her, and of course he was secretly in love with her.

Reality was more prosaic. Her boss was gay, their cases were mostly down to earth, and apart from one notable exception, her skills were replaceable.

At least her workplace fit her fantasy. The investigative firm leased space in a century old brick warehouse. They shared the slightly rundown building with a dog groomer, a CPA, and—in her opinion—a dubious spice shipper. Fortunately, Discreet had a separate back entrance. Not so fortunately, it was in the alley next to the trash dumpsters. Mia hissed as her canvas sneaker splashed in a cold puddle. She shook her foot, but the remedy came too late. She'd have to change into her work heels as soon as she got inside. Her boss, who she otherwise adored, insisted heels set the right business tone.

Mia preferred to put off donning the "right" shoes as long as possible.

"Coffee's here," she called as she did every day.

The heavy door clanged shut behind her, the sound echoing in the high-ceilinged space. Their second PI, Jake Reed, looked up from his perch on the front of his dinged steel desk. He'd been casually flipping through the contents of a manila folder—probably the cheating case they'd been working on. They were presenting a report to the client this afternoon.

Admittedly, Mia didn't have a ton of experience, but Jake Reed was sexiest, most darkly dangerous male she'd ever laid eyes on. Somewhere shy of forty, he topped six feet by a couple inches and had a deceptively relaxed-looking rangy build. Former military, he practiced a form of martial arts whose name she suspected was top secret. Twice in the year they'd worked together she'd seen him subdue angry men with no more effort than a wolf yawning.

Jake observed the office dress code with a series of identical dark gray suits. At least, she thought the suits were a series. If it was the same suit, he managed to clean it every day.

Refusing to pair his shirts with ties saved him from looking like a drone.

"Hey, beautiful," he greeted her in his raspy Clint Eastwood voice.

Mia blushed, which she suspected was his goal. She wasn't ugly or anything, but he was so far out of her league she couldn't take the compliment seriously. Mostly, her reaction seemed to amuse him.

"Black plus a bagel," she announced, handing him his personal bag.

Jake took the sack, peered inside, and pulled out the lidded cup. He regarded her for a moment without prying open the plastic top. She tried not to dwell on how deeply blue his eyes were.

"Thanks, doll," he said—another favorite endearment.

"Sure," she responded, doing her best not to squirm under his erotic smirk. *You're work colleagues*, she told herself. And he was just teasing. "What's Curtis up to today?"

Their boss could be seen in his glassed-in office, lounged back in his swiveling chair talking on the phone. Though the door was open, he spoke too quietly to be heard. He was younger than Jake, his leadership accounted for by his superior people skills.

Though he lacked his employee's edge, Curtis was also a

handsome guy. Running and workouts at the gym hardened his lean physique. His hair was red-gold, his eyes a complementary crystal green. He wore neckties every day. Today's was royal blue. With one hooked finger, he tugged the loosened knot. The absentminded habit signaled that something troubled him.

Even from a distance Mia saw the furrow between his brows.

She'd known Curtis since she was ten, when he'd started dating her big brother. Curtis was as much her family as Mike had been, as dear and as protective. She wouldn't have this job if it weren't for him. In truth, she might not be employed at all.

Bachelors in art history didn't exactly fast track a person to success.

"Anniversary's coming up," Jake observed, answering the question she'd really asked.

He meant the anniversary of Mike's death. Her brother had died of an unsuspected aneurysm five years before, just dropped like a stone one morning on the subway he took to work. Mia had been entering college at the time. She loved her parents, but without Curtis to watch over her, she wasn't sure she'd have survived the loss with her sanity. Mike had been the best brother ever: loving, fun, with an acceptance of her oddities no one else could match. To him, Mia had been normal—better than, actually. When she dreamed about things she'd do in the future, she always pictured him being there.

Mike and Curtis had been the love of each other's lives. Curtis still kept Mike's picture on the right corner of his desk. As far as Mia knew, her stand-in sibling hadn't dated since the funeral.

That made her sadder than she knew how to say.

Not sure this was appropriate to discuss with Curtis's coworker, Mia hung her damp leather trench coat on the coat tree beside the entryway. When she glanced back, Curtis's body language said he was wrapping up the call. She could take him his coffee; maybe say something to let him know she cared. She pinched her lip indecisively. Mia wasn't always great at guessing what people wished to hear.

"Mia," Curtis called, coming to his office door.

She jumped forward and seized his bag. "I got your usual: skinny hazelnut plus a scone."

He smiled like she'd amused him, though she noticed the underlying set of his mouth was grim. "Bring your coffee too. I need to discuss a possible job with you. See if you'd be willing to lend your special skill to it."

Her legs slowed their hurried roll. Mia liked helping in the field—so long as she stayed in the background. If both men were out on assignment, the office got boring. Plus, it felt good to be Curtis's secret weapon. It meant she'd been more than a pity hire. Her instinctive hesitation stemmed from Curtis's expression.

He had a complicated favor to ask today.

"You want me to sit in?" Jake asked. Clearly, he'd noticed their boss's mood as well.

"Yes," he said. "I'd value your opinion."

This was sounding more and more ominous. Deciding changing out of her damp sneaks would wait, Mia grabbed her coffee. She tried to hide her apprehension as she smoothed her creased knee-length skirt—ironing was *not* her thing—and slid into one of Curtis's two guest chairs. To settle herself, she straightened her ponytail. Rather than take the second chair, Jake propped his shoulder on the wall. Though his pose was casual, the look he slid her was measuring.

She was relieved when he slid it away again.

"So," he said to Curtis, now back behind his desk. "Who's our client?"

"Genbolt Industries," Curtis said.

"*The* Genbolt Industries?" Mia's jaw dropped, and Jake let out a low whistle. Genbolt was a multinational corporation—not as recognizable as Apple or GE, but in its own way just as interwoven into the fabric of modern life. "Why on earth would they hire a small potatoes firm like us?"

Curtis coughed with amusement at her question.

"I mean, of course they'd be lucky to have you. Or Jake. You're both awesome."

Jake added his own snort. Curtis touched her brother's picture, adjusted it a millimeter, and sat back with folded hands.

"Perhaps I overstated," he said wryly. "Sam Raeburn's personal head of security is considering engaging us." Mia knew Sam Raeburn was Genbolt's founder and CEO. "Evidently, Raeburn has a job his own people can't be directly involved in."

"Can't be?" Jake repeated, his tone alert.

Curtis pulled his mouth askew. "It's sensitive."

Mia's brain did the party trick it sometimes performed—

4

assembling seemingly unremarked facts into a pattern she hadn't guessed was there. "This has to do with his daughter. The one who slapped him at last month's Save the Kids dinner."

Mia pictured the incident clear as day, though she'd only glimpsed it in passing on an online news site. Two angry faces. One old, one young. A family resemblance. The silver manicure on the woman's hand had been caught mid-lash by an alert photographer. Silk had draped the twist of her slim body. "Zoe Raeburn wore a white Halston gown and a bonkers nice diamond cuff."

The daughter's outfit was irrelevant, but Mia's mouth tumbled out stuff like that anyway.

Though he was used to the habit, Curtis blinked. "Raeburn's daughter is part of it," he acknowledged. "Zoe has become a bone of contention in Genbolt's ongoing rivalry with WorldWide."

"You mean with Damien Call," Jake said.

"Right." Curtis exchanged a look with his employee Mia didn't understand.

"Damien Call, the car maker? The superfast electric ones?"

"That's him," her boss confirmed. "Though WorldWide builds more than cars. Basically, if it's fast and a billionaire would want one, Call has his fingers in the pie. Call's company produces yachts, jets—"

"Rockets," Jake interjected.

Curtis nodded. "All kinds of supersonic shit. Plus the systems they need to run. Software. Circuitry. Power supplies so advanced we might not know what they were if we saw them. Lately, allegedly, Call's been courting the Pentagon. Wants to develop some of his ideas for them. He's already worth a mint. Who knows how high WorldWide would be valued if he won those contracts."

"Contracts Genbolt wants," Mia guessed.

"Contracts Genbolt *has*. Or so I hear. Details of those agreements aren't public."

"Where do we come in?" Jake asked. "I know we've done corporate work before, but this case sounds big."

He didn't seem intimidated, just curious. Curtis shifted his gaze to him. Mia was impressed that he also appeared unfazed. "It could be big if Raeburn's suspicions of industrial espionage are correct. The trick is that it's also personal. Raeburn is alleging

Damien Call seduced his daughter then used her to steal a cutting edge navigation system Genbolt's been developing, one that supposedly prevents manned and unmanned aircraft from being hacked. Raeburn wants us to find proof Call filched the plans . . . without implicating Zoe."

"If we pull this off, it could bring in a lot of work," Mia mused. "You could hire another man."

"I could hire another man *and* double your salary."

"I don't need my salary doubled," she said without thinking.

Curtis laughed.

"Well, I don't," she said defensively. "You're very generous. I pay my bills, and I still save some."

Curtis shook his head, his smile tinged with wistfulness. "Kid, sometimes you are too sweet for your own good."

"You can double my salary," Jake volunteered. "I don't really need it either, but I'd find a way to cope."

"Good to know," Curtis said.

Mia wriggled in her chair. "I still don't get why Raeburn's people came to us. They must have researched different firms. Unless it's your reputation. Because you don't blab about your clients, no matter what. Maybe you handled a tricky case for someone Raeburn knows."

Curtis looked uncomfortable. "Actually, I suspect the reason Genbolt came to us is you."

"Me?" Mia's face flashed hot. She didn't relish being noticed by strangers.

Curtis explained sympathetically. "Damien Call is a security freak. Rumor has it his staff sweep for bugs twice a day. Nobody gets a camera into his offices, including camera phones. That being the case, obtaining the evidence Raeburn wants will be tough. Because of your gift, you're a living recording device."

Mia didn't always think of it as a gift, but thanks to an accident she had when she was eight, she did indeed have the ability to remember anything she observed. "Were you hoping Call would hire me as a secretary?"

"Not exactly."

Mia's brows shot up at his evasion. "What exactly then?"

"Call has a type."

"A type?"

Jake snorted from his leaning post on the wall. "He likes wet behind the ears, doe in the headlights brunettes."

Mia gaped at him and then at her boss. Jake's implication was clear, though she couldn't imagine many scenarios less appropriate than this. She was no siren, nor did she expect her boss to put her in that position. "You want me to be a honeytrap?"

"Not exactly," Curtis said.

Jake laughed again. "I'd call it pretty exact."

"She wouldn't have to sleep with him."

"Oh my God," Mia exclaimed. "You expect me to be able to squirm out of that kind of situation? Damien Call is a billionaire. He's not used to people saying 'no' to him." As her panic swelled, more data she'd unwittingly amassed about Call rose up. She recalled an old newspaper photo of him, kneeling among teammates in shoulder pads and a stained jersey. His expression was that of someone who didn't like to lose. "He played hockey when he was at college. He isn't some 98-pound nerd."

"Damien Call doesn't sleep with women."

"If he's gay, you be the honeytrap!"

"He doesn't sleep with anyone," Curtis clarified. "He likes to watch."

Mia blinked rapidly, curiosity warring with disbelief. He liked to watch? Sensations she didn't want to have at work coiled between her legs. "That's not possible. I've seen him at press conferences. He's . . ."

"A sex god?" Jake sardonically suggested when she trailed off.

"Well, he's not short on testosterone. You can tell by how he carries himself. He's sexually confident. Like a stallion who's corralled all the girl horses into his harem." She fought a blush at Jake's rising hilarity. "Laugh all you want. I'd bet the rent he's not impotent."

Curtis patted his desk as if he could calm her by soothing it. "No one said he's impotent. Just—" he hesitated "—sexually eccentric."

"If he's such a security freak, how would you know that?"

Curtis cleared his throat. His fingers had stopped patting his desk and instead drew circles.

"What aren't you telling me?" she asked.

"There's a group," Jake said, answering for him. "A very exclusive club. Curtis belongs to it, and I attend now and then."

Mia wasn't sure her eyes could get any wider. "You mean a sex club?"

Curtis steeled his jaw and answered for himself this time. "It's for people with particular tastes. Role-play. BDSM. Voyeurs like Call. You don't get in because of money or power but because management decides you're trustworthy."

"And you belong?" Mia's brain was having trouble computing this. Curtis was gay, but she'd always thought of him as a straight arrow. Buttoned-up. Mainstream. Definitely not the sort to swing from the chandeliers. She blurted out her next thought before she could stop herself. "I thought you hadn't dated since Mike died."

The way his face colored up made his eyes extra green. "This isn't dating. It's . . . a more intellectual kind of sex."

Intellectual wasn't a word she associated with sexual activity. Not that she was an expert. She'd only ever had one boyfriend, in her senior year at college. Now she had a million questions. Had Curtis joined this sex club before Mike died? What exactly did he do there? What did Jake do? Did they do it together? Wasn't Jake straight? Was leather involved? Did they maybe spank people? She recalled the cryptic look Jake and Curtis had exchanged earlier. Had they been thinking about acts they'd witnessed or participated in?

Most importantly, how sexy *was* Jake's body under those charcoal suits?

She clamped her mouth shut determinedly. Best not to ask questions whose answers she wouldn't be able to forget.

The tension in her muscles warned her she was wound up. Her hands clamped her coffee cup, and her knees were locked together. She probably looked like she'd joined a convent, though the wild pulsing in her pussy reminded her she had not. Mia might be shy, but she had needs and fantasies the same as anyone. She simply didn't go around joining secret societies so she could live them out.

Hoping her voice wouldn't emerge too hoarse, she spoke. "So, um, what is this club called, if I'm allowed to ask?"

"Diogenes," Curtis said.

"Like Mycroft's club in the Sherlock Holmes novels?"

"I suppose that's the inspiration. Diogenes does have a certain . . . Victorian ambience."

Mia revised her mental picture to include corsets. She really shouldn't have done that. She liked the idea of corsets, and her quivering flesh grew steamy. "I assume you can't bring just anyone there with you."

"No." Curtis leaned forward across his desk, his green eyes watching her closely. "There's another place, a nightclub called Audition. When members need to have a guest approved, they bring them there for vetting. People who've heard whispers about Diogenes and want to join show up too. It's a culling ground for talent."

"Pretty people."

Curtis shook his head. "It's not enough to have the right look or even an interest in S&M. Diogenes' management is very picky. They want people of intelligence and sensitivity who can be trusted to keep what they see to themselves. People who understand power but won't abuse it."

"That sounds selective," Mia said unsurely. "Maybe too selective to include me."

Curtis rubbed his temple as if it hurt. Perhaps, given his personal preference, he wasn't comfortable assessing her appeal. He settled for a dry statement. "You don't see your own charms."

"They'll eat you up," Jake predicted with less restraint. "Like a freaking braised lamb with mint jelly."

"I'm not a lamb," she objected.

"You are," Jake and Curtis said at nearly the same time.

"You are," Jake repeated. He took a seat on Curtis's credenza, the position pulling his crisp trousers taut over powerful thighs. "It's not an insult. Innocence is an undervalued trait."

Okay, maybe she was innocent about some things, but that didn't make her an idiot. "I'm not stupid."

"No one said you were." Jake's hot blue eyes were gentle. "You're . . . unspoiled. At your age, it'd be a shame if you weren't."

He was looking at her like she was twelve years old. Coming from him, about whom she'd spun more than one illicit reverie, the look couldn't help but prick her anger. She set down her coffee and crossed her arms. "I'm an adult."

For just a moment, his gaze gleamed with a different kind of heat. "You are," he conceded. "But you can't deny you haven't been one long."

"If you think I'm a child, maybe you shouldn't be asking me to go along with this."

Curtis broke into their debate with gusty sigh. "You're too perfect for the assignment not to ask."

"Why do you keep saying that? The kinkiest thing I've ever done was have sex in a car. And I didn't enjoy it!" She blushed furiously, as annoyed with herself for confessing this as she was by the memory. Her college boyfriend Steve had promised the roadside adventure would be fun but, per usual, he only meant for him.

"That's why," Curtis said softly.

"What's why?"

"Because you radiate sexual interest and at the same time give the impression you've never been satisfied. If a man ever devoted himself to you, ever truly paid attention to your needs, you'd explode with excitement."

"I would not explode!" Belatedly, Mia realized she was squirming on her chair. She stopped the tiny motion and drew in a calming breath. "Human beings aren't bombs, Curtis. They don't do that."

"You're a born submissive," Jake interjected. "A man like Damien Call won't be able to resist watching you unravel."

He was smiling faintly the way he did, supercilious, his left hand bracing his right elbow while he pushed his right index finger across his lips. He had a good mouth—not full but sensitive looking. The gesture made her imagine kissing it.

Rather than let the fantasy take over, she ground her teeth together. "Just because I get you coffee doesn't make me submissive."

"But you enjoy getting us coffee," he teased. "And, again, it's not an insult."

"I suppose you think you could dominate me."

The curve of his mouth deepened. "That's not even a question."

She inhaled sharply, about to challenge the arrogant assumption.

"Enough," said their mutual boss. "This isn't helping Mia make her decision."

"Isn't it?" Jake asked with sly humor.

A sudden realization caused Mia to sit straighter in her chair, her annoyance forgotten for the moment. "Wait a second. If

Damien Call never sleeps with women, how did he seduce Raeburn's daughter? Unless he's just that good . . ."

Curtis smiled. "Not that I know of. We only have Raeburn's word Call recruited her to spy. His head of security didn't seem aware of Call's sexual hobbies. Until evidence shows otherwise, I'm assuming Raeburn isn't clued in either. He wouldn't know we have a reason to doubt his tale."

"And you didn't enlighten him about Call's kinks?"

Curtis leaned back in his chair, his hands pressed together in a steeple. "I didn't think it was my place. Raeburn's hasn't officially hired us yet."

A light bulb switched on in Mia's head. "This is one of *those* cases. Where you're not sure we should do what the client asks."

Curtis's eyes held a glint of pride at her adding this together. "It is."

"I notice you're not informing Call he's been accused," Jake said.

"No," Curtis admitted. "We don't know what his angle is either."

"So, depending on what we find, we could end up with no client and no paycheck." Jake laughed and shook his head. "I knew there was a reason I was willing to call you boss."

"What is the plan?" Mia asked, still not convinced she wanted to take part. "You bring me to this Audition and hope I draw attention?"

"I hadn't thought it through completely," Curtis said.

Jake crumpled his empty coffee cup, neatly three-pointing it into Curtis's trashcan. "Damien Call has been around the block. It'll take more than a pretty face and a banging body to catch his eye."

Despite not wanting to seem susceptible, Mia flushed with pleasure at Jake's words. She was average height and a little plump. She'd always figured Jake preferred the supermodel type.

"We could dress her up," Curtis suggested. "She has great legs when she wears heels."

"She has great everything. But we need to get her close enough to Call for long enough that she has a chance to snoop."

Curtis scratched the frown line beside his mouth. "You think we need to stage some sort of scene?"

"I do." Jake looked as sober at the prospect as Curtis did. Though he rarely fidgeted, he tugged the open front of his suit jacket. Her coworkers' understanding of each other made Mia feel like the odd girl out.

"Guys," she said. "Maybe you should tell me what you mean."

Both men looked at her. Though Jake's blue eyes lasered into hers, Curtis was the one who spoke.

"We'll get to that." He reached for his phone and punched in a number. "Sweets," he said to whoever answered. "I've got a situation that requires your magic . . ."

◆

Hillary Sweets ran a secondhand clothing shop in Brooklyn Heights. Rich housewives from Manhattan supplied her stock, the kind of women who couldn't afford to wear an outfit twice —much less get caught reselling their pricey designer duds. An expert secret keeper, Hillary been known to sneak one client out the back then turn around and let the next in the front. Less known, at least to civilians, was her sideline in high quality fetish wear. This she designed to order, so successfully she supported half a dozen skilled leatherworkers and seamstresses.

Naturally, Curtis and Jake were familiar with her product. No self-respecting frequenter of Diogenes would dream of buying gear retail.

Aside from admiring her work, Jake liked Hillary as a person. She was attractive, witty, and not at all romantic. They'd shared dinner and a night in bed on a number of occasions. Jake appreciated her enthusiasm for sensory pleasures and that she knew the score. She loved martinis, had two grown kids and an ex-husband. More than that he didn't need to know.

A female less like Mia Beck was hard to imagine.

As he slid out of his shiny black Acura, in which he'd driven the three of them, he was aware of Mia's presence behind him. The girl was his personal erotic Achilles' heel. Though she had a brain, "Innocence" could have been her middle name. Those big brown eyes of hers always seemed to be hoping for something. She spoke what she thought far too often, loved to please those she cared about, and possessed a mouth as sweet and soft as a girl half her age. She wore a bouncy ponytail, for crap's sake, like she'd escaped a Fifties sock hop an hour before. Her body recalled Norma Jean rather than Marilyn, her tender curves taunting red-blooded wolves like Jake to sink their teeth into them. Worse, Mia had no idea how mouthwatering she was.

This, of course, made him burn all the hotter to debauch her.

Off limits, he thought, clenching his jaw as he opened the door for her. The reminder was for her sake as much as his. He'd been cynical before the CIA sent him on his eight-year tour of black ops hotspots. After it, he was just plain broken in many ways. His wiseass front only went skin deep. He couldn't trust, wouldn't love, and might never believe humans as a species were good for much. Signing on with Curtis, who actually had principles, had been his first attempt to climb out of the pit of bitterness he'd sunk in.

He'd promised himself he wouldn't drag a girl like Mia down with him.

Given what Curtis was proposing, keeping that promise would be difficult.

Mia took Jake's hand and got out, blushing slightly at the contact while pretending she was not. She let go too soon and not soon enough. The weather was cool and misty, and she tied the belt of her leather trench coat tighter around her waist. She was proud of that coat, which she'd saved up for and wore every day she could.

Probably she'd love being wrapped all over in black leather.

Jake turned away sharply, his cock grown heavy from the images in his mind. "This way," he said, refusing to glance back at her again. "The entrance is around the corner."

He felt Curtis shoot him a look but didn't return it.

The boutique was as he remembered, the racks organized but stuffed with expensive clothes that smelled faintly of dry cleaning. The old-fashioned doorbells jingled as Curtis shut the door. Habit sent Jake's gaze around, taking in the lack of customers and locating the EXIT sign.

The street outside wasn't busy. He registered no threats . . . apart from what Mia posed to his self-control.

Hillary was behind the counter, paging through accounts on an iPad screen. As they entered she looked up. In her tailored suit and tasteful jewelry, she could have passed for a high-paid attorney.

She broke into a smile of genuine pleasure on seeing him.

"Well," she said, coming around the barrier to kiss his cheek. Her skyscraper heels lifted her even taller than usual. Lean as a whippet, she smelled of Chanel and quality cosmetics. "Jake. I wasn't counting on seeing you today."

He felt unaccountably awkward kissing her in return, aware that Mia's big brown eyes tended to see a lot. He put his hands on Hillary's shoulders, gently controlling how close she could come and how long she could linger.

"You're looking well," he said, rather than explain that the mission they were on also concerned him.

Hillary laughed and turned to kiss Curtis too, though in a less flirty way. After that, she regarded their young colleague. "This must be the moppet you want me polish up."

Her tone was a teensy bit condescending. Mia must not have noticed, because she didn't blush. She was gazing wide-eyed at Hillary. "That blonde is *killer* on you. Your colorist is an artist."

Her compliment couldn't be mistaken for anything but sincere. Since Hillary had reached a certain age, and Mia was too young to sport a single thread of gray in her chestnut locks, it was also an inadvertently good comeback. Disconcerted, Hillary's hand flew to her sleek champagne do. Though Mia didn't know it, this was a coup. Hillary Sweets was nearly impossible to fluster.

Curtis pressed two fingers to his lips to conceal amusement. "We need Mia to look suitable for Audition. Eye-catching but not cheap. More grownup but not overdoing that either."

"Understood," Hillary said dryly, considering Mia more professionally now that she'd recovered from being caught off guard. "Youth is an asset no women should overlook."

"I'm not good with heels," Mia warned hastily. "If I don't have to wear anything too high, that would probably be safer for everyone."

Hillary's smile warmed her face in slow motion, like a cat enjoying a mouse's naiveté.

Jake had a feeling Mia was in for it.

◆

Mia stared at herself in the changing room mirror and mentally went *ulp*.

The dress Hillary had chosen for her was blood red, skintight, and didn't come close to covering all of her. Though it had sleeves, its intricate wrap design exposed portions of her midriff and a lot of her back and spine. When she twisted around to look, her butt was just about indecent. She spotted tailbone dimples, though thankfully not cleavage. She recalled seeing a famous pop star wearing something similar recently. Shocked, she tried to tug down the hem, but her thighs—which definitely did not possess a gap—refused to un-display themselves. The heels she'd been given were midnight black velvet. Surprisingly not pinchy, they were tall enough to cause her ankles to wobble.

"I don't think this outfit is going to work," she said to the shop owner.

Hillary opened the swinging door. "You're kidding, right? I'd do you in that dress."

This was both flattering and alarming. Hillary was as far out of her league as Jake. "Curtis said he didn't want me to look cheap."

"Trust me, sweetie, at $2,000 new, that dress doesn't qualify. Those shoes look like they fit. Come out and show the men."

"Do I have to?" she pleaded.

"Jesus." Hillary laughed as she laid one hand on Mia's arm, the gesture friendlier than she'd made before. "You have no idea what a treasure your body is."

"It's a private treasure," she protested then blushed at how prissy she'd just sounded.

Because Hillary didn't relent, Mia trailed her out of the dressing room. Cheeks blazing, her gaze immediately went to Jake. Not one to let down his guard, he was keeping tabs on the foot traffic outside the shop and had his back to her. He turned slowly as they entered—as if he didn't want to see what Hillary had accomplished.

"Wow," Curtis said. "Talk about a transformation."

Jake's granite jaw tightened. He seemed frozen in position, his hyper-vigilance momentarily in abeyance. His blue eyes narrowed with suspicion.

Hillary guessed the meaning his reaction sooner than Mia did. She laughed throatily. "I take it you approve."

"She'll do," Jake grudged, his always raspy voice harsher than usual. "She still needs hair and makeup."

"I can handle that," Hillary said.

"I can't walk in these shoes," Mia tried, sensing she was losing her say in the situation. "I'm going to fall over."

"Practice," Jake advised without one drop of sympathy.

Mia couldn't prevent her eyebrows from shooting up. Jake

never talked to her like that, like he was the boss of her. Her pulse skipped, a tiny surge of adrenaline centering in the sweet spot between her legs. She was very aware that the dress didn't allow her to wear a bra, and that her nipples were tightening. The heightening of sensation felt good but embarrassing.

Jake cleared his throat. "The shoes are good. They're the sort women wear to Audition."

"Okay," she said unsurely.

"You do look appropriate," Curtis seconded. "We just need to decide what kind of drama we should spin to catch Call's eye."

"Curtis," Jake said, like he was scolding him. Did Jake think he could order him around too?

"What?" Curtis seemed surprised by the tone as well.

"You know there can't be a 'we' in this scenario. Everyone at Diogenes is aware you don't play with girls."

"More's the pity," Hillary murmured to her manicured fingernails. "Gingers are so much fun."

Curtis flushed. "I wasn't planning to . . ." He waved his hands vaguely. "I have to be there. Mia is my responsibility."

"Mia is like your sister."

"Exactly," Curtis said.

"Would you want your sister watching you at Diogenes? Wouldn't her presence inhibit you?"

"Shit," Curtis said, seeing too late the corner Jake had maneuvered him into.

Jake put his hand on Curtis's shoulder. "Some things can't be coached. If this plan has any chance of working, we need Mia to react naturally."

"You mean I have to trust *you* to take care of her."

"Yes."

"No matter what it ends up involving."

"No matter what," Jake confirmed.

"I *am* jealous now," Hillary laughed softly.

Her comment shook Mia from the captivated daze the men's conversation had put her in. "What precisely are you expecting me to do?"

Jake's hot blue gaze locked on hers. Though his face wasn't showing an expression, his nostrils had flared and a hint of color darkened the slanting blades of his high cheekbones. The stubble that shaded his jaw made him seem even manlier. Mia couldn't deny her heart was racing.

"I expect you to do everything I ask," he said. "The moment I ask you to."

His voice was sandpaper with smoke flowing over it.

Wow, she thought as she literally wet her panties with excitement. Both her knees and her hands felt like they were vibrating.

"And if I don't?" The husky words came out with no preplanning.

Jake leaned intimately closer. "If you don't, I expect you to pay whatever price I set."

Everyone else disappeared from the room. There was only him: his eyes, his scent, the pure male danger he exuded. Mia would have given anything to have him lay hands and more on her right then. Her daydreams paled compared to his raw appeal. Her pussy ached to have his cock shoved in it, its creaming walls fluttering.

"Uh," Curtis said from what sounded like a great distance. "Maybe you two should save some of this for later."

Jake drew back from her with his trademark smirk.

"You okay?" Curtis asked, dragging her focus—somewhat reluctantly—to him. "There's still time for you to back out."

Curtis's worried green eyes acted to clear her brain.

"This case matters," she said. "Not just for the firm but maybe even for national security. Someone ought to find out if Damien Call stole those plans."

"That doesn't mean the someone has to be you."

Maybe it didn't. Though she refused to look in Jake's direction, she sensed him beside her: silent, tall, radiating more than a mere 98.6 degrees. Jake acted cool, but now he was aroused—probably throwing wood in his business suit. Right or wrong, Mia wanted more of what he'd teased her with. This plan might be nothing but a means to an end to him, a game his heart wouldn't enter in. Maybe she'd end up broken. Maybe she'd be sorry. For sure, she'd have an intense experience. One hundred percent alive, like she doubted she'd ever been.

Hadn't losing her brother taught her that was important?

"I want to do it," she said softly.

When Jake hissed in a breath, she knew she wasn't thinking about the safety of her country.

CHAPTER 2

MIA had more time to second-guess her bold decision than she wanted. Genbolt dragged its feet making a decision, and as a result their plan was on hold. Over the course of the next few days, Curtis wrangled with Raeburn's people, trying to pin the big man down to officially hiring them. Finally—perhaps because he wanted to take Curtis's measure in person—Sam Raeburn agreed to meet at Discreet's offices.

Mia's first real world glimpse of the CEO was informative. He'd come on his own, without a driver or bodyguard and carrying a black briefcase. Mia found him physically imposing. 5'10" or thereabouts, he was stocky but not fat. His hair was a bristly pewter, his face tanned and weather lined but unremarkable in either beauty or ugliness. She remembered he'd competed in the World Cup, which might explain his sailor's squint. Genbolt's boat hadn't won the race, but that couldn't have been for lack of trying.

Raeburn radiated tenacity, his *I own the world* stride the most striking thing about him. His walk reminded her of the Russian leader Putin—a beefed-up strong man crossed with a bull. The posturing would have amused her if both men's power weren't undeniable.

Genbolt's annual revenues exceeded the gross domestic product of some countries.

When she took Raeburn's beautiful wool overcoat to hang it up, his pale blue eyes swept her. He seemed to note everything about her without registering her as a person. That's how it felt, anyway. He actually did thank her.

Now he was in the conference room with Jake and Curtis while she waited dutifully at her desk. The bursts of male laughter that swept out told her Curtis had succeeded in putting the CEO at ease. She glanced at her watch. They'd been in there five minutes, long enough for her to bring in coffee.

She'd already gathered cups and saucers and cream and sugar that didn't come in packets. The scones came from a bakery down the street, and she'd sliced little bowls of fruit with her own two hands. The refreshments were a cut above their usual, despite which she was abruptly certain she might as well have plopped a box of Pop-Tarts on the table.

Sam Raeburn probably never threw a meeting without a cordon bleu caterer.

He glanced up as she wheeled in the wobbly cart. This time his sharp eyes saw her. She wished they hadn't. Ever since she'd tried on the red dress at Sweets, her wardrobe seemed dowdy. Generally, she was proud of her bargain hunting, but now she felt second-rate.

She cursed herself for not spending more effort ironing this morning. She had a feeling Raeburn noted every wrinkle in her bland beige skirt.

"This is the girl?" he asked, as if Curtis had been claiming a frog was a princess.

"This is Mia," Curtis said. "Mia, this is Sam Raeburn."

Raeburn remembered his manners and rose to acknowledge her. He held her hand in both of his like politicians did, seeming gentle and friendly but really controlling.

"Nice to meet you," she said as calmly as she was able.

He considered her a moment longer. "Can I test her?" he asked Curtis.

Mia prayed he meant test her memory.

"Certainly," Curtis said.

As Raeburn unlatched his briefcase to remove whatever he intended to quiz her with, her gaze slid to the other side of the conference table, where Jake had tipped his chair back against the exposed brick wall. Naturally, their second investigator was relaxed, though to her amazement he wore a tie today.

The little wink he sent her as he flipped it steadied her.

Raeburn set a legal pad and fountain pen on the table, followed by a page torn from a Yellow Pages, the sort you rarely saw anymore. The print included advertisements as well as phone listings.

"How long do you need?" he asked.

"I've got it," she said. "You can put it away."

The page hadn't lain in front of her for more than a heartbeat. Raeburn looked surprised as he pulled it back. She knew he hadn't seen her do anything. Her gift didn't require concentration, or calm, or any other effort. Her brain did what it did because it was wired that way.

Understanding what was expected, she sat in the empty chair beside the CEO to scribble what she'd seen on the legal pad. She reminded herself to keep her hand relaxed to prevent it from cramping. Thankfully, Raeburn's expensive pen wrote smoothly. Fifteen minutes and six pages later, she'd recreated the phone book page in extremely precise detail.

Jake, bless him, had taken over serving coffee in the meantime.

Raeburn set his cup in the saucer when she handed over her little stack.

"You can proof it," she said, "but everything is there."

Raeburn laid out the pages, each of which duplicated a section of the original. She'd have been surprised if he didn't check her work. He did it swiftly, obviously sharp between the ears himself.

At last, he sat back and gazed at her. "That's amazing. You even drew the illustrations in the ads."

"I figured you wanted me to. Otherwise, why pick a page that included them?"

He rocked his office chair thoughtfully. "You can memorize anything? No matter how detailed?"

"If my eyes can see it, I can draw it afterwards."

"What if you don't understand the information?"

"It doesn't matter. I reproduce it visually."

"Were you born like this?"

She hesitated. She didn't want to be rude. She knew getting this assignment was important. "I'd rather not talk about that, if you'll forgive me."

"Of course," he said. "I was just curious."

He didn't seem offended, but she was still unnerved by his attention. The feeling was nothing new. People who saw her do her thing tended to react as if she'd turned into a Roswell style alien.

Watch out for my big gray bobblehead! she thought. The private joke allowed her to smile faintly.

"Okay," Raeburn said, addressing her boss again. "I'm satisfied she can do what you claim. What I'm wondering is why you're sure you can plant her on Call's personal staff. That paranoid bastard doesn't let anyone close to him."

Curtis had prepared her not to react to this assumption—not that it mattered. Raeburn wasn't watching her anymore.

"You can leave that to us," Curtis said. "You're paying us for results, after all. We'll move forward as soon as you specify the smoking gun you need Mia to search for."

Raeburn frowned then seemed to make up his mind. He sat up straighter in his chair, pulling a large rolled up sheet of paper from the relative emptiness of his briefcase. His blocky, powerful looking hands flattened the page on the table. Curtis and Jake leaned forward to see better.

Because she was next to Raeburn, Mia had a clear view of it.

She wasn't sure what she was looking at—possibly a blurred copy of a circuit board or a blown-up view of a microchip. The images were dense, with tiny printed symbols and mathematical formulas. The page was stamped CONFIDENTIAL, and the G/lightning slash/B that formed Genbolt's logo marked the upper right corner. Though the schematic was complex, she knew she'd recognize it if she saw it again.

"This is half the blueprint we believe my daughter passed to Call. Naturally, I can't show you the rest for security reasons. Zoe denies giving it to him, so I need evidence he has it in his possession." Raeburn's cool blue eyes pinned hers. "We know WorldWide has been working on a competing version of this project, but we had good reason to believe their progress was at least a year behind ours. Now, suddenly, they're claiming to be ahead and telling the government they should get development funding instead of us. I don't think that's the way business should be done in this country."

He addressed her as if she had the integrity to share his opinion, which was flattering or diplomatic, depending.

Mia answered him frankly. "I'm not certain me seeing this in Call's possession will hold up as legal proof—assuming I can locate the thing."

"I don't expect the matter to come before a judge. The government prefers to settle this sort of quarrel behind closed doors. Fortunately, given the nature of your memory, you'll only need to glimpse it in passing. God willing, you'll never be in harm's way."

Mia would prefer to avoid that too. She was no risk junkie.

"So we move forward?" Curtis asked politely.

Raeburn rose, re-secured the items he'd taken from his briefcase, and buttoned his multiple thousand-dollar suit jacket. Probably his tailor was worth the extra simoleons. He almost looked trim with the front fastened.

"We move forward," he agreed. "Your retainer will be wired into your account by end of business today."

Curtis nodded and Mia accompanied Raeburn out of the conference room to return his overcoat.

Raeburn spoke to her a final time as he shrugged it on. "You be careful," he said paternally. "Don't take risks you don't have to. And thank you. What you're doing means a lot to myself and my company."

Well, Mia thought as she shut the door after him. She didn't doubt Raeburn could be difficult, but he'd shown flashes of likability. Maybe bigwigs had their own version of charm school.

"You buying that?" Jake asked Curtis from behind her.

"I don't know," Curtis said. "I think we all need to watch our step."

◆

Watching his step seemed essential when Jake arrived at Mia's apartment the following night. She rented a third floor walkup in a 1930's vintage complex built around a nice courtyard. The apartments weren't fancy, but they were secure enough. Jake had been here a few times before, dropping her off after they'd worked late. Though he enjoyed teasing Mia, he'd been careful not to encourage her romantically. Their conversations had been light and impersonal.

Tonight was different. He had a fresh haircut, a shave, and was dressed in his best date clothes. Tonight at the very least he'd hold her in his arms. Tonight he'd probably kiss her . . .

The slight vibration that struck his lips warned him that wouldn't be a hardship.

Cursing would give too much away. He kept the swear word inside and pressed the buzzer for her unit.

"Jake." She sounded so breathless the length of his penis twitched. "I'm almost ready. I'll be down in five minutes."

He didn't say he'd come up. Maybe cooling his heels down

here would cool the rest of him. The night air ought to have done the trick. It was early March and still cold enough for coats. His was black leather: exactly what Mia liked. Watching her squirm naked over it would be fun.

Idiot, he thought as the fantasy sprung vividly to mind. *Try to remember this is a job.*

His first sight of her beneath the stoop light made him forget everything.

She wore the red dress, of course, but she'd also been primped and buffed. Just the right touch of makeup highlighted her eyes and lips, and for the first time ever he saw her with her hair down. Glossy chestnut waves spilled across her shoulders, the silky abandon painfully touchable. Her coat was unfamiliar, a swingy salt and pepper tweed barely longer than her dress's hem. As if he were compelled, his gaze slid past it and kept going. The shoes Hillary Sweets had chosen did unbelievably appealing things to Mia's legs and ankles.

"Is this all right?" Mia asked. "Hillary brought the coat when she stopped by to do my face and hair."

Jake's hands had curled into fists. "It's good." His voice sounded strangely distant to his own ears. "You look like you're supposed to."

Maybe it was just as well Mia wasn't listening closely. Her eyes went round as she saw the car behind him. "You hired a limo?"

"I did. We have ground rules to set on the way over."

A growl he couldn't quite control darkened the assertion. When Mia's soft red mouth parted in surprise he wanted to cover it with his. Though it went against his baser instincts, he opened the limo door for her instead.

"Ground rules," she repeated. "Right."

The part of him that was a natural master loved her slight nervousness. She slid into the back seat ahead of him, her hosiery hissing on the dark brown leather. The window between them and the driver was snugly shut. Jake tapped the glass to let the man know he could pull out. The little light on the ceiling enabled him and Mia to see each other.

When she turned toward him, her knees were pressed together.

"Here's the deal," he said, his cock gone partially erect just from her obedient schoolgirl pose. "Damien Call is a creature of habit. Every Thursday at nine sharp, he shows up at Audition. Maybe one visit out of four he zeroes in on someone who interests him. If that someone passes muster, he brings them to Diogenes. The club keeps expert doms on staff. Call selects one to handle his latest charge. Then he watches what happens. Whoever he's brought from Audition has to agree to everything. Nothing can be done to him or her without permission."

Mia rolled her lips worriedly. Jake didn't think the *him or her* reference registered. "Are the doms on staff trustworthy?"

"They are, but it's not my intention to let anyone lay a finger on you but me."

She flushed and his dick surged to full hardness. "I kind of figured. Do you have a plan for ensuring that?"

Rather than answer, he stroked a fallen lock back around her ear. Her hair was cool and silky, her cheek hot and velvety. He'd never touched her like this before, and Mia sucked in a startled breath. Her responsiveness delighted him. He was willing to bet it would delight Damien Call as well.

With his heart rate rising, Jake leaned closer. "My plan is for you to leave the plan to me. Be yourself. React the way you react. As long as you surrender your trust to me, everything will turn out right."

"Have you . . . done this before?" she asked, her deliciously breathy voice breaking.

"Many times," he assured her.

"Why?" she blurted, reminding him she sometimes lacked an internal editor. He smiled, actually liking that about her.

"Why does anyone do anything? It gives me a special buzz."

"Has it always?"

Mia's eyes were huge, her thick spiky lashes untouched by mascara. A pulse beat crazily in her neck. Jake wet his lips and answered without editing himself. "The first non-ignorable boner I remember getting was from watching a girl be tied up in a movie. I was so excited I had to jack off in the theater john before the film ended. I didn't care that my friends teased me for leaving in the middle. I literally could not control myself until I took care of it."

"So it's bondage that gets you."

"Among other things." He touched the beating hollow between her clavicles, the stroke of his fingertip feather light. The wheels bumped across a pothole but kept rolling.

Mia shivered a tiny bit. "You don't seem out of control tonight."

"I've learned to keep myself in hand." He'd had to, though sometimes—when it suited a mission—his bosses at Langley had ordered him off leash.

Not knowing this, Mia eyebrows waggled. "There's a joke there, you know. Keeping yourself 'in hand.'"

He returned half her smile. "I have a gift I want you to wear."

He retrieved the jewelry box from the inside breast pocket of his coat. Wisely, Hillary had left accessorizing Mia to him. Jake opened the case to show her what was inside.

Mia's hand went toward the gleaming contents but retreated. "Is it a necklace?"

"It could pass for one, but it's a collar." Made of parallel steel chains in varying thicknesses, the thing was decorative but with a hint of brutality. Its links were slightly flattened, resembling those on chunky curb chain bracelets. Here and there a larger steel circle lay.

Mia touched one with her finger. "What are these for?"

"For attaching other things."

She looked at him, her big eyes searching his. He had a feeling his expression was giving things away. "Will you put it on me?" she asked softly.

He wanted to kiss her so badly his mouth watered. "Face the window," he said gruffly in command. "Hold your hair up out of my way."

Mia complied without hesitation. The exposed nape of her neck looked soft, but he didn't kiss that either. He secured the heavy collar, smoothing it with his thumbs before drawing his hands away. Mia turned back around. The hot color on her cheeks created the impression that more than a necklace had been put on.

"Will the people at Audition think I belong to you if I'm wearing this?"

"They'd have thought that anyway," he said.

"Jake," she began, and he sensed she was about to say something serious about her feelings.

"No," he said, firm but soft. "Property doesn't speak unless it's asked a question."

"Property—"

He laid his hand across her mouth, silencing her. "From this moment forward you obey me. If you truly wish to object to something, your safe word is 'daffodil.' Say it, and I'll listen to a request."

He'd succeeded in shocking her. Her lips worked but no sound emerged.

"Good," he said, dropping the lightest kiss onto them. "I know you'll remember."

◆

Mia felt like she'd stepped into an alternate reality, one where things she hadn't known could arouse her did. Waves of excitement crashed through her nerves, simply because Jake had ordered her to obey. Her lips tingled from his glancing kiss the same as if he'd marauded them. Her pussy was growing wet and her nipples tightened. The strength of her reaction was a little alarming.

It made her wonder what their exchange had done to him.

When he shifted to check their progress through the side window, her gaze arrowed to his crotch. He didn't wear his clothes super tight, but a bulge lifted his zipper.

She fought a shiver at the healthy size of it.

She looked away before he caught her staring, but of course the image lingered in her mind. Even without her gift, she'd have memorized it. Jake's erect cock was impressive.

Truthfully, she wasn't sure he was wearing underwear.

She bit the side of her thumb. The heavy collar had warmed around her neck, as if his hands were touching her and not chains. Her clitoris throbbed in reaction.

Property doesn't speak, he'd said.

This is pretend, she warned herself. *Don't get too into this.*

Her body refused to listen. Jake reached without warning to take her hand, sending an involuntary jolt up her clit and deep into her. Mia inhaled loudly enough to be heard. The burst of sensation had almost felt like coming.

"We're nearly there," he said, his gaze penetrating hers. The gleam in his hot blue eyes said he suspected what had happened. His callused fingers gripped hers a bit tighter. "Keep hold of my arm while we go inside. And behave yourself. Management will watch every move we make."

She opened her mouth to speak then remembered he hadn't

asked a question.

"Good," he said like he meant it. "I'm glad you're a quick study."

The limo driver slowed and began a turn. She saw they were in the theater district. As lit-up as Broadway was, she should have noticed this already.

Audition was on a narrower street. The glass and metal awning above its front reminded her of old Paris Metro stations, the flourishes typical of art nouveau style. A line three- and four-deep straggled along beneath it and a ways down the block. The people who waited were well dressed but conservative, as if they worked on Wall Street or legal firms. She saw designer cocktail dresses and bespoke suits—and not a single item of studded black leather.

Her decorative steel collar was the nearest thing to fetish wear in sight.

She discovered this made her happy. Maybe he didn't really mean to, but Jake was treating her like she was special. She couldn't resist stroking the chains as their driver opened the door for them.

Unsurprisingly, Jake ignored the line and led her to the entrance. The bouncer who guarded it was as big as a linebacker. He also wore a good suit. Jake produced a black poker chip embossed with golden Comedy/Tragedy masks. A silhouette of a horsewhip traversed the images.

The bouncer glanced at the token and then at Jake. Jake must have met his approval. Without a word, he pulled the door open.

Mia wondered if Damien Call had to flash a chip.

She didn't ask. They'd entered a red satin antechamber with a coatroom.

Jake removed his leather jacket, handing it to the elegant woman who stood behind the counter.

Whoa, Mia thought, taking in Jake's appearance. He wasn't dressed like he did at work. He'd paired a black silk shirt with knife crease black trousers. He never looked bad, but tonight he looked *sharp.* His shoes were shined and his belt was narrow. Without his usual suit jacket, the perfect shape of his trim strong body was obvious. He had a dancer's ass: tight and muscular.

Mia couldn't believe she hadn't noticed how great it was before.

"Coat," Jake reminded, yanking her from her fugue.

"Sorry," she said.

Jake pressed a scolding finger across her lips.

How crazy was it that him shushing her stirred a thrill?

"Turn," he ordered, his hands guiding her as she struggled not to blush. Every place he touched seemed unnaturally sensitive. She wasn't sure what he intended until he lifted her coat from her.

"You need to check any phones or cameras," the chic coat girl said.

Jake handed his cell over. "Do you have one?" he asked her.

Mia shook her head.

"Take my arm," he said, offering his elbow.

She was glad for the support. The space behind the next set of doors was packed and unexpectedly noisy. European dance music pulsed at her like a shifting wall. Voices laughed, plates and glasses clinking as people ate and drank. The room was circular, and the floor wasn't level around the sides. Staggered tiers like terraces in a rice paddy supported small tables. Most of the seats were full, but some couples writhed on a black onyx dance floor in front of a curtained stage. Their gyrations were suggestive. Mia's overly detail-oriented brain temporarily went into overload. She swayed on her teetery heels.

Jake's arm shifted to her back. "This way. I see a free table."

The table wasn't free yet. Two tuxedoed servers were clearing it. One of the young men seemed startled when he saw Jake. His skin was caramel, his eyes the clear aqua of the Caribbean. The honey brown corkscrew curls that haloed his head looked like a Renaissance angel's.

"Mr. Reed," he said. "We didn't know you were coming."

As the slightest flush touched the young man's cheeks, knowledge slapped Mia in the chest. Jake had played his S&M games with him. And maybe more than games. The waiter was preening the tiniest bit. Perhaps he was crossover staff between Audition and Diogenes. If Jake frequented Diogenes more often than here, this would explain why he hadn't been familiar to the bouncer. Mia gaped at Jake, not having guessed he was so flexible in his preferences. He noted her glance but the inferences she was drawing didn't seem to fluster him.

Not that Jake gave away that sort of thing.

"Gabriel," he greeted the waiter, the name fitting. He touched Mia's shoulder. "As you can see, I've brought a friend."

"But . . . it's *Thursday*."

This seemed to be important. Was it because Damien Call came on Thursdays? Or was there another reason the day was significant?

"Some friends are worth showing off," her escort said smoothly.

The curly haired young man shook his head but recovered. "Shall I tell Management you're here?"

"Thank you," Jake said. "That would be convenient."

Gabriel held their chairs while the second waiter set out a fresh bouquet of dewy-fresh, garden-grown pink roses. Jake didn't bat an eye at the fussing. He ordered wine without looking at a list—something French, she thought. The wine was for her. Gabriel brought whiskey with a separate glass of rocks for Jake. The chunks of ice looked artistic, liked they'd been chiseled from a larger block individually. Jake dropped one into his drink with a pair of tongs.

He smiled at her expression. "Didn't know I was this worldly?"

Here at last was a question she could answer. "I knew you were worldly. Just not cosmopolitan." Since he'd given her an opening to speak, she drew breath for a few more words. "May I ask where Call is?"

Jake's eyes narrowed, but he didn't reprimand her boldness. "He's probably in that corner near the stage on the highest tier. That's his reserved table."

The elevated platform was shadowy. Mia made out the shape of a tall well-built male in the single chair, leaning back casually. She found it difficult to connect the hockey player in the stained jersey with this icon of elegance. Call's perfectly tailored dinner jacket fit as naturally as a second skin. Light fell across his left sleeve, gleaming on a snowy cuff with a bright silver link. His hand rested on a nearly full champagne flute, his graceful fingers as long as a pianist's. He held himself motionless—regally, she might have said. She noticed other eyes sliding in his direction, so perhaps he was still because he was self-conscious.

"Have you met him?" she couldn't resist asking.

"Not directly." He squeezed her shoulder. "Hush now. Management is coming."

Management was a beautiful dark-skinned woman in an incredible turquoise gown. The sparkling garment wasn't simply designed; it was designed for her. Its cloth flowed down her tall slim body like water.

Jake stood and greeted her.

"Mr. Reed," she said, accepting his polite kiss. "What a pleasant surprise."

Mia noted he didn't respond with a name for her. He smoothed the front of his black silk shirt. "I hope you don't mind me showing up unannounced."

"Goodness, no. We'd given up on seeing you on a Thursday, you being such a *private* practitioner."

Her emphasis was subtle, but Mia still heard it.

"Sometimes new toys require new approaches."

Did he mean her? Mia looked up at him. Though he didn't glance down, his hand dropped onto her back, where the cutouts in her dress bared skin. She wasn't sure, but she thought his thumb and index finger were playing with her hair.

"She certainly is new," Management agreed, a hint of doubt in her cultured voice. "Almost too new, if I'm not mistaken."

"She's obedient. So far anyway. And better coaxed than broken, to my thinking."

"And you intend to 'coax' her here?" The woman's skepticism was obvious.

"If you're amenable. You know my reputation. I'm not one to harm anyone."

Management pursed her lips. "She knows what you've planned?"

"I thought it best not to give her a chance to worry. Not that it would necessarily matter. She's very responsive."

Management startled Mia by crouching beside her chair, allowing Mia to look down at her obvious power superior. "Do you trust this man with your well being?" she asked. "Not just physically but also your emotions?"

The gorgeous woman stared directly into her eyes, making the question seem even more important. Instinctively, Mia knew she didn't need Jake's permission to answer.

"I do." Her voice was husky. Management smiled as Mia cleared her throat.

"Very well," she said, rising to her full height again. "Mr. Reed, we'd be honored to have you . . . coax your new toy in our company. Please let Gabriel know whatever assistance you require."

CHAPTER 3

AS soon as Management left, Mia shot Jake a look she hoped would elicit answers to her questions. Jake didn't oblige her.

"Finish your wine if you're going to," he said, his amusement faint but discernible. "There's a room backstage where we'll meet Gabriel."

Not liking the sound of that, she left her wine untouched. She had a feeling she'd want her head clear for what came next.

The space he led her to was a combination of dressing room and erotic prop storage. Most everything she saw made her nervous but also a bit intrigued. If it hadn't been for the people presumably waiting to watch out front, she'd have liked exploring some of these things with him.

"There's a powder room," Jake said, gesturing toward the open door. "You can freshen up and compose yourself."

The idea of composure seemed optimistic. She splashed her blazing cheeks with cold water and dried her face on a towel. The girl who looked back at her from the mirror was wide-eyed. She remembered Jake calling her a doe in headlights. She certainly fit the description then.

You're supposed to be like this, she told herself. *This is what the plan depends on.*

She blew out her breath and went to join Jake and Gabriel. The men were conferring on strategy.

"The rack makes a nice visual," Gabriel was suggesting.

For a second, Mia thought he meant her breasts.

"Yes," Jake said, "but I think I prefer the chair. Simple. Comfortable. Plus, there's the Sharon Stone factor."

"Jesus," Mia blurted, automatically pressing her thighs together.

Jake turned to smile at her. He seemed very much at ease. "Good," he said. "You look ready."

◆

Her photographic brain identified the chair as an Emeco "Navy" model in brushed aluminum, quite possibly an original 1944 version designed for submarines. The things lasted forever, so she'd heard. The chair was simple, its straight unadorned slats begging for body parts to be chained to them. It sat alone on Audition's half-circle stage, lit up by an overhead spotlight.

The sight of it, waiting for her ass to plunk down in it, made her heart beat fast enough to dizzy her.

This was like one of those dreams where she was supposed to sing an aria but didn't know Italian.

Jake stood behind her in the stage's wing. He must have sensed her nervousness. He squeezed her tense shoulders and leaned closer. "You can't fail," he murmured into her ear. "Everything that happens here is on me."

It was nice of him to say this, but she knew they were a team. If this went pear-shaped, she'd share the blame. She forced herself to focus on Management's voice. Though Mia couldn't see her, she was currently speaking on the other side of the closed curtain.

"As most of you know," she said, "Thursdays are special at Audition. Tonight we watch demonstrations of our associates' skills. During the presentation, silence is our golden rule. There are to be no comments or exclamations of any sort, neither to praise nor to criticize. Break this rule and security will escort you out. No exceptions, no second chances. You *will* respect this opportunity to learn." She paused to let her words sink in. "Elaine? Please activate the curtain. Mister R, the stage is yours."

As the curtain hissed upward, Mia realized *Mister R* was Jake. Management was protecting his privacy. A few last coughs disrupted the audience, after which quiet reigned.

Jake put his hands behind Mia's shoulder blades and gave them a gentle push.

"Walk to the chair and wait," he said, projecting sufficiently that she imagined everyone in the place could hear. "Slowly please. People will want to admire your excellent legs."

Crap. He meant walk onto the stage alone. Mia's palms broke into a sweat. She dried them on the skirt of her snug red dress then hoped she hadn't left a mark. Her supposedly excellent legs felt like stiff spaghetti in her tall shoes, ready to snap the moment she unlocked her knees. She'd practiced walking in the heels like Jake advised, but at the time she'd been by herself in her apartment.

The idea of swinging her hips for watchers made her as uptight as trying to prevent them from moving.

"Slower," Jake said, still in the wings. "Don't sit until I tell you to."

Her right knee buckled at his order, but she recovered without twisting her ankle. She assumed the little gasp that rippled through the crowd didn't break the golden rule. The near miss sent heat flooding to her face. Luckily, the stage was small. She'd reached the aluminum seat. She wanted to sit but didn't.

"Stand behind the chair and grip its back," Jake commanded.

Mia gripped it for dear life.

"Breathe," Jake said, and this was an order too. "Slowly in, slowly out."

She tried to do it, but it was hard to calm. She'd never liked being the center of attention. Her comfort zone was in the background where people were less likely to notice her idiosyncrasies. Though she faced the packed audience, the footlights blinded her from seeing them. She wondered if Damien Call were watching in the dark. Did her anxiety excite him? Was he breathing faster in his James Bond at the casino clothes? Perhaps he felt an increase in pressure from his cock prodding his zipper.

These ideas came out of nowhere to arouse her. Or maybe not *nowhere*. She and Jake were here for Call. He was the only observer whose opinion signified.

She could tell herself the roomful of other strangers didn't exist.

She wished telling herself would convince her. Every person she'd glimpsed in Audition—every diner, every waiter, every gyrating dancer—flashed into her retentive mind. Immediately, she longed to tug at her hem. This dress was so short. Were people thinking her thighs were fat? How long was Jake going to take before he joined her?

She turned her head toward where she thought he was and jerked in surprise. Jake was right beside her. He'd crossed the stage silently. Relief flooded her at his nearness. She was safe now. He was with her. Her gratitude was so potent it startled her.

She had a sneaking suspicion this was the reaction he'd meant to cause.

If it were, he didn't give the game away. He shook his head in mild disapproval, his deep blue eyes gleaming. "I see I need to teach you no one exists for you but me. I am the only master you need to please."

She swallowed, unable to look away from him.

"Better," he said in his raspy voice, "but I think you need more focus."

He had something in his hand. He'd been holding it by his trouser leg, and she hadn't seen. Now she recognized a short whip, the same as silhouetted Audition's poker chip, the same she'd seen jockeys use in horse races. About thirty inches long, the riding crop had a rigid handle, a flexible whipping part wrapped in leather, and a narrow slapper bit at the tip—probably to prevent breaking the horse's skin.

As Jake drew his martial arts hardened fingers along its length, Mia's fascinated gaze followed every millimeter of their progress.

"This is your focus aid," he purred. "You'll grow to like it, I think. It should pinpoint your perceptions perfectly."

A sound that wasn't speech broke in Mia's throat.

"You've never been spanked, have you?" he asked.

She shook her head.

"Nor whipped."

She shook it again.

He dragged the leather slapper across his palm. "In truth, your ass is completely virginal."

She blushed. The answer to that was *yes* in more ways than one.

Jake's smile was sexy and saturnine. "Push your lovely ass out, doll. And spread your feet apart. I'm going to *focus* you."

Him calling her *doll* reminded her he was the Jake she knew. He cared about her, and wouldn't embarrass her too much. She only shivered a bit as she moved her legs wider. That was the draft's fault, she told herself.

Jake drew his arm back and stopped. "Remind me, what is your safe word?"

For a moment her mind went blank. "Daffodil," she burst out.

"Yes. Daffodil." He trailed the slapper part of the whip around her pushed-out bottom, the feel of it through the short skirt both tickly and erotic. "Say it any time and I'll stop whatever it is I'm doing. Other than that, feel free to cry out all you like. I won't pay the least attention."

She gaped at him. He thought she was going to cry out? He'd told her earlier to react as she reacted. Didn't he know wailing like a porn star totally wasn't her? Who did that in real life? In her experience, real world sex wasn't that earthshaking.

His lips curved archly at her expression. Apparently, he had a whole arsenal of smartass smiles he intended to use on her.

"Why don't I begin?" he suggested.

"Yes, why *don't* you?" she heard herself goad unexpectedly.

Someone in the audience muffled a giggle.

Jake swung the riding crop sharply down on one butt cheek. The sting surprised her—and the heat that streaked after it.

"That tone of voice isn't acceptable," he warned.

He swatted her again and again, each stroke deliberate and controlled. Right cheek, left cheek, top, middle, and underneath. The blows drove her onto the balls of her feet, though not precisely because of pain.

The aftermath of each strike felt better than the one before, as if the whip were driving electric charges from the muscles of her bottom into her clit. That throbbing button swelled as blood engorged it and all the flesh nearby. Her pussy ached, hot slick fluid filling it. She heard Jake breathing harder, and knew he was aroused too. She wanted to squirm, to writhe—anything to ease the tormenting need.

She couldn't do that without moving her legs together.

Actually, she couldn't do it without his say-so.

He struck her once more, and she did cry out. She couldn't help it. She wanted his hard cock driving up inside her too badly.

He took the cry as his cue to stop but let her know it wasn't out of pity. "Perhaps that's enough for now. We wouldn't want to take all your . . . innocence in one go."

His concern for that trait was questionable. She gasped as he used the slapper bit to stroke up the inside of one shaking thigh and onto her swollen lips. She prayed the audience couldn't see where the whip had gone. She wore a thong, but it wasn't covering much. Jake teased the whip down the other thigh and back to the heart of her sensation.

"Do you know what this part of the whip is called? The one that's touching you right now?" His voice had changed, darkening and tightening as he pulled her deeper under his spell. "It's called the keeper."

He stroked the leather wings up and down her labia. The pressure was too delicious. Mia's sex overflowed. She bit her lip to restrain a whimper. Jake drew the whip end toward him again. Her knuckles tensed around the chair's metal back. She knew the leather would come out wet and that he was bound to say something.

"Don't," she pleaded before he could.

"Don't what?" he taunted. "Tell the world the effect my keeper had to you? They can guess, doll, even if they're not near enough to see."

He understood her too well. She hung her head and her hair fell across her face.

"That won't do," Jake said, suddenly touching her nape gently. "You may stand straight again. Gabriel, please bring the rest of my submissive's accessories."

She straightened, trembling. Jake's warm hand fell to her spine, where her dress was cut out. Up and down he rubbed her bare skin, as if they were a couple of longstanding. As he did, she had the odd sensation of being taller—though this was likely due to her fancy shoes.

Jake towered over her the same as before.

Gabriel had been watching from the wings. He came out at Jake's summons with an armload of silvery chains. Mia would have tensed, except the other *accessory* the server emerged with distracted her.

Gabriel's black waiter pants looked like he'd shoved his fist behind their zipper.

Her breath sucked in. That was some serious wood. Gabriel did nothing to hide it. Apart from his heightened color, which might or might not have been embarrassment, he didn't seem self-conscious.

He was, however, walking gingerly.

"Sir," he said, stopping a foot away. "What would you like me to do with these?"

"Please attach the ends to her collar rings."

There were three lengths of chain, all long and none wider than a finger. The strands were light, possibly aluminum. Gabriel attached them to her necklace with a glancing touch for each. He must have like girls too, because he didn't seem to mind being close to her. His respiration was choppy by the time he drew back from her.

His attention dropped to her breasts. Mia tensed but she hadn't suffered a wardrobe malfunction. Her red dress still covered her. The indecency came from her nipples having turned to volcanic stone.

It was a sign of how extraordinary the circumstances were that this didn't make her want to cross her arms over them.

"Sir," he said, wrenching his gaze to Jake.

"Thank you, Gabriel," Jake said with a hint of wryness. "That will be all for now."

He seemed to know what the other man was experiencing. Was that what being a good dom meant? That you could get into other people's heads?

He didn't have any trouble getting into hers. He took the triple length of chain in his hand as if it were a leash, sparing her from tripping on it as he walked her to the front of the chair. The move didn't make her happy. Simple though the seat was, it had been a barrier between her and watching eyes.

Before her panic could rise, Jake stepped in front of her.

"I'll just tug this down." His body radiated warmth as he leaned close to pull the hem more securely around her butt—the same as she'd have done if he'd allowed it. "Now sit."

His words were as good as a shove. Her basted cheeks appreciated the coolness of the metal, though she had to struggle not to wriggle. The nerves of her clitoris wanted her to a lot.

Jake knelt in front of her. "Legs first, I think. I can tell you're concerned about exposure."

This time he wasn't trying to prevent it. Gently but firmly, he pressed her knees apart until her calves sprawled wider than the chair legs. He took hold of her right foot, tucking the toe of her fancy shoe into the chair's bottom rung from its outside.

"Stay like that," he ordered.

She stayed, though doing so unnerved her. Then again, maybe it was the tingles his every action inspired that kept her in turmoil.

Jake strode around her once with one of the silvery chains, circling her waist and binding it to the chair. He crouched again to feed the links around both her lower leg and the nearest rungs. The loops weren't tight, but there were so many they held her limb secure. His physical adeptness was obvious. With efficient yet precise motions, he looped a nearly identical spiral around her second leg.

Mia clenched the seat of the chair with her still free hands. Having her feet tucked up off the ground made her feel off balance and vulnerable. Sharon Stone's *Basic Instinct* moment hadn't involved this much. Despite Jake's earlier adjustment of her hem, her skirt had crept up. The lacy tops of her fancy stockings—which Hillary had insisted on—were exposed. Mia hoped the shadows hid the more personal parts of her.

She also hoped the club's no camera rule was well enforced.

Jake straightened to his full height and looked down at her.

His efforts had been *almost* businesslike, but she saw he was affected. His black silk shirt clung to him in places where the sweat of his excitement dampened it. She recalled his story about the movie and the girl who'd been tied up: how he hadn't been able to hold back from jacking off. Though the lines of his face weren't giving much away, he was breathing more deeply, clearly liking the picture he'd created using the chains and her body.

The ridge that pushed out his zipper was bigger than it had been on the drive over.

She leaned toward it without thinking, her body yearning for what his had to offer.

Jake stepped neatly out of reach. "Both hands behind your neck. Point your elbows toward the ceiling."

It was the bark of a drill sergeant, reminding her he'd been in the military. Feeling like she was in a dream, Mia released her hold on the seat and positioned her arms as he'd instructed. With the final and longest chain, Jake bound her wrists together.

The sound of the links' clash and rattle was sexual.

"Don't struggle," he said gruffly. "I don't want the links cutting into you."

He wasn't done binding her, and she found she was glad of it. The process of being wrapped was unexpectedly reassuring. He was controlling her, taking the weight of that burden on himself. More slowly now, as if he needed to savor the process, he wrapped the chain around her torso. He used it to separate and draw attention to her breasts, to circle her waist, to immobilize her hip joints. There seemed to be an aesthetic to his choices, not simply a wish to constrain. Whatever he was aiming for, each loop felt as if it were a further step in a sexual act—so many passes, and they'd have to reach climax. He formed a V around her pubis that was like a hand squeezing it. Her muscles shuddered, her nerves jumping crazily.

At last, he ran out of chain.

Though she would have listened regardless, he put his hand on her shoulder to claim her attention. "Tell me, beautiful, do you feel helpless now?"

"Yes," she gasped, the act of admitting it exciting. A moment later, she had a different thought. *Should* she be giving him what he wanted? Wouldn't, maybe, resisting be more fun? She couldn't *really* resist, not to any dangerous degree. He did have her at his mercy.

"Do you want to move?" he asked. "Maybe rub your hungry little pussy against the chair?"

He made her blush. "I don't dare. I don't want the chains to cut into me."

He enjoyed the answer, though her tone had edged toward sarcasm. The gleam in his eyes increased. "Is your bottom pulsing? Can you feel the whip strikes I laid on it?"

She felt them twice as much after he said the words. Her clit pulsed in a matching rhythm, unbelievably sensitized by everything he'd done. She could please him by letting him know that. Rather than give in to temptation, she bit her lower lip.

"Rebellion," he chided, wagging one long finger.

An extraordinary zing shot up her clitoris, as if his wagging finger were tapping it. What had he done to her? She was completely in thrall to him. Then again, maybe they were in thrall to each other. How else could she explain that he knew to pull these reactions out of her? He cupped her breast with the hand that had scolded her. When he squeezed, his callused palm compressed her nipple. She was sensitized there as well. The pleasure was so sharp a cry tore from her.

"I could make you come," he warned. "Whether you wanted to or not, I could manipulate this one nipple and all these people would see you orgasm."

"Don't." Her throat felt sore, her body trembling from head to toe. Part of her knew she didn't want him to listen. Part of her was completely thrilled.

"'Don't' isn't your safe word."

He stole her breath by jerking the chair she was bound to onto its back two legs. She couldn't fling out her arms for balance. They were chained behind her neck. Instinct told her to panic, but at the same time she absolutely knew Jake wouldn't let her fall. Adrenaline flooded her, and Lord knew what other crazed biological cocktail. If she hadn't been bound, she'd have thrown herself on him; just ripped down his zipper, climbed his tall hard body, and rode him until they both climaxed. If a million people had watched, she wouldn't have stopped herself.

"'Yes' or 'no,'" he said, holding her dipped back. "I need to hear one of those two words before I continue."

His handsome face was inches away, his cologne mixing with his sweat to form a scent she'd never get enough of. His arms were steely from the intensity of his grip, his pupils swollen with arousal. When he wet his lips, she lost it.

"Yes," she answered.

He crashed his mouth over his, his tongue instantly claiming the territory inside. Her hormones went *ohmygod*. He tasted so good and felt so good and boy oh boy he could kiss. She strained in the chains that held her, desperate for more of his oral skill. Jake made a rumbling noise in his chest, too soft for anyone but her to hear. His kiss went deeper. His hand tightened on her breast . . .

She came, her body jerking with pleasure and surprise. The orgasm was quick but sharp, and it drew a low moan from her.

Jake pulled free and set her upright again.

She gaped at him, shocked and actually a bit angered by his retreat. At least he wasn't smirking over his victory. She couldn't have tolerated that. His face was flushed as he stared back at her, his hands slightly clenched at his sides. Mia had no idea what lay behind his dark expression until a smattering of applause broke out in the audience. Then annoyance flicked across his features. He didn't want their experience lowered to the level of something done for show.

The applause cut off. Management was striding onto the stage in her amazing blue sparkly gown. She had no trouble walking in four-inch heels. "Thank you," she said to Jake as the house lights came up. "I'm sure we all appre-"

"What the fuck do you think you're doing?" a familiar voice demanded.

It was Curtis, her and Jake's mutual boss. Mia had thought he was leaving tonight's scheme to Jake, but she guessed not. Curtis glared at Jake from the edge of the dance floor in the same clothes he'd worn to work, his arms crossed angrily at his chest. To be honest, Mia wasn't a hundred percent certain his rage was feigned. Curtis looked genuinely pissed.

Maybe he hadn't known how far Jake intended to take this?

"What does it look like I'm doing?" Jake responded unhelpfully.

"You told me you didn't play with coworkers. You said it would 'threaten our dynamic.'" Curtis's face flushed darker as he made quote fingers. "Mia is our receptionist. And under my protection!"

Jake shrugged. "What can I say? You're hot, Curtis, but I like her sexy bits better."

Curtis rushed toward the stage roaring, clearly intending to attack. Mia cursed the chains that kept her from intervening. Fortunately, two of Audition's security guys got between Curtis and the object of his anger.

"You're fired!" Curtis shouted, struggling to wrench free of them. "Both of you are goddamned fired!"

Hey, Mia thought, stung by this in spite of the fact that it probably was an act. How was it fair that she got fired too? What happened to her being under Curtis's protection?

"Get him out of here," Management ordered her security personnel.

It took one more guy, but Curtis was escorted out.

"Lower the curtain," was Management's next command. She ducked behind it as it fell. "Are you two all right?"

Jake squeezed Mia's shoulder. "I think we are. I'm really sorry about the scene."

Management waved away his apology. "Not your fault. That young man earned himself a blacklisting. From here *and* Diogenes."

Well, hell, Mia thought, her sense of injustice switching targets. She hoped Curtis didn't like the club too much. At least he'd been interacting sort of romantically with people. She looked at Jake, who warned her with a small headshake not to plead on her friend's behalf.

"Let me get you out of these chains." He hunkered down to do it. A moment later, his brows lowered. "You're shaking. Why didn't you warn me that was too much? It's important for subs to communicate their limits."

Was that what she was now? His sub? Jake had one hand on her knee and the other behind her hip. Both touches were unusually comforting. Under the circumstances, Mia gave herself permission to enjoy them.

His eyes were so stunning and intent she temporarily forgot to respond to what he'd said. With a little jerk, she remembered. "What you did wasn't too much. It was just . . . a lot. Plus, I think I might be in shock from getting fired. I've never seen Curtis that angry."

She hoped she wasn't talking too much. She wasn't the best actress. Jake patted her upper leg. "This is my fault. I'll help you find another job. You're a good receptionist."

He began unwinding the chains that held her to the chair. She watched him take them off with as much fascination as she'd watched them go on. She sensed him working not to react to what he was doing. That was illuminating. Jake *really* enjoyed bondage. She guessed it was lucky *he* wasn't getting barred from Diogenes.

Standing again was awkward. Her muscles had tensed and her panties were really wet.

"Ma'am," Gabriel interrupted, coming in from the wings again. "Mr. C would like to speak to these two."

Management's eyes narrowed. "Would he now?"

"I think I should take my friend home," Jake said. "She's had an upsetting day."

"I might be able to help with that," Damien Call said smoothly.

He didn't wait for permission but stepped past Gabriel to join them on the stage. He was tall in person, broader than Jake but not bulky. Mia estimated he was around thirty, so younger than both Jake and Curtis. He was handsome in a square-jawed Captain America sort of way—privileged and polished. His hair was gold-streaked brown under the rafter lights. The strands were straight and as perfectly styled as a magazine cover. He seemed unruffled, as if his evening clothes didn't dare wrinkle.

He stopped more than an arm's length away. Possibly his personal space needs were bigger than most people's.

A little tingle of . . . *something* coursed through Mia as his impassive gaze raked her up and down. His eyes weren't polished. They reminded her of a mountain lion—like he was deciding how to eat her up. Though the onceover had been quick, she suspected it was thorough.

Jake stepped slightly in front of her and pulled himself straighter. "We're not looking for help."

"Aren't you?" The men's gazes locked, the battle of wills interesting to watch. Both commanded their own sort of power, and both definitely had a thing for control. Damien Call blinked first, though this might have been because he decided to. "It sounded as if you might be seeking employment."

"Playing at Diogenes is my hobby, not my career. Anyway, you don't know us."

"I don't know *her*," Call corrected. "You I've seen operate."

This seemed to surprise Jake a bit. "You've watched me."

"I especially admired your work with Gabriel. Staff submissives tend to get thick-skinned. You took him higher than anyone I've seen."

"Great," Jake said, but not like he was flattered. Mia concluded he was playing hard to get. "We're still not looking to sign on as Daddy Warbuck's toys."

Call smiled faintly. "I was going to offer you regular jobs. I happen to be in need of a personal assistant. And a driver with security experience."

If Call knew Jake had that, he'd researched him already.

"*You* need a driver?" Jake responded skeptically. "You made your first million designing cars."

Call shrugged. "I don't like driving in the city. Also, quite often, I need to work en route. That's not safe to do when I'm behind the wheel."

He was lying. Mia couldn't have said how she knew. Her subconscious brain sometimes added up nonverbal signs. Though it might not have been strategic, she said what she was thinking. "You don't need a personal assistant or a driver. It's like Jake said: you want us to be your toys."

Call really looked at her this time. "I would like you to be my toys, as you put it. However, I'm perfectly willing to hire you in a standard capacity while you make up your mind and take my measure. I pay well, in case you were concerned."

"We weren't," Jake said flatly. He put his arm around her shoulders, pulling her to his side. That nonverbal message didn't need any special brainwork to decipher.

"As you wish," Call said. "I'll give you my card in case you change your mind."

He took a step closer and handed it to Jake. Without retreating, he looked at her. "Would you like one as well?"

The question took her by surprise. Mia considered for a moment before holding out her palm. Call placed his card in it. He didn't pull back as she expected but left his hand lightly touching hers. The brush of his fingertips was electric. Her gaze jerked to his. His irises were hazel: gold flecked with green and blue—very beautiful, she thought.

"You haven't slept with him yet, have you?"

Mia yanked her arm away, her fingers tightening around his card instead of dropping it. "That's a personal question."

"I know it is." He didn't seem repentant. "If you'd permit, I'd like to make an even more personal request. If you're considering accepting my offer, don't go any farther with him than you already have."

Mia gaped. She really didn't know how to respond to that.

Call's mouth curved with another glimmer of amusement. He was very sure of himself. Very sure of them, she suspected. He'd gotten his way too often not to be.

Jake didn't say a word as the billionaire shrugged his dinner jacket straighter and turned to go. Mia had a feeling Call's assumptions suited Jake perfectly.

◆

Though everything seemed to have gone according to his plan— not that *she'd* been privy to the whole of that—Jake was uncharacteristically jittery during the limo ride home from Audition. First he tapped the door handle, then his knee, and finally he bounced his shiny shoe on the plush brown carpet.

Mia had a number of conundrums to think about, but after a few miles of this she couldn't take it anymore.

"Why are you so antsy?" she demanded. "Didn't you get what you wanted?"

"What?" He looked surprised.

She gestured to his unruly knee. "You're bouncing."

"Oh." He stopped doing it. "Maybe we should discuss what happened."

"Which part?" she asked warily.

He laughed through his nose and twisted around to her.

Seeming relaxed again, he slung one arm along the top of the leather seat. "Are you prepared to have sex?"

Mia blinked. "You mean with you?" He nodded. She didn't know how to answer. She was plenty ready in some ways. In others, she was leerier than ever. The power he'd exerted over her tonight was unnerving. "You don't mean now, do you?"

Amused, he shook his head. "Call seems to expect us to have it in front of him. I didn't know he'd want that. From what I'd heard, he mostly enjoys watching dominance exchanges."

"You think that's why he told me not to go any farther with you until we decide on his offer."

"Yes."

As happened too often, the truth seized control of her vocal chords. "Being told not to do it makes me think about it even more."

Jake's eyelids grew heavy. His attention dipped to her mouth. "Yes," he agreed in his whispery bedroom voice.

Mia couldn't not shiver. When she did, he looked into her eyes again. "I know you don't sleep with men casually."

Was he implying it would be casual for him? What they'd done at Audition already felt intimate to her. She turned her head to the window, noting they were close to the Brooklyn Bridge. The weather was clear tonight. The heavy Gothic arches made quite a picture lit up against the sky. She wondered how many other bridges she'd cross before this was over.

She touched one fingertip to the window to trace a suspension cable's swoop. "We don't have to decide this second."

"Soon we do," Jake said quietly.

This time Mia was the one who turned fidgety.

◆

Jake had the unsettling sensation that he and Mia were connected by an invisible cord of . . . incompletion, he guessed he'd say. If she'd been anyone else, he'd have been fucking her in the car—enjoying it too, he'd bet. Mia might be inexperienced, but she wasn't short on interest in sex. She'd be incredible to have under him. To hell with what the driver might or might notice. Their scene at Audition had been exciting, their chemistry potent. His cock still felt heavy, like it would rise at the least excuse.

Really, it was no wonder he'd fidgeted.

"The lights are on in your windows," he said as they arrived at her apartment building. "Curtis must have used his key. Probably he wants to go over what happened."

Mia gnawed her lip.

"He won't be mad," Jake assured her. "You know that fight was an act."

She nodded like she wasn't a hundred percent convinced. She got out anyway and led him up the three flights of steps.

Halfway up the second, she took her heels off and walked barefoot.

Curtis heard them coming and pulled the door open. Mia didn't give him a chance to say hello.

"You didn't tell me Jake was bi," she said.

"Uh, bi-*ish*." Curtis stepped aside to let Jake in too. He gave Jake a wide-eyed *here we go* grimace. "I'm pretty sure he likes girls better."

"Whatever. You went to the club together. You knew he was playing with Gabriel. That stuff you said about not wanting to mess with your work dynamic was genuine."

"Sort of. I mean, of course it makes sense to keep that option off the table, but we didn't discuss it explicitly. I'm relatively certain we're not each other's type. Would you like a beer? I brought a few over."

Her walk-up had a simple kitchen along one wall of the living room. Mia glanced at the refrigerator, clearly suspicious of his peace offering.

"I'll get it," Jake said. After the night he'd had, he could use alcohol.

He handed out the bottles, opening Mia's for her first. Mia and Curtis sat like brother and sister on her beat-up couch beneath her vintage travel posters, their slouched-back poses identical. They balanced their beers at the same angle on their thighs.

"Are you upset that Jake is bi-ish?" Curtis asked.

Jake wondered that as well. To himself, he identified as het, or pretty near it on the spectrum. Now and then, a man made his radar ping. It didn't seem a big deal to him. Interested to know how it seemed to Mia, he lowered his weight to the arm of a nearby chair.

"I suppose I'm not," Mia said. "It wasn't my business before. And it never bothered me that Mike was gay."

"I always liked that about you," Curtis said.

"I don't think I deserve credit. Mike was impossible not to love."

In Jake's very private opinion, the same was true of her.

"Anyway," Curtis said, turning more businesslike. "I want an update on what happened after I was kicked out."

"Call offered us employment: a driving job for me and a personal assistant position for Mia. He admitted he hoped this would be a precursor to us putting on more intimate shows for him."

"Really," Curtis said. "That was quick."

"We didn't give him an answer. I figured we shouldn't look too eager."

"He knew Jake had security experience," Mia added. "He must have researched him."

Curtis spread his hands. "He'll research you too, but it doesn't matter. Your story is that you are who you are, and you do what you do. The only thing you keep from him is that we work for Raeburn."

"Which maybe we don't." Mia rubbed the couch's slipcover.

Jake had a feeling he knew what was bothering her. "Did Raeburn pay the retainer?"

"I put it in escrow," Curtis said.

"You know this is a fine line we're walking ethically."

Curtis's steady look said he knew it was. "I'll be careful not to cross it. You be sure you don't cross the line with Mia. And you —" He jabbed his finger at the girl. "Don't forget you can tap out any time. It hasn't escaped my notice that Jake interests you, but he's a big leaguer."

Okay, this topic of discussion made him uncomfortable, especially when Mia flushed bright red. "She held her own tonight. If she wants to, I think she can handle this. I could tell Call was impressed with her."

"Apparently, he's also impressed with you."

Curtis sounded slightly annoyed. "Jealous?" Jake teased, hoping to defuse his boss's irritation with humor.

"Screw you," Curtis swore mildly. "Who needs a man who only wants to watch?"

He seemed fine, so Jake relaxed and sipped his beer.

"I want to see what you've dug up on Call," Mia said.

"Thought you might." Curtis handed the folder over. Mia

took it with such eagerness he grinned.

He knew what was inside. He'd done his own background check. Damien Call had been born in Pacific Palisades, California to upper middle class parents. He'd attended exclusive charter schools where he excelled beyond the norm. Now 29, *Forbes* estimated his personal net worth at 5.2 billion. He was single and never married. Current residence: Manhattan. Attended MIT but didn't graduate. Generous sponsor to green-related charities. Parents divorced when he was seventeen. Formed his first company, Sun Motors, a year later. The IPO had broken records, which whetted his appetite to break more. Damien Call was coder and engineer—accomplished on both sides of the equation. He had complicated and expansive holdings around the world. Though viewed as eccentric, he commanded fervent respect from his employees. Sometimes referred to as the Twenty-Four Karat Ice Cube, he was famed for his dispassionate negotiating style. Rivals called him a calculating bastard but admitted he knew his stuff.

Public record of his activities at Diogenes seemed not to exist at all.

Jake wondered which of these facts was causing Mia's brows to furrow. Watching her read was always interesting. She turned pages faster than most people skimmed—and with total absorption. There was no denying her brain was different then. Other things about her too. Jake had never met anyone like her.

Cut it out, he ordered his wandering mind.

Thinking about Mia as one in a billion didn't help him stay businesslike.

CHAPTER 4

DAMIEN Call's corporate HQ took up five of his Manhattan skyscraper's sixty floors. The building was one of the financial district's newer builds. Its boldly curving architecture was very airy, very sleek, and exemplified the Call aesthetic. In case people didn't recognize the streamlined shape of one of his jets in it, the WORLDWIDE logo wrapped the topmost floor. The giant letters were brushed silver, their edges lit up at night to help approaching pilots orient themselves.

Okay, really the lights were for him. Damien liked seeing his company's name glowing above the great city.

He also liked the amazing view the building commanded at the island's tip. Battery Park and the harbor, the East River, even the Brooklyn Bridge was laid out for him. He only had to stroll a different length of windows in his office to admire a new vista. His personal corporate space was bigger than many homes. The custom tiles on its floor—brick sized and laid out in herringbones—bore the same matte silver finish he used on his concept cars. The furniture was modern and spread apart, the rugs antique and understated in soft blue tones. His scattered knickknacks adhered to a navigation theme: mostly old compasses and gyroscopes. His prize possession was the door from an 1890's electric cab with SAMUEL'S ELECTRIC CARRIAGE COMPANY on its side.

Looking at it reminded him he was bringing electric powered vehicles back to the forefront where they belonged. Someday fossil fuel reliance would go the way of the dinosaurs.

Leaning back in his state of the art ergonomic chair, with a brand new sunrise piercing the clear glass walls, Damien could convince himself his spirit was as serene as his surroundings.

"Good morning, Mr. Call," said a smoothly professional—and unwelcome—female voice. "Would you like me to get coffee?"

It was his secretary, Ms. DeWinter. Though it was literally the crack of dawn, she stood a few steps inside his door, notepad at the ready, every wave of her naturally russet hair perfectly arranged. She'd been with him six months now. During the last two, this had been happening more often. No matter what time Damien arrived, Ms. DeWinter would appear within the quarter hour. Though the assistant didn't know it, he'd determined she'd come to an arrangement with José in Security, whereby the guard informed her if Damien's private elevator descended from his penthouse residence to this floor.

Ms. DeWinter seemed to hope Damien would think she was psychically attuned to him.

He didn't want to fire her. She was highly competent, hardworking, and—he'd thought—happily married. His colleagues enjoyed that she was easy on the eyes. If, however, he couldn't break her of this habit, he'd have to cut her loose.

"Ms. DeWinter," he began resignedly. "I didn't call for you to come in."

"No, sir. I was simply trying to anticipate your needs."

Was she flirting? Her cream silk blouse seemed more unbuttoned than usual.

"I don't pay you to anticipate my needs outside of normal working hours."

"Of course, sir, but—"

"No 'buts,' Ms. DeWinter. I'm sure your husband would rather you spend your mornings together."

"He understands, sir. He knows you're an important man."

Damien sighed internally. This would require bluntness. "Ms. DeWinter. I don't want you here unless I've called you. You should also know that, as of today, José is no longer a WorldWide employee. I don't appreciate my comings and going being shared, no matter how benign the intention."

Ms. DeWinter's flush was unmistakable. "Forgive me, sir. I —"

"Go home," he said, cutting off her apology. "Don't return before 8:30."

She practically bowed as she backed away. To his relief, she shut the door behind her.

This was the problem with running a huge company. Even when you signed the checks, some employees inevitably strayed from their assigned course.

He squeezed his temples between the thumb and middle finger of his right hand, blowing out his breath in an attempt to restore his calm. He needed to let this go. He'd never control everything.

Interestingly enough, control was the topic he'd come here to contemplate.

He hadn't slept much last night. He couldn't get what he'd witnessed at Audition out of his mind. Mr. R's new sub had climaxed from a kiss. Not sex. Not a spanking. But from a kiss. He'd watched Mr. R work his wiles before. The man was a master in every sense of the word. Too much of one, maybe. He'd intrigued Damien—men sometimes did—but Mr. R's façade had never betrayed the cracks it did last night.

Last night, something magical had happened. Despite the dom's clear experience, the girl he'd been whipping nearly unraveled *him*. He'd been so hard the back rows could have counted up his inches.

Damien sincerely hoped Mr. R hadn't fucked the girl when he took her home.

He shifted in his chair, now uncomfortably hard himself. He wanted to see it; wanted to watch every millimeter of that raging organ slide into her. The girl was incredibly responsive. Damien knew she'd enjoy it.

He remembered the silken feel of her palm as he gave her his business card. Her big brown eyes had seemed so startled when they snapped up to his. She was an innocent with just enough spirit to make things interesting. He sensed she'd been tempted to accept his offer. Mr. R was possessive—as indeed he ought to be. The girl was a treasure, and Mr. R wouldn't give up control of her for a job. Damien's best hope was that the dom would realize she wanted to explore the exotic world he'd introduced her to with Damien's hand joining his on the steering wheel.

Unless Mr. R were an idiot—which he didn't seem to be— he'd do a quite a lot to keep his young friend happy.

Suddenly, Damien had to know her name. He grabbed his phone, doubly glad now that he'd sent Ms. DeWinter home. Though it wasn't generally known, Damien owned Audition. Not

Diogenes, which annoyed him; the sister clubs really should have been guided by the same person. This morning, thankfully, owning one club was better than none at all.

He had to wait a few rings. The individual who picked up was sleepy but alert enough to recognize his voice.

"Sir," he said. "What can I do for you?"

"I need our background check on the guest known as Mr. R. Please forward the encrypted file to my secure email."

Damien heard computer keys clicking. "Anything else?"

No file would yet exist on the girl. She'd only attended once that he knew. "That's all," he said. "Sorry to wake you."

The girl was Mr. R's work colleague. Damien knew how to do a search. Finding her name—and most everything else about her—would be a piece of cake.

◆

The buzzing of a wasp pulled Mia from the depths of a pleasant dream. In it, Captain America had escorted her to her high school prom where, despite her hopeless unpopularity, she'd been voted in as queen. Classmates watched with envy as she and her handsome tuxedoed date gyrated on the dance floor.

The band's sexy lead guitarist looked a hell of a lot like Jake.

You can hold your own, he was singing raspily.

"Mmph," she said, reluctantly pushing up from her tangled sheets. The buzzing noise that had woken her grew louder, as if someone nearby were using a weed whacker. She twisted toward her bedside window and nearly choked on a gasp of shock.

A helicopter style drone was hovering outside her third floor ledge. It was shiny black, about the size of a fire escape barbecue, and had four bright blue insect legs. The silver WorldWide logo stood out on its dark surface. Beneath its belly, a parcel hung.

Mia tried to get her brain to make sense of what she was seeing. Was it even legal for a drone to be flying here?

As if the thing could tell she was looking at it, a small red light flashed three times at her.

Okay, maybe that's how it asked if it could come in. Glad she didn't sleep in the nude and not sure what else to do, Mia hauled the window open and backed up to make room for it. The drone bobbled slightly but buzzed through the opening without hitting anything. More sensors blinked as it dropped its package gently onto her mattress.

Then it zipped out the same way it had come in. Mia watched it disappear above the roofs with her jaw hanging.

The box sitting on her bed assured her she hadn't been dreaming.

FOR MIA BECK, its plain paper wrapping said. PLEASE OPEN IMMEDIATELY.

In spite of her jangled pulse, she laughed. It must be a present from Damien Call. He'd certainly picked an attention-getting mode of delivery. Even as she worked the package open, a rich dark scent gave away the contents: coffee beans from a local specialty purveyor, so recently removed from the roaster the bag was warm. She pulled the coffee out to inhale and spotted a schmancy stovetop espresso pot. Extricating that revealed two more bubble-wrapped items.

"Oh my," she breathed once she'd opened them.

They were bone china cups and saucers with alternating fuchsia and ivory stripes. Real gold highlighted their delicate rims and handles, which she stroked delightedly. Mia had never told anyone she had a fancy coffee cup obsession. She liked looking at them online, but the sort she favored didn't fit her budget. These were very like a pair she'd drooled over the other day.

"Crap," she said, her heart beating faster for a less pleased reason.

Damien Call knew her name. And her address. And had somehow gotten access to her browser history. Okay, probably this wasn't surprising. He was a computer nerd as well as a carmaker. She felt uncomfortable being spied on but, to be fair, she'd perused a not entirely public file on him last night.

"So we're even," Mia murmured. Maybe. She shifted guiltily on the bed. She was actually planning to spy on him some more.

She looked at the delicate cups. They were so pretty! Heaps better than lingerie or jewelry. Giving in to temptation, she gathered up her treasures to carry to the kitchen. Guilt could wait until after she'd enjoyed her present.

She was savoring her second cup when her cell phone rang. "Hey, Jake! Did you get a special delivery too?"

She realized too late how cheery her voice sounded.

"I did." His tone was amused. "Mine dropped a set of keys on the floor of my living room."

"Keys to what?"

"Come to the front of your building and find out."

"Crap. I'm not dressed. Or anything else. Give me ten minutes and I'll be there."

She took fifteen but trotted down the steps feeling more or less together. Her eyes went round when she saw the sleek silver sports car Jake waited in. For once, her heart jumped for different reasons than seeing him. Awed, she trailed her hand over the smooth as glass but not shiny aerodynamic hood.

"This is the W-22!" she breathed. "I hear there's a waiting list six months long to get one of these puppies."

"Seven." Jake didn't hide his grin. "Production at the factory in Detroit has been slower than expected."

"Have you let it park itself? What about the four-wheel drive and the GPS nav system? Can it actually go from zero to seventy in under five seconds?"

Laughing, Jake leaned to open the passenger door, which was a slick gull wing. "I had no idea you were this into cars."

Mia slid into the hand-stitched bucket seat with an undeniably sensual sigh. "Oh my god, new car smell!" She closed the door, caressed the soft glove leather, then craned around to see behind her. The compact rear electric engine left room for a good-sized second seat. "You're a way more expensive date than me. I got coffee and a coffee pot."

"I'm pretty sure it's a loaner. Call couldn't have meant for me to keep it."

Mia looked at him and smiled.

"He couldn't have," Jake protested, seeming taken aback. "This car costs six figures."

"Did you check the glove compartment?"

"I'm not sure where the glove compartment is."

The dash was minimalist compared to a normal car but Mia found the concealed recess. She pulled out the folded papers tucked inside. "Twenty bucks says your name is on the title."

"No." He shook his head disbelievingly.

"A hundred?"

He took the documents from her. When he opened them, his stunned expression told her they said exactly what she'd predicted. "Holy crap."

"Told you. Me cheap date. You pricey."

"This is crazy."

"Call has a lot of money. I guess it's no big deal to him."

"You got a coffee pot?"

"The cups might have been expensive. I think they were made in France." She was having trouble keeping a straight face.

"You're enjoying this."

Mia let out a snicker. Jake stared at her for a moment before sighing. "He sent a note along with the keys. You're welcome to read it."

He dug it from his coat's inner pocket. The same bold printer font that marked her package was on it.

PLEASE CONSIDER THE ATTACHED A
CONVENIENCE. IT OBLIGES YOU AND MISS BECK TO
NOTHING, BUT IF YOU LIKE, I'D BE PLEASED TO
MEET YOU BOTH FOR LUNCH TODAY AT
WORLDWIDE TO DISCUSS MUTUAL INTERESTS.
SINCERELY, DAMIEN CALL

"Ha!" Mia laughed. "He calls this car 'the attached.'"

"He's original," Jake agreed. "By the way, I swept it for surveillance."

Mia covered her mouth. "I didn't think of that. Did you find any?"

Jake shook his head. "We should probably accept his invitation."

"No more playing hard to get?"

"Not for now," he conceded.

◆

Jake tried not to let the gift of the car throw him off balance. His parents had been humble people, salt of the earth Montanans who knew how to stretch tight budgets. They'd passed their frugality onto him. While the CIA paid specialists like him well, he hadn't spent the money on luxuries.

The only presents he'd received since his parents died consisted of his annual bottle of Christmas scotch from Curtis.

This doesn't mean anything, Jake told himself as he pulled into a reserved guest slot in WorldWide's underground garage. Damien Call sneezed more money than most people made in a lifetime.

Except . . . Jake loved driving, and this vehicle was a dream. The torque alone was incredible. You touched the accelerator and, presto, off it went. Jake was careful about leaving digital footprints. Could Call have divined his preference from digging into his?

No. Lots of men enjoyed sports cars. Call would have sufficient ego to assume anyone would enjoy driving one of his. Anyway, Jake would return it as soon as the assignment was over.

He caught himself stroking the platinum finish as he opened Mia's door for her.

"Bye, car," she said, unashamedly giving the thing a pat. They'd spent the morning tooling around the city. He supposed she'd grown fond of it. He wondered why Call hadn't given it to Mia. She certainly liked it.

Unless Call *had* given it to her. His step hitched as he steered Mia toward the elevator. Maybe Call had guessed she wouldn't accept the gift directly. She'd been tickled by the idea of Call favoring Jake preferentially. That was classic Mia. How people she cared about were treated mattered more to her than the treatment she got herself. If Call had figured that out, he was even more perceptive than Jake had given him credit for.

They had a thoughtful elevator ride to WorldWide's offices on the fifty-second floor.

Mia stiffened as soon as they entered the sun-filled silver and white lobby.

"Wow," she muttered under her breath. "I'm so not dressed for this."

WorldWide's dress code certainly wasn't casual. Everyone who strode past looked like they'd stepped off the runway of a corporate fashion show. Though Jake wore a tailored suit, he wasn't up to their standard. The disparity amused him, but he could tell Mia was upset.

"You look fine," he said, giving her shoulder a gentle squeeze.

"I'm in *jeans*."

She was in jeans and a navy Ralph Lauren V-neck sweater she'd probably nabbed out of a sale bin. The tails of her white Oxford shirt stuck crookedly out the bottom, creased from lack of ironing and sitting in the car. To Jake, she looked cute, mussable, and ready for adventure. How Damien Call would view her outfit was unknown.

To Jake's surprise, the man himself was coming down a shining marble corridor to meet them. As he walked, he removed his suit jacket, draping it over one arm as nonchalantly as if he'd suddenly found the air too warm. One hooked finger loosened his tie as well.

Now that, Jake thought, *is considerate.*

"I'm so glad you made it," Call said, shaking their hands by turns. His grip was firm but not overpowering. "I hope you don't mind. I've taken the liberty of arranging for lunch to be served in my office."

Jake had a brief mental picture of the three of them chowing down on pizza around Call's desk. He shook his head humorously. Loosened tie notwithstanding, he knew that wasn't happening.

As they proceeded down the hall, a trophy secretary in a gorgeous cream-colored suit popped up from her watchdog desk. "Sir," she said. "I could have—"

"No matter, Ms. DeWinter," Call cut her off politely. "Mr. Reed and Miss Beck are friends. I wanted to greet them personally. Please hold my calls until I inform you otherwise."

"You have a meeting with the section managers in an hour."

"They can wait if they need to. No interruptions, Ms. DeWinter. No exceptions."

Ms. DeWinter's gaze drifted to Mia, her lips tightening briefly at her casual appearance. She subsided reluctantly behind her desk. "Yes, Mr. Call. I'll make sure you aren't disturbed."

"Excellent." Seeming to forget the woman as soon as she agreed, Call opened a glass door in the glass wall of his office. "Shall we?" he said, holding it for Mia.

Mia stepped cautiously inside. "Whoa. There's a whole house in here."

There was a good part of one. Apart from Call's spacious desk area, there was a large living room, a small conference table, and a "coffee" kitchen three times the size of the one in Mia's apartment. An intimate table draped in white sat by the best window view. Three chairs waited around it.

Call settled his suit jacket on a hanger and hook near his desk. His pale blue shirt was cut British style, conforming closely to his body. He wasn't huge, but he was built powerfully, his muscles subtly shaping the smooth linen. No love handles spoiled the transition of the shirt into his dark trousers.

Jake recalled from his research that the billionaire liked to box. His sparring partner might actually deserve his astronomical salary. Apparently, he kept Call in fighting trim.

Mia might not have been aware she watched, but her eyes

tracked every move the big man made. She jerked when he turned around.

"Which do you prefer?" Call asked her. "To eat first or talk business?"

"I think I'm too nervous to eat," Mia said in her honest way.

Call smiled and a spark passed between them that made Jake uneasy. Mia was attracted to Damien Call. He realized he'd never seen her look at someone else the way she looked at him.

"Mr. Call," she began.

"Damien," he corrected.

"Damien, I—"

"May I call you Miss Beck?"

She laughed, which might have been what Call intended. His poker face made it hard to tell. "I prefer Mia. Perhaps you could, um, save 'Miss Beck' for special occasions."

The glow of appreciation behind the CEO's eyes increased. "I could do that."

His slight suggestiveness made Mia press her palm to her stomach. "I want to apologize for showing up dressed like this. I wasn't thinking when I got ready this morning."

"I find no fault in your appearance. Did you enjoy your gift?"

"Yes, and Jake's too. You didn't have to give us anything."

"It was my pleasure."

Mia rolled her lips together. Jake knew she was going to blurt something she wasn't sure she should. "Was it also your pleasure to invade our privacy?"

Call leaned back on his glass-topped desk, his hips propped against its edge. He didn't seem at all put out. "That was simple caution. I know where you used to work. Surely you're not suggesting you didn't also dig into my history?"

"That was simple caution too," Mia said. "I just think we ought to set limits on the spying."

Call's smile was smooth and agreeable. "That's why we're here. Would you like to read the contract I've drawn up?"

Mia blinked. "You drew up a contract?"

"They are customary for these sort of arrangements."

Jake decided it was time to step in. He allowed his hand to fall lightly onto Mia's back. "Mia is new to these 'sort of arrangements.' As I'm sure you're aware."

Call's eyes met his and Jake experienced his own inner zing. This man certainly commanded a lot of amperage. Should he get the chance, Jake would enjoy putting him in his place—erotically speaking. Though the muscles of his pelvis tightened, he forced himself not to change expression.

"You and she are playing without a contract," Call observed.

"I know what I will and won't do."

"And she trusts you."

"She's not wrong to."

"Um," Mia interrupted. "Maybe I could read the contract while you two have your stare-off?"

"One moment," Call said. His wafer thin smartphone was lying on the desk. He pointed it at the wall of glass between his office suite and the corridor. A second after he pressed a button, the wall went opaque. "There. Now we're private."

"Cool," Mia said.

"We're soundproofed too?" Jake asked.

"We are," Call confirmed.

Jake's powers of deduction told him Ms. DeWinter wouldn't be pleased by that. Focused on other topics, Mia sat on a boxy modern couch to go over Call's contract. She didn't pretend to read it at normal speed. Call watched her performance with interest but not surprise. Her slender brows arrowed up a couple times. When she finished, she passed the document to Jake.

The nondisclosure paragraphs were as he'd expected. In addition, all parties agreed not to surveil the others or to make recordings without explicit permission. The hiring party—Call—would supply any wardrobe or equipment not already owned by the hires. In return, hires would hear out Call's suggestions regarding the interactions he wished to watch. If suggestions weren't provided, they could improvise as they pleased. In no event were they to pressure Call to participate. Safe words were to be established and, if appropriate to the circumstances, prophylactics used. The hires would submit to examination for pertinent medical conditions. Salaries could be negotiated, but the following were proposed. Hires were to make themselves available to the hiring party around the clock, though personal time off requests would be respected.

Most importantly—the language here was in bold—hires agreed not to advance their sexual relationship when out of the hiring party's presence. Doing so would constitute grounds for voiding the agreement. In any case, the contract would automatically expire but could be renegotiated at the culmination of two months.

Jake could guess which parts had caused Mia's brows to lift.

"This seems to cover everything," he said.

"It doesn't cover the regular jobs he offered us," Mia said. "The driving and the personal assistantship. I don't know about you, but I like to do actual, useful things, not just play sex games 24/7."

Her objection amused the CEO. "I thought HR could go over that with you. You can think about this contract and sign it when you're ready."

Mia and Jake sat side by side on the couch, not touching but adjacent. The cushions were deep, perfect for a man as tall as him. Call was across from them. He hadn't pulled his chair any closer, and this left a body length of space between them. Now he leaned forward and cleared his throat. "I should mention I'd want you to adhere to the bolded passage even before you sign."

Mia leveled a look at him. "You mean the part that says we can't have sex without you there to witness it."

"I believe the clause covers more than that."

Mia wouldn't need reminding of the exact wording. She inclined forward like Call was, her earnestness apparent. "What do you get out of this, Damien? You seem capable of participating. And, I'm not an expert, but you don't strike me as sexually afraid."

Call didn't like this question. He sat upright, his hands contracting on his thighs. This was when Jake noticed what Mia evidently already had. Call had become aroused during their conversation. A substantial bulge distorted his trouser front—though it didn't affect his manner otherwise.

"What I get out of it is my business," he said crisply. He rubbed his thighs. "You don't tiptoe around things, do you?"

Mia winced. "I don't try to be rude, but I'm afraid diplomacy isn't my strong suit."

"Well," Call said, "perhaps I'm . . . too used to people coddling me."

Jake rubbed his mouth to hide the twitching at its corners. Mia wasn't denying the other man's admission. She probably didn't realize she should. Call's gaze sharpened when his attention moved to Jake. Jake erased his amusement, thinking Call might take offense. Instead, the CEO relaxed.

"All right," he conceded. "I suppose we'll find a way to

tolerate each other's oddities. Do you accept the contract in principle, or would you like amendments?"

"I'm okay with it." Mia looked at Jake. "How about you?"

"As long as Damien understands we might say 'no' to him now and then."

"I do understand. I'm not interested in making either of you unhappy."

Jake shrugged, his lounge on the couch deepening. "In that case, I'm good."

Jake's words had a second meaning Damien seemed to appreciate—to go by the smile that flirted around his mouth. "Before we sign anything, would you two consent to a test of your chemistry? I'd like to confirm that the electricity you generated at Audition wasn't a fluke."

"Here?" Mia asked, startled.

"We're private," Damien assured her.

"This is your workplace."

"So it is." Damien flashed a grin that made him look more like a pirate than a sober captain of industry. "I thought, perhaps, you'd like to turn the tables on your friend."

The CEO caught Jake unprepared. Lust streaked through his veins and heated his genitals. Damien wasn't the only one with a hard-on then.

Mia blushed and stammered. "I'm not . . . I don't . . ."

"We'll keep it simple," Damien soothed. "No whips. No chains. Just you in control of him. Do you think you'd enjoy that?"

Mia's gaze jerked to Jake's and an even stronger surge of desire crashed through him. Unlike himself or Damien, Mia's face expressed every emotion. The emotion he saw on it then was longing. Jake's cock pounded so hard it should have shaken Damien's skyscraper. He'd known Mia wanted him. Now, thanks to the con they were playing out, he'd experience her yen for him directly.

Mia swallowed before answering. "I think I'd like that. I've never been the boss of him."

"Have you ever touched him sexually?"

"Not before Audition. Assuming you don't count fantasies."

She covered her mouth. Sometimes she really didn't have a filter.

Damien's chuckle was low and charmed. "Did you ever

fantasize about giving him a handjob? Maybe while you sat at one desk and he sat at the other?"

Jake's mouth opened and immediately shut again. The wisest course truly seemed to say nothing.

"Um," Mia said. "Jake doesn't sit a whole lot. Mostly, he's a leaner."

Damien smiled and rose. "Follow me, Mr. Reed."

Jake shook himself from his daze, unused to taking orders from anyone. Damien didn't turn to see if he obeyed, just led the way to his desk. The curved glass top resembled something that would fly if you pushed it out a window. A riveted steel pedestal with splayed legs anchored it to the floor. The thing was simultaneously butch and artsy, a sculpture you could work on.

Damien wheeled the desk chair away from the block of sunshine behind it. "Please stand here, Mr. Reed. With your hips resting on the edge."

"You can call me Jake."

Damien smiled faintly. "I'll call you what I wish, Mr. Reed."

O-kay. Damien Call had a thing for keeping his distance. Jake noticed Mia had gotten more of a concession on this point. Finding this interesting rather than annoying, he stood where the CEO directed.

"Now you, Mia." Damien gestured for her to come.

Jake's heart beat faster as she approached. Her cheeks and mouth were flushed, her eyes very bright. He wet his lips without thinking. She stopped an arm's length from Damien.

"As you can see," Damien said, "this desk is sturdy and bolted to the floor. No matter what you do to your friend, he'll be able to brace without toppling it."

"That's convenient." Mia's involuntary breathiness turned the wry response erotic. She looked at Damien who, for the moment, stood closer to Jake than her. The current of awareness he'd noticed before passed between the pair. "You have rules for this, right? Or suggestions?"

"I have two rules for Mr. Reed: that his hands remain gripped on the desk behind him, and that he not kiss you on the mouth."

"And for me?"

"That you open his clothes rather than remove them, and that you use no other body part but your hands on his erection."

Damien's voice had gone slightly rough. When Mia shivered

in response, an answering tremor ran across Jake's shoulders. They could tell their would-be boss was really into this.

"Is Jake allowed to come?" she asked.

"Whenever he likes. How long this lasts is up to him." Damien slid his gaze to Jake, his mouth curving knowingly. Damien didn't need to set a time limit. No man would let another male think he couldn't control himself—not if he could help it.

Damien stepped back out of touching range, his side to the sunny windows overlooking Manhattan's tip. He extended his arm to indicate Mia should move in. "The stage is yours, Mia."

Mia moved onto it. Jake could tell she was nervous. For his part, tingling waves of heat surged through him at her nearness. His natural urge was to put his hands on her waist. He had to remind himself not to release his grip on the desk's rounded edge. Mia glanced down him, her attention catching on the ridge behind his zipper. Her cheeks had flushed by the time she dragged her gaze up again.

"I'll just, um, start with your shirt, I think."

Jake smiled but didn't speak. He liked her timidity almost as much as Damien did.

Timid or not, her little fingers were torture undoing his buttons, every spot she brushed on his chest burning. She progressed to his belt and stopped. "I have to pull the tails out to get the rest."

Her need to warn him was endearing. She tugged the garment out carefully. The cotton strafed his straining erection, but she wasn't hurting him. She bit her lip as she freed the final buttons and moved to his belt buckle. He guessed she hadn't undressed many men. The mechanism stymied her for a moment before she conquered it. Undoing his trouser tabs forced her to lean closer, her warm breath fanning his exposed skin. Her ponytail swung with her efforts.

Though Jake didn't look at Damien, he knew the man had a clear view of everything.

"Got it," she declared victoriously.

"Don't stop there," Jake joked. "This is getting interesting."

She didn't have the nerve to sass him back. She took hold of his zipper tab. Their gazes locked, her deep brown eyes seeming to pull him down a well. This was happening. She was going to touch him.

"I'm looking forward to this," she confessed.

His breath rushed out even before she dragged the zipper carefully around him. God, she had a knack for getting to him, for making him want things he ought to leave alone. She had too much honesty, too much unhidden need for him. Jake knew he had a way with women; he'd charmed enough of them for his job and himself. Mia, though . . . Mia made him feel like the sexiest man on the planet just by being her natural self.

He sucked air sharply as her hand slid into his underwear.

She seemed to think the moment was special too.

"Ooh," she said, circling his base with her soft fingers. Her hand and wrist fit closely between his briefs and him. "You're so big and smooth."

He was getting bigger by the second. Mia wrapped him in her hold and pulled. He couldn't stop his flesh from leaping. She wasn't using a lot of pressure, but the sensations that rocketed through his shaft were indescribable. This was *her* hand, the off limits honorary sister of his boss. The muscles of his thighs and ass tightened. In that moment, he was very glad he wasn't supposed to stop this from happening.

He ground his teeth as her stroke rubbed across the flare.

"Is my hand cold?"

He had to unclench his jaw to answer. "No," he forced out. "It's perfect."

"You like this?"

He couldn't believe she needed reassurance. He'd broken into a full body sweat from a single stroke, his breath just about panting. Mia pushed her fist down his length again. His eyes nearly crossed at how good that felt.

"I like it," he promised jerkily.

"You might want to slow down," Damien said.

Mia stopped what she was doing to turn her head to him. The other man tapped his index finger across his lips.

"I'm not going fast," she said.

Damien laughed. "He's reacting fast. So the question is, do you want to embarrass him?"

"Seriously?"

"See where his hands grip the desk? His knuckles have gone white."

Mia looked, and her lips formed a surprised circle. "Wow. I've never seen him do that. Jake is the original cool cat."

"You have power over him. He's as attracted to you as you are to him."

Jake wasn't sure he enjoyed being talked about as if he weren't there. On the other hand, he didn't want to ruin Mia's fun. He couldn't mistake that having sway over him titillated her.

"Press your lips to his breastbone," Damien suggested. "See how fast his heart is beating."

Mia leaned in a bit shyly, one hand still down his pants. She didn't quite kiss him, but her lips were warm as they flattened on his skin. Jake struggled not to push closer. He knew his heart thudded.

He liked the feel of her almost-kiss better than was good for him.

Mia backed up and her head turned to Damien. "What can I do besides jack him off that won't break your rules?"

Sunshine flared in Damien's green- and blue-flecked gold eyes. "You can touch him anywhere you like. Just don't open his clothes any more than they are."

Mia considered the possible territory. Jake wasn't a bear but he did have hair on his chest. He guessed that appealed to her. She slid both hands under his gapped shirt and scratched his skin lightly with all ten nails. That felt amazing, like she was waking a million nerves simultaneously. Seeming oblivious to the storm she was stirring up, she explored his pecs and his ribs and the ridged muscles of his abdomen.

"Lean down to me," she said.

When he leaned, his hands moved with him automatically.

"Those stay on the desk," she reminded.

If she'd been anyone else trying to order him around, he'd have made her work for it. He was a natural top; he didn't bottom unless it was for a good reason. This was Mia, though. She wasn't a fan of confrontation and wouldn't relish a battle to subdue him. Still leaning toward her, he put his hands back where they belonged.

"Thank you," she said politely.

Possibly he should have thanked her. She reached under his shirt and around his back, her smooth nails pushing up his muscles to his shoulders. The position put her between his legs, almost hugging him. He could feel the curve of her breasts, could smell the peach shampoo she used to wash her hair. Damien had told him not to kiss Mia on the mouth, but that didn't exclude the rest of her. Unable to resist, he nuzzled the tender spot where her neck curved into her left shoulder.

She gasped when he sucked it hard.

"That's allowed," he told her, murmuring the taunt against her ear.

Her eyes flashed, and he sensed he'd challenged her temper.

"This is allowed too," she said. Her nails scraped down under the back of his unzipped trousers, both hands running over and then squeezing his ass cheeks. For Mia, this was pretty bold, especially when she continued kneading him. Her thumbs were strong where they gripped the first inches of his cleft. Pleasurable feelings rippled into parts of him she probably wasn't thinking too hard about. "You have a great butt, Jake. I'd really love watching it get spanked."

Okay, maybe he'd refrain from jumping to conclusions about the vanilla nature of her fantasies.

He looked up to find Damien rubbing his smiling lower lip, obviously entertained by their repartee. He wondered if the billionaire honestly thought *he'd* give Jake the spanking.

"Please continue," Damien said, noting his attention. "I'm enjoying this."

His contribution emboldened Mia. "You hear that?" she said. "Damien wants to watch your ass get paddled too."

That was a possible interpretation, one Jake maybe should have thought of first. He hadn't, though, and that unsettled him. Did he *want* their audience to take a more active role?

Mia distracted him by dragging her hands forward around his hipbones. "I hope you don't mind. I really want to touch this part of you again."

Sweat broke out anew on his skin. He wasn't sure he was ready, but he didn't get a say. This time Mia worked both hands into his cotton briefs, forming a tunnel for his cock with interlaced fingers and aligned thumbs. She rode her hold up him once and paused.

Jake didn't realize his eyes had squeezed shut until he had to open them to see why she'd stopped.

Mia's expression was hesitant. "I don't want to give you a burn. I bet Damien has lube stashed around here somewhere."

Jake bet he did as well, but: "I prefer just your hands," he said hoarsely. "I like a good firm tug better than a gliding stroke."

Mia cracked a grin. "Good to know."

He didn't bother trying to recite baseball stats. He would have missed her pleasure in what she did. Hell, he would have missed his own.

That grew stronger with every stroke she took.

"Christ," he said, his grip on the desk beginning to slide with sweat.

She switched to fisting him with one hand and his head fell back on his neck. Her movement was freer, her grip chafing and tugging simultaneously. She concentrated on his shaft, leaving the crown alone, though naturally all that vigorous motion stimulated it as well. Jake tried to control his breathing, but it had grown ragged.

"Too hard?" she asked breathlessly.

He shook his head and spread his legs wider. "God, I want to hold you," he burst out.

He wanted to fuck her, to push her back on the desk and have his very thorough way with her. Mia must have sensed his frustration. She wrapped her free arm around his back, pulling her side snug against his front. Her weight leaned against his thigh. Because he couldn't not, he turned that leg closer.

Mia, he thought as his feelings rose. He wasn't going to say her name aloud. He knew the sound would give his affection for her away. This had to stay a game.

"Rub his crown," Damien ordered quietly.

Mia didn't hesitate. Her fist shifted higher, her thumb crooking over the nerve-laden skin that stretched drum tight around his tip. He was wet from pre-come, which caused her thumb's pad to slide. She tightened her fingers to compensate, suddenly jerking his cock hard and fast out from his abdomen. Her speed almost hurt, but the hurt was good.

She was doing what he would have if he'd wanted to come quickly.

He wasn't going to come slow. The ache of near orgasm deepened and then reached flashpoint. Fire streaked up his penis —hot, sweet, and momentarily mind blanking. His lungs squeezed flat as he ejaculated, air rushing noisily from his chest. He sucked more oxygen to fill it and shocked himself by groaning.

Three hard shots later, it was over but for the sigh.

His eyes opened reluctantly. Mia bit her lip and grinned.

It was impossible not to share her humor, not with the warm relaxation that had loosened his tensed muscles.

"Okay," he conceded. "You got me good."

"Kablooey!" she teased, letting out a snicker. She turned her head to Damien. "Have you got a hanky I could borrow?"

Damien wasn't expecting to be addressed. In the nanosecond before he pulled himself together, Jake glimpsed something that might have been envy.

"Of course," he said, pulling a pristine square of silk from his pants pocket.

"I've got this," Jake said, taking the cloth from her.

He wiped her hand first, enjoying having each of her little fingers in his control—especially when it gave him the chance to feel how fast her pulse was pattering in her wrist. He cleaned himself with less fuss. Mia watched him, seeming interested in the process of him tucking his cock away and zipping.

When she saw he'd caught her gawking, her cheeks went pink.

"You flatter me," he said softly. "And now I owe you one."

That made her redden more. He smiled and their gazes hooked together. Jake knew Mia was imagining an act or two he might perform to discharge his debt. Though she wore a shirt and a sweater, her nipples poked out like pencil erasers.

"Well," Damien said, which weirdly didn't feel like an interruption. "I suppose this settles my question about your chemistry."

CHAPTER 5

MIA'S skin tingled all over but especially where Jake had come on her hand. If she'd been fifteen, she'd have vowed never to wash it again.

She grinned to herself. Though she ached for her own release—and for him to give it to her—she didn't regret the act that had put her in this state. She'd made Jake come. She'd watched Jake come. The image of his face as it tensed and then relaxed was in her memory forever.

She couldn't imagine ever regretting that.

"Shall I call the kitchen to bring up lunch?" Damien asked. "Or would you like more time to compose yourself?"

He seemed composed already. She supposed he was used to watching other people enjoy themselves while doing without himself. *What a strange way to live*, she thought, though he didn't look unhappy.

Actually, he looked satisfied. She and Jake had proved they could deliver whatever X factor he sought from these encounters.

"Oh what the hell," she said, impulse taking hold of her. Jake had left Damien's contract on a side table by the couch they'd sat on earlier. She strode to it and then looked at Damien. "Have you got a pen? I don't know about you guys, but I don't need more time to think before I sign this thing."

Seeming bemused, Damien found a writing instrument and handed it to her. Naturally, the barrel was platinum.

Mia leaned down to scribble her signature. "Okay. Who's in this besides me?"

"Well, I am." Damien added his John Hancock. He offered the pen to Jake. "Mr. Reed? Will you make it unanimous?"

"Sure," Jake said. "Who am I to rain on this parade?"

The atmosphere felt celebratory once they'd signed the agreement. Lunch beside the sunny office window was better than the fanciest restaurant she'd ever eaten in. Between the view and the wine Damien had selected, she was the teensiest bit tipsy. The CEO was a gracious host. Though the conversation wasn't personal, it was pleasant. For much of it, the men compared meals they'd eaten in other countries, both awful and delicious. Jake had traveled more broadly than Mia realized, not just to military hotspots but also places like France and Greece. Jake and Damien both agreed you hadn't really had steak until you'd eaten it in South America.

"Osaka comes close," Jake said, his posture in the chair relaxed. "But those Brazilians know their barbecue."

Damien nodded and then smiled at her. "I'm afraid we're talking too much. We must be boring you."

"Not at all," she said honestly. "I enjoy hearing your stories. I wish I'd seen as much of the world as you. We should probably go, though. You must need to get back to work."

He didn't deny it. "Stop by Ms. DeWinter's desk with me. We'll set up arrangements for tomorrow. For your regular jobs."

Ms. DeWinter almost managed to look unruffled by her boss's lengthy radio silence.

"Good," Damien said. "You're still here. I thought you might have gone to lunch. Please contact our company shopper, Stephanie Giles. Miss Beck needs a suitable corporate wardrobe. Top to bottom. No scrimping. Have Stephanie charge it to my account until we set her up with a clothing allowance. Let's see. She'll need measurements."

Damien took up Ms. DeWinter's notepad, jotting a list of figures Mia presumed were related to her size. He didn't ask if his estimates were correct or even look at her to double-check.

"There," he said, handing the list to his secretary. "That should be everything."

"Sir?" was all Ms. DeWinter managed to get out.

"Sorry," he said. "I forgot to say. I've hired Miss Beck as my personal assistant. And Mr. Reed here will be my new driver."

Ms. DeWinter's composure was considerably rattled now. Mia almost felt sorry for her as she swallowed audibly. "Your personal assistant?"

"I've been thinking it would be nice to have someone

accompany me around. And you have plenty to keep you busy here. Tell Stephanie my apologies for the rush, but we'll need the wardrobe by tomorrow."

"Of course," Ms. DeWinter agreed faintly.

"Excellent," Damien said and turned away from her.

No way did a man as sharp as he was fail to notice he'd knocked his secretarial Cerberus off balance. The sternness of his expression as he gestured Mia and Jake forward suggested the blow was deliberate. Damien was using Mia to squash Ms. DeWinter's ambitions of being everything to him herself.

Mia concluded their gracious host wasn't gracious to everyone.

Jake didn't comment until they'd pulled out of WorldWide's garage and headed up Water Street. "That business with the secretary showed a certain ruthlessness."

"Maybe Ms. DeWinter has been angling for a relationship beyond business."

Jake's strong hands skimmed the steering wheel. "That seems likely, though Call's response suggests he might be cold enough to convince a rival's daughter to commit corporate espionage."

"Are you sorry I signed his contract without getting your okay first?"

Jake glanced at her. "No, I think that was smart. He'll trust you more because you were in the moment and genuine."

"I guess you'd know, considering the job you had before signing on with Curtis."

They hadn't talked about his former profession much. It didn't take a genius to tell Jake was reluctant to. Now he made a noncommittal noise of response.

"Were those stories you told Damien true?" she asked. "About eating steak with arm's dealers in Brazil?"

"They were true. The best cons stick as close to reality as possible. Like you and me actually enjoying what we did in front of him. Live your cover is what they teach at The Farm."

Mia shifted uncomfortably on the bucket seat. Was he warning her not to build too much on the fun they'd had? "How do you suppose he stands it?" she blurted. "Just watching other people and not getting off himself."

"We don't know that he doesn't. Maybe he jacked off in his private bathroom as soon as we were gone."

"But what if he didn't?" Mia was unable to let the topic drop.

"Maybe that's the secret to his charisma: that he keeps himself pent up."

Jake seemed to find this funny.

"It could be the secret," Mia huffed.

"Maybe," Jake conceded. He thought for a moment. "On the other hand, he's only—what—twenty-nine? That's young, libido-wise. He could be jacking off and pent up at the same time."

Mia needed to stop talking about Damien's releases or lack thereof. The idea was making her too squirmy. She fell silent, and Jake did too. When they got to her apartment building, he surprised her by parking.

"I'll walk you up," he said when she looked at him questioningly.

"You'll walk me up? It's broad daylight. What do you expect to happen between here and my door? This fancy car is more at risk than me."

Jake's jaw tightened. "I'll walk you up," he insisted more firmly.

Had something changed because of their experience at lunch, something that prodded him to play gentleman protector? Mia didn't dare let herself believe it. He solved the mystery by pulling a small black gadget from his coat pocket.

"Stay there," he said, waving her toward the slipcovered couch in her living room.

It took ten minutes, but he swept every nook and cranny in her apartment for listening devices. To her relief, he didn't comment on the romance novels in her bedroom.

"Nothing," he said when he came back. He seemed disappointed as he scrubbed the back of his neck with one hand.

"Did you really think Damien would bug us? He specifically promised not to in his contract."

"Inviting us to lunch could have created an opportunity for someone he hired to sneak in."

"That would have been devious."

"Call *is* devious. All those save-the-planet cars and jobs for Detroit are nice, but you don't get where he has by being a boy scout."

Mia supposed this was true—not that she had a right to judge. "Do you suppose he's sweeping his office now? In case *we* planted bugs on *him*?"

"I think he has people do that for him."

True to habit, Jake lowered himself to her single armchair's arm rather than its cushion. Because he seemed to be lost in thought, Mia studied him. He had a narrow distinctive nose. She hadn't noticed until that moment that it had a dint on the end, as if a child had pressed its finger into a bit of clay.

"There's something else I need to do before I go," he said.

He didn't look happy about it. He was slumping as he sat.

"Are you going to tell me what it is?" she prompted.

He sighed and stood and then took her hands to pull her onto her feet. His deep blue eyes were resigned as he gazed down at her.

"What?" she asked, mystified.

He slid his arms around her, lifting her to her toes. Mia gasped at the unexpected contact with his body. A second later, she was glad for the extra air.

Jake's mouth came down over hers. His sensitive lips were soft, his tongue bold, his long arms squeezing her tight to his hard muscles. Her feet left the floor entirely as he kissed the living daylights out of her.

Her mind seemed to melt, every thought but returning his kiss as enthusiastically as she could sliding out of her. Jake clamped one hand on her bottom as she swung her legs up around his waist. Thank God for jeans with stretch. She lap-danced her crotch over his six pack, moaning while she forked her fingers into his hair. The short strands were silky, the way his jaw worked as he kissed her incredibly arousing.

Suddenly her back thumped the nearest wall. Jake had turned and was thrusting her into it.

He broke free, panted twice, and kissed her again.

He didn't groan, but she couldn't stop making pleasured sounds. He'd shifted their respective positions. The massive ridge behind his zipper now dug into everything that was hurting between her legs.

She wanted him there like crazy. Shoved deep. Pumping. Taking her completely. She clung to his muscled shoulders as he drove one hot hand underneath her shirt. The hot hand's palm covered her bra cup and squeezed. An incredible thrill streaked through her as his thumb compressed one nipple. The feeling was as powerful as anything caused by the rocking of his hips.

"Jake," she gasped.

His mouth was on her neck, sucking hard enough to leave a

mark. She wouldn't have expected that to be pleasurable, but she couldn't help writhing. Her fingers caressed his neck without her actually planning to.

"Jake," she said more loudly but not less breathlessly. "We signed a contract. Don't you think this counts as advancing our sexual relationship?"

"Fuck the contract," he growled and covered her mouth again.

He didn't really mean that. He was a professional. He wouldn't sabotage a job that way. Mia more than half wished she were willing to. Instead she pushed at his chest.

Jake kissed her for two more heartbeats before backing off a handspan.

"Don't move," he ordered when she would have unwrapped her legs from him.

Though his pelvis no longer pushed at her, his erection throbbed against her jean's inseam. Along with the rest of her, Mia's lips buzzed as if they'd been painted with hot pepper. She sensed if she didn't say the right thing, she wasn't going to talk either of them out of escalating this.

"You're just ticked that Damien told you not to kiss me."

His eyes narrowed, his lashes incredibly thick and spiky this close up. "That's not the only reason. Anyway it's just a kiss."

"'Just a kiss' is when I peck Curtis on the cheek. The last time you kissed me like this you made me come."

He glowered at her.

"You know it's true," she said. "You don't want to screw up this assignment just because you won't take commands from another man."

"I can take commands. I used to take them all the time."

She stroked his chest soothingly.

"Fine," he huffed and let her down from him.

Her knees were shaking. She had to lean against the wall for a couple seconds before she could stand again. As she tried to recover, she cupped her neck where she feared he'd given her a hickey. Apparently, these signs of his sexual prowess satisfied Jake's need to feel like a conqueror.

He smirked a little when he told her he'd see her tomorrow.

◆

Jake sat in the silver car, waiting for his pounding body to calm enough to drive. Whew, that had been a kiss! He licked his lips, still tasting her on them. He'd adored the way Mia looked against the wall afterward. Weak-kneed. Cheeks aflame. Mussed six ways to Sunday.

Basically, like he'd bedded her already.

The idea got his pulse ticking up again. She'd had a pile of romance novels beside her bed. At the time, he'd found this sweet and funny, but now he remembered hearing women who read them tended to want sex more.

"Cut it out," he said aloud.

This was getting out of hand. He was too old for Mia, too hard . . .

Definitely too hard right then.

He snorted at himself and turned the engine on. The vehicle barely made a noise until the wheels began rolling. Jake loved how stealth the sports car was—kind of like Damien Call, come to think of it. Call wanted this to happen: for Jake and Mia to get so sexually frustrated they'd put on a good show for him.

"*Pent up*," he muttered beneath his breath.

He'd been right to call the billionaire devious.

◆

Mia's wardrobe arrived later that evening, via human and not drone. Damien's little copter couldn't have handled it. As it was, the delivery guy took two trips to trundle it all in. When he set down the last package, the main room of her apartment was overwhelmed.

Damien had been serious about furnishing her from head to toe and no scrimping. Her first discoveries were a dozen suits, hung up neatly in custom boxes in individual zip-up bags. Next came shoes and hosiery and—to Mia's eyes—very pricey silk and lace underwear. The lingerie was politely fancy: nothing red or black or overly pushup, despite which the things made her fingers tingle when she stroked them.

The suits told a similar story: quietly expensive in tones of gray and blue. None of the skirts were short and none of the beautifully tailored matching jackets did more than skim her curves. In her experience, men liked clothes that fit tighter and showed more. Either Damien's mental measuring tape wasn't as accurate as she'd thought, or Ms. DeWinter had added her own instructions—to prevent Mia from drawing more of her boss's attention than she already had. If this was true, she probably hadn't guessed the modest styling suited Mia's preferences.

Her sole regret was that every pair of shoes had not-very-modest heels. She didn't see happy feet in her future.

Her cellphone buzzed with an incoming text. Her heart jumped at the thought that it might be Jake, but the message was from WorldWide. Human Resources expected her at 8:00 a.m. tomorrow, presumably to sign a bunch of forms and have her photo taken for an ID.

When she called Jake to see if they could carpool, he didn't answer. That was disappointing. Had their kiss rattled him more than he let on? Was he avoiding her? She shook her head in negation. Jake wasn't the avoiding type. Probably he was meeting Curtis off the grid somewhere, updating him on the day's events.

Mia would have to take the subway in.

She wouldn't get lost. She knew the lines by heart, but the prospect still unnerved her. She'd never worked for anyone but Curtis, and he was as much friend as boss.

Don't be a pussy, she told herself. *People start new jobs everyday.*

If you counted what they'd done at lunch, she'd started this one already.

◆

Mia guessed she looked like a real employee. Two people nodded at her on the elevator ride to the fiftieth floor. The woman in HR seemed nice, if a teensy bit rah-rah. She explained Mia's generous benefit package, assuring her she'd enjoy working for WorldWide.

"WorldWide demands competence and hard work, but we reward our people well. We've very little turnover compared to other Fortune 500 companies."

"That's good," Mia said. "WorldWide's people must enjoy being able to settle in."

She must have sounded like she hadn't drunk enough Kool-Aid, because the HR lady shot her a funny look. Mia didn't have time to worry. Ms. DeWinter came down to personally collect her.

Her formfitting designer dress made her look like a corporate seductress. Her first words to Mia as they strode away along a line of cubbies weren't meant to be supportive.

"That shirt isn't supposed to be paired with that jacket," she informed her.

Mia looked down at it. She'd put a silver blouse with a soft gray suit. Maybe the combo was monochrome, but she couldn't see that it was *wrong*. "Really?"

Ms. DeWinter jabbed the button for the elevator with a long painted nail. "We expect employees to uphold certain standards here, Miss Beck."

It was probably just as well she didn't have a smart comeback. "I'll try harder next time," she said, straight-faced.

Ms. DeWinter gave her side eye, but Mia knew how to look innocent. The elevator dinged and they stepped in.

"Where are you taking me?" Mia asked. "Does Mr. Call have something he needs me for?"

"Mr. Call is in Atlantic City. Mr. Reed drove him there for a meeting early this morning. —This way," she added as they exited into the lobby on fifty-two.

Ms. DeWinter's walking speed seemed designed to see how out of breath she could get Mia. They rounded the corner nearest to Damien's office suite then clacked halfway down the next marble corridor. Ms. DeWinter turned the knob on one of the identical plain black doors.

"Your office," she said crisply.

"I have an office?" Mia didn't try to hide her amazement. Apparently, she had an office with a view. The space wasn't huge but it was considerably bigger than the cubby she'd expected— maybe as big as her bedroom. The desk and chairs were mid-century modern, the computer so new and shiny she immediately wanted to sit down and play with it.

"You're Mr. Call's personal assistant," Ms. DeWinter explained. "No one's going to stick you in a broom closet."

Mia's genuine astonishment caused Ms. DeWinter to unbend a bit. It occurred to Mia that if anyone knew the lowdown about Damien Call's business life, it was this woman. She remembered what Jake said about the best cons sticking close to reality.

"I'm a pity hire," she confessed with what she hoped was credible sheepishness. "Jake was the employee Mr. Call really wanted to headhunt."

"I'm sure that isn't true," Ms. DeWinter soothed—but as if she were willing to be convinced.

"It is," Mia obliged her. "Jake has all sorts of advanced driver training, plus his bodyguarding skills. He made us a package deal so I wouldn't sit at home and get bored."

Ms. DeWinter seemed to welcome the suggestion that she and Jake were a couple.

"The thing is," Mia went on, "I really would like to be useful. Do you think you could help me get the lay of the land? I don't know much about WorldWide. I'd rather Mr. Call not think I'm totally ignorant."

Ms. DeWinter unbent a smidgen more. "I do have some material you could read. More in depth than what HR will have given you."

"I would *love* that," Mia said gratefully. "Do you want me to come get it?"

As it turned out, Damien Call's executive assistant had a treasure trove of research concerning him and his companies. Mia returned to her office with two fat binders stuffed with clippings and other things. A lot of it Curtis had dug up already, but some of it was new. Ms. DeWinter liked to keep thorough records of her boss's accomplishments.

Mia waited to return the binders until just before she suspected Ms. DeWinter went to lunch. She'd guessed well. Ms. DeWinter was pulling on her coat to go out.

"Surely you're not done reading all that!" she exclaimed.

"I read everything I understood," Mia said, which Ms. DeWinter wouldn't realize actually meant everything. "Do you think— I don't mean to step out of place, but do you think I could take you to lunch just today? I don't know anyone yet, and you seem to have a handle on what goes on."

Thankfully, this wasn't laying it on too thick. Ms. DeWinter accepted, saying she knew a quieter place than the company cafeteria. Also thankfully, given that Damien Call was Ms. DeWinter's favorite topic, it wasn't hard to steer the conversation onto him.

Pretty sure Ms. DeWinter would frown on her eating anything that might stick to her hips, Mia ordered the same Spartan salad as her superior.

"I know I shouldn't say this," she confided once the waitress had gone away. "But, wow, Mr. Call is a hottie! If Jake weren't so possessive . . ." She shook her head. "I bet lots of the woman at WorldWide fall for him."

"Some do," Ms. DeWinter admitted, probably unaware that the way she jabbed her fork at the lettuce made her wedding diamond flash. "But Mr. Call is particular. He's not susceptible to the sort of women who throw themselves at him."

This held a hint of warning. Mia pretended it had nothing to do with her.

"That's admirable," she said. "Some guys would hump a stump if they tripped over it."

"Exactly," Ms. DeWinter agreed. "Mr. Call is a unique man."

Mia took a sip of her plain iced tea. "What about that woman I saw him with on the news—the Raeburn heiress, I think it was?"

For a second Mia worried this question was too gossipy. The secretary's beautiful lipsticked mouth thinned disapprovingly. Luckily, her contempt wasn't aimed at Mia. "Zoe Raeburn was more interested in Mr. Call than he was in her. She was someone he could attend events with, not anyone he'd be serious about."

"So more Paris Hilton than Duchess Kate."

"Exactly," Ms. DeWinter said again. "To be fair, Zoe Raeburn isn't stupid. Her father *is* grooming her to take over his company."

"But she wasn't special."

"No." Ms. DeWinter stabbed a frilly lettuce leaf. "She's called the office a couple times, but I don't think he's seeing her anymore."

She said this with such satisfaction Mia thought she'd better not let on that Damien had his eye on not one but two new prizes.

◆

"Hey, beautiful," called a sly male voice. "Need a ride?"

Mia laughed, knowing it was Jake even before she turned. She'd been heading toward the subway when the silver sports car slowed beside her to match her walking pace. Given that this was New York, it took two whole seconds before the driver behind him leaned on his horn. Seeing Jake's grin lightened her heart startlingly.

"Get in," he urged. "Before I have half the city cursing me."

She hopped in and shut the gullwing door.

"It's five thirty," he said as he rejoined normal traffic flow. "I didn't think you'd still be at work."

"I was waiting to see if Damien would come back. Since you're here, I must have just missed him. How was Atlantic

City?"

"Boring. Call met up with some investors. Gamblers but not gangsters, as far as I could tell. They're helping finance the mini-car he's developing. The man does not quit working. He was on his phone nonstop while I was driving him."

"So no sexy stuff," Mia said.

Jake glanced at her with his lips curving. "Wondering if he got fresh with me when you weren't there?"

"Maybe," she said, enjoying his teasing mood.

Jake smiled at her a moment longer before turning to the road. "No. He was all business. How about you?"

"I made nice with Ms. DeWinter and pumped her for gossip over lunch." She related the gist of the conversation, which he seemed to find interesting. "Sadly, I discovered my personal assistantship doesn't qualify me to access much of the WorldWide network. I couldn't even view Damien's calendar."

"That's a security thing," Jake said. "Probably only Ms. DeWinter knows what he's got scheduled."

"Really?"

"Really. Call is a well-known wealthy person, a corporate celebrity. If just anyone could predict his movements, he'd need bodyguards to go with him everywhere."

Mia hadn't thought about this aspect of Damien's life. "He wouldn't like that."

"No, he wouldn't. Not a privacy freak like him."

"Jake," she said, suddenly overwhelmed by doubts. "How are we going to find out if he has Raeburn's plan? His company is huge, and this is only one part of it. The special navigational system Zoe supposedly stole from Genbolt was for aircraft. What if Damien took it to Arizona, where his aviation operation is headquartered? It'd take me a week just to search the file room here."

"You shouldn't search it," Jake cautioned. "You'd risk raising suspicion for no reason. Call won't have stuck the thing in a drawer where anyone can find it." He tapped his fingers on the wheel as he thought. "His research guys will have seen it, but they might not know its origin. Our best hope is that he kept the blueprint for the microchip or whatever it is where he can study it in private. I'm no techie, but from the look I got, I don't think you could build a system based on that single page. The specs seemed pretty complicated. And how crucial were the mathematical formulas? Would the variables be obvious to an engineer? If not, you'd have to figure out what the drawing was getting at."

"Raeburn claimed Call is pitching a prototype to the government."

"That doesn't mean it's finished. Just that he's made a start. Bottom line, we have to get closer to him. We need him to give away where it is. And in that vein . . ." Jake's profile grew more reserved. "Call invited us to join him at Diogenes tomorrow night."

"Tomorrow." Mia's heart immediately beat faster. "That's soon."

"I'm surprised he didn't make it tonight. He seems to want us to stay worked up."

"What do you think he'll ask us to do?"

Jake was changing lanes to get around a double-parked bakery truck and didn't look at her. "I think we need to take the reins from him—and by 'we,' I mean me."

"You're worried." She twisted around on the seat.

Jake rubbed the groove between his lower lip and chin. "Not about him. He's secure on our hook for now. You and I— We're doing this for the job, but it's still real in a lot of ways. I think I need a better handle on how to master you."

Mia's mouth fell open. She shut it when he glanced at her. He did look concerned. His dark eyebrows had scrunched together. "You haven't had any trouble doing that so far."

"I want to stay at your place tonight."

"My place."

"It's the outward expression of who you are inside."

This was not a phrase she expected to hear from him. "You sure you want to risk it? The last time we were alone together things . . . got heated."

A muscle bunched in Jake's jaw. "I'm a grown man. As long as we don't tie you up, I think I can handle it."

CHAPTER 6

MIA'S living space was just as she'd left it that morning. Fancy coffee cup in the sink. Delivery boxes flattened in a pile for her to take to the recycling dumpster when she felt ambitious. She tried to remember when she'd last cleaned her facilities. Not recently enough, she suspected.

"You hungry?" Jake asked as he locked the deadbolt. "I'll call for Indian."

He didn't appear to feel weird about being there.

"Sure," she said. "Indian's good. I'll just . . ." She waved vaguely toward her apartment's most disreputable area.

"Take your time," he said, his face amused. "I can guess what you want to eat."

She nodded, tossed her new jacket on the couch, and went to give her bathroom the quickest scrubbing of its life. Since she was there, she washed off her work makeup, including the concealer that had hidden Jake's hickey from yesterday. She touched the spot carefully. The telltale bruise had almost disappeared.

Jake is spending the night, she told her bemused reflection.

She shook herself, not wanting to think too hard about that in case she got more uptight.

The way his forehead furrowed when she came out didn't lessen her self-consciousness. "Are you wearing your new wardrobe? Why is it so baggy?"

"It isn't baggy," she said, wondering why everyone felt the need to critique her clothes. "It's comfortable."

"My eighty-year-old granny wore shorter skirts."

"I'm supposed to look professional."

Jake rolled his eyes. "Have you seen the female execs at Call's office? They dress like they all want to seduce the boss."

Mia put her hands on her hips. "That's a sexist thing to say."

"Okay, maybe only half want to sleep with Damien." Mia frowned and he grinned unrepentantly. He picked his phone up from the counter. "I'm calling Hillary Sweets. She can send one of her seamstresses over to nip and tuck."

"Jake—"

"No arguments. You've got a nice figure. You're not going to embarrass yourself if those suits fit the way they should."

Mia saw she wasn't going to dissuade him. "I think Ms. DeWinter might have added a size to Damien's guestimate."

"Or two. That woman is determined."

Jake started dialing and then stopped. He cocked his head to consider her. "Those romance novels . . . The ones stacked beside your bed. They're all historical, aren't they?"

Mia ordered herself not to flush. She'd been hoping he hadn't noticed them. "What if they are?"

"Just having a thought. I might need to put in an extra order when I speak to Hillary. Why don't you change into whatever you wear at home while I talk to her? Shoo," he added when she resisted.

She shooed, despite her annoyance at being bossed around. Retreating to her room gave her a chance to compose herself. As she pulled on a T-shirt and jeans, she admitted another truth.

She liked being the center of Jake's attention.

◆

Mia survived Hillary's seamstress's house call. She was an older woman who didn't speak much English. Somewhat to Mia's surprise, Jake was fluent in Cantonese. Whatever he said to the seamstress as she chalked and pinned had her giggling uncontrollably.

Before she left, the woman piled all but one of Mia's new outfits across her arm.

"You see knees," she said to Jake. "I promise."

Mia found this so charming she couldn't be sorry Jake called her.

Dinner was a surprise as well. In the year they'd been at Discreet, they'd become more comfortable with each other than she realized. They talked about work and Curtis and assorted casual things. She washed the plates and glasses while Jake took out the trash. They watched a little TV together on her small couch. She was very aware of him beside her, of how tall he was and how warm. He wasn't wearing aftershave and smelled mainly —and rather deliciously—of soap and man. He was restless, she thought, shifting now and then on the seat cushion. Overall, though, hanging out with him was easy.

That, of course, was before bedtime.

Her pulse began to skitter when he clicked off the news. He looked at her, the blue of his eyes suddenly hotter. "Do you shower in the morning?"

"Night," she said, willing him to ignore the involuntary jump in her voice's pitch. "I'll just . . . go do that now."

He nodded. "I'll poke around. I snoop better without an audience."

"Right," she said. "Because that's why you came over."

He smiled and she knew she'd sounded like an idiot. She got up from the couch before she could make it worse, her lips clamped firmly together.

Maybe she could shower forever and not come out again.

◆

Mia's old-fashioned, no-frills bath had a shower and tub combo. The water pressure was chancy but the heat was plentiful. She didn't sing like she usually did. Her voice wasn't really suited for any ears but hers. She was rinsing the last of the shampoo from her hair and face when someone with bare feet stepped into the tub behind her.

Though she knew it had to be Jake, she squeaked like Norman Bates had joined her.

"It's me," he said.

"I know it's you." She refused to turn around. In her opinion, her rear view was enough of an eyeful. "Get out of here. This shower isn't big enough for two."

"I didn't come to shower."

Crap. The sensual growl he put in his voice got to her. She shivered and went liquid at the same time.

"Mia," he crooned teasingly. "Turn around and look at me."

She wedged her hands beneath her armpits and debated. "Are *you* wearing clothes?"

His chuckle was devilish. "As it happens, I am not."

Seeing Jake naked *might* be worth turning around for.

"Promise you won't laugh?"

"Mia," he said, something tender in the sound. "I swear you don't need to worry about that."

She turned and put her arms down with more defiance than she felt. She knew she wasn't ugly, but still it was difficult. Naked meant vulnerable and gave people things to judge. Who knew what Jake thought was attractive?

He scanned her unhurriedly from head to toe, like he wanted to memorize every inch of her. She was so nervous she forgot to look at him. Finally his eyes returned to her face. His expression was serious.

"You make my heart stop," he said.

Her heart felt like it had stopped too. "I'm nothing special."

"You are. You're amazingly beautiful. If it weren't for that stupid contract, I'd be all over you right now."

She caught her lip in her teeth. His mouth hooked upward at one corner. "Don't you want to look at me?" he joked.

She did, but she didn't want to rush. She studied his face, the same handsome lines and planes she saw everyday at work. The steam from her shower had beaded up on its surfaces, the heat bringing extra color into his skin. This late in the day stubble shadowed his strong jaw. She looked at his Adam's apple, at the hollow between his clavicles. His shoulders were broad and beautifully shaped, his arms hanging gracefully from their joints. He had lovely muscles: distinct but smooth—not like men got from gym workouts. Jake used his body. To fight. To move. Maybe to kill, in his former profession.

It was hard to think of him doing that. He stood there patient and relaxed, letting her study him. Beneath his ribs, his diaphragm went in and out slowly.

"You have good legs," she said—and he did. They were long and well developed, with what seemed to her the perfect covering of dark hair.

"Are my legs all you like?" he asked huskily.

She let her eyes rise to the spot they'd wanted to focus on. The shower spray spattered down her back and spine, incapable in that moment of distracting her. Nothing obscured her view but the vaporous air. Jake was erect, rising thick and long from the patch of fur at his groin—a good deal bigger than her last boyfriend. Up and up his phallus stretched, to the broader, darker knob of the tip. A little bead welled from the center slit, ready for action. Moved by that, Mia couldn't stop her tongue from sweeping across her upper lip.

"Your legs aren't all I like," she admitted.

"Do you want to stroke my cock like you did before?"

"Jake."

"Just answer," he said. "You don't have to do it."

Her pussy pulsed with desire. "This is playing with fire."

"*I* want to touch you," he said. "Kiss you. Stroke you. Run my tongue in circles around your nipples until they get even redder than they are. I want to suck them while I shove my cock deep inside you. I want to grip your gorgeous ass in both hands while your thighs tighten around me."

The pictures he was painting undid her. There was hardly any room to retreat. She stumbled back against the faucets behind her.

He caught her forearm, maybe afraid she'd fall. Mia tugged away from him.

"You made your point," she said as sharply as she was able when she was so short of breath. For a second, he seemed surprised by her reaction. Then he recovered.

"What point would that be?" he asked.

"That you—" She waved at him. "Find me attractive without my clothes. That you don't need to tie me up to get hard."

"That was never in doubt. You've been making me hard since the day Curtis hired you."

"I haven't!" she denied.

"You have," he insisted. "Every day. Every night. And right now I'm going crazy from wanting you."

She gaped as he slid his hand down the front of his own body. His fingers strafed through his chest hair, skimming over his abs and navel, until he reached low enough to give his ball sac a squeeze. He let go while she was still blinking, wrapped his grip around his rod, and started wanking right in front of her.

His stroke was slow, the way he handled himself uninhibited. His bicep did bulge then. He wasn't stroking his penis straight. Instead, he forced it to bend slightly. Waves of nuclear heat rolled through her as the walls of her pussy clenched.

She concluded he liked extra pressure on his right side.

"Daffodil," she blurted.

The motion of his arm faltered. "What did you say?"

"I'm using my safe word."

Now he gaped at her. "I'm not doing anything to you."

She knew she was blushing crazily. "I want you to stop doing that to yourself. It makes me want to touch you too much. You know how this will end if I do."

He laughed, no doubt because she'd sounded like a schoolmarm.

"All right," he said, forcing his hand away, his breathing not quite even. "You got me. I can't ignore that command."

◆

If Damien's contract didn't drive Jake insane, Mia and her safe word would. He brushed his teeth, peed, then left Mia to finish showering in peace. To his dismay, when he examined her slipcovered couch he discovered it wasn't convertible.

Well, shit, he thought. Mia only had a double bed. She'd sleep out here, he was sure, but he wasn't going to ask her to.

This lumpy-ass secondhand couch wasn't big enough for her either.

He rubbed the back of his neck. They'd share then. Tonight was about bonding and building trust. What better way than to sleep together in close quarters?

Aware that his control had limits, he pulled his briefs back on.

He was sitting up in her bed, paging through her romances, when she walked in wrapped in a towel.

"Um," she said, jolting to a halt.

"We're sharing," he informed her.

She seemed to understand he wasn't opening it for discussion. Somewhat to his relief, she grabbed some underwear and a T-shirt and returned to the bathroom to put them on. Seeing her naked once tonight was sufficiently frustrating. Mia had no idea how tantalizing her body was.

She was soft and curved and, man, did she have great tits. Her nipples made his mouth water, and her ass caused his fists to clench. Her legs belonged around his hips. Her expressions of surprise were totally worth inspiring. When that mouth of hers formed an O . . . Jake shook his head and shifted uncomfortably. No man could see those soft rosy lips without wanting them circling his erection.

He was picturing that a bit too vividly when she slid awkwardly under the covers and into the bed with him. She stayed sitting up like he was.

"You didn't put the lid down," she said.

"Sorry," he said. "I was distracted."

She was silent for a second. "Are you really reading that?"

"Skimming," he said. "For research." Realizing she wasn't sleepy, he set the book aside. "Why do you keep these around? I mean, I understand you enjoy the stories but with a brain like yours, you must have them memorized."

When he looked at her, her cheeks had flushed prettily. "I like reading words on the page. I like when the story unfolds a bit at a time, even if I know how it ends." Her knee bumped his thigh as she shifted to face him more. "Do you like to read?"

"Not much fiction. I like political exposes. And old movies."

She smiled. "Me, too. Not the political books. The old movies."

He sensed he was treading a delicate line. It wasn't his intent to convince her he was a good match for her. "*Casablanca*," he offered carefully.

"Bogey," she responded, her eyebrows wagging in approval.

"Ingrid Bergman was no slouch either."

"She was a knockout. If I swung that way . . ." She laughed. "Well, if I swung that way, she'd be out of my league."

Mia had blown her dark hair dry and left it down. Jake stroked the soft length that fell across her cheek. No one seemed out of her league to him.

"Tell me about the first time you were with a man," she said.

His eyes widened. "You want to hear about that?"

"It seems relevant."

He supposed it was. "I was cultivating an asset for my . . . government job, a woman who worked at an embassy for a country of interest."

"So you were a male Mata Hari." She was teasing him a little.

"Occasionally. My duties weren't usually so exotic, but my superiors were aware I had a knack for domination that appealed to some women. Anyway, this embassy employee I'd been dating asked if I'd be interested in a threesome. I assumed she meant with another woman, but a second man showed up. Making my apologies wouldn't have been strategic, so I gave it a shot."

"And you liked it."

"More than I expected. I'd never thought about being with a man before. Fortunately, he turned out to be a good source of intel too. My superiors complimented me on the bang up job I did."

"Har har."

He tapped her little nose. "You should get some sleep."

"I can't have a blow by blow?"

"No." Certainly not when giving her one was likely to wind him up.

Her sudden naughty grin should have warned him what was coming. "I guess if I want to know what you got up to, I'll have to hope Damien Call finds you irresistible."

She did have the ability to surprise him. "Don't hold your breath," he said. "'Restraint' seems to be his middle name."

In the interest of encouraging her to drop the topic, he turned out the bedside lamp and lay down on his side. After a moment, Mia did the same behind him. Given the size of her bed and the size of him, this didn't leave much space between them. Naturally, he soon had a half hard-on. He was willing it to relax when he heard the sound of snorting laughter behind him.

"Is something funny?" he asked his companion.

"I'm in the superior spoon position."

"The what?"

"If we were snuggled up, I'd be spooning you." She imitated a monster voice. "*I am the spoon master! I am dominating you!*"

She was too silly. Jake had to laugh with her. "Go to sleep, Mia."

She laughed a little more before wriggling deeper into the covers. "Jake?"

Jake mentally rolled his eyes. "Yes, Mia?"

"I did guess the point, didn't I? In the shower. About you wanting me to know I attracted you. I wasn't jumping to crazy conclusions."

"You weren't. I want you to trust my genuine interest in playing these games with you. That's as important as trusting I won't hurt you."

Mia mulled this over. "Good night, Jake," she said after a few heartbeats.

"Good night, Mia."

To his amazement, he dropped off in no time.

CHAPTER 7

DAMIEN Call had one of the city's shorter commutes. A private elevator whooshed him from his penthouse on the sixtieth floor of Ten WorldWide Plaza to his office on fifty-two. There, the door was disguised as a liquor cabinet. As Damien exited, he reminded himself to wait for the shelves to swing aside fully. Whenever his shoulder bumped them on his way out, the glasses he stored there clinked.

This morning patience didn't come easily. He was full of energy, eager to begin the day. Once again the sun was shining, the city outside sparkling like a fresh-washed toy—his toy, he liked to think. When darkness fell on its streets tonight, he'd have new things to look forward to.

Both prospects had his blood buzzing. He dealt with Ms. DeWinter's usual morning questions as quickly as possible. Free then, he strode around the corner to greet the employee who'd put the extra spring in his step. He'd never had a dom's submissive work for him before. As to that, he'd never hired a dom to do anything but dominate. Though it involved risk, the uniqueness of the situation gave him a charge. Damien was in uncharted territory, gambling and maybe gambling big.

The part of him that *didn't* always want to be in control enjoyed that.

Mia's office door was open. She was hanging up her coat and had her back to him. He saw he'd guessed her size accurately. His chest tightened as he took in the hug of her slate blue skirt around her lush bottom. The hem bared at least four inches of excellent thigh. Her calves looked great in the coordinating heels, their muscles stronger than he'd expected in such a soft woman. The tapering of her ankles helped him understand why some men liked kissing women's feet.

Every part of Mia was seductive.

Even better, for the next two months her seductiveness was his.

"Miss Beck," he said, not wanting to alarm her when he stepped over her threshold.

She spun, her adorable high ponytail bouncing. Her coiffure was hardly corporate, but he knew he wouldn't ask her to alter it. The hairstyle was the real her underneath the dress up.

"Mr. Call," she said.

"Damien," he corrected without thinking.

"We're at work. If you call me 'Miss Beck' and I call you 'Damien,' everyone will think I'm an idiot."

He scratched the side of his mouth. He didn't want that. "Very well. I'll call you Mia if anyone's around."

His solution seemed to amuse her. She laughed softly.

"How was your first day?" he asked. "I'm sorry I didn't get a chance to touch base with you yesterday."

"It was good. Your employees are more gung ho than I'm used to, but I admire how much they admire you. You inspire loyalty."

She'd given him what sounded like a genuine answer. He was tempted to say he hoped he'd inspire her loyalty too.

"I have a confession to make," he said instead. "I don't know what work to give you. Ms. DeWinter handles quite a lot. Plus, I pay services to perform the functions a personal assistant would."

"I thought I'd walk two steps behind you and make you look important. And schlep things. Water bottles. Laptops. Sunglasses. You know, your general handmaiden-geisha thing."

He laughed, enjoying her irreverence. He was glad she was comfortable with him.

"I'm not entirely kidding," she said. "From what I've seen, personal assistants are status-enhancing accessories. On a more practical level, I have a great memory. I can take notes at meetings without seeming like I am. Although, maybe you can do that too."

"To a certain extent I can. You don't mind running the occasional errand?"

"Have you seen my pay package? I wouldn't mind dog walking if you had one. You should also know I'm not generally mouthy. I totally know how to be invisible. Or you could just ignore me, let me sit here all day, if that suits your needs better."

"Do you *want* me to ignore you?"

She shook her head. "I know it's not PC, but I like the idea of the handmaiden-geisha thing."

Damien fought a smile. The faintest tinge of pink had risen into her cheeks. He guessed she really did like that.

"We'll give it a try," he said. "And see how it suits us both."

To his surprise, he didn't hate the idea of her shadowing him.

◆

Approximately twelve hours later, Damien Call was engaged in one of his favorite rituals: preparing for an evening out. He'd already showered and was shaving for the second time that day. He admitted to being slightly vain about his looks. The lines of his face were clean—even a little hard. In his opinion, the scruffy gold-brown stubble he was prone to didn't improve them. He liked the chilled look a fresh shave gave him, especially if he coupled it with slicking back his sun-streaked hair. He couldn't hide his libido. The predator always lurked behind his eyes. But intelligence lived there too. He knew which was in charge.

Today, he'd enjoyed being in charge more than usual.

He was pleased with his and Mia's experiment. She'd accompanied him to four of his less sensitive meetings, one of which Jake had driven them to across town. Though the associates he met seemed intrigued by his new accouterment, true to Mia's promise of invisibility, they soon forgot she was there.

Damien didn't forget. For one thing, she seemed to make every interaction run more smoothly. She forestalled the inevitable power jockeying between his VP's by pouring everyone's coffee. She found extra chairs and cued up two tech-challenged executives' presentations. Her memory was so good he could give her notes without waiting for her to jot them down. She took care of incidentals he hadn't realized impaired his productivity. Significantly, she did all of this without him feeling his private space had been invaded.

Marveling at that, Damien pressed a towel to his now smooth face.

How was it that Mia was nonintrusive while at the same time being unrelentingly attractive? His body had hummed—all day, it seemed to him—with awareness of her nearness. More than once, he'd considered ducking somewhere to find a quick release.

He'd refrained of course. Damien believed in the value of delayed gratification—for himself and others. The moment you *had* to have a climax was when it was most potent. The distinction lay in how difficult refraining had been today. Everything Mia did struck him as erotic, as if she truly were the geisha she'd joked about. Damien had met geishas on business in Japan. Though Mia wasn't clumsy, she couldn't claim their trained grace. She had gentleness maybe, or humility, or perhaps he just liked her pheromones.

He had reason to know that could happen.

He frowned as he buttoned his perfectly starched dress shirt. The idea of Mia exerting an extra tug on him was uncomfortable. Keeping the upper hand in this arrangement mattered. Jake was no pushover. At the least, Mia's will ought to remain subservient to his. Jake should answer to him as well, but considering Damien expected him to master Mia, he had to allow the man some leeway.

As if his thoughts had traveled through the ethers, the phone he'd left on the bathroom counter rang. Jake was calling him. If he were canceling their appointment at Diogenes, Damien would be irked.

"Yes?" he said crisply.

"Damien." Jake's voice sounded even raspier on the phone. "Have you got time for a couple questions about tonight?"

Questions Damien didn't mind. "Of course, Mr. Reed."

Damien smiled at the ensuing pause. Jake didn't like being addressed that way by him.

"Your contract said if you didn't provide suggestions, Mia and I could improvise."

Intrigued in spite of himself, Damien turned his back to the mirror and leaned on the counter's edge. "I take it you'd like to improvise tonight?"

"I have an idea I think Mia will respond to. The thing is, my plan will work better if you fall in with it."

"I believe my terms were clear, Mr. Reed. I do not wish to participate."

"I understand. This is more along the lines of you adding to the atmosphere."

"The atmosphere."

"Have you got non-modern formal wear? Some of that British lord of the manor stuff?"

"You mean traditional black tie?"

"Yes. With one of those starchy white shirts that take cufflinks. And maybe suspenders."

Damien already wore a shirt such as he described. "I can oblige you there."

"Great," Jake said. "Also, do you want me to pick you up, or would you rather be surprised like Mia?"

Damien sensed himself being led down a path. For whatever reason, Jake wanted to spring tonight's scene on him.

"My tolerance for surprises has limits," he warned. "I would like to see you tie up Miss Beck again."

He knew this was Jake's core kink and that he was unlikely to refuse.

"Okay," Jake said after a brief pause.

"In addition, I'd like to stipulate that your activities not involve sexual intercourse or full nudity."

"Agreed," Jake said almost too readily.

"In that case, I'll transport myself to Diogenes."

"Great," Jake said. "See you there."

He hung up, leaving Damien to stare in disbelief at his smartphone's screen. Arousal fought with annoyance inside of him. He was looking forward to seeing Jake operate. The man was an artist, possibly an ideal alpha. On the other hand, while Damien appreciated Jake's ability to reduce Mia to jelly, he strongly suspected the other man had cut off the call to dodge further instructions.

That crossed a line Damien shouldn't turn a blind eye to.

◆

Laypeople often believed that to get what you wanted, you had to target weaknesses. In Jake's experience, you got farther discovering an individual's comfort zone. Once you knew that, you could push against it. Better still, you could lull your subject into a sense of security. Damien's erotic comfort zone seemed to be watching other folks lose their cool. His self-control felt superior when theirs was less. Jake was relatively certain he could capitalize on that.

Mia had been with him when he spoke to the CEO. She looked at him as he tucked the phone away. "You have a funny expression. Did Damien ask for something you don't want to do?"

"Everything he asked I've already planned. I let him think he was steering me." Jake studied Mia's worried face. His fingers curled with longing to cup her velvety cheek. "I need you to play make-believe with me tonight, to be your natural self but as if you were someone else."

"Okay," she said unsurely. "Except I'm not Meryl Streep."

"You don't need to act, just let yourself fall into the moment. You won't even need to talk much. You can leave that to me." Despite his words, her little brows remained furrowed. "If it makes you feel better, we won't have an audience. It will just be you, me, and Damien."

She pursed her lips, her manner turning considering. "Can you draw Damien into pretending too? More than just asking him to dress up? Maybe we could get him to participate while he thinks he's just watching."

She'd taken Jake's idea farther than he had himself.

"Maybe we could," he said approvingly.

◆

Reaching Club Diogenes required a drive north of New York City, past the tolerance of most daily commuters. Set amid rolling acres and surrounded by mature trees, the mansion originally belonged to a nineteenth century oil baron. Because he'd wished to buy it, Damien had traced its ownership. The property first became a sex club in the Roaring Twenties. The Great Depression and Prohibition seemed not to slow it down. The club nearly folded in the "free love" sixties but rose from the ashes under the guidance of the oil baron's many-times great grandson.

As near as Damien could discover, the club changed hands again seven years ago, right around when he'd paid their astronomical entrance fee. From what other members said, the transfer of power had gone off without a hitch, the quality of service not suffering.

Probably it shouldn't irritate him that he couldn't dig up the individual's name who made his pleasures here possible. He'd acquired Audition. That coup would satisfy most people.

Since he hadn't wished to drive, in case he decided to imbibe, he'd called the club's private limo firm. The black Town Car stopped beneath the grand portico, where a Diogenes staff member trotted out to open the door for him.

The young woman wore full bellhop livery. "Lord C," she said, offering him a hand. "We're so happy you could make it."

Damien lifted his brows at her. He was no lord, nor did he ask the staff at Diogenes to call him anything but mister. The bellhop bowed to him.

"This way, sir," she said. "Everything is in readiness."

This must be part of Jake's plan to entertain Mia. Damien followed the staff member into Diogenes' palm-dotted Turkish inspired lobby. The usual skimpily dressed employees lounged attractively on settees, waiting for someone to summon them to a scene. He noticed curly haired Gabriel locked in the embrace of a taller man over by the large fireplace. Jake's previous favorite seemed engrossed in the kiss, as close to fucking the other male as he could get with their clothes still on. Damien guessed the young man wouldn't be assisting Jake tonight.

Perhaps it was just the three of them?

Someone removed Damien's outer coat. Under it he was dressed as Jake requested, in traditional black tie with a crisp pointed collar and polished shoes.

The bellhop's warm onceover flattered him.

"Sir," she said. "Your stable master, Mr. R asked if you would condescend to make use of these."

She handed him an opera hat, a walking stick with an eagle head, and a pair of supple kid leather gloves—suitable for any well-dressed Victorian gentleman.

Damien looked at them and his pulse picked up. The items were all authentic, though—strictly speaking—white gloves belonged with white tie. Damien pulled them on anyway. They were his size. His hands felt good as he worked his fingers in and loosened up the leather. If he were so inclined, these would enhance the delivery of a spanking.

The bellhop must have thought so too. She couldn't seem to tear her eyes from them. Amused, Damien gripped the walking stick and gestured its end forward.

"Shall we proceed?" he suggested.

The bellhop jerked back into action. "Yes, sir. Mr. R has your wife sequestered next to the blue room."

His *wife?* This fiction was getting more elaborate by the second. He donned the top hat as they walked a carpeted corridor. Diogenes Club was huge, and he wasn't sure where the blue room was. His sense of adventure heightened as they climbed a back staircase. His trousers whispered against his legs, making him aware that his balls were heavy and his cock was stirring. Though its length remained lax enough to swing, he doubted that would stay true long.

His palms were tingling with excitement.

They left the stairway on the third floor. Damien heard none of the carnal noises he sometimes did at Diogenes—no cries of pleasure, no groans, no beds or walls being thumped against. Jake must have reserved the whole area.

"This is your door," the bellhop said, indicating one with an old brass key sticking out. "My name is Regina. Please call me if you or your partners need anything."

He looked at her. He was a man, and she was very cute. Despite this, the thought came to his mind that he'd rather watch Mia spank this girl than do it himself. As to that, he'd rather let Mia paddle *him*.

The way his cock twitched at that idea unsettled him. Damien had his quirks, but he wasn't a bottom.

Rather than speak, he nodded in acknowledgment. Regina retreated partway down the corridor. Damien turned the key in the keyhole.

He saw at once that the room was empty—and where it got its name. The walls above the dark wainscoting were silvery blue, as was the rug and the pooling brocade curtains that had been drawn shut across a pair of tall windows. A ponderous nineteenth century four-poster, also draped in blue fabric, filled the space between them. All the furnishings were true to period, from the washing bowl on the dresser to the leafy ceiling medallion from which a patinaed gasolier descended. The space was intimate, the single chair barely an arm's length from the foot of the heavy bed. The seat was already wedged in a corner and couldn't be withdrawn further.

Damien suspected that wasn't an accident. He was being offered an up close and personal view.

The room was warm. He removed his hat and jacket, laying each carefully aside. The gloves he kept on, and he retained the walking stick. Because pacing would have betrayed too much restlessness, he sat and crossed his legs.

His cock was thick but not erect. Too aware of it, he shifted in the chair. Regina had said his wife was sequestered *next* to the blue room. Did Jake and Mia need to be informed he'd arrived?

He noticed a second door on the opposite side of the bed. Despite his wish to maintain his self-control, his breath sucked in as the old brass knob turned.

Jake entered the room alone. Damien's "stable master" wore downstairs servant garb: plain black trousers, suspenders, a loose white shirt with no attached collar. The front of the shirt lay open, baring a wedge of muscled chest. The dark hair on Jake's head was tousled, his sleeves rolled up to expose corded arms. Both the flush on his cheeks and the sheen of sweat on his brow suggested he'd come from some exertion. The tightening of the cloth at Damien's crotch reminded him Jake was one of a select group of males who piqued his interest.

When Jake inclined his head deferentially, the pressure on his prick increased.

"Sir," he said. "I've prepared your wife for her discipline. Do you wish me to bring her in?"

Damien wasn't accustomed to being involved in a scene this way, as if he were a player. He hesitated then decided he'd allow it. Jake had gone to some trouble to set this up.

"Please do," he acquiesced.

His breath caught for the second time as Jake led Mia gently in by the wrist. Her head was bowed, her chestnut hair falling shyly across her face. A beautiful Victorian corset in pale green silk accentuated her already tempting curves. Her breasts swelled above the bodice, and two black velvet bows marked the spots where her nipples were nearly popping free. The matching thong she wore bared her rounded bottom, which was every bit as bitable as he'd imagined that morning. Her feet were bare, her toenails painted innocent pink.

The outfit transformed her. Mia was no longer a modern girl. She was property.

Was Jake sweating because he'd helped change her?

"That's far enough," Jake said when they reached the foot of the four-poster.

Mia lifted her face to the other man. To Damien's surprise— and perhaps to Jake's—one glistening tear rolled down her dove-soft cheek.

"There," Jake said, wiping the drop away with his thumb. "I know you're frightened, milady, but you've earned what's coming."

"I haven't," she protested. "I only tried to do what's right."

Jake's sympathy turned stern. "You disobeyed your lord and master."

"Please," she said, the word tremulous.

"If you wish to beg forgiveness, you must address your husband."

Mia slid Damien an unsure look.

"Do it," Jake ordered, giving her bottom a scolding swat.

If she stepped any closer, she'd touch Damien. She dropped to her knees on the rug instead. Her clenched hands dug into her thighs, perhaps in a show of spirit or just to avoid brushing him. She, at least, was honoring Damien's terms.

"Please, sir," she said to the floor. "Don't let this brute punish me."

Damien's cock surged with interest, the throb of blood in it quick and hard. His grip tightened on the walking stick. He wasn't sure what the script for this drama was. "If you've sinned . . ."

"I haven't!"

"You went against Lord C's wishes," Jake contradicted. "He ordered you to pleasure me and you refused."

Mia tossed her head defiantly. "I only have your word for that."

"You know his preferences," Jake scoffed. "What's more, he knows yours. That quim of yours is too hot to be satisfied by a single man. If your husband wants me to help him fill it, who are you to gainsay him?"

"I am an honorable wife!"

"You are an unruly vixen. You need to be disciplined. Lord C —" Jake turned his gaze to him. "Please explain to this chattel what you expect of her."

A thrill went through him as both their eyes supplicated him. This time, Damien knew exactly what to say. "I expect my wife to submit to my chosen servant as she would submit to me. I expect her to trust that any demand I make is for her own damn good."

Jake smiled in triumph, his blue eyes gleaming devilishly. "Shall I tie her to the bed, sir? Shall I . . . educate her concerning her nature?"

"I command you to," Damien said unequivocally. "See that

you don't let her off lightly."

"The ropes are in that drawer," Jake said. "In the table beside your chair."

Damien debated ordering Jake to step past him and get the things himself. With a mental shrug, he twisted around to open the compartment. Two lengths of braided yellow silk lay within, the material soft but strong. As he handed them to Jake, the tips of their fingers bumped. Jake's hand jerked slightly and Damien hid a smile. He already knew Jake was susceptible to his chemistry.

He couldn't deny the contact gave him a buzz as well.

"Climb onto the bed," Jake ordered Mia as if the moment hadn't occurred.

The bed was tall. With the corset hampering her movements, Mia had to grip the post to clamber up onto her knees.

"Left hand," Jake said, already breathing harder at the prospect of tying her.

Mia hesitated and then offered her hand to him.

He had a knack for making bondage pretty. He wrapped a stack of coils around her wrist before securing it to the post with a sailor's knot. He did this quickly, as if he didn't dare linger. Despite the precaution, the bulge of his crotch grew larger.

When Mia noticed, she gnawed her lip.

"Right hand," he instructed. "Now!"

She tore her gaze from him and obeyed. He bound her second hand to the opposite post, that rope cuff matching the pattern of the first. Mia tested the knots and then looked at her captor. Her soft rosy lips were parted, her eyes startled. She reminded Damien of a silent movie heroine, unable to imagine how she'd come to be tied to the railroad tracks. When she trembled, the reaction was utterly natural.

Damien's cock went so stiff it hurt.

"What are you going to do to me?" she asked anxiously.

Jake's lips curved. "I'm going to force you to admit the truth: that your pussy is too hungry to be contented by one man."

"My husband is all I need!"

"We'll see." Jake broke through Damien's daze by extending his arm to him. Damien tensed. Jake seemed to be urging him to get up.

The impression was misleading. "Might I borrow your walking stick?" he asked politely.

Damien handed it over—though for a second he found himself mysteriously reluctant to release it.

Mia's expression was horrified.

"You're not going to beat me with that!" she exclaimed.

Jake stroked the stick between his hands, a motion that mesmerized his victim. "Do you remember your safe word?"

"Daffodil," she said.

"Do you wish to use it?"

"Not yet," she admitted.

"Then push out your pretty bottom. Naughty wives like you need to be warmed up. Knees apart, if you please."

He tapped her inner thighs with the walking stick. Mia spread them and flushed brighter. The thong that covered her little mound had a noticeable damp spot.

"How nice," Jake said. "You're wet already. That will make the job of breaking you easier."

He stepped around the bed until he stood slightly behind her, giving Damien a clear view. Mia wriggled helplessly in the ties, unable to restrain herself.

Her excitement was seductive.

"Now," Jake said with obvious relish. "Shall I decide how many lashes you receive, or will you leave that to your husband?"

"I belong to him!"

"Give her four," Damien said. "She isn't strong enough for more."

Jake landed four sharp strikes across the meat of Mia's buttocks, hard enough to sting but not to leave welts. Damien's "wife" gasped loudly for each one.

"There," Jake said, one large hand caressing the curves he'd struck. Stuck in the chair, Damien tensed his own ass in sympathy. "Your husband and I know what that's done to you. How it's made you aware of your lustful nature. How you're wet and hot and dying to be plugged by a good thick cock. Sadly for you, you haven't earned that privilege yet."

Close to her now, Jake slid two fingers beneath her sopping thong. Mia squeaked as they rubbed lovingly between her labia.

"You want me," Jake purred. "You'd kill to be taken by me right now."

His rubbing fingers pushed into her. Damien held his breath at the wet noise they made. Mia couldn't stop her neck from arching.

"I'll resist you," she promised huskily. "What you're asking of me is wrong."

"I'll show you *wrong*," Jake said.

He laid the walking stick on the covers in front of her, continuing to work her pussy with his first hand while his second slid up her corset front. As she writhed with pleasure, Mia's breasts fell free of the low bodice. Damien's fingernails dug into the gloves he wore. Her breasts were round and pretty and tipped with tight red nipples. Jake pulled one stiffened berry between his thumb and fingers, drawing a groan from her.

Damien could easily imagine squeezing the tender bud himself.

"Don't," she begged even as her hips twisted around the fingers that speared her sex.

"'Don't' isn't your safe word," Jake replied tauntingly.

He pulled his hands from her without warning, moving to the end of the bed again. Clearly flustered to suddenly not have him stroking her, Mia straightened from her former butt thrust-out position. As she did, her soft sweet breasts settled back into the corset cups.

Damien would admit to regretting that.

"You're cruel," she accused.

"I'm honest," Jake said. "If you want relief, all you have to do is be honest in return. Admit you need me. Admit your husband isn't enough for you. It's what he wants. Your supposed virtue is nothing but your pride talking."

She tossed her hair, her expression gone mulish.

"Very well. I see you need more incentive." He shrugged free of his suspenders and began unbuttoning his shirt. Mia huffed and turned her head away.

"Watch," Jake commanded. "Or you won't like the next caning I give you."

Damien knew threat was empty, but it did the trick. Mia watched Jake warily as he continued stripping off the garment. The man's upper body was very nice, his muscles lean and defined. Naked from the waist up, he tossed the shirt away and rolled his broad shoulders. His nipples were dark, their centers pointed with arousal.

When Mia wet her lips, Damien realized he'd done the same thing half a second ahead of her.

"Fine," she said. "Your chest is attractive. That doesn't mean

I'm surrendering."

"I'm not done yet," Jake said smugly.

His hands went to the waist of his trousers, obviously about to undo them. Damien's grip tightened on the arms of his chair. He'd been clear about no full nudity and no intercourse tonight. Was Jake going to defy him? If he was, did Damien really want to object? The hump that pushed out Jake's zipper was impressive, and Damien did have an interest in seeing it. Perhaps he *wanted* Jake to convince Mia to take him here and now.

Maybe her gratification didn't need more delay.

He was running out of chances to call a halt. Jake popped his top trouser button and followed with the rest. White linen undershorts swelled into the opening, lifted by the rise of what they were covering. Jake rubbed his thumb and fingers over the straining cloth. The material was fine enough for his veins to show. Aroused by that, Damien bit the inside of his cheek.

Mia betrayed her longing with a small moan.

"This is what you've been dreaming of," Jake said. "What you fantasized about even as your husband covered you on your wedding night. You want us both to take you. You want us to take turns fucking you."

Though her head shook from side to side, she couldn't seem to tear her gaze from his hand's motion. Jake noticed this, of course.

"Maybe I need to show you more," he said.

With a quick digging motion, he eased his erection free. The thing was a cudgel, its hardened state vaguely threatening. Pre-come glistened on the head, evidence of how wrought up Jake was. The tip of Damien's cock suddenly felt wet too. How would he feel with a hand wrapped around and exposing it? In that moment, Jake's hand or Mia's or even his own appealed.

His whole body prickled to think of it.

Mia swallowed. "Jake—"

Jake's hand moved, stunning her to silence.

"That's right," the stable master crooned. "Watch me stroke myself. I know you wish these were your hands. Hell, I know you wish your pussy were rubbing over me. I'd fill you just like he does. I'd ride you like I exercise his expensive horses, long and hard and sweaty until you can't help but scream your pleasure. By the time I spill, he'll be so excited he'll take you too. You'll never tire us both. Together, we'll fuck you right into submission."

The hoarseness of Jake's voice increased as he slowly stroked his cock up and down. His lack of inhibition was fascinating. He behaved as if he'd forgotten Damien—though Damien was only feet away. "What'll it be, milady? Are you ready to beg me to take you yet?"

Mia squirmed within the ropes that held her arms outspread, looking as if Jake truly were torturing her. She'd pressed her lips tight together to keep the truth inside. Jake stepped closer, his legs bumping the footboard. Mia's enraptured gaze followed his reddened cock to its new location.

The next time Jake's fingers approached the bulbous crest, they gave it an extra squeeze.

Damien knew exactly how sensitive he was there.

"This is too much for you, isn't it?" Jake's insinuating murmur was hot as smoke. "I bet you want to say your safe word like before. I bet you're terrified of what you'll agree to if I don't stop tempting you."

Damien's frontal lobes belatedly came on line. "What do you mean 'like before?' Isn't this the first time you've jacked off in front of her? Mia claimed she hadn't seen you naked yet."

Even as he asked, he knew the answer. Something had changed since their lunch in his office. The pair was too in synch not to have ripped through another barrier to intimacy.

Jake could have denied the charge but shrugged. "We might have played a bit in her shower last night."

"We have a contract. You agreed not to advance your relationship on your own."

"So I saw her naked. And she saw me. We were just fooling around." Jake's sly grin said he knew it had been more. He was goading Damien. Like an unruly sub testing for cracks in his master's limits, Jake *wanted* to be called out.

Under normal circumstances, Damien wouldn't have let himself get sucked in. He'd simply have walked away. The problem was he liked Jake and Mia. They felt realer than anyone he'd played with before. As to that, he felt realer when he was with them. He'd didn't want this game cut short.

So show him your limits, he told himself. *Let Jake know what happens when he ignores the rules you set.*

Though his heart beat faster, he forced his face to go frigid. "On your knees."

Jake's dark eyebrows shot up. "Excuse me?"

"You've broken your word. You need to perform penance."

"To you." Jake's tone was derisive.

Damien was aware of Jake's military training. Despite outweighing the other man, nothing Damien had picked up from his sparring partner would enable him to defeat the former operative. His sole advantage was his ability not to telegraph his intent. He backhanded Jake across the cheek before the other man guessed the blow was coming.

"No!" Mia cried in genuine distress, not realizing the gesture was symbolic. She wrenched at her bonds as if she'd fling herself at Damien.

"It's all right," Jake soothed her. He hadn't reacted except to touch his face. In truth, he'd barely flinched. Damien made a mental note concerning the man's exceedingly cool temper.

"He *hit* you," Mia protested.

"No harder than I hit you. Look, he didn't leave a mark."

Mia frowned at the place he showed her. "It's red."

"Enough," Damien said. "Jake, do you agree to submit to me?"

"I'll do it," Mia said, still trying to shield her friend.

Damien shook his head. "It has to be Jake. You're his sub. He's responsible for both your infractions. Understand, this isn't about forcing him to do things he doesn't want. It's about him bowing to my will. If you're worried, he can share your safe word."

Jake gave Damien a level look—and not because he didn't want to say *daffodil*. "It's not my nature to submit."

Damien's random fantasy about Mia and the bellhop came back to him. "No man's nature is all one thing or another. The real question is do you wish this arrangement to continue?"

He knew what he wanted Jake to answer, though he did his utmost to conceal it. Flashing one's cards prematurely didn't win poker games.

Jake's jaw worked, his unusually blue gaze boring into Damien's.

"All right," he said at last. "What penance do you give me?"

CHAPTER 8

THE CEO wasn't the cool cucumber he pretended. Mia couldn't mistake his relief at Jake's answer.

Her relief that they hadn't gone too far and shot their plan to hell was short-lived.

Damien was standing now, as close to her as Jake. His perusal of her trussed-up body sent tingles along her skin. "Mia brought you to climax in my office. It seems only fair that you return the favor. Lay her down on the bed and pleasure her with your mouth."

Mia had two strong but contradictory reactions. The first was a stab of pleasurable anticipation that shot directly between her legs. The second was embarrassment. She and Jake had barely kissed on the mouth so far.

"Um," she said dubiously.

Damien's steady tricolor eyes pinned hers. "Do you dislike receiving oral sex?"

She fought not to squirm and lost. "No. I mean, I don't think so. I've only had it done to me once."

"By him?" Damien's tone was sharp.

"By my first boyfriend. I don't think he was really into it."

Damien's eyes creased faintly with amusement. "I don't believe Mr. Reed suffers from that handicap."

"But it's . . . it's *personal*," Mia said.

"Yes," Damien agreed. "Personal and exciting and very much a sign of trust between two people. Not unlike being naked in front of a new partner. Or do you count that as 'just fooling around' too?"

"I guess not," Mia admitted, surprised by his insight. "Not for a woman anyway. Men don't seem to mind taking off their clothes as much.”

“So this is appropriate. You engaged in an intimacy behind my back. Now you should experience this one in my presence.” He must have seen her nose wrinkle. “I won’t judge you, Mia. I think your body is beautiful. I sincerely hope Jake has the skill to drive you to great heights. I also hope you’ll trust me with your uncensored reactions.”

“What about you?” she asked impulsively. “Are you trusting us with yours?”

Caution shadowed his eyes. “That’s not our agreement.”

Shouldn’t it have been? Was this truly how he wanted to live his life? She had enough self-control to keep the words inside. Maybe Damien knew this and was grateful. He stroked her cheek lightly with one finger, the gloves he wore preventing his skin from touching hers. The effect the contact had on both of them was interesting. His pupils dilated, and her shoulders shook with a small shiver.

For just a second, she thought maybe he wanted to touch her more. If he did, he didn’t give in to the urge. His arm dropped, though his face remained close to hers. His breath smelled of cinnamon.

“You know Jake will make you enjoy this,” he said softly.

He was too smooth for her to argue with. She let out a resigned sigh.

Damien chuckled and turned to Jake. “Mr. Reed, perhaps you should put away that marvel of hydraulics for the time being. I assume you can get . . . my wife past her embarrassment.”

Mia guessed they were back to role-playing. Another hot shudder vibrated her tailbone. She liked the story Jake had made up for them. She watched with interest as he tucked his cock back into his pants. Though he was mainly still erect, he was businesslike about it.

“Getting Mia over her embarrassment will be my pleasure,” he promised.

He reached for her hand, which she’d clenched unthinkingly around the braided silk. “Relax,” he said, giving her fingers a coaxing rub.

She loved his touch—and the gentle sureness with which he moved her wrist. To her surprise, what she’d thought was a complicated knot turned out to unwrap easily. Jake performed the same trick on her second hand. Her wrists were still attached to the posts, but her arms could move more than before.

"Turn around," he said. "Lie down on the covers."

He helped her obey. When she'd finished, her hands lay above her head, held there by the slackened ropes. She felt abandoned in that position, as if she really were a Victorian gentleman's lustful wife. Fires kindled in Jake's eyes as he looked down at her. Mia's breathing deepened.

"I need to take these off," he said.

He meant her thong panties. Damien didn't protest as Jake drew them down her legs. Mia tried not to dwell on how damp they were.

"So pretty," Jake praised, stroking her legs along the way. He made one knee jerk by tickling the vulnerable skin behind it. He smiled at that and sat on the mattress. Her tiny mint green panties dangled from one finger. "I'm tempted to sniff these, but you've probably blushed enough. I'd rather your blood pooled elsewhere."

"Thank you," she said more tartly than she'd intended.

He grinned, tossed the panties aside, and swung over her on his hands and knees.

Oh boy, she thought as the mattress dipped beneath his weight. He was hot and big and her hands weren't free enough to push him off anything he had a mind to explore.

This, she had no doubt, was the point in leaving her wrists tied up.

"My," he said. "So much to feast on. Where should a humble horse man begin?"

He feinted a kiss toward her mouth. Was Damien's prohibition against frenching still in effect? Jake acted as if it were, nuzzling into her neck instead. That was sufficient to make her wriggle, especially when his hands slid up to cup her breasts again.

She gasped when he pushed her right nipple free of the corset top. As he took it into his mouth, her spine bowed off the covers, her hands automatically gripping the silk ropes. Jake wasn't afraid to use real suction. His lips and tongue worked a wicked magic on a long chain of nerve endings. In seconds her clit was pulsing, her sex overrun with cream.

She gasped even louder when he let go of her.

"You'll want to scoot that chair closer," he said to Damien. "I believe your wife is about to lose control."

She heard the chair scrape the carpet but couldn't look away from Jake. His knowing smile held her mesmerized.

He caressed her torso through the boned corset's silk. Each of her ribs received his stroke, then her waist and belly. Mia's body tensed as his hands molded over and rubbed her thighs. He was coaxing her knees apart, opening her most personal parts to his gaze and more.

His smile gentled as he sensed her tension. He kissed the inside of one sprawled knee and then the other.

"You don't have to do this," she blurted.

"Mia," he said, his voice amused but also gravelly. "You can't imagine I'm being forced. This is my privilege."

"I—"

"Shut up," he laughed, covering her open mouth with his palm. "Be a good wife and please your husband."

When he put it that way, she had to obey. He caressed the groove between her thighs and hips.

Then he laid his mouth over her pussy.

She jerked, but his tongue was only tickling her. He moved his hands to hold her labia from his way. His thumbs felt good when they pressed down and rubbed. A low noise escaped her throat. The weight of his muscled forearms trapped the loll of her thighs. She couldn't get away even if she'd wanted to. That idea made her pussy well. The tip of his tongue flicked her clitoris, which was way more sensitive than she expected, as if a jolt of electric current were shooting straight up it.

Shit, she thought—or possibly said aloud.

Jake chuckled against her mound and did the flicking thing again.

She cried out and gripped the wrist ropes harder. Her pelvis seemed to rock up by itself, her legs suddenly wanting to crook around his broad shoulders.

"Just this one," Jake said, obliging her by arranging the left to drape down his powerful back. Her right leg he held down even more firmly.

So Damien could watch, she realized. That leg would have blocked his view. She groaned, impossibly turned on by that. She wouldn't look at the other man, couldn't—her eyes were screwed tightly shut—but she was suddenly hyperaware of other signs of his presence. She heard his quickened breathing and the little shifts he made in his chair. Was he leaning closer? Were his knuckles white? Could he see the expression on Jake's face?

Thinking about all that made her thrash uncontrollably.

"Fuck," Jake said, perhaps in response to the rise in her excitement. "I can't wait anymore. I'm giving you what you need right now."

She'd needed it forever, it felt like. Since before their first kiss. Since before Audition. Maybe since the day they'd met. She moaned as Jake's mouth engulfed her with total possession. He was sucking her clitoris and lashing it and digging his thumbs into the strongest nerves that branched away from it. She groaned as one thumb crooked into her passage. Jake pressed one spot and then another like he was working his way around a clock. His breath panted against her, hungry sounds breaking in his chest. Damien had been right. Jake was into this. The ache of near orgasm rose from deep inside her pussy.

"Please," she moaned, the word torn from her.

Jake's exploring thumb found a spot inside her that was erotic gold.

Her eyes flew open as she came. *This* was a climax. Intensely pleasurable sensations burst in her core and spread outward. Her toes were curling, her thigh muscles tightening with ecstasy. Her head rolled from left to right. Damien had risen to watch the end, and he'd pulled off his fancy gloves. His bare hand gripped the bedpost, covering the final loop of her silk wrist tie. His knuckles were white, just as she'd fantasized.

When she lifted her gaze to his, he didn't look away.

Though she couldn't read his emotion, the potency of his stare seared her. What a soul he must have. Saint or sinner, he burned inside like a sun.

Finally the sweetness of her orgasm faded out.

Jake lifted his head from her. She sensed Damien shifting his attention to the other man even as she did herself. For the moment, Jake was focused on her. With his fingers feathering her thighs, he licked his lips and lifted one brow in question.

Mia laughed with the bit of air she could gather. Though breathless, her body was deliciously relaxed. "Five out of . . . five gold stars!" she slurred. "Or are you . . . waiting for . . . something . . . other than a review?"

He chuckled and rubbed her hip. "A review will do for now." He groaned as he pushed to the side of the bed to sit. "God, that got me all worked up."

He looked ruefully at his lap, where the large bulge of his erection was pushing up. "I don't suppose—?"

"No," Damien said in response to his unfinished suggestion. "You'll enjoy it more if you wait."

Jake smiled, slow and mischievous, a reaction Mia had no trouble interpreting. It hadn't escaped either of their notice that waiting was Damien's special obsession.

♦

The pair's matching grins unsettled Damien—especially Jake's. The man hadn't been granted a release, but he appeared to be on the same satisfied page as his cohort. Decision rose in Damien before he could squash it down.

"You two are coming home with me."

"Excuse me?" Jake said. "That wasn't our agreement."

"You need oversight," Damien said. "You've already proved you can't be trusted on your own. You'll stay with me and we'll . . . bond."

"*You* want to bond," Jake said. "With us."

"Do you deny that was a successful scene?"

"Very," Jake said. "And I admit that was thanks in part to you. Obviously, we both find you inspiring. However—" He slitted his eyes at Damien. "We didn't agree to let you take over our whole lives."

Damien hadn't been a hundred percent sure he wanted them to agree—until Jake resisted. He crossed his arms stubbornly. "Move in with me or the deal is off."

"*Move in?*" Mia blinked then abruptly shut her mouth.

"I have plenty of room and any amenity you could wish. Plus, it would only be for two months."

"I don't know," Jake said. He looked at Mia.

"It's up to you," she responded, deferring the choice to him.

Did Damien resent that? For an instant, it seemed he did. He shook off the sensation. "There's *lots* of room," he insisted. "You'll still have your privacy."

Jake rubbed his jaw and considered. Knowing nothing else would get him his way, Damien held the other man's gaze without wavering.

"I'll want a concession," Jake said, obviously shifting to bargaining mode.

"What concession?"

"I don't know yet, but when I tell you, you won't refuse."

Damien got the *Godfather* reference. He also got that Jake wouldn't ask the impossible. Jake might be sly, but he seemed honorable.

"Agreed," Damien said and held his hand out to shake on it.

When Jake returned the clasp, his hold was warmer than Damien expected. Damien shook dozens of hands a day and thought he knew every style: from grips that crushed or tried to ingratiate, to nervous sweaters and germaphobes. Jake's was neither sycophantic nor pugnacious.

Jake shook hands as if he liked Damien.

◆

After all the planning and drama, Mia found it strange to have the scene over. It was though. Damien left to inform the limo service he didn't need to be driven home. Mia sensed he wanted a chance to pull himself together. She understood the urge. She wasn't back to reality yet herself.

Once Jake had undone her ties, she sat up and rubbed her wrists. His smartass smirk was nowhere in evidence.

"You're worried," she said, noting his serious expression. "Didn't this turn out the way you hoped? He's invited us to his home. We'll be able to search there."

Jake bent down, searching for something on the floor. "Yes. That was a lucky break."

"But?"

He retrieved her panties and handed them to her. "But I can't read him as well as I'd like. I'm not sure what he wants— aside from us putting on a show for him."

Since her companion seemed distracted, Mia pulled the thong on without blushing. "I think he wants more than a show. Underneath, anyway."

Jake grunted and rubbed his nape. "Here's the thing: who is Damien identifying with when I dominate you? Am I his proxy or are you?"

"Why can't the answer be both of us?"

"It can," Jake said, but he didn't seem satisfied with that.

"You thought *you* were Damien's stand-in. Because he's been following your scenes here."

"I suppose I did. Obviously, he's top dog in his business life. Sometimes people switch roles from work to private. . ." He stopped speaking to stare into mid-air. "Actually, I'm not sure I'm asking the right question. There's something else going on with him. Some other reason he is the way he is."

"He's a mystery wrapped in an enigma," Mia suggested. Jake laughed, the furrow between his brows relaxing. Mia liked that he wanted to talk things through with her. Probably, she ought to do the same.

"Jake," she said. "Something's been bothering me. Damien seems to . . . like us. I don't know if he's guilty of what Raeburn claims, but he's still a human being. If he discovers we did all this to manipulate him, he'll be hurt."

"Yes. I'm not thrilled about that myself." He didn't suggest they call off the job, just laced both hands behind his neck and stood thinking silently.

Though she didn't think he was posing, he looked yummy like that—all bare-chested and muscular.

Jake had his mouth on me, she thought, the idea suddenly surreal. What did their adventures mean to him, really? Wasn't he, in his way, as big a mystery as Damien?

"Your shirt's over there," she said, pointing it out to him.

He shook himself from his thoughts and smiled.

"You're a trooper," he said, which was hardly a role she'd daydreamed about filling.

◆

Jake had returned to his driver role. Mia watched him open the silver car's rear door for Damien. The CEO glanced at him before sliding in.

"You too," Jake said, surprising her.

"I thought I'd ride shotgun."

His mouth twisted. "I'd appreciate it if you didn't. You're too distracting for safe driving."

She wore the loose jeans and pullover hoodie she'd brought along for after—not exactly siren wear. "For real?"

"For real," he said with a faint smile.

"I assure you I don't have cooties," Damien added from the back seat.

She had to slide in then. Up till then, she and the CEO had ridden together in roomy limo compartments. Now Damien seemed very close, which was unexpectedly pleasant *and* awkward. Despite the recent orgasm she'd enjoyed, part of her wanted to swing onto his lap and grind on him like a stripper. The impulse didn't go away as Jake put the electric vehicle in motion.

Damien cleared his throat. "Your attire appears quite . . . comfortable."

Him being self-conscious allowed her to relax. She turned toward him until her knee nudged his nearer leg. "Do you always talk like that?"

"You mean so formally? I'm afraid so. When I was a boy, my classmates called me 'the professor.'"

"I bet you were a cute kid."

He pulled a face. "I was a dichotomy. The brain and awkwardness of a nerd and the looks of, well . . ." He trailed off.

"A Greek god?" she suggested teasingly. The comparison didn't seem to please him, though it was pretty accurate.

He shook off his irritation and shifted around to her. "What about you? What sort of child were you?"

She hesitated. This was a genuine get-to-know-you conversation, the kind that might deepen Damien's feelings of betrayal when their arrangement reached its inevitable end.

Damien's face stiffened. "If my question is too personal, you need not answer."

"It isn't that." Mia sensed Jake checking on them in the rearview mirror. Jake kept telling her to be herself, though the self she was didn't really like telling this story, not when Jake hadn't heard it either. "According to my mom, I was weird even as a baby. She claimed I crawled to my own drummer—usually away from everyone."

Seeming interested, Damien propped his chin on his hand. "You were introverted."

"Yes. I played by myself more than with other kids, assuming you don't count imaginary friends. My brother Mike was eight years older. He was better at fitting in. Outgoing. He was my best friend, I guess. My protector."

"Go on," Damien said when she paused.

To hell it with it, she thought. "When I was eight, I fell out of an apple tree."

Damien laughed. He covered his mouth and stopped. "Sorry. The way you said that was amusing."

"That's all right. I guess it does sound funny. I didn't fall that far, but I hit my head on a rock and knocked myself unconscious. I'd been playing alone in an orchard near our house. Mike found me. We don't know how long afterward. It turned out I had a serious brain injury. A portion of my left temporal lobe was damaged. Whatever new connections my brain made to compensate for the loss resulted in this memory thing I have now."

"You developed a form of savant-ism," Damien said. "Your left brain filter for suppressing superfluous detail must have been switched off."

"That sounds like what the doctors said. Anyway, I ended up more of a weirdo than I'd been before. You're looking at a girl who didn't have a boyfriend or a date until I left high school. For a long time, I'd blurt out everything I knew on a subject every time I was asked a question. Mike helped me practice getting the compulsion under control."

"Fascinating," Damien said—but not like he thought she was a freak. "I'd be interested to hear how your brother did that. He must have been very bright himself."

"He was," she said around the sudden lump in her throat. She didn't explain that Mike had channeled her impulse into drawing her memories. That skill was too tied up in her and Jake's hidden agenda.

She dropped her eyes and Damien cocked his head to the side. "You miss him."

His comment reminded her he'd researched her. He already knew Mike was dead. "Every damn day," she said honestly.

He reached out to cover her hand. The spontaneous touch surprised her.

"Your brother left you strong," he said. "You should be proud of that."

She had the oddest impression this was the real Damien Call: this warm, steady, openhearted human being. She didn't dislike the eccentric who'd put her and Jake at his beck and call—who was she to judge, after all? But if this was the real him, how on earth had that other Damien come to be? This Damien was the sort of man a woman could fall for.

"Thank you," she said, a thready breathlessness in her voice.

Damien drew his hand back from her.

CHAPTER 9

IT was late, and the shining lobby of Ten WorldWide Plaza was as quiet as a mausoleum. Damien signed his companions in at the desk, thankful the night guard was new. If he hadn't been, he might have betrayed surprise. Damien never brought guests to his residence.

Probably he shouldn't be doing so tonight.

He shouldn't have touched Mia in the car either. He needed to be careful. Triggering her to fall for him would mean the end of their enjoyable arrangement. He cast a sidelong glance at her. She seemed all right, not dewy-eyed or anything.

"This is *your* elevator," she said, watching him activate the handprint control.

"Yes," he said. "I'm the only actual resident of the building. I'll need to code your prints into the system."

That realization sparked discomfort. This was his private space. He shrugged internally. He could renege their access if circumstances changed. It wasn't the end of the world that he hadn't thought this through.

"There's a corporate hotel across the street," he added as more practicalities occurred to him. "I'm sure they'll send over toothbrushes and whatnot."

They stepped into the private elevator, the three of them close to filling it. Naturally, the ride to his floor was swift. The mechanism was his design, and he didn't design slow things. Despite the quickness of the journey, one or two ideas of what the three of them might do in the confined space arose. His cock was noticeably restless by the time they arrived.

"This is me," he said unnecessarily.

His front door had been salvaged from an old Buddhist

116

temple. Constructed of solid bronze, the panel's size and weight had necessitated it being hoisted to the skyscraper's top by crane. At the moment, all it required to open was his handprint.

"Hold on," Jake said. "Let me check inside before you two go in."

"I'm sure it's safe," Damien said.

"Just in case," Jake responded.

Mia let out a little snort as Jake went to look around. "He does this protector thing at my place too. I think we have to humor him."

Being referred to as part of a *we* gave him an odd feeling.

Jake returned shortly. "Okay. Everything seems fine."

Damien's nerves were uncustomarily tight as they went in. His home was outside the norm. Jake probably wouldn't care. Damien suspected the former CIA operative had slept in plenty of strange places. Mia, however, might feel uncomfortable.

She walked as far as his living area and turned in a slow circle. "Wow, wow, wow, wow, wow," was her comment.

"Is it all right?" he asked.

She laughed. "It's better than Superman's fortress! Talk about open plan!"

His residence took up the entire top floor of the WorldWide tower. The architect had designed it to give the impression of being a single immense room. Half walls shielded areas benefitting from seclusion, but above them was a great gulf of air. Surmounting that, an exposed steel framework supported a super-strength glass enclosure roof. The lengths of glass that comprised it rippled like frozen ribbons, the effect sleek and graceful rather than industrial. Damien loved the engineering feat his home represented, and the way it let in the sky.

The city that never slept glittered 360 degrees around them.

Mia gawked with her head tipped back then turned to grin at him. "I notice you don't have a lot of furniture. Where are Jake and I going to sit?"

She was teasing. He had enough chairs for that. "I don't entertain a lot."

Her eyes met his. He felt her looking into him, trying to discern why. Was she pitying him or just curious?

"I guess I might keep this place to myself if it were mine," she conceded. "Can Jake and I have a tour?"

Relief flooded him at her enthusiasm. "Of course. It would

be my honor."

◆

From the perspective of their mission, the most interesting part of the tour was Damien's home office. This was a cube of glass within the larger glass sculpture.

"That's locked," Damien said. "Some of the things I keep there are sensitive."

Mia admired Jake's absentminded nod of acceptance.

"Where will we sleep?" he asked.

The guest area Damien showed them didn't seem to have gotten a lot of use. It included two queen size beds, a few chairs, and a walk-in dressing room with frosted glass for walls. It was nice but impersonal—like an upscale modern hotel.

The lack of a single painting disappointed her. At home, the best she could afford were framed prints. Given Damien's deep pockets, her inner art history major had been hoping for a close encounter with a Chagall or a Hockney or *something*. She guessed she'd have to settle for the space itself. Admittedly, it was spectacular. The windowed roof twisted like a structure by Frank Gehry.

"You're on the opposite side of the penthouse from me," Damien said. "You'll have your privacy when you need it. Here's the bathroom you can use."

The bath was boxed by more frosted walls. Jake stuck his head inside and whistled. "You're going to like this, Mia."

When she went to see, her heart skipped a beat. She didn't know whether to gasp at the seamless acres of Carrara marble or the zillion body jets poking out of the farthest wall. It, too, was open plan. "I think that shower and I need to be alone."

Jake laughed.

"No, really," she said. "You men get out of here."

"What if we don't want to?" Damien asked silkily.

That caught her unprepared. For one thing, he was saying *we,* as in him and Jake, and that pushed a few buttons. For another, they'd already played out a scene tonight.

Then again, she was the only one who'd gotten an orgasm out of it. The tips of her fingers went buzzy with interest.

"You want to watch me shower?"

Damien's eyelids were hooded, his Greek god mouth slightly pursed. "Actually, I was thinking I would help."

♦

Damien saw he'd surprised her. He hadn't planned to initiate another erotic encounter. Not tonight, and certainly not with him in an active role. Something about having Mia in his territory was changing up his habits. Mia was unique, and obviously the connection between her and Jake was strong—stronger perhaps than either of the pair realized. They weren't simply a couple. They were a natural team. They fell into a united strategy seemingly without effort. Their role-playing at Diogenes was evidence of that.

As long as Damien didn't break the connection between them, wouldn't Mia's feelings for him stay within safe limits?

He told himself he was making a reasoned choice, taking a calculated risk and not reckless one. Yes, he wanted Mia quite a lot and, yes, it had been a long time since he'd allowed himself to lay hands on a woman. But he wasn't giddy. His mind was too disciplined for that.

"You want to help her shower," Jake said dubiously. "With me there too."

Damien flashed a grin. "I said I didn't want to be pushed to participate. I didn't say I never would. Do you object?"

This was directed to Mia. She shut her mouth and shook her head. Her cheeks were very pink. "You only live once, I guess. Might as well live out a few fantasies."

Damien filed this intriguing response away. "And you?" he asked Jake.

"It won't be my first rodeo with another guy."

Damien didn't expect the jolt of excitement the words inspired. Though Jake's tone was casual, the cagey glint in his eyes put Damien on notice. Jake hadn't forgotten Damien making him submit at Diogenes. Any dominant worth his salt would be watching for opportunities to turn that table. If he weren't careful, Damien might be signing on for more than he could handle.

But that wasn't an immediate worry. For now the chain of command remained as he'd established it. Or he thought it did anyway.

Mia pointed sternly at him. "I'm stripping in the bedroom. You two be bare-assed by the time I get back or don't expect to get anywhere with me."

Jake's mouth twitched with amusement. "She means it. I

know that tone."

Damien took his word for it. He removed his clothes without fuss, leaving them folded on the low bench beneath where the guest robes hung. When he finished, Jake was already naked. The driver-slash-bodyguard leaned casually on a marble wall, with both his arms and ankles crossed. His body was graceful and athletic, his cock casually half-mast. He wasn't self-conscious about giving Damien a onceover.

"You sure are fit," he said. "No boardroom flab on you."

"Nor on you," Damien returned dryly. "I gather your former government employer didn't chain you to a desk."

Jake's lips crooked up at the corners. "My former government employer liked me to stay busy."

His sly inflection suggested the slang meaning. Damien contemplated the extensive experience Jake must have—and not only with women. His own shaft began to rise. Jake's smirk intensified as his gaze dropped to Damien's groin, which sped up developments there.

"That answers that question, I guess," Jake said. "You do have eclectic tastes."

"I'm back," Mia announced from the bathroom door. "You two play nice or I'm leaving."

They turned to look at her and Damien lost his breath. He'd loved her in the corset, but just plain naked she really was something. *Old-fashioned* best described her figure. Her feminine curves dried his mouth: her just-full-enough breasts, her waist, the surprising length of her shapely legs. She looked soft and silky and fuckable. Though she blushed at their attention, she didn't hide anything. Not her breasts. Not her neat triangle of curls. Her nipples tightened, and she appeared to be pressing her thighs together—hopefully with arousal and not fear.

Damien might not have the patience to allay that. He was having trouble not leaping on her that instant.

"If you hadn't stolen my breath, I'd whistle," he said, hot desire beating through his whole body. "That is a world class reveal."

"Yeah," Jake agreed. "What he said."

Mia smiled and cast down her lashes, her shy pleasure enchanting. "You should probably turn on the shower. That control panel looks like it's for a jet."

Damien was still blinking.

"She means you," Jake chuckled. "You're the computer programmer."

"Right. I'll take care of it."

He turned jerkily, the motion making him aware that his erection was now at vertical. The control panel was a waterproof touchscreen on the wall. For a few blank moments as his hard-on throbbed violently, he couldn't remember how to work it.

"Do you want music?" he asked over his shoulder.

"Ooh," she said. "Put on Clean Bandit."

Damien was clueless. Fortunately, his house system found whoever this was online when he repeated her request. Upbeat dance music pounded into the room as the pulsating sprays turned on. To his delight and distraction, Mia began shaking her booty. Damien didn't go clubbing. He couldn't tell if she were dancing well or badly, only that she seemed to be having fun.

He decided then and there to code her voice into his system too. She shouldn't ever be deprived of this pleasure.

"Well," Jake said, taking in the show while still leaning on the wall. "This is my new favorite song."

Mia laughed and bounced toward Damien. He couldn't move. The animation of her body entranced him. She danced into the complicated array of jets, her bare feet slapping on the wet floor.

"Dance with me," she urged, offering her hands to him. "That's allowed, right? And you can't look any stupider than I do."

She didn't look stupid to him. Damien slid his palms over hers, twining their fingers together so that hers were trapped. With her arms secured, he walked her butt-first into the warm marble wall. Mia gasped as her ass cheeks hit it, her brown eyes wider but not frightened. Too tempted to stop himself, Damien leaned into her. Her soft breasts flattened beneath his weight, his engorged cock branding her belly.

He wasn't prepared for how incredible this felt. The full contact of his front with her hot wet body caused his lust to go nuclear. With a throttled groan, he pushed one hard thigh between her smooth two.

He couldn't fail to note her pussy was creaming.

"Why don't we dance like this?" he suggested huskily.

He wasn't thinking, or not with his up-top brain. Forgetting everything he'd ordered himself not to do for years, he tilted his head and tongue-kissed her.

◆

The intimate kiss overwhelmed Mia's already revved up system —partly because she didn't expect it and partly because it was just that good.

Damien held back nothing as he marauded her orally. The motion of his tongue was graphic, the message it sent unmistakable. He wanted to be inside her. He didn't seem inexperienced. He had no shyness, no inhibition about touching the female form. If anything, he was greedy for the feel of her. His body was bigger than Jake's, his muscularity and his broadness triggering instinctive feelings of helplessness. Coupled with that, Damien's hands held hers captive beside her head. His strong fingers kneaded hers, his pelvis and chest rubbing rousingly along her body.

She couldn't escape, but she hardly wanted to.

She liked everything about his body: its hairiness, its weight, even the press and roll of his testicles. He was flat-out delectable when he let go like this. He tasted good, and smelled good, and the rocking of his thigh between hers was propelling her like a rocket toward orgasm.

Damien seemed to be racing toward it too. She didn't think she'd ever felt a cock throb as dramatically as his was. The smooth heat of it shoved tight against her belly was beguiling. She tried to wrest one hand free. She wanted to touch him, to stroke him before he came.

Maybe he understood. He groaned down her throat, suddenly releasing one set of trapped fingers.

He was too quick for her. Before she could lower her arm to him, he wedged his hand between their bodies and thumbed her clitoris.

Mia cried out. Two long fingers had just curved inside her sheath, joining his thumb in pushing lightning along her nerves.

"Come," he hissed. "Fucking come for me."

She couldn't quite. She longed to break, but standing up like she was interfered with her reactions.

Then another thing she didn't expect happened, though maybe she should have.

"Why don't I help you with this?" Jake said.

He was right behind Damien, the shower's spray instantly

plastering his dark hair.

Damien stiffened in surprise. He turned his head and then gasped like a gunshot. Jake had done something Mia couldn't see. The pressure of Damien's muscular body on hers increased.

"I've got my thumbs up his butt," Jake informed her helpfully. "I found some lube in his cabinet, and now I'm massaging the nice nerves he has in there."

Mia couldn't speak. A tingling flood of excitement had stolen the power from her.

Jake bit Damien's earlobe. "You should have stocked condoms in this bath. Then I could fuck you too."

Damien shivered at the threat. A second later, Mia caught the reaction.

"I didn't . . . give permission for this," Damien panted.

Jake grinned like a devil born. "If you want me to stop what I'm doing, you can use her safe word. We all know you remember it."

He was taunting Damien, and Damien knew it.

Damien opened his mouth to retort but sucked in air suddenly instead. His cock jerked hard against her belly.

"That would be his prostate I just found," Jake told her. "I've got my finger in him now and I'm stroking it like I did your G-spot when I went down on you."

Damien writhed against her and moaned.

"You'll come pretty soon like this," Jake warned. "Especially with the way you like to deny yourself. Tell me, have you masturbated since that hand job she gave me in your office?"

"I don't see how that's your business." Somehow, in spite of his insane arousal, Damien managed to sound haughty.

"It's my business because knowing I'm seducing a goddamn monk pushes all my sex buttons. So what's the answer, boss man? Have you or not?"

"Not," Damien snapped.

Mia's sex buttons punched down in unison, the ache inside her suddenly multiplied by ten.

"Excellent," Jake said. "You'll really enjoy this then. By the way, if you want to get her off before you, you better get your hand in gear again. Let me know if you need instructions. I definitely remember what she likes."

Mia heard Damien's molars grind with anger. "No woman . . . only likes one kind of touch."

Jake winked at her over Damien's shoulder, but Damien was right. Jake had issued a challenge and he was going to rise to it. He resumed caressing her purposefully. Though his technique was different from Jake's, it felt just as effective. The pad of his thumb rubbed her clit up and down, pushing the slippery sheath along the little rod. Completely crazed now, Mia clutched his back with the hand he'd freed.

"Swing your leg up," Jake suggested. "Might as well give him room to work."

Mia hooked her calf around his hip.

"Jesus," she gasped as Damien's fingers slid wonderfully deeper.

"Go," Damien ordered. "I want to feel you do it."

Her neck arched back. She was almost there. Damien released her second hand to clamp his around her butt. He hitched her higher and ducked his head, his hot mouth sealing hungrily around her nipple.

The fervent tug of his lips was instantly addictive. She gripped his nape to hold him where he was. She tensed, gulped air . . .

One of Jake's palms slapped the wet marble beside her ear. The sound was a match struck to the fuse of her excitement. Two men were overpowering her now, two large bodies straining toward release like she was herself. Jake thrust against Damien's ass, his other hand doing presumably pleasurable things inside it.

Damien choked out a noise, but he wasn't objecting.

Jake's actions didn't allow the man to hold back. The CEO turned desperate, growling and undulating like he'd push straight through her. He was so excited he had to release her breast.

"God," he said, his eyes shut with sensation. "*Yes.*"

Mia couldn't tell who he was talking to. Both of them maybe. His body flashed hot against hers.

It was the end for both males. Jake grunted, and Damien stiffened, and hot jets shot from his cock up her stomach.

Her climax broke an instant later, as if theirs had touched it off. Long, rippling sensations ran like wine through her pussy and then flowed out through the rest of her. Her sheath pulled at Damien's fingers while he groaned loudly.

Hearing that was the cherry on top of her afterglow.

"Christ," Damien said, sagging against her.

The skin between them was slippery, his ejaculate

temporarily out of reach of the shower.

"Move back," he said to Jake. "We're going to squash Mia."

Jake moved back with a throaty sigh.

"Don't let me fall," Mia said to Damien.

He held her upper arms as he stepped back, giving her knees a chance to steady. "You okay?"

She opened sleepy eyes and smiled. Damien's brow was creased, which deepened her amusement. The music played on, but she was too tired to dance. The hot sprays felt good where they pulsed on her.

"All right," he said, releasing her. "I guess I have my answer."

He swept his wet hair back with one hand. The motion made his big bicep bulge.

"Are *you* okay?" Jake asked with a hint of teasing. "That was some noisy groaning I heard from you."

"I'm fine," Damien said curtly. "You . . . did a good job of disarming me."

"*Disarming* you." Jake's eyebrows wagged. "Is that what we're calling it?"

Damien rolled his eyes. "Next time, ask."

"What fun would that be?" Jake said disingenuously.

Damien was probably too relaxed to be angry. "I'm going to bed. I'll see you two tomorrow."

He grabbed a robe as he left but didn't put it on. His back view was extremely nice: big shoulders, strong butt, solid muscles running impressively down his long hairy legs. His calves were sexy, Mia thought. Next time she'd try to get her hands on them.

When her glance strayed to Jake, she wondered if he realized he was ogling Damien too.

◆

The looseness of Damien's strides suggested the release they'd given him had done its intended job. Their host was relaxed now, the hormones that flooded him in the aftermath hopefully as effective as a sleeping pill. Jake didn't speak until he was sure the other man was out of earshot.

"That should keep him out of our hair for a while."

Mia had been rinsing off, her pretty body shining in the spray. Now she gave him a funny look. Had she not realized why Jake pushed Damien to let go?

"Didn't that mean anything to you?" she asked.

Okay, those were words he never relished hearing, and they were doubly unwelcome now. He pushed off a niggle of discomfort to answer her coolly. "I enjoyed it, obviously, but we're here to do a job."

Her mouth twisted worriedly. "Damien is a person."

Jake admired Mia's tender heart but not right that moment. "He's a person who might have committed a serious crime. I'm going to give him fifteen minutes to drop off and then pick the lock to his office. If I find the stolen plans, I'll come back and get you so you can take your mental photograph."

She bit the tip of her thumb. "What if the plans aren't there? And what if he catches you? He'll toss us out before we get a chance to search anywhere else."

This was a valid point. Jake considered what he thought Mia could comfortably pull off. "Fine, you go check on him. If he's asleep, stand guard and make sure he stays that way. If he's up, tell him you couldn't sleep and ask if he wants a nightcap. That should keep him occupied."

"What if he, um, wants to do something else?"

"That's up to you," Jake said. "Any time you want to back out of this, you can."

This answer bothered her for some reason. Whatever the reason was, she didn't share it with him.

"Okay," she said. "I'll do what you suggested."

◆

Mia had thought Damien tugged Jake's affections too. Clearly, he was better at turning his feelings on and off—and also at acting. She supposed he'd gotten good at detachment back in his Mata Hari days. That detachment now seemed to extend to her. A memory of how warm he'd been at Diogenes returned. Maybe the idea of her and Damien fooling around without him did bug him. Maybe he just wasn't ready to admit it.

And maybe denial wasn't a river in Egypt.

She snorted to herself as she slipped across the dark penthouse. Thankfully, the lights of the city outside the windows kept her from stumbling on Damien's sparse collection of furniture. She'd already found her way to the wine storage near the kitchen, where she'd picked up her props. Her nervousness wasn't unpleasant. She guessed she understood why some people liked playing spy. Not that she'd make a career of it. Enjoying this adventure while it lasted was good enough.

If Jake had his druthers, it might be over after tonight.

She froze as she spotted a small glow moving erratically to her left. Cold sweat broke out on her skin, but it was just Jake searching Damien's glass cube office with the aid of a small penlight. She blew out her breath and ordered her pulse to calm. Jake must be counting on Damien not looking in this direction. Or maybe he was far enough that the billionaire wouldn't see. From her memory of their tour, Damien's sleeping area remained a ways off from her.

Keep it simple, she ordered as anxiety kicked in. *Don't try to tell fancy lies, and you'll be all right.*

Probably she would. She'd done okay so far.

She recognized the shape of a platform bed. A body lay motionless on its back underneath pale sheets. Her heart went crazy. She couldn't tell if the body was asleep. Did she dare tiptoe closer? Suddenly she felt rude. A man like Damien wouldn't like being snuck up on.

She nearly dropped her excuse to be there when he sat up.

"Mia?" he said. "Is that you?"

Shit, she thought. "Yes," she answered in a whisper. "Sorry. I couldn't sleep and I wondered if you might be up too."

"Where's Jake?"

"Dreaming of sugarplums, last I saw."

Damien laughed, which made her feel better about saying something so goofy.

"I brought a nightcap." She held up the wine bottle and stemmed glasses. "I think it's white. I didn't turn on the light to check the label."

"I case you woke me, you mean," he said, sounding entertained by that.

"I guess I wasn't being logical."

"Hold on." She heard sheets rustle and then a low murmur. A small lamp turned on. Damien's bedhead was cuter than she was prepared for. His gold-brown hair stuck out in boyish tufts like a regular person's.

"Is this okay?" she asked now that she could see him. "Do you want to talk to me if we're not doing a scene?"

He smiled. "I was awake. And you're not unpleasant to talk to."

He patted the bed beside him. Mia sighed with relief and climbed on.

◆

Perhaps he should have squelched the reaction, but having Mia sit cross-legged among his covers in a borrowed bathrobe made a wisp of happiness rise in him. He took the bottle she offered from her hand.

"A sweet Sauterne," he said. "You chose your midnight indulgence well."

"Accidentally. I don't know much about wine."

He managed the cork and poured. "You'll like this. Even neophytes find it lovable."

Mia took a cautious sip. "Mm. It tastes like apricots and honey."

When she licked her lips, he wanted to tongue-kiss her like he had before. He told himself not to push his luck. Whatever trait made women too susceptible to his charms seemed to have a biological component. Fortunately, when he'd lost control earlier, he'd done it in the shower. His various body fluids would have washed away. He'd been thinking about that as he lay in bed, staring up at the shaped glass roof, remembering Mia's soft body in front of him and Jack's very hard one behind

What Jake had done to him was a bit of a revelation. Maybe Damien's interest in men wasn't inconsequential. His cock stirred as he considered being impaled by the man's erection and not his hand. He wasn't averse, though the pictures that rose in his mind included Mia. The idea of the three of them twined together seemed to have the most power on his libido.

His cock hardened more, tempting him to take action on its behalf. Damien frowned at that.

One release in an evening ought to be sufficient.

He shifted, telling himself the hum of desire didn't bother him. It was, after all, a familiar companion.

He undid his self-talk by wondering if Mia were aroused too.

She took another sip and looked at him. "That was the first time a man played with you, wasn't it?"

Her perceptiveness surprised him. She seemed so guileless and young he didn't expect it. "I suppose it was."

"Why didn't you ask Jake to stop?"

"I enjoyed it, didn't I? He's very skilled. And I certainly didn't mind the effect it had on you."

She flashed a sheepish grin. "Maybe it's twisted, but watching man on man stuff is total catnip to me. It's like getting access to the ultimate boy's club."

"No girls allowed in our tree house?"

She shoved his knee with her hand. "Don't tease. Men like the idea of lesbians, don't they?"

"Sometimes." He set the Sauterne on his side table. When he turned back, Mia was watching the play of muscle in his chest and abdomen. He was used to attention from women, but hers especially pleased him. "Your brother was gay, wasn't he?"

"I think you know the answer to that question." Her gaze was level. She didn't seem to need him to pretend he hadn't come across this in his research.

"Yes," he admitted. "When did you realize he liked men?"

"He came out when he was eighteen, when he and Curtis started dating seriously. My parents were shocked. Mike was athletic. Star of the soccer team. Always popular with girls. They had plans for him, and him being gay disappointed them. I was ten, but I don't remember being surprised myself. Maybe on some level I always knew."

"Didn't your folks have plans for you?" Damien asked.

Her dry laugh belonged to a different, more cynical girl. "Mike was the favorite child. From day one, I was something of an embarrassment. Too weird. Too sensitive. Too bad at fitting in. The funny thing is—" She hesitated before continuing. "My parents loved Mike so much, they both came around about the 'gay thing,' as my mom calls it. They made Curtis part of the family. My parents send him Christmas and birthday cards. Sometimes they forget me but not him."

The back of Damien's eyes pricked unexpectedly. "They didn't come around about you—after your accident, I mean."

She shrugged uncomfortably. "They're not deliberately neglectful. They love me. I just can tell they wish I were more like him. They wish . . . They never say it, but I think they'd rather I'd died instead of Mike. I understand that, I guess. Mike had a stronger bond with them."

Damien squeezed her knee.

"Sorry," she said. "I sound pathetic."

"No," he said very firmly. "You're anything but. I also expect your brother would disagree with their position."

129

She smiled faintly. "Probably. Mike was a very giving guy. He had a bad boy streak now and then, but Curtis used to call him Saint Michael."

"Curtis, your old boss."

Mia inhaled and then let out a sigh. Damien hadn't thought much about the man who'd so recently employed her. He'd been more interested in the convenience of her being available to hire. "Do you think Curtis will forgive you for getting involved with Jake?"

She blinked at him, thoughts he could only guess at passing behind her eyes. "I think so. I hope so. When he has a chance to cool down. He's been an important part of my life."

Would two months be enough to settle the man's temper? That would suit Damien. A twinge of something he couldn't identify prodded his breastbone. He'd never wanted a limited contract to last longer, but he'd also never been this involved with a pair he was observing.

He fell silent and Mia did too. A slap of wind buffeted the roof above them and was absorbed, a sound he was well used to. His building was engineered to withstand more than hurricanes. Mia rubbed the stem of her wine glass. He noticed she hadn't taken another sip. He had the oddest urge to ask her to stay with him, to sleep with him through the night. He hadn't cuddled a woman in a long time. Maybe he could convince her she was good enough to come first with anyone.

"You must be tired now," he said instead. "You'll want to get back to Jake."

She seemed startled. "I— Are you tired? I don't want to leave if you'd still like to talk. Not that you're the one who's been blabbing."

He smiled. His hand was still on her knee where he'd left it. He lifted it to brush the side of her face with his fingertips. Her hair was pulled back in a messy ponytail. "I enjoyed our conversation. I believe it's relaxed me enough to sleep."

"Or bored you."

"Not at all," he said honestly. "You remind me people are more than the sum of the metadata one can dig up."

"Um. Glad to be of service?"

He leaned forward to kiss her cheek. "Go to bed, Mia. I'll see you in the morning."

◆

For the life of her, Mia couldn't concoct a reason to stick around. Damien's bedside light was on, so she couldn't stand guard over him either. She had to leave and hope Jake had finished his rummaging.

She guessed he had. He was in their guest "room" when she arrived, sitting up against one headboard.

She sat on the other bed facing him. "You don't look like you found anything."

"I didn't. And only the office door was locked. I searched every drawer. Maybe Damien destroyed the original plan. He could have scanned it onto his computer."

"We're not hackers."

"We're certainly not good enough to hack him." Jake rubbed the stubble on his cheeks. "I'm beginning to wonder if this assignment isn't a fool's errand."

"At least we're having an adventure."

She was trying to cheer him up, but he grimaced in response. That hurt a tiny bit. She had mixed success in hiding her reaction when he leveled a look at her.

"Be careful about liking him too much, Mia."

"Don't you like him?" she couldn't help asking.

"I wouldn't let liking someone blind me to what I had to do."

"Were you this cold when you were cultivating assets for the CIA?"

To her surprise, Jake flinched. "I am what I am," he warned once he'd recovered. "You should remember that as well."

"Fine," she huffed. "I promise not to like either one of you."

That, at last, caused him to crack a smile.

"By the way," she said. "Damien hasn't been with a man before. If there's a next time, you could go easier."

This time, she had the satisfaction of seeing him flush.

"I didn't know that," he said gruffly. "He seemed . . . into it." His gaze sharpened. "What else did you two talk about?"

That was satisfying too, until she remembered she'd done most of the talking. Jake seemed amused when she admitted this. "Tell me anyway. You never know what might be important." He patted the mattress beside him.

"You want us to sleep in the same bed?"

"Damien will think it's strange if we don't."

Mia kind of doubted that. She guessed her face said so. Jake's expression turned stubborn. "I'll feel safer if I know where you are."

He was who he was, all right: overprotective, overbearing, with marshmallow underneath.

"Fine," she said aloud, "but only because you're asking so nicely."

He made room for her on the mattress—taking the superior spoon position, she noticed. They snuggled together with maybe not so surprising ease.

"Now," he said, his body warm, his head above hers on the pillow. "Don't leave out anything."

CHAPTER 10

AN ocean of dappled sunshine greeted the opening of Jake's eyes. He lifted his forearm to block the glare. His waking brain informed him it was Saturday morning, and this was Damien Call's penthouse. Mia was curled up beside him, evidently still unconscious.

Her presence in the bed felt too comfortable. Falling asleep twice with her shouldn't turn the act into a habit. He made up for the treacherous ease by slipping out without disturbing her.

He pulled on the trousers he'd worn the night before, did what he needed in the bathroom, and went foraging for food.

Damien's residence in daylight was remarkable. Jake was no expert, but he could tell the architecture was award worthy. Light flooded the sculpted metal and glass dome, glinting here and there with rainbows, animated by shifting clouds and bird shadows. The space beneath seemed weirdly empty—and for more reasons than the widely scattered modern furniture. It was too serene, Jake realized as he padded through it toward the kitchen. Too impersonal. He didn't spot a single photograph of Call's friends or family. No paintings hung on the few walls there were, not even framed magazine covers of his cars. He saw a bit of dust but no clutter.

It was as if Damien were hiding his personality from himself.

And speaking of hiding things . . . The story Mia shared last night about her brother being her parents' favorite wasn't one Jake had heard. All Curtis had told him was that the Becks were white-bread and a tad judgey. Jake got the impression his boss wasn't as attached to them as he was to Mia. That was satisfying to him right then. No girl as special as Mia ought to be made to feel inferior.

Not by me either, was the thought that came to him.

Damien was already in the kitchen when he reached it. The CEO sat at the breakfast bar in business attire, drinking coffee and reading a newspaper one-handed on a sleek tablet screen. The shiny silver case matched the trademark paint on his electric cars. Curiosity pricked Jake. He hadn't known WorldWide was dipping its toe into the device market.

"There's yogurt," Damien said without looking up. "And toast. And navel oranges in the bowl."

"Thanks." Jake wondered if Mia liked any of those things. He poured himself coffee from an apparatus that looked like it belonged in a science lab.

"Cream's in the fridge," Damien added, thumbing onto another page.

"That's good. Mia likes her caffeine pale."

The mention of Mia brought Call's head up. Damien had a killer poker face. His expression told Jake nothing. If his own ears hadn't heard the man loudly groan out an orgasm, he wouldn't have believed anything could move him.

"Is Mia still asleep?"

"Yes. She said you and she talked last night."

Damien grunted noncommittally and shifted on his designer stool. "I forgot to remind you. Did you plug in your car last night? It could probably use a charge."

Suddenly Jake realized Damien was self-conscious about having people in his home. He was the opposite of cool and trying to conceal it. If being a host hadn't distracted him, he'd never have overlooked maintenance for the vehicle.

"I used the hookup next to the parking space." Impulsively, he decided to twit the man. "You should know Mia thinks she's a cheap date compared to me. I got a sports car. She got a coffee pot."

Damien's mouth fell open. "I didn't think she'd accept an expensive gift."

"I'm not accustomed to them myself," Jake said wryly. "Just so you know, I plan to return it when our contract is up."

"As you wish, though you could consider keeping it to set an example for less ecologically conscientious car owners."

He was completely serious, which meant Jake couldn't resist yanking his chain some more. "In other words, for the good of mankind, I should hang onto it."

Damien might have recognized his leg was being pulled if Mia hadn't walked up before he could. She wore a robe and she'd brushed her hair down her shoulders until it shone. The expression that crossed Damien's face was illuminating. His hard features softened, his hazel eyes warming as they sought hers.

"Good morning," he said. "Did you sleep well?"

Jake felt a bit like the cheap date then. This hadn't been his greeting.

"I slept great," she said froggily. "Is that coffee?"

Jake prepared another cup as she wriggled onto the stool beside Damien.

"Thank you," she said. "What are we doing today?"

A zing shot through Jake without warning, one he wouldn't have predicted and was unable to control. His morning wood hadn't been as hard as this sudden erection. Damien shifted on his seat and Jake knew as sure as sunrise that he'd just stiffened too. Damien's eyes met his, and the zing strummed his cock again. Damien knew what had happened to Jake and was turned on by it.

Shit, Jake thought, totally off balance now. He had a raging boner for both of them.

"What would you like to do?" Damien asked politely.

"I could choose?" Mia responded.

"Within reason, certainly."

Her eyes cut to Jake. Damned if he didn't know what she was thinking. She wasn't going to suggest they have a picnic in the park or fly Damien's jet to Paris. No, she was going to press for the next level up in their intimacy.

Don't, he thought, though his throbbing body was begging *do.*

"If Jake wouldn't mind," she said, "and if it doesn't upset your timetable, I'd like to have actual sex with him. With kissing too, if that's all right with you."

◆

Jake's face tightened, so Mia probably shouldn't have asked for this. She couldn't help if intercourse was what she really wanted. If this mission ended tomorrow—which it might—not having had him inside her would be the thing she kicked herself most over. Not that she could be blamed. If Jake hadn't wanted her to think about doing him, he shouldn't have come to breakfast without a shirt. Any woman would get itchy over him and his stellar abs. On top of which, she was *asking*, not forcing him. Plus, Damien could still say *no*.

Jake jerked his head away, so she turned her gaze to their host.

Damien rubbed his lower lip. "You want plain old sex. No bondage. No role-playing or props."

"Well, you'd be there." Her cheeks flashed hot as she realized what she'd said. "Not that you're a prop. Just that you're not plain old."

He pressed his lips together like he was trying not to laugh. "I'm gratified to hear it. What do you think, Mr. Reed? Are you up for a straightforward erotic encounter?"

Jake glared at him. "I'm sure you know I'm as 'up for' it as you are."

His verbal air quotes caused her to jerk. Were they—? She couldn't help checking out their groins. Adrenaline instantly flooded her. They were hard. Both of them. Like, grab-a-tape-measure hard, because Guinness world records might be at stake. Mia's thighs clenched, her pussy squirming with interest.

If Damien had asked what she wanted then, she'd have given him a greedier answer.

"Oh boy," she said softly.

The men stop playing stare wars to regard her. Jake's eyes slitted as he registered her excited state. Was he angry? Her body didn't think it mattered. It twitched with anticipation the moment he zeroed in on her. The thought crossed her mind that she liked when he focused on Damien too.

Face it, she thought. *You wet your panties for everything these guys do.*

Jake's jaw unclenched enough for him to speak. "She might not want props," he said, without turning to Damien. "But we still need a few supplies."

"You want to take her here?" Damien asked.

Jake's expressive mouth slanted. "People say the kitchen is the heart of home."

"Very well." Damien rose from the stool. "I'll get what you need. Please wait for my return."

"Are you angry?" Mia blurted as soon as he'd stepped away.

"Like that would stop you," Jake growled.

"You can say *no* if you want."

His hot blue eyes shot fire at this suggestion. "Mia. For such a brilliant girl, sometimes you're an idiot."

He'd been on the opposite side of the kitchen's shiny black island. Her pleasure at being called brilliant slowed her reaction to the fact that he was now stalking toward her around it. She slid off the stool nervously. Damien's swanky guest robe was oversized on her. Though she'd tied it snugly, she couldn't forget that she was naked under it.

Naked and wet, as it happened.

"Damien said wait," she reminded.

Jake gripped her arms and yanked her onto her toes. "Fuck Damien."

He kissed her more gently than she expected, everything considered. His lips molded over hers, his tongue sliding in to stroke and tease. Her insides melted as she slid her hands up his muscled back, stretching up him to get closer. His powerful arms wrapped her waist obligingly. The kiss deepened and slanted. Jake's big hand palmed her bottom through the waffled cotton, massaging the rounds of flesh.

When his hand suddenly tightened to pull her against his erection, a pleasured noise broke in Mia's throat.

She could have kissed him like that forever, but Jake wandered. He kissed the corner of her mouth, and her cheekbone, and dragged his open lips down and up her neck.

"This is for me," he murmured beside her ear, his breathing not quite even.

He still sounded slightly angry. Mia touched his face and looked up at him.

"I want this," he said, understanding what she was asking. His expression turned rueful. "For better or worse, I want to be inside you."

Mia bit back a grin. "Forgive me if I hope it's better."

His thumb stroked her jaw, his eyes gazing into hers. "Sweet little Mia."

She didn't like the wistfulness in his tone. "Jake—"

"Don't change your mind," he warned.

She hadn't planned to. She didn't get a chance to say so. Damien had returned.

"Condoms," he said, smiling faintly as he held up the box. "And lube, though that might be unnecessary. Do with them what you will."

It occurred to Mia that she'd like to watch Damien dress

Jake's cock. She pressed her lips together to prevent herself from asking. Asking would be pushing. Damien was back in his comfort zone, so relaxed and pleased about what was unfolding that she didn't want to ruin it.

"Is that dining table sturdy?" Jake asked, jerking his head toward the dramatic plank thing that sat nearby.

"It's solid redwood." A grin split Damien's handsome face. "It's also marine sealed for quick cleanup."

Jake snorted with amusement. "Good thing I don't have to worry about getting it messy."

Mia sucked a startled breath as Jake swung her up in his arms. He carried her to the table and sat her on its end. She saw at once that it was the perfect height for Jake to enter her standing up.

"Take any seat you like," he said to Damien.

She suspected Jake knew what that would do to her. Her borrowed robe grew damper under her.

Jake considered her. "You haven't left me much unwrapping."

"No," she agreed breathlessly.

He pushed her knees apart and stepped between them. His body heat warmed the breeze that tickled her pussy. She loved how deliberately he was breathing, and that Damien chose a chair hardly any distance away from her. Jake's glance slid to the other man and returned to her. A deeper flush stained his high cheekbones. He began undoing the simple knot that held her robe's tie closed.

"I want to keep that," she said.

His eyebrows went up. "You want the tie."

"Yes, please."

He removed it, placing it in her waiting hand. Mia set it on the broad table behind her. The whorls of the wood were pretty, the lacquer that sealed it smooth. She stroked its satiny surface as she turned back to Jake.

"All right," she said. "I'm ready now."

He chuckled silently. "You're ready, huh?"

He parted the robe around her, baring her, gently slipping the cotton down her arms. Nothing hid her then. Not clothes. Not the steam from a shower. Not the shadows that came with night. She sat naked in the sunshine, being watched by two admiring men. Happily, they weren't looking at her flaws; they were focused on what they liked. Jake's fingers caressed her breasts, his thumbs circling her nipples so that their centers drew tight and hard. He pulled his touch down her belly and onto her thighs.

When his hands smoothed upward from her knees, he pushed her legs wider.

"Let's see how ready," he whispered.

She tensed as he rubbed his thumbs along the inner side of her folds, but it was a good tension. The desire she couldn't wait for him to meet was rising. He looked at what he was doing and licked his lips.

"So pretty," he said. "So pretty and wet for me."

She felt pretty, more than she ever had. She heard Damien's light breathing quicken, saw his hand grip the table's irregular edge from the corner of her eye.

"Show me what you have for me," she said.

Jake had a hump the size of the Brooklyn Bridge. He undid his waistband button and took hold of his zipper's tab.

"You mean this old thing?" he joked.

She couldn't look away as he dragged the teeth carefully open around the ridge. She reached for him before he could dig his erection out.

"Let me."

He closed his eyes as she stroked the hot velvet of his shaft. That was a true pleasure, like holding life itself in her palm. A foil packet appeared like magic beside her leg. Mia put its contents to their intended use, taking great satisfaction in making sure the latex was properly smoothed down. Possibly, she was too long about it. She hadn't forgotten Jake liked rubbing his cock's right side when he masturbated. It seemed important that she pay that part of him extra attention.

Her consideration didn't go unnoticed. When Jake lifted his lids again, his irises smoldered. Mia shivered, and his mouth curved slowly into a smile. As his lips pulled higher, she noticed his eyeteeth were sharp—as if he really had alpha wolf DNA.

He put his hand lightly over hers on his cock. "I think you haven't quite got me where you want me. Why don't you fix that?"

The rasp behind his suggestion was dead sexy.

"Pull me closer to you," she urged.

He scooted her to the table's edge. His tight butt made the

perfect shelf for her heels, but his hard-on's angle was too high. She tipped it downward slowly, very conscious that Damien was watching. Jake's breathing got faster. He leaned straight-armed on the table, and she touched his crown to her gate.

She swallowed at the feel of their flesh kissing.

"Don't rush going into me," she said. "You know he wants to see."

Jake's fiery blue eyes darkened. "I know. I'm going to lower you to the table."

He cupped the back of her head to control her descent, his torso following hers as she went back. Finally, he hovered over her on his elbows. His skin was hot, his body beginning to perspire.

The tip of his cock nudged a fraction into her.

"Wait," she said as he gathered himself to thrust.

Though he checked himself, she could tell she was straining his patience.

"One second," she promised. She fumbled blindly for the bathrobe's discarded tie. She found it after a second, wrapping one end around her left wrist and the other around her right. A foot of white cotton stretched between.

Jake watched this with fascination, his personal kinks rendering the simple act powerful. When she snapped the tie taut between her wrists, he jerked.

"Now," she said. "I'm ready to be taken."

He hissed a curse that sounded more like praise. "You'd better be ready, doll."

His hands took hold of either side of the table's edge. Realizing she'd better brace, she swung her self-administered bondage over his head and onto his back. *Then* he pushed, his shaft so thick with excitement she doubted he could have entered quickly no matter what.

"God," she moaned, her neck arching off the table as her heels dug into his ass.

Despite her urging, he went in slow. He felt so good—smooth and hot, stretching her pulsing wetness until he truly seemed to be claiming her. Halfway there, she remembered she wanted to watch his face. She forced her eyes back open. Their gazes met. A bead of sun-struck sweat rolled down one high cheekbone. He pulled in another breath, using it to help him forge in the last inches.

A tremor shook him as he held deep, a mini-quake of lust.

"Don't move," he ordered her.

She didn't want to. She was memorizing the sensation of him filling her. She'd had one bed partner before him, and he'd just made her feel like there hadn't been any. Her body recognized him as her first true lover, the first her heart desired, the first she craved to give in to with every cell.

His hot gaze slid down her body, to the notch and press of their pelvises. The hitch of his diaphragm said the sight aroused him.

"Can you see?" he asked without turning to Damien.

"Very well," their watcher said quietly. "Please don't worry about me."

Mia stroked Jake's back with the stretched out tie. "Please move, Jake. Before I go crazy."

He pushed even deeper and then drew back. Her hands fisted on the belt as a groan rolled from her. He thrust in and out, not fast but thoroughly, every inch of him stroking her inside. The heaven of him moving caused her to eyes to drift shut again. His motions weren't perfectly controlled. He was too excited, the things their bodies were doing too new and delicious. He moved one hand between them to thumb more friction into her clit.

Mia swallowed a pleasured noise.

"I need to . . . catch you up to me," he said.

Her body undulated, her heels sliding higher on his back to splay her knees wider. Jake laughed breathlessly and dropped his chest closer.

"That's not helping."

"I don't want to help." She tugged at him with the tie. "I want you to go at me."

She opened her eyes and found him staring back at her.

"You want me to fuck you."

"Yes," she agreed. "I want you to fuck me."

"Well, then." He took hold of her upper thigh and gave her what she asked for.

She cried out, because the increase in speed and force instantly felt like ecstasy. He grunted and kept going. She clutched him—with the belt, with her hands, her heels urging him on energetically. God, she couldn't get close enough. Instinct had her shifting one leg higher than the other.

"Mia," he huffed. "Mia . . ."

The way he said her name caused something fiercer than pleasure rise in her.

That rose too, of course. His thrusts were too compelling, too strong and deep not to push her up the slope. She groaned and arched, her pussy tightening on his cock with her first contractions of climax. Jake gasped out a curse and really picked up the pace. Their combined weight thumped the heavy table, the rhythm ragged but effective.

"Come closer," he said, shoving his left hand beneath her back.

She didn't have the breath to say *yes*. His right hand anchored her hip. He was using the holds to brace her, to keep his pumping from pushing her away. He drove her through the peak and beyond, so that she flew up and leaped again. She felt him swell between her walls then, felt his fingers grip so hard she knew they'd leave marks. He jerked as he plunged deep and shot in her.

"Ah," he cried, the noise unexpected and exciting. "Ah."

Mia's calves slipped on his perspiring ribs.

Finally, his spine relaxed.

"Whew," he said, wiping his sweaty brow on his sweaty shoulder. "Give a guy a workout."

Mia smiled at him and he smiled back. The tie had come loose. She'd let it go, she guessed. Her hands had found their way to his chest, where they stroked his chest hair and muscle. Jake's eyes looked sleepy, but his heart pounded crazily. Hers wasn't much calmer.

He dropped his head to rub their noses together.

"Mia," he said. "Thank you for wanting that."

◆

Damien's heart had lodged in throat, emotions rioting inside him that he was reluctant to identify. He'd pushed for this. He'd wanted to see Jake and Mia's passion, for it to be genuine and extreme. It was why he watched anything. To see those heightened moments, to steer them into happening. They were his then a bit, just not enough to be dangerous.

Never once when he watched before had he felt he might be missing out.

Be careful what you wish for, he thought.

He forced himself to release the table edge, which he'd gripped tight enough to cramp his fingers. He didn't massage the tendons, only pulled his arm away.

Mia was the first to look at him. She drew breath as if she would speak.

Damien stood up before she could.

"That was very good," he said.

Jake pushed up on his arms, his body still connected to Mia's. The hard man's gaze was too discerning for comfort.

Damien smoothed his tie. "Entertaining as that was, I wasn't planning for us to play this morning. I have to visit my hanger in New Jersey. There's a problem with a jet the engineers want my input on."

"I'll take you," Jake said.

"That isn't necessary."

"It's my job." He held Mia's waist as he pulled gently out of her. In seconds, he'd tucked away and zipped up. Despite the reassuring pat he gave her knee, Mia appeared surprised.

Damien was as well. He'd thought the man would want to linger. "I was planning to drive myself."

Jake rinsed his hands at the sink and dried them on a towel. "Give me seven minutes to finish cleaning up and dress."

Seven minutes sounded specific. Bemused, Damien watched him stride off.

"Well." Mia shrugged the sleeves of her robe back on. "I guess that interlude is over."

Her wry tone didn't hide the fact that she was ticked.

"I'm sure he didn't mean to insult you. Men sometimes compartmentalize activities."

Mia rubbed her temple. "That's one way to look at it."

"I do apologize. I didn't know we'd be spontaneous."

She smiled at him, and suddenly he felt stupid for saying *we*. He'd only been observing.

"I don't suppose you need a PA today," she said.

"Regrettably, no. My engineers would find it odd. I do . . ." He hesitated. "There's a charity function I need to attend tonight, an auction for funding scholarships in the sciences. Perhaps you'd be kind enough to accompany me."

"As your PA?"

"As my date. It's formal. You'll need to obtain a gown."

"I could call Hillary, I guess."

He assumed she meant Hillary Sweet, who was well known among Diogenes members. She'd know exactly what Mia ought to wear. "Use your corporate card. Your wardrobe allowance will cover the expense."

Mia's brown eyes blinked and he had no idea why.

"Okay," she said. "I guess my job today is shopping."

"Don't buy jewelry," he added, which took her noticeably aback.

"I wouldn't dream of it," she assured him.

Jake reappeared in appropriate driver garb. "You ready?"

Damien was almost. He retrieved his tablet from the kitchen counter, turning its touchscreen to face Mia. "Press your palm print on this. I'll add you to the house system so you can get in and out by yourself."

Mia did as he asked and grinned. "Now I've got the keys to the castle!"

Her pleasure in this pleased him. Most women he knew would have been more excited about the evening gown.

He and Jake walked side by side to the elevator. Damien pressed his thumb to the call button. "You're a lucky man, Mr. Reed."

"That I am," Jake agreed—but not as if he really comprehended how fortunate he was.

◆

"Don't even bother," Hillary said when Mia began flipping through the designer dresses on her boutique's racks.

"Why not?" she asked. "Aren't these nice enough?"

"They're plenty nice, but they're secondhand. You can't risk what you're wearing being recognized as some other guest's castoff. The women you'll meet tonight will already have their claws out for you."

That sounded alarming. "They won't know who I am."

"They'll know Damien Call, or think they do, and that man is quite the catch. His reputation for keeping his arm candy at arm's length only makes him more attractive. I heard Zoe Raeburn wasn't spared the jealous snark, and she's a society princess."

"So what *can* I wear?"

"What all New Yorkers do when they need to look indomitable."

"Black," Mia said.

"Black," Hillary agreed. She reached for her phone. "Let me call my best cutter. If we keep it simple, I think we can kit you in black velvet."

"This is good of you," Mia said gratefully.

"You're paying me, aren't you? Besides which, real women need to stick together."

Mia laughed. "*We're* the real ones then?"

Her humor seemed to tickle the elegant storekeeper. "You're all right, kid. I think you'll land on your feet, no matter what convoluted game those men are playing."

Her approval gave Mia a warm feeling.

"I really admire you," she said impulsively. "You seem to have it all together."

"I don't know about all of it," Hillary said. "I'm just a person, same as you."

"A person with a *plan*, one you're accomplishing."

Hillary smiled. "I've accomplished a few. So will you. Maybe sooner than you think."

Mia fought a tiny frown. She couldn't help hoping the fulfillment of one plan wouldn't happen immediately.

◆

Despite its sporadic tensions, Mia's day had a number of bright spots. One of them was popping out to show Jake and Damien the result of Hillary's team's efforts.

"Tada!" she said as the men entered the living area together. Jake had his jacket slung over one shoulder, but Damien was still buttoned up. Rather than dwell on how happy she was to see them both, she spread her arms and turned. The fitted black velvet column merited displaying in the round. "Look, it has an Angelina Jolie slit."

She stuck her right leg forward to demonstrate.

"You look beautiful," Damien said seriously.

Jake covered his mouth to contain a snicker. "You might want to practice your posing if you intend to do that tonight."

"Do you think I'll get a chance?" she asked with faux innocence.

"We can only hope," Jake replied straightfaced.

She broke into laughter, which confused Damien. "I won't pose," she promised, in case he thought she would. "I know your date should be dignified."

"You can be anything you like," Damien said, but she rather doubted that.

Jake sank into a very modern white chair and sighed.

"I stopped at our places while I was out," she said. "Picked up some clothes and personal stuff. Curtis relinquished his copy of the key to your apartment."

She'd given Curtis an update at the same time, since communicating via email or phone seemed tricky. She didn't know for sure Damien wasn't tracking their messages. Seeing Curtis had definitely been one of her day's highlights, his bone-cracking hug reminding her she missed him.

Visiting Jake's apartment, which she'd never been invited to before, had also been interesting. She hadn't snooped exactly, but she'd looked around. He favored simple well-made furniture—and not a whole lot of it. She'd confirmed that six identical dark gray suits did indeed hang in his closet. His shirts, briefs, and socks were similarly uniform and high quality. Given his kinks, she hadn't expected such conservative choices.

The single personal decoration was a beautiful color photograph of street kids playing in a city somewhere in India. It hung on the wall in his living room. She wasn't sure what the picture meant. Maybe a reminder to protect the innocent.

Jake's expression said he longed to grill her on what she'd poked her nose into.

"Talking to our former boss must have been fun," he said carefully.

"I'm afraid he's still mad at us," Mia said, trying not to act too hard. "It might be a while before he cools off."

Jake responded with a strategically vague hum.

Damien appeared not to regard their conversation as suspicious, because he checked his watch. "We should probably get dressed."

"We?" she asked.

"I'm bodyguarding tonight," Jake informed her.

"I thought you'd be more comfortable with that arrangement," Damien said.

Did he think she wouldn't enjoy herself if it were just the two of them? It wasn't an unreasonable assumption, but suddenly she wasn't sure it was correct. That was weird, wasn't it? That she didn't mind the idea of being alone with him?

She was thinking so busily she couldn't respond at all.

"I have something for you to wear with the dress," Damien said. He dug into a bag he'd been carrying, coming out with a jewelry case the size of a hardback book. The case was covered in rich brown leather and embossed with the logo of a prominent diamond store.

Mia stared at it and at him, her hands refusing to reach for it.

A hint of devilry turned up one corner of Damien's mouth. "This is so you won't accuse me of treating you like a cheap date."

She gaped at Jake, who was grinning too. She couldn't believe he'd shared that story.

"Open it," he urged. "I helped Damien pick it out."

She guessed this was a new form of male bonding. She took the box and pried up the hinged lid. The amount of ice that glittered out at her made her blink. After a moment, the dazzling sparkles resolved into a multi-strand platinum necklace.

Whoa, she thought, completely flabbergasted. *How freaking many carats is this?*

More than she could count was her best estimate.

"It's designed to resemble a rope," Jake said helpfully. "Depending on your neckline, you can wear the knot and tassels in front or back."

So it was bondage jewelry. No wonder Jake liked it. She stroked the diamonds in the trailing part tentatively. "I'll need a bodyguard if I put this on."

"Do you like it?" Damien asked.

Like didn't cover her emotions. This was a necklace literally fit for a queen. The idea of wearing it mortified and appealed simultaneously. Despite Jake's earlier joke about her posing skills, both men obviously assumed she could carry it off without looking ridiculous.

She found that incredibly flattering.

She had to swallow before she could speak. "I've never worn anything this stunning. You must know I can't keep it."

Damien's devilish smile deepened. "If Jake decides to keep his car, I really think you'll have to."

Jake's head jerked to him in surprise. "You *are* devious."

He sounded admiring. Damien preened slightly.

"I have my moments," he concurred.

CHAPTER 11

MIA resolved to enjoy her Cinderella moment. She wasn't complaining that she had two princes instead of one. The men were sexy in their black tie, and both of them smelled divine—like she was getting a double dose of testosterone. Jake had supplied them with concealed earpieces, which amused Damien.

"I won't play pretend bodyguard," Jake said. "If I'm here in that capacity, I'm going to do it right. Just tap the earpiece off if you need privacy."

"This is a charity dinner," Damien said as they exited the car in front of the ritzy downtown hotel. "I doubt we're in danger other than from undercooked chicken."

"It's a crush," Jake countered. He handed the keys to a valet. "And never mind your safety. Mia looks like a million bucks. I want to keep track of her."

Mia stroked the necklace that was making her nervous.

Damien coaxed her hand down and squeezed it. "You're fine, Mia. Jake and I will keep an eye on you."

The placard outside the ballroom said *WELLES FOUNDATION SCHOLARSHIP DINNER*. Inside, the standard sea of white-draped tables channeled the milling crowd into the spaces between them. The attendees were all shapes and ages and dressed to impress. The fundraiser must be a hot ticket for New York's deep-pocketed intelligentsia. Mia's fancy gown wasn't out of place and neither was her necklace.

"If I were a jewel thief," she mused, "this is the event I'd hit."

Damien laughed, the soft sound echoing through her earpiece. "Let's find where they've set up the auction. I want to make sure WorldWide's listing is correct."

An official looking woman in a long sparkly gown spared them the trouble of searching. "Mr. Call," she said, lifting her arm as she hurried over. "The young people will be so excited that you've arrived."

"Ah," Damien said, seeming not to know who she was.

"Greta Harris." She pointed to her nametag. "We spoke on the phone."

"Of course. Greta. How nice to meet you in person. This is my friend, Mia Beck. Could you direct us to the venue for the auction?"

"I'll take you, if you don't mind. Last year's scholarship recipients are there. It would mean a great deal for them to speak to you. You're their hero."

"I'm sure I'm not all their hero," Damien said. "But I'd be happy to."

Damien's little bow—or perhaps his unexpected humility—brought a flush into Greta's cheeks.

"This way," she said, flustered.

Mia bit her lip to hold in her amusement. Damien didn't have to try much to charm women.

Like a silent protective shadow, Jake followed them to the auction room.

Here there were no tables, just chairs in rows in front of a podium. The crowd around the edges of the room was smaller than in the ballroom. A handful of adults watched over a couple dozen kids of high school age and younger—science prodigies, she assumed. Six girls straggled among the boys, and none looked comfortable in their dress up clothes. One boy wore a faded T-shirt under his too big suit jacket. For no reason she understood, the shirt was captioned *Byte me, Einstein.*

"Come on," Jake said quietly, echoing her thought. "What techno geek doesn't like Einstein?"

All the kids perked up when they spotted Damien.

Greta herded him along their line like a visiting dignitary, which Mia guessed he was. Damien spoke to each kid politely, but she noticed some interested him more than others. The ones who didn't gush but jumped straight into arcane technical discussions got his full attention. The boy in the *Byte me* shirt, who struck Mia as surly and bad mannered, got Damien's business card.

"He'll probably tear it up," Damien confided laughingly

afterward. "He's convinced he's smarter than me and, God knows, he might be."

Mia liked him more than she could say for not minding.

She felt rather than saw Jake grow more alert behind them.

"Heads up," he said as she and Damien turned.

She saw at once why he'd warned them. Sam Raeburn, the CEO of Genbolt, was powering toward them like a tugboat. He had the physicality she remembered, as if he needed—and was entitled to—more space than other folks. His tailor was as skilled as ever. His tuxedo slimmed his stocky frame the same way his suits had. Mia had to admit his pale blue eyes and pewter hair gave him a striking appearance.

No one could mistake him for anything but a VIP.

She tensed at the prospect of pretending they hadn't met then realized this might not be a problem. Raeburn's gaze slid over her as if she were a complete stranger. That gave her a start. She knew she was dolled up and painted, but did he really not recognize her from Curtis's office? Mia didn't think she could have changed that much.

Apparently seeing no need for hellos, Raeburn curled his lip at Damien. "Enjoying your rock star status with the under-eighteen set?"

"Who wouldn't?" Damien said lightly.

Raeburn seemed not to like this answer. Maybe he wanted Damien to get mad. His attention strayed to Mia. "You're switching up your type, I see. I thought you usually went for blondes."

Damien's hand was behind her back. Mia felt it stiffen. "Excuse me?" he said disbelievingly.

"Well, there was that Swedish Victoria's Secret model, and then the German lawyer."

This insulted not just Damien but her.

"Don't forget your daughter," Damien said softly. "She's blonde too, as I recall."

"I'm surprised you remember, what with your revolving door."

"I hardly have to remember when you're so intent on keeping track. Or is it keeping score? Men like you seem to view every interaction as a competition for a trophy."

He'd struck a nerve. Raeburn's sun bronzed skin reddened. He lowered his voice but spoke more hostilely.

"You think I don't know who you are, that I'm as dazzled as you've got some people." He threw up his hands and waggled thick fingers. "Saint Damien. Why don't we hire him to design missiles? He came out with a car that runs on batteries—like no one else built one of those before."

"No one else builds them as well as me."

"How can you tell," Raeburn scoffed, "when you're how many months behind on production?"

Damien's expression chilled. "Some people believe in doing things right rather than blowing smoke up the government's ass every time their 'breakthroughs' turn out to be jack shit. If you want to catch up, you should probably try to poach some of my employees. Oh wait, you've already attempted that."

Okay, Mia thought. These two had history . . . and not the pleasant sort. She wondered what had happened to the Raeburn she'd first met. That man had been imposing but he'd had charm. Damien seemed different too, as if Raeburn—and their rivalry—brought out his darker side. They were like fighting cocks circling each other, looking for a vulnerable place to peck.

She rubbed Damien's arm, about to suggest they find the bar.

Raeburn eighty-sixed that plan by spitting his next retort. "If you think I'm going to let myself be lectured by some wet-behind-the-ears, arrogant—"

"Better wet behind the ears than an unscrupulous twentieth century holdover. Your company has had its teeth clamped on the government teat so long you'd starve without it. You don't care if you're incapable of delivering on your promises. Your greed makes you a danger to every man and woman in our armed forces."

"Say *anything* like that again, and you'll hear from my lawyers."

"Your lawyers can kiss my lawyers' ass."

Damien poked Raeburn's breastbone like he meant to drill through his shirt. Not about to stand for that, Raeburn grabbed Damien's lapels. Mia guessed this was enough to spur Jake to intervene.

"Is there a problem here, Mr. Call? Because I don't think these kids need to see you two get into it in front of them."

The reminder of their audience caused them to step apart, though Damien was the one who looked embarrassed. Raeburn was slower to release his hold.

"Great," Jake said. "Don't sit near each other at dinner."

Raeburn glared at Jake as if to demand who the hell he thought he was. Jake responded by doing something with his jacket that caused the CEO to stiffen and back off.

Mia realized Jake must have flashed his holster when Damien hissed at him. "You're carrying?"

Jake offered a blasé shrug. "I'm licensed to."

"Which of us were you going to shoot?"

"Whichever one seemed like he wanted to draw blood most."

Mia laughed at his deadpan answer. Jake certainly had a unique bodyguarding style.

◆

Damien strode stiffly out of the auction room. Despite only saying what was true, he was ashamed of himself. He shouldn't have let that idiot Raeburn get his goat. He could have defended Mia's honor some other way—and Jake was absolutely right about a bunch of kids who looked up to him not needing to witness him losing it.

Why bother getting angry when Raeburn didn't have a leg to stand on? Yes, the W-22 delays secretly exasperated him. He wasn't going to accelerate production until he was certain the factory could maintain quality. That was the right choice—the only choice for him.

"Fuck," he muttered beneath his breath.

Mia squeezed his hand as if his state of mind worried her.

"Sorry," he said, stopping so he could look at her. "I should have been more controlled."

"You were angry."

Damien noticed Jake had halted along with them, though he faced away to observe the corridor. Damien realized he'd been a jackass in front of both his companions. That bothered him more than he was comfortable admitting. "I wanted you to have a nice time tonight."

Mia grinned from beneath her lashes, seeming surprised and pleased by his confession. "The night isn't over yet, Mr. Call."

An unexpected vise tightened around his chest. What she said was sweet, but the sensation reminded him of this morning, when he'd watched her and Jake rub noses after sex. Damien worked so hard to avoid women falling for him. What if he decided he wanted one to succumb? Worse, what if that particular woman turned out to be unobtainable?

"Those women Raeburn talked about were just dates," he blurted. "I don't have a revolving door."

"You kind of do," Mia said with her sometimes inconvenient honesty. "I mean . . . Hell, I don't know how to un-say that."

Jake sniggered behind them, the sound audible through their earpieces. "She's right, Damien. You kind of do. Especially now that we can add men to your menu."

A buzz of gratification rose in him. Was Jake saying this because he liked being included?

A moment later, his emotions swung the other way.

Great, he thought. Jake *and* Mia considered him a man whore. But if that were true, shouldn't he be getting it more often? He heaved a gusty sigh.

"Very well," he surrendered. "Let's try to enjoy dinner."

◆

Since he was Mr. Moneybags Science Celebrity, the charity had given Damien a power table. It was located near the stage, where Mia presumed the speaker could more easily encourage him to scribble a big check. She doubted Damien minded. He'd certainly proved himself no tightwad with her and Jake.

His name was on the sign that stuck up from the floral centerpiece, though the individual seats didn't have place cards. Possibly this explained why someone already sat in one.

"Shit," Damien said, his step faltering beside her.

A moment later, Mia recognized who the early arrival was.

His office Cerberus, Ms. DeWinter, looked unusually glamorous in her plunging gold lamé gown. Her wavy russet hair was styled more softly than she wore it at work, and her makeup was more vivid. She rose as Damien neared, beaming with unmistakable and embarrassing fondness.

"You made it," she said. "I'm so glad."

"What are you doing here?" Damien asked, stupefied.

"Well, I know it's a *little* forward, but when you didn't instruct me to return Zoe Raeburn's call, I thought you might need a plus one."

Mia guessed her logic escaped Damien. His mouth worked with nothing coming out.

"Hello, Miss Beck," Ms. DeWinter said, belated noticing her.

"Are you attending with Mr. Reed?"

"She's with me," Damien snapped.

Ms. DeWinter looked confused. "Why would she be with you?"

"Because she's my date. As you most definitely are not."

"Uh boy," Jake murmured at the distressed expression that claimed the woman's face.

"You know," Mia said. "I think I'll powder my nose while you two sort this out."

"No," Damien said, catching her wrist before she could escape. "You're the last person who needs to leave."

"It'll be easier to explain without me here."

"Damn it."

His jaw had tightened, but she knew he saw her point. As he released her hand, she leaned in to kiss his cheek. "I'll be back. I'll leave you Jake for protection."

"He'll have to shoot *me* if you stay away too long," he grumbled.

◆

Coward that she was, Mia stashed her earpiece in her clutch purse. She didn't need to overhear Damien's sure to be awkward conversation with his besotted assistant.

The bathroom off the hotel lobby was old school fancy, with a uniformed towel attendant, a second door labeled *Ladies Lounge*, and multiple shell-shaped sinks. Mia used a stall, washed her hands, and checked her makeup in the long gilded mirror. Since her lipstick hadn't strayed from where it belonged, she glanced at the exit door. Her side trip hadn't taken long. Probably Damien and Ms. DeWinter were still at it.

"Is the lounge open?" she asked the female attendant.

"Of course, miss," said the woman. "You're welcome to sit in there if you need a rest. We stock Advil and everything."

That really was full service. Mia smiled as she pushed through the separate door.

What she found behind it nearly made her back out again.

A spectacularly gowned blonde sat hunched on one of the fussy couches, quietly sobbing into her slender hands. Mia didn't share some men's aversion to female tears, but she wasn't an indiscriminate nurturer. For one thing, she wasn't good enough at saying the right thing.

Maybe, just this once, she'd be forgiven for not hand-patting a fellow member of her gender?

She would have slipped away if her brain hadn't chosen that moment to do its memory thing. Suddenly, she *knew* the hands the woman was crying into. She'd seen them in a photograph, slapping the face of an older man. This was Zoe Raeburn, Sam Raeburn's daughter, the very woman who supposedly stole Genbolt's secret plans and gave them to Damien.

Curtis would repossess Mia's decoder ring if she didn't seize this opportunity to detect.

As an added plus, she could put off returning to Damien's table a bit longer.

"Hey," she said sympathetically, slipping onto the settee beside Zoe. "Are you all right? Would you like an Advil? The attendant said they keep a stash in here."

"I'm fine," Zoe said—not very convincingly, considering she could barely speak. "I don't . . . have a headache."

"How about tissues? I have some in my purse, or I could get you a cool damp towel."

"Tissues would be great," Zoe admitted.

Mia dug out the little packet and handed it over.

Zoe sat back to dab at her ruined face. "I must look a holy fright."

"You're a bit racoony, but I've seen worse."

Zoe laughed shakily. Her tears were abating, and she pulled herself straighter. She was taller than Mia—probably naturally elegant. Despite her emotional storm, when she looked Mia in the eyes, she radiated the female version of her father's king-of-the-world presence. If Damien considered her "just" a date, he really had high standards.

Zoe let the hand that held her squashed tissue fall. "You're very nice," she said to Mia.

"Well, um, I'm sure you'd do the same if our roles were reversed. Did some guy do you wrong?"

Mia hoped this wasn't too leading. If it was, Zoe must have been in the mood to share. She exhaled heavily. "It's always this way for women, isn't it? Our fathers betray us, and our boyfriends, and then we betray ourselves. We get so used to distrusting men we don't recognize a good one when he's right in front of us."

"The good ones are hard to find," Mia said, suspecting

originality wasn't required here.

Zoe's shoulders hitched, and she wiped at her eyes again. "Is it too much to ask for a second chance? To explain? To apologize?"

What did Zoe have to apologize for? Hadn't she betrayed her father for Damien's benefit?

"I'm sure it's not," Mia said uncertainly.

Zoe sagged back and sighed. Mia concluded Raeburn's daughter had a teensy flare for the dramatic. Zoe turned her head, seeming to really notice Mia for the first time. Dramatic tendencies aside, she was intelligent. Her light blue eyes sharpened. "You're Damien's date for the fundraiser, aren't you?"

Mia didn't have to fake surprise. She hadn't expected Zoe to know this. "Um, yes. I'm here as his guest."

Zoe waved her crumpled tissue dismissively. "I don't hold it against you. No woman could say *no* to him. He's sexy and brilliant and charming and emotionally unavailable. That's catnip for us women. We're always falling for men who withhold themselves from us."

Zoe was working up to an Oscar worthy performance, a prospect that alarmed Mia in spite of wanting her to talk. She decided to try the tack she'd used on Ms. DeWinter. "I don't know Damien well enough to say. Our dating is just a convenient arrangement."

"That's what *I* thought, until the stupid man sneaked underneath my skin." Zoe grabbed Mia's hands without warning. "I could have helped him, if only he'd let me in. Anyone can tell he has intimacy issues, but he doesn't want to get over them. He couldn't even see how right I was for him!"

O-kay, Mia thought. Did every woman who hung around Damien go nutso?

"Maybe you shouldn't let yourself get this worked up over him," she suggested. "He's just a guy—an interesting guy, but still. Maybe date some other rich handsome dude and put Damien behind you."

"You'll see," Zoe direly predicted. "One day you'll be lunching in his private office, thinking you've got him exactly where you want him, and the next—" She snapped her fingers so loudly Mia jumped. "You're sobbing your heart out in a public restroom, wishing you could delete his memory from your poor tormented brain."

Mia didn't know how to apply reason to this statement. "Why don't I get you that damp towel? You probably need some alone time to figure your way through this."

Alone time wasn't the right phrase to use from a detecting point of view.

Zoe's mood shifted to resolute. "You're right," she said, standing up and smoothing her fancy gown. "I *do* need to dry my own tears. Thank you for reminding me."

She glided out of the lounge to do it, leaving Mia to stare in dismay at the swinging door.

Well, she thought. She'd just learned a whole bunch of nothing pertinent.

◆

Judging it was probably safe, Mia returned to Damien's table in the ballroom. Thankfully, Ms. DeWinter was gone. Jake lounged in the chair she'd vacated, next to a frowning Damien.

"Not firing her right away is going to bite you in the ass," Jake was warning him.

"I told her not to come in on Monday. HR can drop the official anvil when she's not in the office."

"You're firing Ms. DeWinter?" Mia asked.

"Unfortunately." Damien shook his head dourly. "I really thought she'd last longer."

This seemed a strange statement, but Mia wasn't sure how to probe deeper.

"You were gone a while," Jake observed.

"That's a story for another time," she said, not wanting to get into it in front of Damien, especially since she hadn't sorted out what Zoe's meltdown meant. She glanced from one man to the other. "Neither of you look cheery. Are you sure you want to stay for dinner?"

"I'm afraid I'm here for the duration," Damien said. "WorldWide donated a W-22 to the auction. It's good PR for the company. I'll be expected to say something. You two don't have to remain, of course."

"Sure we do." Mia pulled out a chair and sat. "We're in this together."

"Agreed," Jake said.

Damien regarded him with raised eyebrows. Obviously, he didn't expect the support.

"Hey," Jake said, treating him to his trademark smirk. "After the start it's had, this night can only get better."

◆

Damien didn't know about better, but he got through it. WorldWide's media team had created a snappy highlight reel for the donated car, and it played for the auction's bidders without a hitch. His own spiel got laughs where it was supposed to. The W-22 earned a record bid from a loud but likable Manhattan realtor. Damien only had to pose for a few pictures. The realtor handily sucked up all the press's attention.

When the valet brought Jake's car back around to the main entrance, Damien realized he didn't want to be driven.

"You two sit in the back," he instructed his companions.

Jake and Mia exchanged a glance but didn't argue.

He calmed as he drove, his normal self gradually replacing his not quite natural public persona. Damien sometimes thought his favorite thing in the world was quiet. Quiet spaces, quiet people, quiet but interesting thoughts. His brain felt bigger then, like it could solve any conundrum. Jake and Mia left him in peace, sitting close together but not speaking. After a couple minutes, Mia rested her head on Jake's shoulder. A pang of wistfulness touched him.

Jake met his gaze in the rearview mirror. "Mia's tired," he said.

Did Jake think her action needed justifying? Damien couldn't tell. "I'm sure she is."

To his surprise, he experienced more than the usual sense of homecoming as he parked in his secure section of Ten WorldWide's garage. Jake helped Mia out, and Damien plugged the car into the charger.

His phone vibrated as they walked to the elevator.

"Hm," he said, checking the short text he'd just received. "I need to stop at the lobby desk."

"We'll come with you," Jake said. "Then we can all ride up together."

Damien started to deny this was necessary but shut his mouth. He didn't mind. In spite of its newness, Jake and Mia's company was already pleasanter than solitude.

◆

As they stepped into the elevator, Jake rolled his shoulders uneasily. He still had a warm spot where Mia's head had lain. He couldn't have nudged her off. That would have looked weird to Damien, who thought of them as a couple. The problem was Jake had *wanted* her to rest against him. He'd wanted to put his arm around her and hold her there. To be absolutely truthful, he liked how much she liked him. He liked her back just as much and more maybe.

Untying the bond between them—as they'd eventually have to do—was going to be tricky.

The doors opened at the lobby. Jake began to exit but bumped into Damien's back. The other man had stopped moving for some reason.

"Fuck, fuck, fuck," the CEO muttered beneath his breath.

That was a lot of fucks. Jake touched Damien's back while simultaneously reaching under his jacket to unlatch his holster.

"I've got this," Damien said.

He strode out before Jake could ask what the problem was. Seeing no immediate danger, he let Damien move ahead as he obviously wished. The security guard sat calmly behind his desk, definitely not on alert. Another man stood not far from him in a good quality suit and overcoat. Above average height, his shoes were shined and his scarf cashmere. His non-showy but large gold watch suggested wealth, though maybe not billionaire status. The silver that streaked his medium brown hair put him in his late fifties. His manner was in no way threatening—the opposite really.

He had the air of a person who wanted a favor.

"Cheekbones and jaw," Mia said beside him. "That could be Damien's dad."

Mia had a knack for facial recognition, so Jake didn't doubt her guess.

The guard jumped up as he spotted Damien and his scowl. "Mr. Call. My apologies if I should have let this gentleman up. I told him I couldn't without your express okay. He claims he's your—"

"I know what he claims." Damien's words were clipped and exceedingly controlled, making it even clearer that he was furious. "You were absolutely right to make him wait. I value my privacy, and that includes from relatives. In the future, do just as you've done tonight."

"Yes, sir," said the guard, his eyes not concealing his curiosity.

"Damien," the other man scolded, though he seemed unsurprised by his behavior.

Damien leveled a hard look at him. "I'm not speaking to you here."

"Fine, son. We'll go anywhere you like. Are you and your friends coming back from an evening out? I'd love to be introduced."

"Fuck you," Damien hissed, so enraged he was shaking.

This was enough for Jake. He didn't know what the danger was, but emotionally at least there was one. "Wait here," he murmured to Mia and went to Damien.

"Hello," said Damien's father, offering Jake his hand. "I'm Roderick Call. It's nice to meet you."

Up close, the resemblance between Damien and Roderick was striking. Though his father carried a few more decades and pounds, he and Damien had the same greeny-blue-gold eyes, the same Captain America jawline.

Jake ignored his extended hand and addressed Damien. "What would you like me to do?"

Damien blew out a breath that told Jake his presence was welcome, even if he didn't respond directly. "I'm not getting into a scene with you, Dad."

"Then come out for a drink. Bring your girlfriend, if that's what she is. I'd be happy to meet anyone you care about."

Damien appeared to weigh this option. Jake had a feeling he was going to try to keep him and Mia out of this—not because he wanted to be alone with his father, but because he didn't want them to be uncomfortable.

"We'll come," Jake said firmly.

Damien looked startled. "You don't have to do that."

"Either we come, or I toss your dad to the curb. Those are your two options."

Damien's father dropped his head to smile. He seemed to enjoy seeing Jake stand up to his son.

"I'm up for tagging along," Mia said, because of course she hadn't waited like Jake asked. "Assuming you don't hate the idea of me being there."

Jake suspected Damien wasn't capable of hating anything Mia proposed.

"Fine," the boss man surrendered. "We'll all go for a drink."

◆

They went to the quiet hotel bar down the street, where the staff seemed familiar with Damien's habits. Greeting him without fuss, the host led their group to a corner booth away from the sprinkling of other guests.

Though Mia was ready to drop, she ordered a glass of wine. Damien and his father requested the same top shelf scotch.

"Glad to see we still have something in common," his dad observed.

"Cut it out," Damien snapped, low but sharp.

Mia sat next to him in the booth. She didn't know why Damien was upset or if he wanted comfort, but unable not to, she laid her hand gently on his thigh. To her relief, Damien put his hand on top of it. His palm was slightly damp but warm. He patted her absently.

"Okay, Dad," he said. "Get it over with. Spit out what you've come here for."

"No small talk?"

"We are miles past that, and you know it."

His father's tone had been cajoling, but now his face hardened. Mia guessed he wasn't as soft as he'd been pretending. "As you wish. I've come to suggest, yet again, that we bury the hatchet."

"And how are you suggesting we do that this time?"

"As you know, my sixtieth birthday is coming up. Your stepmother would very much like you to be there."

Damien stared at him as if he'd asked him to dance naked in Times Square . . . and then set himself on fire. "That woman isn't my stepmother."

"Damien—"

"You're as much of an idiot as ever. She only wants to play more games with me."

"Son, you need to get over this delusion."

"You need to pull the fucking wool off your fucking eyes."

"It's been twelve years. You can't believe the situation hasn't changed since then, that *she* hasn't changed. If she ever was what you thought."

Damien huffed in disbelief. "She's *always* been what I thought. You're the one who can't face the truth."

"This can't be misplaced loyalty to your mother . . ."

"You're right about that," Damien broke in bitterly. "Janine made sure Mom was poisoned against me too."

"*I'm* not poisoned against you," his father said. "I love you. I want us to be part of each other's lives."

The hand Damien hadn't put on top of Mia's clenched around his napkin. "As long as she's part of your life, that's not going to happen."

"Damien—"

"No," he said. "Just no. I don't know how to be any clearer. She's using you to get to me. I won't go along with it."

"You've got to realize how irrational—not to mention arrogant—that sounds."

"Tell me she didn't suggest you try seeing me again. Tell me she hasn't been nudging you for weeks."

"Because she knows how much I miss you!"

Damien's father seemed to believe what he said. Damien exhaled slowly. He sat very still for a moment before he turned to Mia. She wasn't prepared for the intensity of his expression. His face was stiff, his eyes like ice over twin bonfires.

"Do you wish to finish your wine?" he asked.

She shook her head. "I only ordered it to be polite."

His hazel eyes softened the tiniest bit, maybe with amusement. "Good. We can leave now then."

He slid down the seat and dug out his wallet, dropping three crisp hundreds onto the booth's table. Jake had extricated himself by then. Only Mia and Roderick remained sitting.

"Talk to him," Roderick pleaded as Damien offered his hand to help her out. "You seem like a nice girl. Families shouldn't be allowed to fall apart."

Mia wasn't sure how deep she ought to wade into these waters.

"I respect his choices," she said carefully. "Sometimes that's what you do when you really love someone."

As soon as the words were out, a rush of blood caused her cheeks to sting. She'd been thinking of her brother, of how she'd learned to accept Mike for who he was.

If a person didn't know that, they might think she'd said she really loved Damien.

CHAPTER 12

DAMIEN must have walked back to Ten WorldWide on automatic pilot, because he couldn't remember doing it. His brain was locked in its own private loop, cursing him for letting his father open up that old Pandora's box. Permitting Mia and Jake to accompany him had been weak, as if he were a kid whose hand needed holding to cross the street.

They'd have questions now, ones he didn't want to answer.

Jake was unlocking the penthouse entry with his palm print. The other man hadn't said a word, or not that Damien remembered. Damien was numbly grateful as he strode into and across the residence. He had a goal at least. The north access to the terrace, where he had his helipad and his shed for drones, was on the opposite side.

The wind hit his face as he pushed the glass door open. This was the sixtieth floor. The gusts were stronger here than on the street but not dangerous tonight. The competing spires of the city rose beyond his building's edge, lines of windows glowing in broken dashes as they raced upward into the sky. Damien tugged his bowtie loose and undid his collar. The cold felt good, and the deep breaths he took. He could let this go. He could put the past behind him.

He did it every day, after all.

He'd been there perhaps a minute when a small warm hand slid into his and curled over it.

"It's cold out here," Mia said, though she still wore her coat.

He saw Jake had followed him out as well. He stood a few steps from Mia, watching them silently—watching over her maybe.

You don't need to be watched over, Damien told himself.

Mia's thumb rubbed his hand. He gazed down at her, viscerally aware that the rope of diamonds around her neck pleased his inner control freak. In truth, everything about her pleased him. He wondered at that. How had her particular arrangement of quirks and features become so damn appealing?

"What is it like?" he asked.

She blinked, the slow descent and rise of her lashes mesmerizing him. "What is what like?"

"To feel safe because certain people are around you. Infants must know, when their parents hold them. Maybe lovers. I'm not sure I've ever had the sensation someone would be there if I really needed them."

Was he asking Mia to pity him? His mood was too unusual to be certain. And he should have known she wouldn't answer the way a normal person would.

She tipped her head to consider his question. "You might not be missing as much as you think. The sensation of being safe is probably a misconception in most cases."

He stroked her cheeks with his thumbs, amused and glad of it. "That's a very cynical answer, one I wouldn't expect from someone with a spirit as sweet as yours."

"I'm not trying to be cynical. It's just the truth. You only know how reliable people are when they're put to the test."

Damien's gaze slid to Jake. "He'd be there if you needed him."

She shrugged. "If someone were trying to kill me, sure."

Jake barked a single laugh.

"He'd take a bullet for you too," she added.

Maybe he would. Something like giddiness brushed him, an invisible feathered wing. Damien slid his hands down Mia's coat sleeves to squeeze her soft fingers. "Let's go somewhere. Côte d'Azur. Belize. My helicopter can be here in ten minutes. We'll take Jake with us too."

Jake snorted. "Obliged, I'm sure."

"I get it," Mia said. "If I were you, I'd be tempted to run away from what's bothering me. Unfortunately, you're too smart not to realize that's what we'd be doing."

"Maybe I wouldn't care."

"Don't you want to tell me . . . tell *us* why you and your dad are at odds? Don't you want to get it off your chest?"

"I feel like I could," he said, "but maybe that's a

misconception too."

"Well, I won't force you, but let's go in. I'm freezing my butt out here."

She tugged his hand, and he didn't resist the pull. Jake held the door for both of them.

"I would have chosen Belize," he said as Damien passed him.

Damien knew this was a joke, but he wasn't ready to laugh. Mia took his coat and sat him on the single couch in the living area. He felt surreal, like his brain was ticking over at quarter speed.

"Drink this," Jake said.

He held out a glass of water. Damien drank and then, because there was no table nearby, set it aside on the floor.

Damien liked his furniture spread out. When Jake pulled two light chairs closer, it startled him.

"You're talking to us," Jake said, gesturing for Mia to sit in the second one. "Ever since we left your dad, you've been acting like a zombie."

Damien leaned forward and dragged both hands down his face.

"You can tell us," Mia assured him. "Think of the things we've already done together. Neither of us will judge."

Maybe they were right. Maybe he would feel better to get this off his chest. He pressed his palms to his thighs, pushing his torso upright again.

"All right. When I was seventeen, my high school guidance counselor seduced me."

Mia's eyebrows rose.

"She didn't force me. She was attractive. I was flattered and hormonal. Plus, I looked old for my age."

"I remember. You said you had the brain of a nerd and the body of a Greek god."

She'd supplied the second half of that description, but he didn't correct her.

"I was physically mature," he agreed, "though perhaps not emotionally. Anyway, I wasn't going to turn her down. She was my first sexual partner. She denied it later, but I don't think I was the only male student she'd deflowered." He shrugged uncomfortably. "It's a gray area. Boys at seventeen often are sexually active. I don't know how many would have complained if she'd approached them."

"It's a power differential," Mia said. "She was an adult. And had authority over you."

"Yes." He sighed. "Be that as it may, my youth and inexperience seemed to be part of my appeal for her. Perhaps because she knew what she was doing, the encounter was more successful than it might have been. I allowed her to talk me into repeating it three more times."

He rubbed his jaw, remembering the hurried and increasingly awkward sessions in her cramped office at the high school. Would he always smell chalk dust and Shalimar when he thought of her? He shook his head to throw the sense memory off.

"Then what happened?" Mia asked.

"I suppose it dawned on me that I was embarrassed. I didn't have the slightest urge to brag to my peers, despite this counselor being the object of many fantasies and me no longer being a virgin. Her wanting to sleep with someone my age felt wrong. She had a . . . forceful personality. I screwed up my nerve and told her I wanted to stop seeing her."

"I take it she didn't like that," Jake said.

"No. She told me I shouldn't be afraid of the difference in our ages; that she and I were meant to be. We were in love, and love transcended boundaries. She rented a secret apartment where we could meet and tried to give me the key to it. She slid notes into my locker scented with her perfume. When I didn't cooperate, she began calling my parents' house and asking to speak to me about school business."

"She stalked you," Mia said.

"Yes. I didn't know the name for what she was doing, but I realized I couldn't give in to the harassment. As I saw it, resisting was my only viable option." His palms were wet, so he dried them on his trousers. "I went to my father. Told him everything that happened. He runs—and ran—a successful chain of dry cleaners, so he wasn't without influence in our township. He agreed to speak to her, to warn her to leave his son alone or lose her job. I'd never felt so grateful to him. I hadn't been sure he'd support me. Now I was relieved it was finally going to be over.

"Except it wasn't. I don't know how Janine did it, but somehow during their conversation she seduced him. She convinced my father I'd pursued her; that she'd given in because she was weak and upset over a bad breakup. She swore we only had sex once and that she was mortified about it. She was truly sorry I'd become fixated, but it would never happen again. She actually suggested he get me counseling."

"And he believed her," Mia said, not making it a question.

"He wanted to. He was forty-seven and tired of being married to his wife. Janine was twenty-six and hot and told him whatever he wanted to hear about himself. Almost before I knew it, my parents were divorced and she was marrying him. My mom . . . had her own issues. During one screaming match the two women had, Janine insinuated *I'd* arranged for her and my dad to hook up, that I'd *wanted* it to happen. Suddenly, I was to blame for everything. My mother cut me off completely. I haven't spoken to her in over a decade."

"Jesus," Mia murmured.

Damien heaved a sigh. "It was pretty fucked up. I don't know if it should be a consolation, but at least, since I never publically accused Janine, there was nothing for reporters to dig up when I started making news with my companies."

"Do you think she's repeated her behavior with other minors?"

This question came from Jake. Damien appreciated how unemotionally he'd asked. He shook his head. "I've kept an eye on her, unobtrusively. I have the tools for that, you could say. After she married my dad, she quit her job at the high school. I'd think she was genuinely devoted to him if I didn't know she's still obsessed with me."

"Still?" Mia asked.

"She finds ways to get messages to me a couple times a year. She'll send a gift, purportedly from my father, and drench it in her perfume. Or I'll get an email of a naked woman—no face and from a spoofed address—but I'll know it's her. I can't go home to visit him. She always tries to maneuver me alone. She likes that I can't prove what she does to my dad. It might be her favorite part of the game she plays."

"You don't want to confront her?"

"It seems to feed her when I try. And it's not like the courts lock up stalkers and throw away the key. So long as she's focused on me and not violent, I guess I can live with it."

Mia mulled this over.

Jake leaned forward in the chrome and black leather chair he'd chosen, his six-foot-something frame causing the sling seat to creak. At some point, he'd shucked his coat and undone his tie. His collar was unbuttoned and his shirt cuffs rolled up. A spot of heat expanded in Damien's chest. Had he noticed before how tan the skin of Jake's corded forearms was? Jake rubbed his callused hands together in a loose fist.

"So," he said, drawing Damien's eyes to his. The expression in Jake's was sympathetic. "You don't allow yourself to get close to women because you're afraid Janine will harm them."

Damien surprised them both by laughing. "I don't allow myself to get close to women because I'm concerned they'll harm *me*."

"You," Jake said, utterly gobsmacked.

Damien let himself enjoy that for a heartbeat before he sighed. "Janine was just the first in a series. I haven't had a single woman fall in love with me who didn't end up going overboard."

"Are you sure they aren't normally interested?" Mia asked. "Ordinary people can get intense when they especially like someone. Daydream about them. Think of ways to please them. They aren't necessarily unhinged."

Extra color rose into her cheeks. Per usual, she gritted her teeth and ignored the reaction. For once, Damien didn't care if the flush was for him or Jake. It was adorable.

A moment later, weariness settled back over him. "I'm afraid I don't mean normally interested. I've concluded there's something in me, something physical that brings out the crazy in females. Perhaps I have odd pheromones."

"You don't think it's your bags of money?" Mia suggested.

Jake choked on his amusement.

Damien smiled. "I expect some women like my money better than they like me, but I wasn't rich when I met Janine or my next girlfriend. We got together my sophomore year at MIT. I was gun shy, I guess. It took me a while to want to be close to anyone. Two weeks after we slept together, she began exhibiting stalking behavior too. I tried to convince myself I was imagining it, but then she showed up with a homemade Taser at a lecture I was attending. She wanted to make sure I wasn't talking to other girls. In the end, I had to drop out to get away from her." He shook his head in remembered frustration. "I *liked* MIT. There were lots of people there like me. Heck, I played on a hockey team. But at least that girl has forgotten me. She wasn't a natural whackjob like Janine."

"Two examples aren't enough to prove a theorem," Jake

pointed out.

"No," Damien agreed, "but there have been others."

"Ms. DeWinter!" Mia said. "Except—" Her nose wrinkled. "You didn't sleep with her, did you? She has a husband."

"I haven't slept with her," Damien confirmed. "And I hoped her being happily married would protect her from whatever odd influence I have."

"Married women still like billionaires," Jake said. "And get obsessed with celebrities."

"True," Damien conceded.

Mia sat straighter. "Zoe Raeburn has her own money. And she's totally gone on you." She wriggled self-consciously in her seat when Damien's brows lifted. "I, uh, ran into her in the restroom at the fundraiser. She was crying because you haven't returned her calls."

"Hell—" Damien burst out.

Mia patted both his knees. "She might not be under an unnatural influence. She could have fallen for your brains or charm. You have both, you know. And the wounded thing. Women go for that too."

"The 'wounded thing?'" Damien's face felt stiff.

"Maybe that's not the best way to put it. People like rescue fantasies, right? Being rescued. Being the rescuer. Since you're loaded, they can have both with you."

"Oh, that's infinitely more flattering than 'wounded.'"

Mia's mouth twisted at his sarcasm. "My point is you're likable. I like you and I'm not crazy."

"Yet," he said darkly.

"Really?" Her eyes went round. "You think I'm going to go nuts too?"

Damien relented. "Probably you won't. You seem genuinely in love with Jake. I've observed that provides a shield."

Mia's gaze darted to the other man. "I'm not— That is, we haven't—"

Damien's patience expired without warning. "Fine. Pretend you're not in love with each other. How you want to fool yourselves is your business."

"Well, certainly Jake isn't!" Mia spluttered.

Damien blinked. She honestly believed Jake wasn't in love with her? And here he'd been thinking she was more perceptive than most people.

"Maybe we could set this debate aside," Jake said.

Damien looked at the other man. Jake's lips had pressed together with disapproval. Surely he was aware of his own feelings. What was wrong with these two? Didn't they know how fortunate they were?

He opened his mouth to say so.

"It's late," Jake said, forestalling him. "We could all use some rest."

He got up and stretched. The movement did things to his rangy body that drew his *and* Mia's eyes. His ribcage was solid beneath the shirt, his dress trousers inching lower on his lean hips. Suddenly, Damien wasn't tired at all.

He was sorry when Jake dropped his arms again.

"*Will* you sleep?" Jake asked, as if the question had just occurred to him. "I could make you tea or something."

"Don't *you* treat me like I'm wounded," Damien snapped. "Or as if I'm your sub."

Jake's deeply blue gaze sharpened. "If you were my sub, I wouldn't be offering tea. I'd be fucking you in the ass up against the wall outside."

Damien's body already felt more awake, but these hard words knocked a fresh shock through him. His cock stirred and swelled. He had to return the challenge. His dominant nature demanded it.

"You could try," he said softly.

CHAPTER 13

JAKE wasn't a natural hand patter. He had to force himself to do things like offer tea. He guessed it wasn't Damien's nature to accept cosseting. That was fine. Jake preferred a more muscular approach anyway.

Rather than engage Damien head on, thereby obliging the less-experienced fighter to defend himself and possibly get hurt, Jake grabbed the light metal frame of the couch and jerked it toward himself. The sharp tug tipped the whole thing backward with Damien in it. He landed without harm but plenty of surprise.

Then, before he could recover, Jake pounced on him.

He ignored Mia's yelp of dismay. In two quick moves, he rolled Damien off the couch and forced his face onto the shaggy area rug. Damien tried to escape, but he was trained to box and not wrestle. Jake planted a knee on his back and bent his arm up between his shoulder blades. When Damien's struggles persisted, Jake pinned his thumb.

Damien gasped at the pressure he was exerting. "That hurts!"

"It's supposed to," Jake growled even as he eased up. "Lie still where I put you."

Both Mia's hands were pressed to her mouth. Jake gauged her condition. She was shocked but not horrified.

He was pretty sure he could snap her out of it.

"You," he barked like a drill sergeant. "Get Damien's shoes."

She blinked in confusion. "His shoes?"

"They're what you usually take off before you strip someone's pants."

She hesitated then knelt at Damien's feet. Due to her snug black gown, she couldn't shift quickly. Damien wriggled like a fish as she removed his footwear and socks—as if her soft little fingers tormented him even there. Jake enjoyed the CEO's energy and strength. He was a big man himself. He didn't often get to dominate males who had more muscle weight. He discovered it was satisfying—more like a fair fight, he guessed. His own cock pounded with readiness to perform the acts he'd threatened.

"Don't I get a say in this?" Damien huffed.

Jake thought that question missed the point.

"We'll make this simple," he said, his voice harshened by arousal. "Your safe word is 'stop.' Don't say it if you don't mean it, because I will."

Damien's head twisted to the side, gaping in disbelief. Jake's lips curved at his stunned expression.

"Do you want to say it?" he asked. "We can end this right now."

They both knew the answer. Damien's mouth worked, his hips squirming slightly but tellingly. "No."

"Good. I'm going to reach under you to undo your trousers. Mia, get ready to pull them down."

"You could just let me up," Damien said exasperatedly.

Jake leaned closer to his ear. "I don't want to let you up, *sub*."

Damien glared at being called this, but his pelvis squirmed again. Probably he couldn't help it. Jake was willing to bet the CEO was even harder than he was—and Jake was damn hard, as it happened. He smirked, put a tad more pressure on Damien's trapped arm, and worked his hand beneath him to unfasten his waistband. The clasps took a couple seconds to free, after which Jake palmed the CEO's giant zipper bulge.

"Shit," Damien breathed in a different tone than before.

Jake allowed his fingers to stretch around his new possession. Damien cursed again.

"This is a good hard-on, sub." Jake rubbed it teasingly up and down, measuring its girth and resistance, enjoying how it twitched. "Nice and stiff and thick. I can't wait to order Mia to wrap her pretty mouth around it."

A shuddered rolled up his new sub's spine, betraying Damien's interest in this prospect.

Jake didn't let him get comfortable. He took hold of his zipper tab and slowly dragged it down his erection. The sensation of it lowering would be slight, but Damien was worked up. He let out a strangled moan.

"Now," Jake said softly to Mia. "Get his trousers off."

Mia pulled until they were gone. Damien's ass cheeks contracted under his boxer briefs. The underwear was dark gray, some European brand Jake didn't recognize. He spared a second to wonder if they were comfortable.

He laughed silently to himself. If he weren't careful, Damien's rich boy tastes would rub off on him. He put on a stern face.

"Remove those too," he ordered Mia.

Mia removed the underwear. Jake's palms began to itch. Damien still wore his shirt and was naked from the waist down. The effect this had on his powerful body was interesting. He appeared more vulnerable half undressed than entirely. Perhaps his full nude beauty precluded humiliation. In that state, he simply was too stunning. Jake noted he had long legs and a good strong butt—not narrow but muscular. Shallow dimples graced either side of his tailbone.

Knowing no one had disciplined this ass before gave Jake a serious power surge.

"Take his hands from me," he ordered Mia. "I need mine free."

Damien twitched, possibly guessing what he planned.

"I'm not strong enough to control him," Mia protested.

"He won't pull free," Jake said. "He'll be afraid of accidentally hurting you."

Jake understood Damien's type. Control freak streak notwithstanding, he *wanted* to submit. Laying down his responsibilities even for a minute would be a relief. All he needed was a sound enough excuse to give in. In this instance, not hurting Mia was sufficient.

She shifted around to kneel above Damien's head, taking one large male hand and then the other. As Jake expected, Damien let her.

With their hands wrapped together, the difference in their sizes couldn't have been more obvious or more erotic.

"Hold tighter," Jake instructed, his voice gone thick. "Our sub needs to know you've got a secure grip."

Mia did as he asked. She was breathing faster, the rise and fall of her satiny breasts causing the diamond rope around her neck to twinkle. The hourglass fit of the velvet dress, and her kneeling inside it, was a picture he'd remember when he was ninety.

She gripped Damien firmly enough for her biceps to tighten.

"You like that," Jake observed, seeing the strength she put into it. "Having your would-be master at your mercy."

"Yes." Her answer was excited and breathy. "Are you going to spank him now?"

At the sound of her anticipation, another half-swallowed moan broke in Damien's throat.

"I am," Jake confirmed. "I'm stronger than you, so I think that's a better choice."

The suggestion that *she* could have spanked him moved Mia. Her fingers tightened on Damien's hands.

Damien murmured a curse half a second before Jake let fly.

Damien was no fragile flower. Jake gave him a good long basting, hard enough to sting and leave him red all over, right up to his two dimples. Damien bucked under the rain of blows and gasped.

"Are you still hard?" Jake demanded then.

He knew the answer. Damien's hips had tried to arch off the carpet after each contact, betraying how aroused he'd grown. Apparently, Damien decided to play stubborn. Rather than respond, he clenched his jaw.

"*Answer*," Jake ordered, lifting his arm high to demonstrate that he meant business. "Or are you afraid to admit the truth of what your master has done to you?"

His palm struck Damien's ass with a resounding smack. Damien groaned and writhed. His hips thrust their highest yet.

"Yes," he burst out reluctantly.

Yes, wasn't good enough. Damien had witnessed plenty of master-sub sessions. He knew the required formula.

"Yes, what?" Jake barked.

"Yes, master, I'm still hard."

Jake immediately rolled him onto his back.

Damien lay there panting, his pupils huge and glittering. Though his body language hinted at abandon, his expression was angry. To be truthful, Jake welcomed that. Anger was heat, and heat burned off inhibitions. Jake wanted Damien to break through whatever remained of those.

"Oh my god," Mia said.

Jake's attention followed hers to Damien's crotch.

Oh my god was right. Damien's erection was big enough to

hurt. His skin stretched drum-taut around it, his engorged veins standing out sharply. Any doubt that he'd enjoyed the spanking evaporated. Damien's entire penis pulsed in time to his heartbeat, the little jerks vicious and exciting. His shaft was dark from the blood in it—and so full Jake would have needed extra lube to take it. The appeal of that idea disconcerted. Jake preferred the take-charge position with other men. Only now and then had he let himself be taken.

He'd let Damien, he realized, if the man wanted to do that.

"He's dripping," Mia murmured.

He was. Little drops of pre-ejaculate squeezed from his slit and ran down the quivering head. Having both their attention on the spot didn't slow the reaction. Damien's powerful thighs shifted restlessly.

"Are you going to stare at me all night?" he demanded.

"Are you going to stare at me all night, *master*?" Jake corrected.

Damien rolled his eyes.

"Say it," Jake said, "or I won't order her to go down on you."

Mia hardly needed ordering. Her little tongue had just snuck out to wet her scrumptious lips. Still, Jake was confident she'd wait for his say-so. Mia knew the value of being a team player.

"Are you going to stare at me all night, master?" Damien complied grudgingly.

"No, I'm not." Still crouched beside him, Jake stroked the inside of Damien's nervously clenched thigh. The big man shivered, conveniently confirming that he was sensitive. Jake lifted his gaze to Mia. Obedient assistant that she was, she bit her lip and waited.

It was all so perfect he wanted to laugh with joy.

"Miss Beck," he said formally instead. "If you'd be so kind, please kiss our submissive's cock."

"'Ours?'"

"Well, there is a chain of command. But he's at the bottom now."

She smiled, liking that answer. "May I suck him too?"

"You may. But don't make him come."

Her brown eyes glowed. "You're saving that for yourself, aren't you?"

He smiled, pleased that she understood. "Why don't we switch places? It will increase the challenge to his self-control if

I sit him up to watch what you're doing."

Damien muttered something angry beneath his breath.

Neither Jake nor Mia paid attention. Jake moved behind Damien, dragging him up until his back was supported by Jake's chest.

"Hm," he said, noticing Damien's loosened black bow tie.

He removed it. He bent both of Damien's arms behind him then bound his wrists comfortably but snugly together. Jake enjoyed that, of course. Bondage always got him going.

"Could I have yours?" Mia surprised him by asking.

"My bow tie?"

"Yes, please," she said politely.

Curious, he took it off and placed it in her waiting hand.

"Now," Mia said, one finger pressed playfully to her mouth as she considered Damien's aroused genitals. "What in the world shall I tie this bow around?"

"Don't you dare," Damien said.

His protest delighted Mia. "Of course I dare! Jake is sharing you with me. You're my sub tonight too."

She lifted each of his ankles, spreading his legs wider and scooting between them. Damien began to twist, her actions triggering responses he was unable to restrain. Mia was no one's dominatrix, but she was playing the part now. She caught his knees to make him stop.

"Now, now," she scolded. "This will please me and Jake. I'm sure you want us to enjoy what we do to you."

"No bows," Damien insisted.

"Fine." Mia broke into a grin. "I'll secure it with a knot."

Fortunately Jake's neckwear wasn't the pre-tied sort. Mia looped the narrower stretch of black silk beneath his testicles, lifting them up against his shaft. Though she was careful about it, Jake tensed empathetically. She wound the rest of the tie once around Damien's shaft, securing the arrangement with a crooked but apparently snug knot.

Jake squirmed slightly on his haunches. He had no trouble imagining the feel of that constriction.

Mia stroked her thumbs along the flat bands of cloth that surrounded Damien. "How's that?"

"Fine," he said grumpily, his tone contradicted by the leaping of his cock.

Mia pretended to pout. "Only fine? Let me see if I can

improve on that."

She braced her hands on Damien's thighs so she could lean forward. He tensed, going completely stiff as she engulfed his tip in her mouth and licked.

Jake wrapped his arms around Damien's chest. He could feel the other man's heart knocking, the increase in his skin temperature. Being able to imagine what Mia *and* Damien experienced was interesting.

"You can give him more than that," he encouraged.

Mia's mouth sank lower. She was sucking him now, using her tongue from the sound of it. Her fingers kneaded Damien's thighs. The knotted bow tie gave her a handy place to stop. Damien's limbs trembled.

"Relax," Jake advised her. "Suck him nice and easy. And don't forget to breathe."

Her lashes lifted. The most amazing sense of connection arrowed between her eyes and his. It was like he and she shared a mind, or at least the same desire to tantalize Damien. She drew up slowly, lips ringed tight, letting Jake watch the other man's pulsing cock emerge.

"Fuck," Damien breathed. His spine was arching, the hands Jake had tied in the small of his back fisting.

"How long has it been since you let a woman go down on you?"

Damien grunted, his hips twisting as Mia sank again. "I don't know. Years. Jesus, that feels good."

"Well, hold on," Jake advised in his ear. "I'm not tired of watching her do that."

Mia wasn't tired either. Her mouth pushed down, rose up, slow and wet and nearly as enjoyable to observe as it must have been to feel. Her breasts swelled enticingly with her motions, threatening to escape her evening gown. Damien's body rolled even with Jake holding it, struggling helplessly to get deeper each time she went down on him.

When his voice came out as a whimper, Mia rose up and released him.

He panted, trying to recover. Jake suspected he'd come extremely close to shooting down her throat.

Maybe Mia knew. She sat on her stockinged feet, a gorgeous riot of color staining her cheeks and cleavage. Her lips were swollen and her eyes shone with stars. Jake had known a lot of women, in every part of the world. Mia was the sweetest siren he'd ever seen. When she licked her soft flushed mouth, both he and Damien reacted.

"I want to kiss him," she said throatily.

Damien swallowed.

"Do it," Jake ordered.

Catlike, she came up their captive: nuzzling his throat, his jaw, rubbing her soft cheek along his shaven one. She brushed her lips over Damien's. Jake was so close he heard and felt Damien's breathing catch.

"You tasted good," she said and pushed her tongue inward.

Damien moaned, maybe tasting himself on her. He accepted the kiss completely then pushed forward and gave it back to her. Mia crooned out a little sound. Erotic chills raced up and down Jake's spine.

Damien and Mia kissed like they'd been craving it for a while.

Long minutes passed while they drew on each other's mouths. Finally, Mia cupped his cheeks and drew back. "You're a good man, Damien. You deserve kindness."

She was in the moment—sincere, Jake would have bet—but if she'd been trying to make the CEO to fall for her, she couldn't have chosen her words better.

Since this situation was bound to end, Jake thought a bit more lightness might be in order.

"Spare the rod, spoil the sub," he quipped.

"You spanked him because you thought he'd like it," she pointed out.

"He'll like what I do next as well."

He pushed onto his feet, helping Damien rise at the same time. The man had good coordination. He avoided stumbling on the way up. He labored under more handicaps than bound wrists. His cock had increased in size from Mia sucking it.

The tie she'd knotted around him was digging in slightly.

"Does that hurt?" he asked.

"Only in a good way," Damien admitted.

Jake smiled, took the man by the shoulders, and gave him a sharp quick kiss with a bit of tongue. This seemed to surprise Damien. His eyes were wider when Jake drew back. Jake couldn't resist an urge to tease.

"You do taste good," he declared. He turned his attention to Mia. She was wide-eyed too. He waved her forward. "Please lead the way to Damien's bedroom. I'd like our sub to be comfortable while I have my way with him. And take off your clothes while you go. I wouldn't want him to give in to . . . trepidation on our walk."

Jake doubted any amount of trepidation could discourage Damien's killer erection. Mostly, Jake just wanted Mia to get naked. As he'd expected, she was no slick stripper. *Adorably awkward* better described her disrobing style. She made the process more challenging by refusing to simply let each item fall. She picked them up and draped them over her arm instead.

Watching her wriggle around to undo her bra clasp one-handed was humorous.

"You can just drop those things," Damien said, still thinking of himself as her host—despite the fact that Jake was marching him behind her by his tied wrists.

"Nonsense," Jake contradicted to remind him of his place. "Mia is observant. She knows our sub likes his home tidy."

Mia flashed a grin over her shoulder. "I do. Plus, I might need to find these things later."

She paused to drag her lacy panties down her legs. She'd come a long way in a little while if she didn't hesitate to strip down to nothing in front of them.

"Wow," Damien murmured once she straightened again.

Jake didn't rebuke him for speaking out of turn. Mia's back view in motion was praiseworthy. Her heart-shaped butt jiggled just enough, the bare soles of her feet oddly alluring. She reached behind her neck for the clasp of the diamond rope necklace.

"Leave that on," he and Damien chorused.

She snorted but let it be. "You two *are* birds of a feather."

They'd reached Damien's bedroom area. Mia turned on a light and looked back at them. Her front view stole their breath then.

"Beautiful," Damien said softly.

She dropped her load of clothes on a chair, her eyes glowing happily. Jake's trousers felt tight enough to strangle his erection. He was so ready to do this.

"On your bed," he ordered, giving Damien a gentle push.

Damien swung onto the mattress and sat on his feet. With his arms bound behind his back, the excited in and out of his diaphragm was especially obvious. He looked at Jake warily. "I have condoms in my bathroom."

Jake enjoyed his caution. He wouldn't want his new toy growing complacent.

"I'll get them." He turned back after a step. "Feel free to keep your mistress happy while I'm gone. Mia, if you want to, untie his wrists."

The glance the pair exchanged amused him. When he returned, he wasn't surprised to find them on their knees kissing. Damien's hands were free, and he was sliding them up and down Mia's silky back. Evidently, now that he'd broken his fast and gotten a taste of her, he didn't want to give it up. Jake liked the tenderness with which he held her, the way Mia melted into him. It got to him—as if he shared the pleasure Damien and Mia took in caressing each other.

He was beginning to understand the billionaire's obsession with watching.

They broke apart as he approached.

"Oh," Mia said, because he was naked too.

Damien tried to be more nonchalant than her. As his gaze dropped to Jake's erection, he gave himself away with a shoulder twitch. Jake had already donned a rubber and slathered it with lube. Damien received the intended message that foreplay was over.

"Lie on your front," Jake instructed Damien.

The CEO shivered and complied.

"Sit next to him," he told Mia.

She sat and crossed her legs like a well-behaved schoolgirl—one with expensive taste in jewelry. The rope of stones hung between her trembling breasts, the picture made prettier by the docile lowering of her head. Jake's heart banged faster inside his chest. Sometimes Mia was too much of a natural at this.

He'd have to work at maintaining his self-restraint.

He swung over Damien on the low platform bed, using his knees to force the man's legs apart. Force was a tool he knew how to apply. Use too much and you risked putting your partner off. Use just the right amount, and anyone with a hint of sub would get pleasantly wound up. Surrender was the ultimate goal of sex, even for dominants.

What else was a climax?

Jake knew Damien wanted one of those. He drew his hands down the other man's muscled back, savoring his strength and responsiveness. Damien tensed when Jake's gliding touch reached the bend of his waist, so likely he was ticklish. Jake smiled but let that pass. The CEO's ass cheeks invited kneading, especially since they still were red. Damien's arms were bent up, his hands resting palm down on the covers beside his head. As Jake massaged his glutes more deeply, his fingers curled under.

Experienced top that he was, Jake let him take in the new sensations, and the reminder that he'd been spanked. When his butt began to tense again with arousal, Jake reached for a pillow to prop up his hips. The new position exposed him, preparing him for assault. Damien breathed faster. Maybe he was nervous, but Jake doubted it.

His own cock throbbed with anticipation. Ignoring the ache, he spread Damien's cheeks and placed his tip at the tight entrance. He wasn't going to rush. This was the other man's first time. Whatever else they were doing here, Jake was damned if Damien wouldn't enjoy it.

"Bear down," he said. "That relaxes your muscles."

The second Damien did, he shoved his well-lubed tip inside.

Sensation spangled through his nerves at the sudden pressure around his glans. Mia inhaled, so she'd seen what he'd done. Jake pushed carefully farther into the smooth passage. Damien's body didn't resist. He moaned, writhing deliciously around him. A heartbeat later, Jake was fully surrounded.

He dropped to his elbows and nipped Damien's earlobe.

The CEO wriggled frenetically. He was definitely trying to get closer. "Shit. I didn't know it would feel so good."

"You didn't know it would feel so good, *what?*"

Damien laughed breathily. "All right. I didn't know it would feel so good, master."

That answer was sufficient. "You have a lot of nerves in your first inch or so. Under the right circumstances, they hook up to sexual sensations. You probably noticed that when I played with you in the shower."

"I . . . remember."

His voice was choppy, his urge to beg fighting with his struggle not to succumb. Jake decided to show pity. "Ready for me to move?"

Damien arched, the motion pushing his ass harder into Damien's groin. His loosely curled fingers turned into fists. To his credit he didn't immediately say *hell, yes.* "Am I . . . allowed to come?"

"You are." Jake pulled back gradually, noting the man's longing reaction. "However, you know you'll enjoy it more if you don't give in right away."

"Right," Damien said, not sounding so sure he could refrain.

Satisfied his condition was what it ought to be, Jake turned his attention to Mia. Her gaze was glued to the spot where his rigid cock was half drawn from of Damien. She bit the side of one finger.

"Mia," he said softly.

Her eyes jerked to his. The hypnotized look in them sent a jolt of pure lust through him. "Yes?"

"Spread your hand across the small of his back. I want you to feel me go in and out. I want you to know what me fucking Damien does to his body."

She placed her hand where he instructed, her palm crossing Damien's spine and the muscles that torqued his hips. She shuddered as she registered his sweat. Her nipples beaded tighter, the diamonds that hung around her neck flashing with her heartbeat. Sensing something going on, Damien turned his head to her. When he saw how she'd reacted, he reached for her upper thigh and squeezed.

The urge to touch her was understandable. The position she sat in exposed her sex. The gleam of liquid between her folds told both men how very wet she was. Jake's balls began to hurt from his eagerness. He wished he could fuck her and Damien— and not one at a time.

Since that wasn't possible, he orchestrated the next best thing.

"Slide two fingers into her pussy," he said to Damien. "Gently."

Damien didn't need the warning, but Jake enjoyed giving it. Two fingers curved into Mia's drenched passage, followed by his thumb tucking over her noticeably swollen clitoris. Mia gasped when he gave it a little rub.

Jake sensed she was still self-conscious.

"His hand is yours," he said. "Do with it what you like."

She cupped it, lightly covering Damien's fingers with hers. She looked at Jake. "*We're* yours," she asserted.

He hadn't expected that. Another jolt ran through him, a primitive satisfaction at the acknowledgement of his ownership.

Desire abruptly flared too high to control. His body wouldn't let him delay longer. He had to start this now.

He pushed his hips into Damien, thrilling to the man's grunt of surprised pleasure. He was hot inside, and Mia's hand between them made the long delicious thrust seem like a true claiming. Jake couldn't conquer Damien by himself. He didn't want to, if it came down to it. They both liked women: *this* woman. Mia made what they were doing feel like a complete vanquishing.

He crushed himself as deep as he could go. Damien's free hand fisted in the bed covers.

"Please," he gasped, his ass a hard cushion that rocked insistently back at Jake. "More of that."

Jake should have resisted. He was the master now. With any other partners, he could have. Then Mia made a sound as Damien began fingering her.

The devil on his shoulder said what could a few thrusts hurt? He gave Damien six, then seven, and then suddenly he was pumping hard and fast, bliss driving up his dick in waves. Damien groaned, his brow rolling from side to side on the bed as he strove to coordinate the hand that finger-fucked Mia.

He must have pulled it off. Jake knew the moment she forgot herself.

She lurched up onto her knees, clutching Damien's hand against her pussy, writhing on the fingers that penetrated her. Her hand still star-fished across the small of Damien's back, and she'd come close enough to bump Jake. She leaned her weight on her straight left arm. Damien seemed to like the pressure this put on him. He groaned louder, his pelvis struggling to tilt up to the angle that allowed Jake to penetrate most deeply.

Jake shifted tack to accommodate the implied request.

Damien let out a low growling noise. "Oh yes, *there*."

Jake's thrusts had found his prostate. He kept going, not caring that he ought to make Damien wait. His cock felt too good. Actually, his whole body did. He pumped and grunted and finally gripped Damien's hips to hitch them to exactly the right position for satisfying the screaming nerves of his dick and balls. He pummeled Damien's ass as forcefully as if he were spanking him. Excitement threatened to undo his control. He had to bite his cheek to keep from blasting every drop of seed that second.

"Beat him off," he ordered Mia, his voice gone harsh. "Reach under and tug his cock."

Mia obeyed, but it didn't feel like enough. Jake had to jack him too. He slapped his hand around Mia's, around the hot thick organ. Their fingers stacked like puzzle pieces meant to work together. Jake felt the knotted bowtie, the bondage *she'd* tied around Damien. It was tighter than ever on Damien's shaft, his extreme arousal causing it to constrict.

The final thread of Jake's control snapped.

He humped Damien so hard he could have been trying to stab the man. Damien sucked a great gulp of air, his passage clenching around Jake's cock. He was coming. The instant Jake's brain recognized this, his own orgasm exploded. Hot ecstasy flooded his body. Mia cried out sharp and high. Damien's fingers had brought her off. Jake's cock contracted more intensely, cum shooting copiously.

"God," Damien groaned, pushing toward Jake with all his strength. He was still going, pumping seed on the bedcovers.

A long ripping sound announced that he'd torn the sheet.

Damien collapsed and trembled, and Jake had to catch himself on his palms. Mia touched his arm.

She was utterly beautiful: part vulnerable doe and all gorgeous sex goddess. Even though he had no breath left, he needed to lean over and kiss her. Her lips clung to his as he cupped her cheek. Their tongues stroked together, their accelerated heartbeats vibrating through their mouths. His free hand fell to Damien's back, caressing the man's warm skin between his shoulder blades. Damien made a rumbly noise like he was happy. Mia pulled free of him.

He watched her lick his kiss from her lips and savor it.

"Doll," he said, knowing she liked the old-fashioned endearment. "You make a man feel lucky to be alive."

◆

Damien lay pole-axed for at least a minute before he could move again. Jake and Mia's bodies still touched his here and there. He heard their murmurs as they kissed, but they didn't bother him. Mia had kissed him too, not long ago. Jake had done way more than kiss him. He'd taken charge of Damien's body, giving and taking pleasure from it in ways that continued to shake it now. Damien tried to identify the feelings he experienced from all this. He was relaxed, he knew. And sexually replete. Something warmer hovered behind that, something that might have been comfort.

Maybe I feel safe, he thought.

That was a strange idea.

He scooted out from under them to sit up.

"How are you?" Mia asked.

He couldn't help it. His mouth stretched into a grin. "Good."

She grinned back. "You ripped the covers."

He glanced down at them, stunned to see it was true.

"I need to clean up," Jake said, arms lifted in a bone-cracking stretch. "Want me to bring back a towel?"

Damien agreed this would be pleasant. He wasn't sure how it happened; he didn't feel like he'd decided, but by the time Jake returned he and Mia lay on their sides gazing quietly at each other with the sheets pulled up to their waists. They weren't right against each other, but the position felt intimate. Without actually talking about it, they'd left space for Jake in the middle.

"We're staying?" Jake asked, tossing Damien a warm, barely damp washcloth.

Even as he used it, a powerful yawn seized his jaw.

"Sure," he said when he could, the idea of bunking with them suddenly more appealing than sending them away. "Tomorrow's Sunday. We can sleep in."

"Mm," Mia said. "I love sleeping in."

Jake playfully swatted her bottom as he climbed in. "Why doesn't that surprise me?"

He grabbed a pillow for himself, seeming completely comfortable as he arranged himself between them. He ended up with his head facing Damien.

"I've done this before," he reminded, easily reading Damien's expression.

"Not me," Mia said sleepily. "Up till now, I've only shared a bed with my college boyfriend and you."

Jake's startled look made Damien feel better about his own scant experience with sleepovers. His arm's length relationships with previous partners precluded them.

"I'm honored to be added to your list," he said.

Mia snickered. "Wait till I start snoring."

"She doesn't," Jake assured him.

Mia pretended to.

Her silliness amused him. Deciding he could do this, Damien

squirmed around to lay on his other side, his usual position for sleeping.

"Off," he commanded the light. The bulb obliged him by extinguishing.

The bed was big, but there were three of them.

"Here," Jake said, reaching behind him to pull Mia's arm around his waist. When she was settled to his liking, Jake rested his hand on Damien's back. He didn't ask permission or make a fuss. He just did it.

His thumb rubbed the skin it touched gently.

The contact felt fine. Casual. Friendly. Maybe even reassuring. Damien closed his eyes. He kept the penthouse cool, but human beings generated thermal energy. Despite only being covered by a sheet, the temperature of the bed was perfect.

"'Night," Mia said.

"'Night," Damien returned.

"Mmph," said Jake.

Damien smiled to himself. The realness of Jake's mumble was perfect too.

CHAPTER 14

MIA'S companions went unconscious before you could say *threesome*. Their breathing steadied and slowed and a last fraction of tension ran out of Jake's back muscles.

This left Mia awake alone.

How content she was to rest with the men concerned her. They'd settled together in Damien's bed too easily. Sure, Jake being worldly helped, but that wasn't the sole reason. She'd relaxed with Damien too. Lying there staring at him across the pillows hadn't been hard at all. The sex—well, she'd be delighted to repeat that. Damien was very good with his hands, especially considering what Jake had been doing to him at the time. Watching both men throw themselves into it had made her go off like a rocket.

Knowing they'd wanted that to happen, that her being there got them worked up too, was the icing on an already scrumptious cake.

Sadly, the arrangement she was getting so cozy with depended on a lie. Simple logic said it couldn't last much longer.

I have to know the truth, she thought. For all their sakes. Dragging out the situation would just cause a bigger mess.

She inched from the bed, aware that Jake at least was a light sleeper. She escaped without disturbing him. He'd only searched the office portion of Damien's house. She was no trained spy, but she could scout around the rest. Maybe her unprofessional eyes would spot something that hadn't occurred to him.

Because it seemed the quickest way to cover up, she grabbed Jake's discarded dress shirt from Damien's bathroom.

Even not naked, creeping around the giant, nearly empty penthouse was eerie. The only noise was the wind outside and

187

the occasional click and hum of hidden electronics. She took her time, trying to imagine what Damien would consider a secure but convenient spot to stash confidential things. She'd reached the entry before any possibilities jumped at her.

A ten-foot-tall aluminum wall set off the foyer. Shaped sort of like a comma, the round bit that formed the dot could have been a coat closet. If it were, the door was stealth, its curve fitting flush to that of the cylinder. Mia bent closer. A dark opening took the place of a knob. Inside it, she spied the reflective gleam of a palm reader.

She straightened and pinched her lip. Damien had added her and Jake's palm prints to his system so they could come and go via his front door. Would her print work on this reader, or would trying set off alarms? She could wait and ask Jake's opinion, but what if this was their best chance to check it out?

Crap, she thought and stuck her hand inside.

She nearly snatched it back when a blue scanner light came on. No klaxons started blaring, so she forced herself to stay motionless while the light rolled across her hand. A LED that had been invisible clicked green, but nothing else happened.

"Open," she said, remembering Damien's order to the bedside lamp.

With a soft hiss of air, the door retracted.

Inside wasn't a closet but a tube-shaped elevator large enough for four people. Mia entered cautiously. The dim illumination revealed three buttons: *P, O,* and *G.* She presumed *P* was "Penthouse," *G* "Garage, and probably *O* stood for "Office." Her trusty mental map said she was directly above Damien's suite on fifty-two. If she were him, she'd love being whisked straight to work from her apartment.

Maybe more importantly, if he had such easy, unobservable access, his office might not seem more public to him than his home. He could work on any project he wanted, any hour of the day or night—including projects he wanted to keep secret. He'd felt safe enough to play sex games at his desk, under a contract that forbade recording. Though he could have lied when he signed it, it seemed possible he had no surveillance at all in there.

The button marked *O* mocked her.

Do or do not, she challenged. Jake would probably risk it. Whether he'd want her to she didn't know.

Chances were no one would be on the corporate floor at this

hour. Even Damien's busy bee employees had limits. And if she were discovered by a wandering security guard, her current getup would support a story of being the boss's overly curious, insomniac girlfriend.

Mia almost lost her nerve at the prospect of being caught, but then she recalled Zoe Raeburn's dire prediction.

You'll see, she'd said. *One day you'll be lunching in his private office, thinking you've got him exactly where you want, and the next you're sobbing your heart out in a restroom.*

Something had happened on fifty-two that Zoe Raeburn was tangled in.

Mia jabbed O before she could stop herself.

The elevator sank so swiftly her heart lifted toward her throat.

The mechanism was as silent as Damien's electric cars. It stopped soon after starting without the slightest jolt. The door opened by itself.

She saw she'd reached his office, though the only light came from the city outside the tall windows. Her shoulder bumped something as she stepped out, causing glass to rattle. A liquor cabinet concealed the elevator, ensuring the private entrance stayed secret.

She glanced left, but the wall of glass between the office suite and the corridor was fogged. The area behind it was dark as well. As long as she kept the lights off in here, she ought to be safe from discovery.

This should have been a relief, but as she padded farther into the room, the back of her neck prickled. Damned if she didn't feel like someone was watching her.

That's just nerves, she told herself. *And maybe your guilty conscience.*

She didn't want to be spying on Damien. She'd have preferred their three-way romantic venture be absolutely real. She'd grown attached to him, and he certainly seemed trustworthy.

So prove it, she thought. *Prove he hasn't been duping everyone.*

She walked to where Damien had put the table for their initial lunch meeting. To her right, at the distant end of the room, the door to the dark bathroom gaped slightly. To her left, the curve of windows led to his sleek glass desk and a trio of tall shelves. Possibly Zoe had sat right where she was standing.

Mia tried to put herself in the other woman's shoes.

If Sam Raeburn's claim was true, she'd had the plan she'd stolen from Genbolt with her. Perhaps she'd thought of it as an offering to earn Damien's affection, to coax their dating-for-show relationship to the next level. Clearly, that hadn't worked. Raeburn said Damien seduced his daughter into stealing the schematic. Given what she'd come to know of the man, Mia had trouble believing that. Easier to believe Zoe had done it on her own initiative. Maybe, though, Damien was ambitious enough to keep the plan afterward. She'd seen firsthand that he and Raeburn hated each other. Could Damien have convinced himself holding onto the advantage was justified?

Her gaze drifted to the shelves that stood adjacent to Damien's desk. True to his fondness for breathing space between his belongings, the groups of books were spread apart. She imagined him working here in the middle of the night, dreaming up new rockets or supercars. If he rose from his chair and walked to the shelves, one cluster of books was at the perfect height for him to reach comfortably.

She went to it.

The books were antique and the titles all had to do with ships. She pulled them off the shelf one by one.

Even before she removed the last, her pulse went crazy. She'd found a safe set into the wall. Instead of a combination dial, it had a palm scanner—exactly like the ones for Damien's elevator and front door.

No, she thought. No way would her print give her access to this too. Damien would have excluded her from it . . . unless it hadn't occurred to him. By his own admission, he rarely entertained. She and Jake might be the only people he'd ever added to his house system.

She blew out her breath and dried her hand on Jake's shirt. She'd come this far. She might as well finish it.

Her hand shook when she flattened it on the screen.

As before, a blue light rolled over it and then a green LED came on. Her voice was so hoarse she had to say "open" twice.

The safe door clicked as its seal released. Mia swung it open and reached in.

The first object she pulled out was a thick manila folder about her. She rolled her eyes at the irony and set it aside. She already knew Damien had looked into her background. Her next catch felt more promising. It was a single sheet of thick paper, quite large and folded into four sections.

Mia spread it out on his desk, where the city's nearby skyscrapers provided just enough light to read. As she smoothed the creases, her stomach sank.

This was it, the same complicated circuit thingie Raeburn had shown her, except this plan was complete. Her finger slid to the upper right corner, her subconscious mind computing comparisons faster than her waking one. Okay, there were a few differences. The Genbolt logo had been removed from this version, and here and there in the margins cryptic notes were scribbled.

That the underlying design was identical Mia couldn't deny.

"Shit," she muttered beneath her breath.

She was so distracted she missed the nearly silent hiss of the elevator leaving and coming back. Her first clue that she should have paid attention was the lights snapping on.

Her head jerked up. Damien was stepping into the room. He'd pulled on his gray boxer briefs but that was all. She'd been right about one thing. He did regard this office as an extension of his home.

"What are you doing here?" he asked. "I woke up and you were gone."

Her mind raced for excuses, but she knew none of them would work. The safe was open behind her. She had the stolen plans spread out on his desk.

"I can't believe you did it," she said.

"Did what?" he asked.

He still didn't look suspicious. *Enjoy this moment,* she told herself. *In half a second, he'll know what you've done.*

She swallowed and felt a lump. "You stole the specs for the navigation system Genbolt is developing. Or maybe Zoe Raeburn stole them. I can't decide if you asked her to or not. I'd like to think you wouldn't deliberately turn a woman against her own father."

Damien came to a halt on the other side of the desk. He was squinting in confusion, possibly too sleepy to add her words together. He looked at the page her fingers were resting on. His brows furrowed as his gaze met hers.

"That's not Genbolt's," he said. "I came up with that design myself. Why are you even—" He stopped speaking as a series of thoughts rolled rapidly behind his face. His expression sharpened. "Jesus, he's trying it again. That bastard hired you to spy on me. You and Jake together!"

Mia wished she could deny this, but she had her own grievances to air. "Obviously, Raeburn had cause to hire us. He showed me this design. Half of it anyway. It's a match except for you erasing his logo. Whatever rivalry you're playing out between you, that's no excuse for keeping what doesn't belong to you."

"It does belong to me!" Damien said. "He sold Zoe the same lie. I left her alone in here for five minutes, and she faxed half of it to him. On my own damn machine. Raeburn couldn't show you the whole schematic because it was never his." He caught sight of the open safe and waved angrily at it. "The lock I had then wasn't as secure. Then again, what good does security do when you trust the wrong people?"

Mia ignored that sting. "Why would Zoe steal half a plan?"

"Because partway through she realized what you haven't, apparently. This is my draftsmanship, my handwriting." He grabbed a pen and flipped the page over, scribbling a quick formula on it.

"Look," he insisted.

Mia didn't need to bend the paper back to compare. The lettering was the same, even the energy of the strokes. Damien had written the cryptic notes *and* the original plan. Raeburn must have added the Genbolt logo.

"When Zoe realized her father deceived her, she stopped what she was doing. She confessed everything to me. That's why she's been calling me. She wants me to forgive her."

"Oh my God," Mia said. "Damien, I'm so sorry. I got this all backwards."

Damien's eyes met the plea in hers icily. She knew the axe had only begun to fall. Damien was too intelligent not to put everything together.

"You never lost your job, did you?" he said. "The drama you staged at Audition was a con. Raeburn hired your PI boss to sic you and Jake on me. That memory of yours is as good as a camera. You must have patted yourselves on the back when I fell for it. Your boss knew exactly what I'd go for. I bet he took notes on everyone he saw me with at Diogenes. I couldn't have been a bigger patsy if I'd tied myself in a bow. —Oh wait, I let you do that to me."

His tone was sardonic and self-loathing. Mia couldn't bear to hear it. "Curtis didn't think you were a patsy. And he knew you might not have done it. He thought the technology sounded important enough to be sure, one way or another."

"Important enough to lie to me."

"I feel really bad about that. I felt even worse when I thought you were guilty. I wanted you to be innocent."

"And somehow that doesn't make me feel better." He looked at her, his hazel eyes so piercing she gripped the desk's edge to brace herself. What he said next was every bit as bad as she feared. "I want you and Jake out of here. Go upstairs, pack your things, and go."

"We weren't trying to hurt you," she pleaded. "Jake and I genuinely like you. What we shared tonight was absolutely not a lie."

"I don't doubt you enjoyed it," he said coolly. "I did myself. The fact remains, however, that both of you betrayed me."

"I know this has happened to you before, but we—"

"Just go." He cut her off to point toward the elevator. Few men could have looked that dignified in their underwear. Mia realized he wasn't going to listen to her apology, no more than he'd listened to Zoe's. He couldn't let himself forgive her—even if he wanted to. Too many people he should have been able to trust had failed him.

She started walking but stopped and turned. Everything about him seemed angry and terrible. She'd done this to him, in spite of how much she cared.

"What are you going to do?" she asked miserably.

His beautiful face tightened. "I'm going to do my damnedest to forget we ever met."

◆

Jake didn't expect to fall asleep with two people and wake with none. For one thing, he didn't usually sleep that soundly.

He sat up and checked the mattress. Though the side where Mia had lain was cool, warmth lingered on Damien's. That caused a small alarm to start sounding in his head. Wherever they were, they hadn't left at the same time. He fought to control his unease as he swung out of bed. Probably Mia had left to pee or maybe get a snack.

She wouldn't sneak off to play detective by herself. Not

when Damien might get up and look for her.

She wasn't in the bathroom and neither was his shirt. Because his trousers were there, he pulled them on. He padded to the kitchen but had no luck. He scrubbed the back of his neck. Could the pair have gone out on the terrace?

A barely audible hiss drew him to the entryway. An elevator he hadn't known existed was opening in the curved separator wall. Mia stepped out, looking upset.

"What's going on?" he asked.

Mia pressed her lips together and shook her head.

That really worried him. He took her shoulders between his hands. She was wearing his shirt. A little part of his brain had a second to be pleased by that. The second ended when she burst into tears.

"Sweetie," he said, cuddling her against him. "Tell me what happened."

"He caught me," she sobbed. "I found the plan in his office and he caught me."

This was *not* good news, but Jake rubbed her back anyway. "Where is Damien?"

"Still on fifty-two." She pushed back to drag her hands down her teary face. "We were wrong, Jake. He didn't steal the circuit thingie from Raeburn. Raeburn tried to get Zoe to steal it from Damien."

"You're sure? He didn't just say that to fob you off?"

She nodded like an earnest child. "The plan was in his handwriting. He made a sample while I watched. Fuck. I should have thought to get one before." She was sniffling and wiped her nose on her sleeve. "Shit. Sorry. This is your shirt."

In spite of everything, he laughed. "Never mind that. I take it he was angry when he realized what we'd done."

"He told us to pack our things and go!" Her voice cracked and she had to dry her eyes again.

"Did he say he was calling the police?"

This question made Mia stop and think. "No. He should have, though, shouldn't he?"

"Maybe not. We are his guests. He might not want this laundry aired publically."

"He also didn't warn me not to give the whole plan to Raeburn. Zoe only stole half before she figured out her dad's game. Damien knows about my memory. He knows I could copy it."

"Maybe he knows you wouldn't. However furious he is about our deception, he's learned a thing or two about your character."

"Maybe." She looked at her feet as if she were ashamed. "He was hurt, Jake. He really feels betrayed."

They knew he might. That's how it worked in the spy business. Rather than remind her of that, Jake stroked her hair. He guessed she'd gotten pretty attached, even in so short a time. Maybe he had himself. His chest felt uncomfortably hollow as he let out a sigh.

"Let's go pack," he said. "Like Damien wants. We need to talk to Curtis. Decide how we're going to handle Sam Raeburn."

"Jake—"

"I know. You liking him makes it hard."

"Damien didn't believe me when I said we both did. He thought it was only sex."

Jake knew he shouldn't encourage her. Lies like the ones they'd told were rarely pardoned. This was Mia, though, who loved novels with happy endings and whose spirit practically shot rainbows. He used his thumbs to brush wetness from her cheeks. "He's angry, Mia, and the wound is fresh. He won't know what he believes for a while."

"He's not a forgiver," she said, wagging her head dolefully.

Jake pulled her close again and hugged her. "We'll see," he said, his cheek pressed into her hair. "You may be more forgivable than you realize."

♦

Damien must not have wanted to have it out with them face to face. Jake and Mia finished packing without him reappearing in the penthouse. Jake left a Post-It for him in the kitchen, explaining that he was driving Mia home in the W-22 but would arrange for the car to be returned soon. He debated adding an apology then simply signed his initials.

Mia left her diamond rope necklace coiled on the counter beside the note.

Jake called Curtis en route to Mia's place. Though their employer had been asleep, he met them there. The way Mia flung herself into Curtis's arms to cry reminded Jake they viewed each other as family—and that in some ways Mia was still a kid. Curtis soothed and patted and tucked her into bed. When he bent down to kiss her forehead, Jake's throat tightened.

Curtis came out of the bedroom and shut the door behind him.

"Wow," he said. "She really liked that guy."

Jake didn't think the sentiment was past tense. "I think he really liked her too."

"Hence the 'never darken my door again' parting."

Jake sighed. "I made coffee. You want some?"

"Sure." Curtis let out his own resigned exhalation. "It's not like I'll get the chance to finish that dream I was having."

They sat together at Mia's small table.

"How do you plan to handle Raeburn?" Jake asked.

Curtis riffled his red-gold stubble with the back of his fingernails. "I'll tell him we tried to get the evidence he wanted but came up empty. Maybe he'll buy that Mia got too nervous to continue. Hopefully, giving back his money will smooth his feathers some."

Jake recalled the temper Genbolt's head honcho displayed at the charity function. "That might be optimistic."

Curtis shrugged. "I'll play it by ear. I can blow smoke with the best of them. And as long as he doesn't figure out we know the truth, I don't think he'll kick up too bad."

Jake rubbed the rim of his coffee mug. "I know a few ears I could discreetly drop that truth in. It seems wrong for Raeburn to get off scot free."

"Let's sit on that option for the moment. I don't want us to get a rep for violating client privilege. Plus, Call is no helpless lamb. He can report Raeburn himself if it suits him. He has friends in government."

Jake supposed he did. The situation just bugged him.

"There is one good thing about this," Curtis said. "The two of you can come back to work. The office was too damn quiet with just me in it."

"Aw," Jake said, feigning sympathy. "You should have borrowed a dog from the grooming place."

"Careful," Curtis responded. "I might decide to replace with you with a real bloodhound."

His coffee finished, he pushed back and rose from his chair. When his gaze slid to Mia's shut bedroom door, he pinched his lip in concern.

"I can stay with her tonight," Jake said.

Curtis turned back and considered him. His crystal green eyes were uncomfortably observant.

"She's upset," Jake said.

"Uh-huh. And this assignment didn't change your relationship with her at all."

"Well, sure it did. Some."

"I saw that 'some' the second you helped her out of Call's fancy car. You treated her like she was made of glass."

"She's a kid. She hurt someone she cared about and she's feeling bad."

Curtis opened his mouth as if to argue but then decided to drop it. "How about I pick you both up here tomorrow? We'll have breakfast and talk this thing through with clearer heads."

By *thing*, Jake hoped he meant the aborted job. "Make it lunch," he said. "Mia and I had a hell of a night."

◆

Mia slept late and still felt like crap. Her throat was sore from crying and her eyes felt boiled. Too depressed to care, she shuffled through her morning routine listlessly. Damien's enraged, wounded face kept rising in her mind, his final words echoing in her ears.

I'm going to do my damnedest to forget we ever met.

When she discovered Curtis had drunk the last of her coffee cream, it was the final straw. Jake hadn't noticed. He took it black.

"I'll get more," he volunteered.

It wasn't rational, but she hated him right then. He'd spent the night on her couch and not with her in her bed—like the job was over and now so were they. He didn't seem upset about Damien. As far as she could tell, his only worry was that she'd throw another sobbing fit like last night.

"*I'll* go," she said, grabbing a light sweater. "The store's only down the street, and I could use the air."

"It's no problem."

"I said I'll go," she snapped when he rose from the chair. "Jesus, I won't have a breakdown from walking down the street."

Hurt crossed his face, something she couldn't recall seeing on it before. Great. Now she was being a bitch to him as well.

"Sorry," she said, touching his arm. "I just need a little room."

The walk did her more good than she expected. It was a beautiful Sunday morning: sunny and finally warm. Because she didn't actually hate Jake, she picked up a bagel and newspaper as a peace offering. She and Jake could go back to being friends if he insisted. Mia would just torment him by wearing bondage-themed clothes to work.

Maybe she'd start walking to the office in gladiator sandals. She could unlace them re-a-lly slowly at her desk.

She was smiling at that idea when the back doors to a florist van opened. The vehicle was double-parked slightly ahead of her on the block. Two big men hopped out, dressed like delivery guys often did in jeans and logo shirts.

A bucket of fresh daffodils caught her eye.

One of the men stepped into her path. Suddenly, she noticed the delivery guys had matching beards and sunglasses. That wasn't quite usual.

A millisecond later, she observed another, considerably more significant detail. The man who'd blocked her had a gun tucked into the front of his jeans waistband.

He put his hand on its metal butt. "Come with us," he said.

Mia dropped her bag and ran.

She got two steps before the other man caught her. He grabbed her right off her feet, one hand clapping over her mouth to prevent her from screaming. She tried to anyway, kicking and thrashing with all her might. Neither of the men seemed very concerned by this.

The first man was already in the van bay.

"Get her in here," he said to his cohort.

The second hoisted her and himself up. As he did, Mia used a burst of determination to kick the heavy bucket of daffodils out into the street. The bucket fell with a great *sploosh* of water, the flower bunches scattering out in their cellophane wrappers. The man who held her looked at them.

"Leave it," the first man ordered. "We need to go."

He closed the doors. The engine was already running. Whoever drove put the van in motion without delay. The first man produced a roll of silver duct tape. Mia knew it was for securing her. Her body shook all over, her burst of adrenaline crashing. She wanted to resist but wasn't accomplishing anything by fighting.

"Good," said her first abductor when she stopped. He

dragged out a length of tape, severing it with his teeth.

"Pat her down for a phone," said his accomplice. "We don't want it pinging the cell towers."

Crap. Mia thought. She didn't have a phone. She'd only been walking down the block.

The entire kidnapping hadn't taken a whole minute.

CHAPTER 15

JAKE recognized Curtis's *shave and a haircut* honk. Since Mia wasn't back from the store, he grabbed her extra keys and trotted down.

Curtis drove a black '06 Lincoln LS. According to him, the model was just old enough to blend in anywhere. When Jake arrived, Curtis leaned out the window. The aviators he pulled off were more stylish than the car.

"Where's Mia?"

"Store," Jake said. "You used the last of her . . ."

He trailed off and glanced down the street. She wasn't among the scattering of pedestrians on the sidewalk. She'd left a quarter of an hour ago. He supposed she might be dawdling on account of being annoyed with him . . .

"What?" Curtis asked.

Jake's brain jumped to a split-second conclusion.

"Something's wrong," he said, already jogging toward the corner.

He sped up as he heard Curtis get out behind him. The convenience store was small. It took three seconds to scan it from the door. Mia wasn't inside.

He raised his voice to get the male cashier's attention. "Has Mia Beck been here? Yea high. Dark hair. Came in to buy cream."

"Mia was here," the young man agreed, so Jake guessed he knew the store's regulars. "She left a while ago."

Jake's heart gave a sickening thump.

"Out here," Curtis called. "I found her shopping bag. With her wallet still in it."

Jake had sprinted right by the thing. Inside the eco-friendly canvas tote was a cream carton, a paper-wrapped bagel, and a *New York Times*. Mia hated the *Times*. She must have bought it for him. It was the most useless reaction ever, but for just a second his eyes stung.

He blinked and spotted the next item of discouraging evidence.

"Flowers," he said, pointing them out to his companion. "Fresh ones."

The large plastic bucket lay on its side in the street, the pool of water it had contained not quite finished running off. Curtis stared down at it with him. Was it an accident that the flowers were daffodils? That had been Mia's safe word. Had she been trying to leave a sign?

"She's been grabbed," he said.

"By Call?" Curtis asked. "Is he that hung up on her?"

"By Raeburn," he said, sure of it. "Somehow he figured out she had eyes on Damien's design."

"Shit." Curtis dug out his cell, his thumb starting to press 9.

"No." Jake appropriated the phone to punch in a number of his choosing. "The police are too slow. We'll waste time convincing them she hasn't wandered off. I'm calling Damien. He can task a satellite to find her. Or, hell, send out a fleet of drones."

"You're sure we can trust him?"

"My gut's sure. He'll want to help her, no matter how mad he is."

The line was ringing. His gut would have to be good enough.

◆

Damien was working out his anger on his at-home punching bag. He cursed when his cell phone rang but went to look at it. The call could be business. His rage over his gullibility shouldn't make him neglect that.

The caller ID said *Curtis Ewing*. That was Mia's former and—he supposed—current boss. He growled at the likelihood that he wouldn't enjoy the conversation then accepted the call anyway.

Hearing Jake's voice and what it had to say dropped him on his ass on his workout area's weight bench. Mia had been snatched? And Jake wanted him to help?

"Give me ten minutes," he said when Jake seemed to be finished. "I'll get back to you with news."

He rang off. The iciness of his face warned him he was in shock. He forced himself to concentrate. WorldWide had a satellite, but tasking it wouldn't be instantaneous. Sending out a wave of drones did no good unless they knew where to search, plus he'd be stuck here operating them. Another option occurred to him. It wasn't comfortable, but he thought it had a better chance to produce positive results.

He gritted his teeth and dialed Zoe Raeburn's personal cell number. She was sure to take him calling as a sign he was coming around romantically. Fuck it, though. If it got them what they needed, he didn't care.

Zoe picked up on the second ring.

"Zoe," he said before she could speak. "This is important. Your father kidnapped the woman you met in the bathroom at the scholarship fundraiser. He thinks she memorized the blueprint you tried to steal from me. I need to know where he'd feel comfortable taking her to interrogate."

Naturally, Zoe didn't accept this without question—despite knowing what her father was capable of. Damien attempted to convince her as efficiently as he could.

A hanging silence suggested he'd gotten through.

"If I tell you, will you see me again?"

Damien leaned forward to squeeze his temples. A big part of him wanted to say he'd do anything she wanted, as long as it saved Mia. He reminded himself showing weakness wasn't a smart negotiating stance.

"Is that how you want to do this?" he asked. "To blackmail me into dating you? I thought you *weren't* your father's daughter."

"Maybe I just have more faith in us than you do."

He tried to blow out his breath silently. "I told you, Zoe, there never was an 'us.' A woman's life is at stake."

"The woman you replaced me with," she retorted. Her gusty sigh forestalled him from arguing more. "Fine. Dad bought an abandoned paper mill in New Jersey a month ago. He's planning to convert the property but hasn't done it yet. The place is empty. There's nothing near it but a buckled two lane and pinewoods. If I wanted to go Gitmo on someone, that's where I'd take them."

Damien suspected she enjoyed the twinge her mention of Gitmo would give him. Zoe was no monster, but she wasn't a saint either. Ignoring that, he got the best directions she could supply, given that she didn't have an exact address.

Now all he had to do was break the news to Jake that he was coming too.

◆

In addition to duct taping her immobile, Mia's captors had dropped a hood over her head. The van drove for quite a while before she was taken out. They didn't cut the tape off her ankles and let her walk. Instead, they gripped her beneath the arms and hauled her, feet trailing in the dirt, into what seemed like a large building. The noises the men made dragging her in echoed. She strained to hear other sounds—traffic, people—but wasn't rewarded. A door on a track slid grittily shut. She smelled mildew and chemicals. She was placed in a chair and secured with more tape to it.

Finally, they pulled off the burlap hood.

The light wasn't bright but it still hurt her eyes. When her vision cleared, she saw she sat in a defunct paper factory. Giant rolls of newsprint moldered to her right on huge machines. The strutted ceiling was high above her and the floor below cracked cement. Her chair was pulled up to an old steel table. Sheets of paper lay across it, along with a cardboard box of used #2 pencils.

Okay. Mia could guess where this was going. Though the knowledge didn't improve her situation, it steadied her a bit. One of her abductors tore the tape off her mouth. Mia worked her stiff jaw. She concluded there was no point in screaming.

"We meet again," said a familiar voice.

Sam Raeburn must have been standing behind her. He pulled out the opposite chair and sat. If Mia hadn't been expecting him, she might not have recognized him in his humble garb of faded flannel shirt and chinos. He seemed broader without his suits, more like the old school thug she supposed he was at heart.

His cool blue eyes were just as she remembered.

She struggled to speak calmly. "I guess this means Curtis broke the news that we can't complete your assignment."

Raeburn smiled faintly. "I guess this means I didn't believe him." He gestured for someone out of view to come closer. "Please repeat to Miss Beck what you told me."

One of Raeburn's flunkies pulled Miss DeWinter to his side of the table.

The appearance of Damien's besotted executive assistant was a surprise, as was her condition. The plunging gold gown that had made her look so glamorous at the charity dinner was considerably worse for wear. More than one bout of tears seemed to have smeared her makeup, and her usually sleek russet waves had straggled beyond repair.

The hold Raeburn's man had on her slender arm added to the impression that she might not be here voluntarily.

"Jesus," Mia burst out. "Are you okay?"

"*Slut*," was Ms. DeWinter's feral response to that.

"Now, now," Raeburn soothed. "Just tell her what you saw."

"You broke into his office!" she accused. "You tricked him into putting your palm print in his system: you and that horrible Jake person. I saw everything from his bathroom while I waited for him to come back."

"You were hiding in his bathroom?"

"I was *waiting*," she said haughtily. "I had to straighten out our misunderstanding. He knew I still my access card. He *meant* for me to speak to him."

This was a bigger load of crazy than Mia could argue with. "Why tell Mr. Raeburn what you saw?"

"He'd approached me before. He knew Mr. Call relies on me. He thought I'd get him what he wanted, but I was loyal."

"Not this time, though."

Ms. DeWinter tossed her head. "Someone has to put you in your place."

Ms. DeWinter seemed not to understand she was now sharing that *place* with Mia. Or maybe she did. The assistant was pretty good at denying obvious things.

Raeburn appeared to have enjoyed this exchange.

"There you have it," he said. "I know you've got what I want inside that interesting head of yours. All that remains is for you to put it on paper."

Mia suspected once she did she was toast. She knew Damien was the plan's true creator, and that made her a liability. To make things trickier, now that she saw the lengths Raeburn would go to get it, she realized the navigation thingie must be pretty damn important. Even if she believed he'd let her go afterward—an increasingly unlikely scenario—she didn't dare hand it off to him. Maybe he'd simply take credit for designing the system, or maybe he'd do something worse.

When he and Damien butted heads at the charity dinner, Damien claimed Genbolt had already behaved in ways that weren't in the best interest of U.S. troops. Her present situation made the assertion even more credible. This was cutting edge technology. What if Raeburn sold it to the highest bidder?

Mia didn't want to be responsible for betraying her own country.

Hopelessness threatened to overwhelm her, but she fought it. *You just need to stall,* she told herself. *Jake and Curtis will find you soon.* They were smart. They'd realize she'd been taken.

"Not to be trite," she said. "But you can't get away with this."

"Can't I?" Raeburn asked. "We're in the middle of nowhere. No one knows where you or Ms. DeWinter is. I have all the time in the world to convince you to cooperate."

He couldn't believe that. He had to know Jake and Curtis would search for her.

Before she could decide if she should say so, he folded his big hands on the table and leaned closer. "Fortunately, I don't need all the time in the world. My associates—" he nodded toward her captors "—possess a number of enhanced interrogation skills. Do you honestly think it would take more than ten minutes of waterboarding to break a sweet little girl like you?"

One of his associates cracked his knuckles. Mia couldn't contain a shiver. She'd seen news footage of that form of torture and had been horrified. She couldn't swear she'd stand five minutes of simulated drowning.

Sadly, Raeburn had no trouble reading her reaction.

"You know," he said, "I suspected we'd end up here the moment I saw you with Call at that charity dinner. I tried to warn you, but you wore your heart on your sleeve the same as my daughter. Women never understand men like him don't commit."

That's what his talk about Damien changing up his type had been aiming at? To prove he was a playboy?

"I thought you didn't recognize me that night," she said. "You're a better actor than I realized."

"You're not the first to underestimate me," he said blandly. He took one of the pencils from the cardboard box and laid it in front of her on the top sheet of blank paper. "Now, shall my associate free your hand, or will we be doing this the hard way?"

Shit, Mia thought. Raeburn was an engineer, not as brilliant as Damien, but he'd know if she presented him with a copy that made no sense. Though she racked her brain, she couldn't think how else to delay.

"Cut me loose," she surrendered.

One of the goons moved to do it. Both had taken off their sunglasses. Maybe it was the effect of their matching beards, but they looked alike enough to be brothers. Once her right hand was free, Mia shook the circulation back into her fingers. So nervous she felt sick with it, she picked up the pencil.

She was immediately sorry Raeburn had seen her do this trick before. When she failed to sketch quickly enough to suit him, one of his associates "encouraged" her with his fist.

The fact that Ms. DeWinter had enough humanity to flinch didn't make her feel better.

◆

Jake didn't have many buddies, but he'd kept one from his training days at The Farm. Sawyer Hayes ran a security firm loosely headquartered in New Jersey. He did "tricky" private jobs, including for Uncle Sam if and when requested. Jake had barely finished explaining their situation when Sawyer volunteered himself and an employee to rescue Mia.

He arrived in a dusty off-road pickup with enough equipment stowed in the cargo bed compartment to wage war on an army of corrupt moguls.

Because Sawyer wasn't the type to let another man take the wheel, Jake squeezed into the crew cab with the others as a passenger. The drive to the location Damien obtained from Zoe felt like it was multiplied by ten. Jake knew he was annoying his seat companions, but his nerves weren't in a state that allowed him to sit still. If anything happened to Mia . . .

He didn't want to finish that statement. Truthfully, he wasn't sure what he'd do. Mia *meant* things to him no one had before.

Ironically, what kept him from disintegrating was Damien's outward calm. Though the CEO had to be nervous, he had sufficient ice in his veins—or maybe sufficient emotional distance—to keep from fidgeting.

If he could keep it together, Jake would too.

They stopped short of their destination to pull off the two-lane and under cover of the pines. Damien took out the little spy plane and laptop controller he'd obligingly brought along.

"Give me fifteen," he said to Sawyer with his not so playful toy underneath one arm. "I'll pinpoint the target and you can decide the best way for us approach."

Sawyer pulled a face that told Jake he didn't like Damien's use of the word *us*. Jake understood his reluctance to involve a civilian in an op but wasn't inclined to intervene. Regarding the drone at least, Damien knew what he was doing.

If they could take Raeburn by surprise, they ought to.

Fortunately, Damien's reconnoitering took ten minutes and not fifteen. From the drone's bird's eye perspective, the paper plant was easily identifiable.

Adding to the evidence that they had the right place, the florist van that abducted Mia hadn't been concealed. The camera confirmed its presence, also sending back footage of the terrain around the derelict factory. Though they didn't know how many hostiles were inside, the single guard they spotted on patrol shouldn't be hard to disable.

Despite how useful this all was, Sawyer remained grumpy.

"I'm not staying with the truck," Damien informed him, his gaze rock steady as he stared down the scowling man. "The smart choice is to keep the drone up until the last minute, so you know if circumstances change. You need me to operate it. Plus, I'll carry the screen."

He lifted the laptop to demonstrate.

Sawyer refused to look grateful. "I'm not arming you. And no arguments about vesting up."

"Agreed." Damien's sculpted lips twitched the tiniest bit. "I should probably inform you I brought my own pistol."

"Jesus H," was Sawyer's response to that.

Jake guessed his old friend decided to let the debate go. He returned to Jake to gear up.

"I don't like it," he muttered as he shrugged an M16 over his hard-as-granite shoulder. "You I trust. Curtis I've drunk and gone hunting with. This yahoo is a complete stranger."

The *yahoo* was wrestling with the straps of a black flak jacket. Since Damien had probably never worn a ballistic vest, his awkwardness was understandable. Sawyer jerked his head impatiently toward his employee, whose name he hadn't seen fit to share. The silent, fit-looking man went to help Damien.

"He's not a complete stranger," Jake pointed out. "You know

who he is."

"And that's another thing," Sawyer griped. "Since when do you hang with billionaires?"

Since they're so freaking kinky hot, was the thought that rolled through mind.

"Mia matters to him," he said aloud. "And he can take orders."

"Oh can he?" Sawyer snickered, knowing a bit about Jake's side interest.

"Order him toward the back," Jake suggested. "I know you'd rather hogtie him to the bumper, but if you let him come, he'll owe you. Just think how many more toys he's invented or can dream up."

Sawyer's eyes took on a speculative gleam. "If Damien Call gets killed, two zillion people will shit their pants. You're gonna have to explain it."

"Agreed," Jake said as lightly as he could.

His sudden and intense discomfort at the thought of Damien dying told him something he hadn't admitted to himself. For no reason he could explain, the realization that he had *more* at risk than just Mia calmed his nerves. He was ready to do this.

"We need to go," Curtis interrupted, his face ten years older from the hardness that had gripped it. "Mia's plucky but she's no G.I. Jane. If Raeburn tortures her to get what he wants, she'll never be the same."

"All right," Sawyer said, relinquishing his irritation over Damien. "Let's put this fat cat down."

He didn't mean *down* as in *in the ground*. He meant out of commission. In that moment, the fact that Jake was okay with either didn't cause him much concern.

◆

Mia dragged out her designated task as long as Raeburn let her get away with it. She asked for water and was given it. Ditto for pauses to shake out her cramping hand. The blueprint was large and complicated, which helped somewhat. The simple physical act of recreating it took time. Finally, though, she was done.

She slid the completed drawing reluctantly across the table to Genbolt's CEO, who turned the sheet around to study it right side up. He'd brought the half he'd shown her earlier for comparison. He stood up to pour over them side by side.

Mia fought not to squirm. The longer this took, the better.

The silence allowed her to inventory her assorted aches and pains. Her head was throbbing and her feet had fallen asleep due to the tightness of the duct tape. Thanks to her periodic "encouragements" from the bearded flunkies, one of her eyes had puffed shut. She didn't think the man had meant to strike her there. She'd needed both eyes to work. She'd simply cringed in the wrong direction at just the right moment. The blows to her cheek, on the other hand, had been intentional. Where the skin had split, blood trickled slowly down her skin. The warm syrup sensation was peculiar.

She wondered if she looked like a horror movie set at IHOP.

Her desire to laugh warned her she was in shock—literally punch drunk, she guessed.

Keep it together, she thought. Her brain was the best defense she had.

Raeburn appeared to have finished comparing her drawing with his half version. He squinted at the new bits.

"What's this?" he demanded, pointing at a formula.

Mia met his suspicious eyes and shrugged. She prayed he couldn't see how fast her heart was beating. "I'm not a scientist. I just redrew what I saw."

"Don't play games with me. I've already proved I'll do what it takes to get this out of you."

"Maybe Damien's ideas are too advanced for you to understand."

Her scorn for him had crept into her voice. Raeburn pinned her with a cold stare.

Mia shifted on her hard chair. "If you don't believe me, call one of your experts."

Raeburn's grimace said maybe he couldn't loop in his employees. They might not know about his more questionable business practices. Mia hoped this was the case, but then he snapped his fingers at one of his associates. "Take a picture of this with your burner phone. Send it to Kozlov for an opinion."

When he turned back to her, Mia put on her calmest face, praying she'd gotten better at acting in the last few days. She didn't know what Raeburn's tech would say. Damien was an honest-to-God genius. His plan *might* be too advanced for the scientists at Genbolt to decipher.

Raeburn continued to stare at her while his associate made

the call. She didn't like the attention, but chances were the blood and the swelling of her eye made it hard to read her thoughts. Where were Curtis and Jake anyway? She'd like to be rescued now, thank you.

"Boss," said the bearded guy. "Reception in here is crap. I need to try from outside."

"Go," Raeburn said. "I'll keep an eye on her."

A bead of sweat rolled down the channel of Mia's spine. Her right arm had been cut loose to make the drawing. She'd drawn it back from the table, and her free hand rested on her thigh. When it curled into an anxious fist, she realized she still held a pencil. Was it sharp enough to attack Raeburn? Could she lure him close enough to her chair to try? No doubt Jake knew a dozen ways to kill a man with a writing implement.

Next chance she got, Mia would ask him to teach her one.

"I'm not going anywhere," she began to say.

"I hear something," Ms. DeWinter interrupted—for which helpfulness Mia could happily have used the pencil on her.

Raeburn pulled a gun from where he'd tucked it beneath the back of his flannel shirt. He pointed it at the door the guy with the phone had left from.

"Don't shoot," that same fellow said.

He had his hands up. A man Mia didn't know was marching him back into the building. He'd jabbed a semiautomatic pistol tight to the flunky's neck, effectively turning his prisoner into his shield. This seemed a good development to Mia, except the second bearded guy had drawn his gun now too. He and Raeburn aimed determinedly at the man in the flak jacket.

"Drop it," the newcomer ordered. "If you fire, I'll make you shoot him and then I'll shoot you."

"I can get him," the second bearded guy murmured to Raeburn. He looked like he could. His arm muscles bunched as he sighted.

"He said drop it," a new voice repeated behind them.

Mia's head jerked around. For a second, all she could see was Jake. His shoulder braced a black military rifle, which he squinted down like he meant business. He wasn't the person who'd spoken. That was another man she didn't know. To her amazement, Damien stood behind both, pointing his smaller gun two-handed. He was pale but determined.

Her heart jumped crazily. He'd come to save her too?

"Do you need to hear it a third time?" Curtis asked. "Drop. The fucking. Guns."

Mia's usually charming boss stepped out from the shadows between two giant paper machines, also armed and aiming his M16 like he'd held one before. Mia barely recognized him. He looked so hard and serious.

The bad guys must have thought he was serious too. Since they were surrounded, the second bearded guy put his hands up, crouching slowly to place his weapon on the floor. Mia *almost* had a chance to relax.

"No!" Ms. DeWinter cried, completely freaking Mia out by darting over to pick up the surrendered gun.

Mia guessed she *really* didn't want to see Mia end up on top.

As the secretary grabbed the gun and turned, a rifle let out a single bark, taking the Ms. DeWinter in the shoulder. The feat of marksmanship came too late. The standoff was broken. Raeburn hadn't put down his pistol yet. He twisted around to point it at the men behind Mia. His trigger finger tightened and her brain went white. She didn't even think. She flung herself desperately forward, still taped within the chair. Her shoulder hit the steel table slightly beneath its edge. Her feet had just enough leverage to slam her weight upward and turn the thing over.

Raeburn's gun exploded, but the upended table had already crashed into him. He stumbled, Ms. DeWinter screamed, and bearded guy number two flattened himself on the floor with his hands stacked behind his head.

"Go, go, go," urged one of her rescuers.

The building's cavernous acoustics made it sound like a hundred boots ran at once. Thirty seconds later, all the bad guys were controlled, their wrists and feet being trussed in zip ties by the men who'd wrangled them to the floor. Mia was pretty trussed up herself. She'd fallen on her side with the chair attached to her.

As she wriggled to get loose, she was a little disappointed she hadn't got the chance to attack someone with her pencil.

"Hey, sweetie," Curtis said, coming over to help her. He tipped her up and stroked her hair from her face. His first good look at her shocked him. "Holy shit. Mia."

"I'm okay," she said, irrationally embarrassed. "Nothing's broken. He just gave me a black eye."

"And a split cheek and a busted lip."

"Stand back," Jake said. "I want to cut that tape off her."

His face was coldly angry. For no reason she could explain this opened the floodgates on her emotions.

"Jake," she exclaimed, her tears spilling out. "I'm so happy to see you."

"Sheesh," Curtis said, backing off to give Jake room.

"You too," she added. "Thank you for rescuing me."

Curtis laughed as Jake sliced through the tape with a box cutter. "I'll check on the crazy chick in the evening gown, the one Sawyer's employee winged."

Right then, Ms. DeWinter wasn't Mia's main concern.

"Is Damien okay? Did Raeburn hit him?"

"He missed," Jake assured her. "Your quick thinking spoiled his aim." He'd crouched down to free her ankles but now he rose. "Can you stand?"

She shook her head. "My feet are asleep."

He touched her cheek very gently, his eyes like intense blue flames. "You are some doll, all right. A real firecracker."

"Would you help me up?"

He helped her, thankfully not commenting on her shakes but holding her tight against his side. His grip was so firm she barely needed her legs.

"Oh!" she said. "The guy with the phone! He went outside to send someone a picture of Damien's plan."

Jake patted her. "We caught him before he got a signal. His phone is already secured."

One of the men she didn't know came over.

"This is Sawyer Hayes," Jake said without letting go of her. "He organized your rescue. Sawyer, this is Mia."

"Pleased to meet you," the man said with military politeness. He was tall and wiry and had a sun-lined face. He must have had nerves of steel. The hand that shook hers was bone dry and callused from edge to edge. Even Jake wasn't that steady. Sawyer's light brown gaze shifted from her to him. "Raeburn is threatening us with his lawyers. And his friends in the government."

Jake snorted. "I guess he doesn't believe peons like us have friends there too."

"He claims Genbolt is too important to national security for the administration to allow it to go under."

"Which he's convinced it would do with him in jail."

Sawyer rubbed his jaw. "It would cause a damn big scandal."

"He committed corporate espionage! And kidnapped a citizen! We caught him red-handed."

"He's donated a lot of money to politicians over the years. You and I both know red hands wash clean sometimes."

"Fuck," Jake said, but not like he disagreed.

"I'm just saying if we don't finesse the situation, it might get away from us."

"Fine," Jake said. "Arrange what you can with the folks you know. We'll go along with the story they want to spin."

Sawyer threw a glance over his shoulder. Damien stood alone in a square of sun, holding up what Mia assumed was the plan she'd drawn. He appeared to be studying it. "What about the billionaire? Those two have a couple buckets of bad blood between them. Electric car boy might push for a public trial."

Jake's expression was hard to read. "Electric car boy is a free agent. I don't control him. Your friends might not be able to either. WorldWide is a power in its own right. On the other hand, if they're willing to include him in the negotiation, he'll make sure Raeburn doesn't get off easy. One more thing—"

Sawyer turned quizzical.

Jake's arm tightened around her waist. The tension in his muscles made the limb feel like steel. "When you find out which of them hit Mia . . ."

"Oh yes," his friend concurred with an air of relish. "I'll take care of that precisely. You just take care of her."

Whatever he meant by *precisely*, Jake seemed satisfied Sawyer would handle it.

◆

As he stood in the block of sun surveying the plan Mia had reproduced, Damien was sharply aware of her. He'd watched her boss rush to check on her earlier, and had monitored every jerk of Jake's hand as he cut her free of the chair. The sight of her battered face had shocked him, the idea that anyone could strike her. Still, he hadn't gone to her himself. Apart from doing his bit to help, Mia wasn't his business.

Considering how she'd used him, she wasn't his anything.

Somewhere behind him, Curtis and Sawyer's man were patching up Ms. DeWinter. Damien had zero desire to check on her. Thankfully, she wasn't trying to speak to him. Addled though she was, she seemed to realize she'd gone too far by colluding with Raeburn and trying to shoot Mia.

Damien shook the paper he held at arm's length straighter. His memory of his former employee turning toward Mia with the gun made his stomach turn over. It would have been his fault if she'd succeeded. He'd seen the signs that the secretary was unbalanced. Jake had even warned him not firing her right away would bite him in the ass. Damien owed Sawyer's man a debt for taking her out of action and sparing him that burden. If Mia had been seriously hurt . . .

He frowned. He'd allowed his thoughts to stray again. He forced his attention back to the large sheet he held. The variations in Mia's copy perplexed him. Half of it was incredibly exact, down to the smallest line. The rest was . . . off, but not in a random way. She seemed to have substituted bits and pieces of other tech into the design. Though they almost made sense, they wouldn't have held up under scrutiny.

He didn't understand why she'd done it. Why not give Raeburn what he wanted? Why risk being injured worse than she already was? Why would someone who'd done what she and Jake had care if Raeburn got his way?

He dropped his arms, his gaze traveling to her in spite of his resolve. Jake and Sawyer were too far away to hear, but they were speaking seriously. Jake held Mia to his side as if she were an irremovable extension of himself. She leaned into him the same way, her arms hugging him. Had Damien really shared his bed with both? Had he truly touched and been touched by them? That reality seemed distant.

Then Mia looked at him.

Damien felt his face stiffen. He couldn't trust her. No matter how much pleasure they'd exchanged, he'd simply been a mark for the two of them. If he kept reminding himself of that, eventually the necessary barriers between him and the hurt would solidify. He'd get through this. He always made his life what he needed it to be.

Mia turned away. Jake was speaking to her, gentle fingers rising to her bruised and uplifted face. He skimmed the tips around her injuries.

His tenderness caused a complicated ache to settle deep inside Damien's chest.

CHAPTER 16

JAKE had new reasons to be glad he'd called his old buddy. Among his many connections, Sawyer knew paramedics at a private ambulance company. He called them to the paper mill to treat their casualties. Ms. DeWinter needed to go to a hospital, but Mia was okay with bandaging and a few stitches. The female paramedic supplied her with an ice pack for her eye and an appointment to check her in a few days.

Mysteriously, Raeburn's underlings now had injuries exactly where Mia's were. Sawyer was very good at *precise*. Jake reminded himself to send his friend a bottle of Stolichnaya.

Since Mia was steadier on her feet, Jake simply opened the rear door to Sawyer's truck and handed her inside. Curtis slid in the other side. Sawyer would drive, of course, while his still nameless man rode shotgun.

Damien had informed Sawyer his helicopter pilot would pick him up.

Mia hadn't commented, but Jake knew Damien's refusal to ride with them bothered her.

"Whew," Curtis said, pulling his door shut. "Let's not have another day like that for a year or ten." He smoothed Mia's hair behind her shoulder. "I'm glad you're okay, kid. Your brother would haunt me if I let you get hurt."

Even with all she'd been through, Mia wanted to comfort him. "Never happen," she said. "Not with you and so many other heroes to protect me."

Curtis smiled and gave her thigh a pat. "Does this mean you'll come back to the office? You know, in a couple days?"

"Of course! But, uh, maybe I'll stick to getting coffee and computer work for a bit."

"I'm sorry for getting you into this."

"You didn't," Mia said. "I got myself. And I'm not sorry—despite appearances. Parts of it were a great adventure."

Her voice had roughened. Jake knew she was thinking about the *adventure* they'd shared with Damien and that she'd miss it. He couldn't stop himself. No matter what the gesture said about his feelings, he took her hand and held it. "You did good today. You used your wits and hung tough until we could get to you."

Mia tipped her head back on the seat and closed her eyes. "I knew you'd come. You're too smart not to have found a way."

When her thumb rubbed his knuckles, the motion was too soothing to relinquish. She wasn't hiding it. Curtis could see plainly, despite which neither of them let go for the rest of the ride home.

◆

"I'm not sleeping on your couch tonight."

Jake appeared at her bedroom door for this announcement, wearing only jeans and holding the extra pillow from her sofa. Mia had cleaned up, popped a pain pill, and put on her comfiest pajamas—a pale yellow pair with silhouettes of kittens. They were silly, but they made her feel like herself again. She was looking forward to zonking out.

Jake's continued presence had everything to do with her being calm enough for that. She turned to him as she scooted backwards on the mattress to sit against the headboard. Jake's stubborn expression—like he expected her to argue—secretly amused her. "I didn't want you to sleep there last night."

"You didn't?"

"No." Since they were having this out, she screwed up her nerve. "It made me feel like you were pushing me away. Like we were over because the job was done."

Jake took a step into the room. "I should push you away, but I don't think I can."

"Well, if I get a vote, I don't want you to." She clutched the covers to her waist. "I don't want us to be just friends. I want us to be lovers."

However she expected him to respond, it wasn't that his worry would increase. He rubbed the furrow between his brows. "I want that too. Except . . . Mia, I'm not always an easy person. I know I joke, but there's a lot inside me that's dark."

"From the work you used to do with men like Sawyer."

"Some of it comes from that. I lied to a lot of people in my previous line of work. And committed more acts of violence than I care to think about. Whatever reasons you do that, it changes you. Truthfully, though, I was born with a dark streak. I couldn't have been a good operative otherwise. From the start, I didn't want to drag a nice girl like you down with me."

Mia's throat constricted. That's what he thought? That knowing an incredible man like him could ever drag her down?

"Everyone's born with a weight or two. I'm certainly not all sunshine and rainbows."

"Aren't you?"

"Not even close! Not when Mike was my parents' favorite. Not when this memory thing turned me extra weird. All through school until I went away to college, I was the girl even freaks didn't want to be friends with."

"This was *after* your brother helped you control your compulsions?"

"Yes. My cooties just didn't wash off for some people."

"I didn't—" He stared at her. "I wish I'd understood that before."

"It's not your fault you didn't. I don't like people thinking I'm pitiful. My point is . . ." She hesitated. "I suspect Damien gets what I went through better than you do. Maybe I'm wrong about that. Maybe I've underestimated how much you understand. I guess you felt different when you were younger too."

Jake didn't seem offended. He sat on the edge of her bed. "I was different in different ways. That doesn't change the fact that you're still a kid compared to me."

"I'm not a kid, just not as experienced as you." Mia took his hand and held it. She wanted to be sure she got through to him. "Please tell me you'll give us a chance to work."

He pulled her wrist to him where his chest was hard and his skin was warm. His second hand stroked her forearm to her elbow. Though his gaze held hers as if he were taking her seriously, he didn't answer her directly.

"Damien really came through today," he said. "None of us wanted him along. We were afraid to risk two high profile CEO's getting killed. But he's a stubborn SOB. He contacted Zoe Raeburn to find out where her father had taken you."

"And she told him?" Mia was genuinely surprised. She shook

her head. "I bet she asked for some tit for tat in return."

"Damien didn't say, but I expect he'd have given her anything she wanted."

Something in Jake's tone made Mia tilt her head. "What are you getting at?"

Jake chafed her arm. "What I'm getting at is I know you wish he'd done more than just come through in a pinch today. I know you'd like to stay lovers with him too."

She looked at him. They were having everything out, she guessed. "Is that wrong?"

His gaze dropped to where his hand curved around her skin. "It's not wrong."

He didn't sound completely sure. "Do you . . ." She thought how to phrase it then decided he'd done fine. "Do you wish you could stay lovers with him too?"

He shook his head, but it wasn't quite a *no*. "I never expected to feel what I do for you. I figured if I'd ever had the capacity in me, it was long gone."

"What do you feel for me?" she asked softly.

"I love you," he said straight into her eyes. "I'd been thinking I might, but when I almost lost you today, I knew. I'd never felt that panicked and miserable in my life."

Mia started laughing then pressed a hand to her mouth. "Sorry. I've never been happy to make someone miserable before. I love you too, Jake. I have for a while, I think."

"Good." He smiled warmly back at her. "I'd hate to be miserable alone. Which still leaves the question of Damien."

She supposed it did. Looking back, maybe he'd seen what was between her and Jake from the beginning.

"I feel something for him," she said, seeing he wanted an honest answer. "It hurt when he threw us out, but how can I be sure it's love? Everything developed so fast between the three of us."

"But it didn't feel pretend."

"No. It didn't feel pretend."

Jake had one jean-clad leg bent up on the mattress. She dropped her hand to his calf and rubbed. He seemed temporarily lost in thought.

"Falling in love with even one person seems lucky to me," she said.

"I hope it is," he answered absently.

This time she laughed openly.

"I *do* hope it is," he repeated.

"Because you're such *awful* boyfriend material, being so capable and sexy and taking me on adventures and rescuing me when I need it."

"I didn't rescue you by myself."

She clasped his face between her hands. "I love you, Jake, even if you're defective."

"Sheesh," he said, rolling his eyes at her.

"I'm sleeping now," she announced. "Do you want to be the superior spoon or shall I?"

"Fuck," he said through his laughter.

"That was a real question."

"Fine," he said. "I want to be the superior spoon."

She wriggled down and let him, loving how he tucked her safely into his warm body. His arm held her loosely to him, his heartbeat steady against her back. A happiness she'd never known rolled in waves over her. Jake loved her, and she loved him. It was amazing and miraculous. He sighed behind her, gradually letting his tension go. His chin rubbed her hair as his breathing slowed.

The moment felt utterly sumptuous.

"What *are* these pajamas?" he asked after a minute.

Oh he could make her grin.

"They're my favorites," she said, hugging his arm tighter. "So don't insult them. They're perfect for catnaps." He snorted and she waited a heartbeat. "Jake?"

"Yes, beautiful?"

"You're a good snuggler. If I weren't so exhausted, I'd totally be taking advantage."

He kissed her hair. "Good to know," he said.

◆

Jake hadn't lied. He'd never been in love before—not like this anyway. The world seemed golden, every atom in it a blessing. He didn't want to take a minute with Mia for granted, or cause her a moment's pain. She'd had enough of that in her life. He let her use the shower first in the morning, and made her coffee, and asked if she wanted anything from the store.

"I can be back in five minutes, in case you're nervous about being left alone."

Mia burst out laughing. "Ow," she said a second later, because her merriment had tugged the healing cut on her lip.

Jake popped up from his chair. "I'll get you a pain killer."

"Stop," she said, taking him by the hands. "I'm okay. I'm just not used to seeing you like this."

He subsided into his seat. "I don't know how to do this romance thing."

"I bet you do." The glint that entered her eyes made him uncomfortable in a different way.

Holding her last night had pumped up his testosterone, especially since he was post-action. When he woke with the luscious butt snuggled to his groin, his usual morning hard-on had just about killed him. A damned marching band didn't drum harder than his cock. He'd ignored it for her sake, because she couldn't be recovered yet.

"You've been through an ordeal," he said unsurely.

Her smile deepened. "But I had a good night's rest."

"Your eye is still swollen, and your lip is hurt."

"I guess you'll have to find somewhere else to kiss me."

She swung from her chair and straddled his, rolling like a stripper up the hump in his jeans. She was wearing yoga pants, and the softness of her mons could be felt through them. Jake's scalp tingled with sensation, his toes curling against her tiny kitchen's linoleum. He gripped her waist, but somehow his hands didn't stop her from rolling up him again.

"Mia," he gasped, his hips rocking up to her. He tried to distract himself with a joke. "Not bad for a someone with no training in lap dancing."

"Who needs training? I'm just doing what comes naturally."

He was shirtless. Her warm hands kneaded his bare shoulders like she enjoyed squeezing his muscles. With that to steady her, her pelvis rolled up him more firmly still. Jake lost his self-control. Mia squeaked as he surged onto his feet holding her. Her legs clutched his waist, but he wanted her on her bed, where he could take his time and drive deep inside of her.

Ten long strides took him to his goal.

He lowered her to the covers and began stripping off her clothes. He loved how this was all it took to flush her from her soft cheeks, to her trembling breasts, to the lovely curve of her inner thighs. When he had her naked, she rose up on her elbows.

"Yours too," she said, nudging his thigh with the ball of her bare foot.

Jake shucked his jeans and underwear in one quick motion.

Mia bit her lip and grinned. "You look . . . very ready, Mr. Reed."

He was almost. He climbed over her to retrieve the box of condoms from her bedside drawer.

"Hey," she said, noting what he'd brought out. "How did those get in there?"

Too impatient to let her play, Jake ripped a packet with his teeth, sat back on his heels, and covered himself quickly. Knowing he was good to go made his hard-on bounce eagerly.

"You slept pretty late," he said. "And I figured I couldn't stay hands off forever. I snuck out to the store."

"So—" Her fingers tiptoed up his thighs. "This morning, when you woke up with the boner to end all boners, they were already there?"

She'd noticed his condition. Jake admitted he liked that. He shivered as her hands crept higher, their tips brushing the curve of his testicles. "I have superhuman restraint. Do I get bonus points?"

"I think you've earned them." She reversed her hands down his thighs then drew them up her own sides and stretched. This put her curvy little body on full display for him. The confidence was new and very appealing. The hungry ache in his cock deepened. "What would you like to trade your points for?"

So many options ran through his mind they were maddening. He rolled onto his hands and knees over her. "How about I trade them for kisses?"

He bent to the tender skin just behind her ears then the column of her neck and her collarbones. He dropped light kisses and little licks, using his lips to tease a long path of nerves awake. When he settled into suckling one tight nipple, she clasped his head to him.

"Jake," she sighed. Her spine writhed on the rumpled covers. Her legs were restless, her heat rising.

He switched to the other breast, his hands sliding possessively down her sides. When he reached her knees, he pushed them down and apart. A slow shudder rolled through him. Just the thought of restraining her nearly drove him insane. She was everything he'd ever wanted and a few things he hadn't guessed besides.

Mia seemed to enjoy knowing this. The brown gaze that met his wasn't so innocent.

"I think my friend from this morning is back," she purred.

"*Your* friend."

His voice was ragged. When she slid her hands down his ribs and abs, he breathed even more crazily.

"This friend." She stroked his painfully erect cock between her thumbs and fingers. Her touch was light, tracing him up and down through the snug latex. Jake's tip jerked and grew wetter. "He's kind of new, and there's still plenty to explore, but I'm getting to know him bit by bit."

She pushed her stroke to his base and cupped his testicles.

He sucked in air at her just-right squeeze. She was getting to know him, all right. If he wasn't careful, she was going to make him come from that.

"Maybe," he suggested a little shakily, "you'd like to learn more about him from the inside."

"Take my hands off you," she said, a hint of a dare in it. "Hold them above my head."

One of his hands was enough to trap both her wrists on the pillow. That she'd invited him to do this pushed him to the edge. He always liked bondage, but somehow doing it to her was larger-than-life intense.

Jake was so wound up he was shaking.

Mia's eyes gleamed with knowingness. "I hope you appreciate my sacrifice. I really like touching your body."

"I'll let you go in a bit," he promised.

Her body undulated, one knee rubbing his hip—perhaps to compensate for him holding her hands captive. "No hurry. I'll get mine back when your guard is down."

She would, and that made everything perfect.

Jake nudged her legs wider with his knees, his free hand steering his cock to her. Her lashes fluttered as the tip touched her.

"I love you," he said as he pushed in.

She was wet and hot and her long moan of pleasure went to his head like wine.

"That's so good," she praised. "I love how you fill me up."

He couldn't wait. He was already rocking in and out. As he smiled down into her eyes, he realized he wasn't holding her wrists anymore. His arm was still above her head, but *she* was gripping it. When he slid one hand beneath her butt, she braced her heel at the top of his ass muscles.

Her strength increased the depth he could go into her. With every stroke, the tension in his groin increased deliciously. God, he wanted to come. He was trying to be careful, but maybe she didn't need him to.

"Can you take more?" he asked a bit breathlessly.

"Oh yes," she said, her fingernails digging in. "Please give me everything."

He gave her more, and more yet, and then they went at it full throttle. Her too-small bed thumped the carpet while erotic cries rang out from her throat. Her hips knocked his, their flesh slapping noisily. It wasn't enough. Jake pulled his arm from her grip, wanting both hands free for maneuvering her.

Steadying her gave him almost too much of what he craved. Pumping into her so fiercely was unbelievably pleasurable, as if not just his cock but every inch of him participated in taking her. He couldn't stop what he was doing, despite how impossible the stimulation made controlling his excitement. His nerves were singing, his balls drawing up with need. He stretched his thumb to her clit, working to rub the swollen flesh despite her thrashing and its wetness.

She clutched his back and ground her mons against him, her neck arching off the mattress as she forgot herself. She was so alive. His every thrust shook her body. Her breasts bounced. Her skin flushed. He wanted to see her like this always, to make her unravel so beautifully. He was her slave then, mastered by his desire to pleasure her. He ground his teeth in a desperate bid to restrain his body's demand that he let go.

"Jake," she cried. "*Jake*—"

Her pussy tightened, pulling so strongly at his cock that all his sensations surged to the point of no return.

"God," she groaned.

Jake's climax rocketed out of him—from his balls and cock and even his tailbone. The merciless bliss tore a growl from deep inside his chest. He choked out her name, one last pulse of seed shooting. A honeyed glow rippled outward from his center. He had just enough strength to hold his weight off her on his elbows.

Mia collapsed beneath him with her arms flung wide and her eyes heavy. "Mm," she said. "That is *soo* much better."

She made him chuckle. "You needed that, huh?"

Her mouth curved into a grin. "I wasn't the only one."

Incredibly, his spent cock stirred inside her.

"Hm," she said, her tone of interest making it react more. "Maybe this isn't over yet."

"Mia," he said before she mustered the strength to move. He knew he wanted to be serious.

"Yes, Jake?"

He stroked the skin of her warm shoulders. "What you said on the roof to Damien, that I'd be there for you if someone were trying to kill you . . ."

Her eyes opened, her gaze focusing on him. "Yes?"

"I want you to know, that isn't all I'd be there for. I'd be there for everything, big or little. That's what *I love you* means to me."

"That's what it means for me as well."

His heart settled from its knocking. "Good."

Her hands found his ribs and rubbed. "We'll be friends too then?" she said, a tiny bit tentative. He understood better now what that word meant to her.

"Absolutely," he said firmly.

CHAPTER 17

THE next two weeks were the best of Mia's life. Though she returned to Discreet after one more day off, she didn't feel like she'd rushed. From the start, she'd loved working for Curtis. Knowing she and Jake would go home together made the most mundane tasks feel rewarding. They split their nights between her place and his, his apartment having more elbowroom.

At first, she was surprised how often Jake wanted to make love—definitely every night and often more than once. Sometimes they didn't get all the way through the door to their apartments before they started tearing at each other's clothes. When Jake apologized for his sex drive, she laughed at him.

Please, she'd said. *Haven't you noticed I can't get enough of you?*

He'd rewarded her for the question by ravishing her especially thoroughly.

She knew this was their honeymoon phase. Undoubtedly, they were both on their best behavior. All the same, the ease with which they accommodated each other felt promising.

Jake was laughing more, and maybe she was as well. Curtis started teasing them for having too much fun around the office. Curtis seemed happier himself. Mia wasn't sure, but she thought he *might* be dating somebody. She hoped he was. He'd mourned her brother long enough. A great guy like him deserved a nice romance. Everybody did, it seemed to her.

That being the case, she gave herself permission to dream a bit about the future.

One tiny flaw shadowed her happiness, one smidgen of wistfulness.

Damien wasn't part of it.

◆

Damien had spent much of the last two weeks in an endless round of closed-door meetings. The power wrangling in DC was more intense than he was accustomed to, but he thought he'd adjusted. He'd met with individuals from DARPA, the DOJ, and various other government acronyms. He and—interestingly enough—Jake's crony, Sawyer Hayes, told the story of Raeburn's felonious behavior more times than they could count. Sawyer wasn't as rough edged as he'd initially seemed. Damien had developed a reluctant respect for him.

Sawyer might be a savvier dealmaker than Damien.

The final meeting in Damien's marathon was with Zoe Raeburn and the Genbolt board. He'd braced himself to see her in person, but she'd been as coolly professional as he could wish. Eschewing tears or flirtation, she'd gotten straight to facing the fact that WorldWide had the upper hand in their bargaining. He didn't go easy on her. He saved his pity for the people Genbolt's duplicity and corner cutting had put at risk.

Thanks to the unofficial-official backing he'd received, the deal they hammered out was one with which he could live.

Effective immediately, the public would be informed that Sam Raeburn had retired to pursue personal interests. Zoe would guide Genbolt until the board approved a replacement. In reality, Sam Raeburn was being shipped off to one of the CIA's more comfortable secret "black site" prisons. As long as Damien's tech proved important to the country's welfare, he was likely to stay there. A consulting committee comprised in part of senior scientists from WorldWide would scrutinize Genbolt's current government projects and suggest areas where substance might be substituted for Raeburn's smoke-and-mirrors shenanigans. Damien didn't kid himself that all Genbolt's abuses would be undone. If even a portion were, he'd consider his time well spent.

Overall, he'd achieved more than he hoped when he began. The downside was that in returning to New York, he found little to distract him.

Compared to the wringer he'd just been through, company meetings were too easy. Damien hired competent people. They could accomplish quite a lot without him. He'd had to keep himself together to handle the Raeburn mess. Now it felt like his strings were cut.

He didn't *want* to do anything. Not go to Audition or Diogenes. Not work out with his trainer. Not dream up new designs or admire those of other folks. He spent far too many hours studying Mia's copy of the stolen blueprint and pacing his penthouse.

As promised—or perhaps threatened—Jake had returned the car Damien gave him. He'd done it while Damien was in DC and hadn't left a note. Mia's diamond necklace was in the catchall bowl on his kitchen counter where he'd thrown it. He kept telling himself to get rid of it; maybe give the proceeds to charity. Thus far, he hadn't brought himself to touch it again. The rejected gift was yet another reminder that his home felt empty in ways it never had before.

Actually, his life was what felt empty.

No more Mia at the office. No more Jake driving him around. To his dismay, he knew precisely how many days remained in their broken contract. The tiny part of him that wanted to compel them to honor it deserved to be sneered at. *He'd* kicked them out—and with good reason.

The difficulty lay in that he'd been happy. For a few shining hours with Mia and Jake, he'd been happy. It was like a color he'd been blind to all his life and they'd corrected his vision.

He told himself a cure that didn't last was pointless. Truthfully, it was cruel. He was better off without it.

He was better off without them.

◆

Jake and Mia were watching TV at Jake's place when news of Raeburn's retirement aired. The sight of the CEO's broad face caused Mia to sit back with her heart pounding. Raeburn's hard pale eyes looked the same as they had in the paper mill. Unprepared for the fear that rose inside her, she tried to conceal it.

"Huh," she said. "I guess that's what your friend Sawyer meant about red hands washing clean."

Jake's arm was slung behind her on the couch. Maybe he guessed her reaction. He rubbed her cheek soothingly. "That's just the official story. He's actually going to be locked up."

Mia turned to him in surprise. "He is?"

"He is. Sawyer filled me in off the record. He'll be held in a secret compound somewhere outside the country. It won't be like going to Rikers, but it'll be secure. He and Damien made a deal with the government."

Well. That was news. And a profound relief. She studied Jake's face but his expression was carefully neutral. "Have you spoken to Damien?"

He shook his head. "I thought about it." He stroked her hair, which was still damp from the shower. "Do *you* want to speak to him?"

She wanted to more than she felt comfortable admitting. She loved being with Jake. Heck, she loved being *in* love with him. There was just that little spot in her heart only Damien had filled, the one that felt like it was made for him.

"I admit I'm worried about him," she said. "And I miss him sometimes. But I can't badger him to forgive me for what I did. He'll think I'm one more in his series of crazed stalkers."

"Calling him once isn't stalking."

"He was so mad," she said. "And we didn't know him that long."

"You're afraid he'll reject you."

Maybe she was. She'd experienced enough of that in her life. She'd always survived it, but that didn't mean it was fun. Probably it said something about the strength of her feelings that she didn't want to risk being rejected by Damien.

"I'd rather wait for him to reach out," she said. "If he wants to, that is. We haven't heard a peep."

Jake fingered a lock of her drying hair. She could tell he was thinking.

◆

In the aftermath of rescuing of Mia from her snatch and grab, Jake had set up an alert to notify him when articles were published on certain names and topics. Two days following Raeburn's "retirement" announcement, something he hadn't anticipated showed up in his inbox.

Frederica DeWinter, former WorldWide employee, had committed suicide. Her husband had discovered her in the bedroom of their shared home, clutching what he'd told police was a keepsake book. Sadly, she wasn't found soon enough to pump the sleeping pills from her stomach. The pills had been prescribed, and foul play wasn't suspected. Ms. DeWinter was survived by her husband and a maternal aunt. A small memorial service would be held in a nearby church.

Jake was willing to bet the keepsake book recorded Ms. DeWinter's obsessive interest in Damien Call. He was also willing to bet her husband had destroyed it.

He glanced toward Curtis's office, where he and Mia were going over a new client's paperwork. If asked, Jake would share this with her. If he weren't, he'd rather not mention it. *Later,* he thought. When he was sure she'd put the last of her shakes behind her. The longer she went without a reminder of her ordeal, the steadier she'd be if she encountered one.

Damien would know about this development, of course. He was an information junkie. Jake wondered if it would upset him. Or maybe he'd be relieved his former assistant couldn't cause more trouble.

Thoughtful, Jake pressed his thumb to his lips. Perhaps it was time he addressed the biggest unfinished business that had been nagging him.

◆

Either Jake was lucky or he'd developed a better sense of Damien's habits than he realized. He found him at the first place he tried: the boring and apparently unpopular hotel bar down the street from his penthouse.

Jake observed his target's condition before moving in. The CEO sat alone and unnoticed at a booth in the back. Though he wore a suit, his collar was unbuttoned and for once he'd forgone a tie. He didn't seem to be pounding back the drinks, but was turning an inch-full tumbler in a circle.

His expression was morose.

A bit of self pity then. Jake could handle that. A true bender would have been more challenging.

Damien was too self-engrossed to look up when he approached.

"I know why you like this place," Jake said. "No-fucking-body else drinks here."

Damien glanced up. It seemed a cause for optimism that he didn't object to Jake's presence.

"They stock my favorite scotch," he explained.

Jake slid into the bench opposite the same as if he'd been invited. "You're a famous billionaire. Any bar in the city would do that."

The bartender was keeping a subtle eye on Damien. Jake signaled him to bring another of what the CEO was having.

"Fine," Damien said. "You got me. I didn't feel like drinking alone at home. Lately, my walls have been closing in on me."

His sardonic tone said he was aware of the irony. Damien didn't have enough walls for that.

Jake waited for the drink to come and the bartender to depart. "I assume tonight's mood has to do with the not so dearly departed Frederica DeWinter."

Damien exhaled slowly. "I'm thinking I ought to feel bad about her death, but all I can manage is relief. We couldn't press charges for her involvement in Mia's kidnaping, not when Raeburn was getting his kid gloves deal. We'd have risked her blabbing to the press. Maybe if I'd spoken to her . . ." He shook his head. "I had HR inform her she was banned from all WorldWide properties. After what happened, I didn't want to lay eyes on her."

"I'm pretty sure lots of people would feel the same."

"But why do I deserve to have this turn out conveniently for me?"

"You didn't make her go unhinged."

"Didn't I?"

"No," Jake said. "I sincerely doubt you did."

"But—"

"No," Jake said, firmer yet. "I know you've had some weird experiences with women, maybe more than your share, but you didn't even sleep with Ms. DeWinter. And before you say you should have known, stalker types sneak under people's radar everyday. It's not always possible to tell how gone an individual is. There's something else I want you to consider. You won't want to, but I think you will because you're used to weighing all possible options."

"Okay," Damien said slowly.

"This arm's length thing you've built your life around? Maybe what you're worried about isn't that every woman you get close to will go crazy. Maybe the real truth is that, because of what happened to you as a teenager, you've decided you can't trust anyone who loves you. You've concluded that if they love you, they'll screw you over—like your parents and that guidance counselor did. It may be . . . *may* be that you're subconsciously drawing people into your life who repeatedly justify that strategy."

Damien gaped at him. "You're saying I invited you and Mia into my life because I secretly hoped you'd betray me? That's a handy method for abdicating your culpability."

"We didn't betray you, Damien. We lied to you in the course of conducting an investigation. As soon as Mia realized the truth, she and I backed your side. Raeburn got nothing out of us."

"You don't even feel bad for deceiving me."

"Mia feels terrible," Jake didn't mind saying. "I know the score when it comes to deep cover work."

Damien snorted. "*Deep cover work*. That's a nice term for it."

Jake lifted his drink and tipped back a throat-burning swallow. He set the glass back down a little too heavily. There was no way to say this except straight out. "Mia is in love with you."

Damien blinked. "Sure she is," he said after a telling pause.

"I might be too," he added.

His heart thudded in his chest as he met Damien's seemingly stunned reaction. Telling Damien he might love him wasn't nearly as pleasant as telling Mia had been. Jake's hands were so clammy he wiped them on his trousers.

"You might be in love with me," Damien repeated dazedly.

"Well, I know I respect you," he said. "When you're not being an ass. You're brilliant, and you've got principles, and I care what happens to you. Being with you is . . . pleasurable. I enjoy seeing you happy. And I want Mia to be happy. She—"

He stopped. He shouldn't act like Mia's preferences were the only ones he was thinking of. "We both liked the way the three of us felt together. Not just the sex but everything. Mia is afraid you'll reject her if she approaches you."

"And—what?—she asked you to approach me on her behalf?" Damien's disbelief was clear.

"She wouldn't do that. She doesn't know I'm here. I think she deserves the world on a platter, but if you can't shake off your blindness and self-pity, you don't deserve her." Damien started to speak, but Jake cut him off. "I won't share her with someone who doesn't understand what she's worth. As for that, I won't share myself. I'll make sure she never feels cheated if she ends up with only me."

His eyes burned with the declaration. To hell with what

Damien thought. He let the tears stand in them.

Damien's brows had shot up. Jake saw a certain . . . curiosity had replaced his anger.

"I can't imagine she would," Damien said. "Feel cheated, that is. You're a staunch defender."

"I'd be your defender too," Jake said. "But not if you won't man up."

◆

Anger surged hotly to Damien's face. Jake thought he needed to *man up*? Did he have no idea what Damien had been doing the last two weeks? Then it occurred to him that of course he did. Sawyer Hayes was his bud. Jake was talking about a different kind of courage.

The courage to make a real connection to someone.

The courage to risk being hurt again.

Jake clearly had that. He hadn't simply claimed Mia loved Damien; he'd said he might himself. Damien's mind raced to make sense of this. Jake had no reason to lie anymore. He might be mistaken, but Damien didn't think he was deceitful.

He'd waited too long without speaking. Jake pulled a paper coaster across the table and produced a pen. He scribbled a few quick lines.

"Mia's twenty-third birthday is next week. Curtis is throwing a party for her at this address. Consider this your invitation."

Jake stood and pushed the coaster toward Damien. "It won't be fancy. Leave your white tie at home. And I know it's hard, but try to bring a gift that costs less than a hundred bucks. Or none at all. Mia won't complain."

"Will she know I'm coming?"

"Are you suggesting you don't have the stones to show up unless she does?"

Jake's words were more confrontational than his eyes. The emotion in them was so sympathetic Damien swallowed.

"Look, man," Jake said softly. "I know you've run your life in a certain way for a lot of years. Maybe you still believe you have to. Just . . . don't miss your chance to discover Mia is worth the risk."

Too dumbfounded to respond, Damien watched Jake stride away. As he did, it occurred to him that the departing man was worth a few risks himself.

CHAPTER 18

THE address Jake gave Damien was for their PI office in Brooklyn. The time he'd jotted was 6:30. Damien arrived a bit past seven. Despite Jake's warning that the party was casual, he wore a beige linen suit with an open collar and no necktie. He'd tried donning khaki pants and a golf shirt, but had felt as if he were putting on a false front. Or maybe he was just contrary.

Jake Reed wasn't his master.

He hadn't complied much better with regards to his birthday gift. That was a bottle of 2010 Marcassin Chardonnay, which exceeded Jake's suggested cap by more than a few pennies. Damien told himself it didn't matter as long as the wine suited Mia's taste. The bow he'd dressed it up with had only cost $2.50 from the bin by the register. Jake would have to be satisfied with that as evidence of restraint. Damien could have had it wrapped professionally.

The main entrance to the firm was inside an old brick building that housed a handful of businesses. Gritting his teeth to control his nerves, he tucked the bottle in the bend of his arm and rapped lightly on the door. He heard music playing inside and loud laughing voices. The small of his back broke into a sweat. He hadn't been this anxious meeting power players in DC. Was his suit ridiculous? And his expensive wine? Mia was twenty-three, and far more of a regular person than he'd been at her age. Though Damien was twenty-nine, he often felt as if he'd skipped his twenties. He'd had to grow up quick in order to be taken seriously.

Probably Mia's guests were eating pizza and drinking beer in there.

Damien knocked again and still no one let him in. If Jake

hadn't told Mia he'd invited him, Damien would strangle him.

Fuck it, he thought and opened the door himself.

Mia's boss Curtis was on his way to answer it. He was in ripped jeans, beat-up running shoes, and a snug gray T-shirt.

"Oh," he said. "Hey!" He ran one hand through his red-gold hair as if slightly disconcerted. "Jake mentioned you might come. Welcome. We're having cake in the conference room."

Damien waded inside cautiously. The crowd was mixed to say the least. Some looked as if they might work in the building's other businesses. The younger females could be acquaintances of Mia's from college, he supposed. Damien didn't spot her among them, and no one seemed to be missing her. He'd thrown parties like that early in his career, where none of his guests particularly required his presence to enjoy themselves. But maybe inviting a group had been Curtis's idea. Though Damien hadn't been focused on taking Curtis's measure during the rescue, he had seemed more extraverted than Mia.

The suspiciously well-groomed males could be the gay man's buddies.

Don't judge, he reminded himself as members of both genders checked him out. He wasn't exactly swinging one way these days.

"Eyes in your head," Curtis warned one of the more obvious oglers, poking two fingers toward him in emphasis. "This one's here to visit someone else." He grinned at Damien over his shoulder. "Feel free to smack anyone grabby."

He didn't have to. The partiers went back to entertaining each other.

The group around the table in the conference room was smaller. Damien was surprised to recognize Sawyer Hayes and the seamstress who worked for Diogenes—Hillary Sweets, she was called. Jake was there, of course, and a large, partially eaten bakery cake. As if he'd been putting off facing her, his gaze settled on Mia last.

She had a beer halfway to her mouth. She choked on a swallow when she saw him.

Fuck, Damien thought. The bastard *hadn't* given her a heads up.

"Damien," she said, recovering from her cough. She kept her hand pressed to the neckline of her sixties-style paisley minidress, inescapably drawing his attention to her very nice cleavage. Her hair was down and not in a ponytail. "I didn't know you were coming."

"Jake invited me." He held out the wine bottle. "I brought you a birthday gift."

She accepted it with some confusion and looked at Jake.

"Happy birthday," the bastard said with a smirk.

And with those two words, Damien's mood transformed. Suddenly, everything was all right. Jake said *happy birthday* as if Damien's presence was his gift to Mia—as if Damien were that important. Perhaps he was. Mia's cheeks went pink a second before she looked back at him.

"He's an idiot," she said. "*I'd* have invited you if I'd known you'd come. And thank you for the wine."

She pulled back a swiveling chair for him. He sat and smiled like the idiot she'd accused Jake of being.

"Do you want cake?" she asked. "Or food? We have plenty of pizza left."

He shook his head and smiled harder. He was certain he couldn't eat. He was too full of the realization that Jake hadn't been playing games with him. He *did* believe Mia loved him. And maybe it was true.

"Man needs a beer," Jake announced, twisting off a cap and setting the bottle in front of him. "You drink beer, right?"

Damien flashed a grin at him too. "As long as it doesn't come in a can."

"Duly noted." Jake sat back and wet smiling lips.

Lust flooded Damien's system at the sight—for Jake and Mia both. His trousers got snug in two heartbeats. He'd have given quite a lot to be alone and naked with them right then.

Curtis cleared his throat in a manner that might have concealed laughter. "We were discussing Mia's maternal birthday card when you arrived."

"God," Mia groaned. "Do we have to?"

Curtis stuck out his hand. "You know I won't be satisfied until I see what she sent this year."

"Is it a thing?" Hillary asked curiously.

Mia bent to dig something out of her purse. "It's a thing that flatters him more than it does me."

Curtis took the envelope she pulled out and extricated its contents. Damien's brow wrinkled. The front of the card simply said FOR YOU in plain gray letters.

Curtis opened it and read. "'On your special day.' At least she remembered it was special. 'Send Curtis our love'—that's me, of course. I'm always in there somewhere."

"You're usually in there first," Mia said.

"True. But to continue. 'Please buy yourself something nice with the enclosed. Best wishes, Mom and Dad.'"

"You'll notice she signed for both of them," Mia put in. "Then again, Dad did sign the check."

"Well," Hillary said, clearly trying to be put the best face on this. "Checks are one size fits all."

"Yes," Mia agreed. "You should have seen what I got when she tried to buy me presents."

"Oprah books," Curtis said. "Lots and lots of Oprah books."

Mia shook her head ruefully. "Mom does not approve of me reading romance novels. I think she figured if she exposed me to the 'good stuff,' I'd be cured. Curtis finally spilled the beans that I was donating them to the library."

"She'd have *kept* sending them," Curtis said. "You'd have died buried in Oprah books."

Mia laughed. "Thankfully, I had you to save me."

Damien knew how to observe people, and he thought he sensed an edge to Mia's humorous manner—the sort a person might bury because the person annoying her was a friend. Why had Curtis insisted she show the card? Was it for his benefit? Was Curtis saying: this is what Mia comes from, treat her better than these others?

Damien was on board with that more than Curtis realized.

Whatever Curtis's reasons, he wasn't the only one telling tales.

"Jake's dad taught him to skin a bear when he turned twenty-one." Sawyer volunteered this fascinating tidbit, the mischief in his eyes suggesting he didn't have Jake's permission to divulge.

"No-o." Mia turned to Jake. "An actual bear?"

Jake wagged his head, seeming unable to refuse answering her. "He scared the piss out of me. He was seventy-something at the time, chasing this poor grizzly through the Montana woods with his old shotgun. He was hitting it, but it was huge and it just kept running. I didn't know whether to be more afraid of my dad dropping dead of a heart attack or six hundred pounds of enraged bear finally turning around and charging him. I kept saying, "Stop, Dad. Just let it go.'"

"I take it he didn't," Damien said.

"Apparently, Dad's neighbor claimed this particular grizzly killed his dog, and my dad was determined to put it down. I'd joined the marines by then. No way could I explain I didn't share his relish for slaying and skinning it. I had the damnedest time convincing him I didn't want the pelt."

Sawyer saluted him with his beer. "You, my friend, are a man of many layers."

Damien saw he'd enjoyed goading Jake to tell the story.

"Wait," Damien said. "Your dad was seventy when you were twenty-one?"

Jake let his eyes rest warmly on Damien's. The look in them said he was willing to let him in the same as Sawyer or Mia. "I was a change of life baby. Mind you, apart from a few very eccentric incidents, my folks were great. Always loved me and told me they were proud. My mom attended every sporting event I ever played and cheered me, win or lose. I never minded that they were older than the parents of other kids my age. I guess, on some level, I knew I had to appreciate them while I could. Neither my mom nor my dad is around anymore. Once or twice I was grateful they didn't see where I'd ended up, but mostly I just miss them."

"That's sweet," Hillary said. "In a twisted, backwoods sort of way."

"Yes," Curtis said. "Thank you for sharing that heartwarming tale."

Jake pelted him with balled-up napkin, which Curtis dodged. They had a rapport, Damien saw, one they both enjoyed.

"And now," Curtis said. "Since I believe the civilians are sufficiently distracted in the front, I have one more present for Mia."

"I thought the party was my present."

"Not this year," Curtis said.

He set a small wrapped box in front of Mia. His face was serious beneath his smile. Interested to see the gift, Damien leaned forward as she pried up the lid.

Inside, half a poker chip nestled on white batting. At first he thought it was an entry token from Audition. The embossed Comedy/Tragedy mask was identical to the one his club used. Then he saw this chip was larger and plated gold. Actually, the gold might have been solid.

The half-chip's broken center shone with the metal too.

"I don't understand," she said. "You can't have bought me a membership to Diogenes, or even half of one. They've got to cost the moon."

Curtis propped his hip on the conference table's edge. "It's not a membership. Do you remember when your brother taught himself to count cards because he got tired of losing every game to you?"

"Sure," she said. "He got really good."

"Mike won that chip in a poker game with Diogenes' previous owner, who thought he'd win because he could count cards too. Your brother turned out to be better, probably from practicing against you." Curtis reached into the pocket of his gray T-shirt. His hand emerged with the other half of the broken chip. "Even though Mike was young, when he and I committed to our relationship, both of us made a will. He split ownership of the club between you and me."

What? Damien thought.

"What?" Mia said, falling back in her chair with her mouth open. "You and I own Diogenes?"

"I've been keeping your half in trust. Mike wasn't sure what you'd think about him patronizing that sort of establishment. He asked me to hold off giving it to you until you were twenty-five or I thought you could handle it—if that came sooner." Curtis smiled gently. "I know Mike was your big brother, but he valued your good opinion. He didn't want to disappoint you even in memory."

"He never disappointed me," she said faintly.

"I should probably warn you that you haven't instantly become rich. Most of the club's income gets plowed right back into it. You have a nest egg, though, and you're likely to be well set by the time you're forty."

"*I* can't run Diogenes," Mia said with a hint of panic.

"Some day you might be able to," Curtis returned calmly. "In any case, you don't have to now. Management and the ruling board take care of the day-to-day, or the night-to-night, if you like. Along with me, you'll get regular reports and you'll have an opportunity to vote at quarterly meetings. You'll have to sign a confidentiality agreement, but I don't think you'll have trouble keeping it."

"Why are you letting us in on this?" Hillary asked, referring to herself and Sawyer with a tilt of her head.

"Because Diogenes is like any corporation. It has its own corporate culture and intrigues. I want Mia to have strong allies and advisors who aren't entrenched—allies and advisors besides me."

Possibly Curtis knew Damien had been asking the same question as Hillary. The man turned to regard him with palpable amusement. "I'm aware you've been trying to discover who owns Diogenes, and that you'd very much like to buy us out. I'm advising Mia against that. However your relationship with her and Jake develops, her independence is important."

"Of course," Damien said, though privately he struggled with the idea of letting that quest go. On the other hand, Curtis considered a relationship between himself and the pair a given? Had Jake discussed it with him, or was it simply that obvious?

Perhaps Curtis read his thoughts on this topic too. The dimple in his cheek deepened.

"Wait," Mia said, distracting Damien. "If you own half of Diogenes, causing the scene you did at Audition couldn't have got you banned."

Curtis chuckled. "I wondered when that would occur to you."

"You're a sly one," Jake said admiringly. "All this time I was impressed by your sacrifice."

"Me too," Hillary said. "I hear gossip. You're popular over there."

"Everybody loves a ginger," Sawyer joked.

Curtis rolled his eyes. "We're agreed then? The people in this room are available to advise and back Mia up should the need arise?"

"You're including me?" Damien blurted.

"I'm including you. Hopefully, you'll stick with these two long enough to become family."

Damien fell back in his chair and blinked. This seemed an extraordinary expression of trust and faith in him.

"When I make up my mind, I make it up," Curtis said. "I think you'll find Mia and Jake do the same."

"This is the best birthday present *ever*," Mia exclaimed.

Damien knew she wasn't referring to her club ownership.

◆

Jake was even gladder than he'd expected that Damien showed up—not just for Mia's sake but his. The need to bide his time until the three of them could talk was less welcome. He shook his head at his own eagerness. If he'd thought being a couple was new and challenging, trying to form a working threesome would surely take the cake.

This didn't matter when he saw Mia's barely contained happy glow. Curtis had surprised her, and so did the support she was getting from everyone.

"Jesus, she's cute," Sawyer chuckled quietly beside him. "And so is Moneybags, if you like that Adonis-in-a-suit type. Good thing Curtis thinks I'm family. On my own, I'd never convince you to come up for air."

"Don't be stupid," Jake said absently. He smiled when he noticed Mia reaching under the table to squeeze Damien's hand. "I'll see you the same as ever."

"Uh-huh." Sawyer pushed his rolling chair back and rose. "Hey, everybody. I hate to be a party pooper, but I've got a previous engagement. Curtis, thank you for inviting me tonight. Mia, happy birthday. I'm pleased and honored to be included on your team."

"Thank *you*," she said. "I'm so glad Jake has you for a friend."

"I'm yours now too. You can call on me anytime."

For a man like Sawyer, this was no light promise. Warmth welled up in Jake: a mix of gratitude and pride and maybe love for Sawyer too. Jake was lucky to have a friend like him, lucky to have survived the various hells they'd experienced together.

In truth, he was blessed to live in a world with every one of the folks who surrounded him. Curtis had simply started out as his boss, someone who'd let him earn a living with his skills without killing anyone. And Hillary was his ex-lover! What deity had he ingratiated to make a woman he'd respected but hadn't loved morph into a friend? Jake hadn't had this consciousness of good fortune since he was a kid.

Life wasn't so dark when you had people worth opening your heart to.

"I should be skedaddling too." Hillary smiled at Mia as she got up. "Don't forget lunch next week. I know you have things you'll want to hash over without all these male ears around."

Mia went to hug her goodbye. Hillary didn't miss the emotion in her eyes.

"No more thank yous," she scolded. "I suspect I don't make close friends any easier than you do."

There were a few more farewells and backslaps to get through, but soon enough Jake and Damien and Mia stood together in the small parking lot behind the warehouse.

"Well," Damien said, jingling his keys nervously.

Mia put her hands on his shoulders, rose onto her tiptoes, and frenched the hell out of him. Jake rubbed a smile as he watched Damien's stiffness inevitably unkink. He knew how passionate Mia's kisses were, how they sank straight into a man's bloodstream and hardened him like iron.

By the time she dropped back onto her heels, Damien's arms had surrounded her.

"Thank you for coming," she said. "Thank you for giving me . . . for giving *us* a second chance."

Damien glanced at him, his eyes cautious but also hot. Jake suspected the other man was thinking of kissing him as well.

"I wanted to." Damien's chest lifted with a breath. "I missed both of you."

Mia sighed happily. "Can we go to your place to talk? Or Jake's, if you'd rather. Mine is too squishy for three people."

"My place is good," he said, rubbing her back gently.

His and Mia's hips remained close together, and—perhaps without thinking—his caresses strayed onto her ass. The sight aroused Jake, the suggestion that Damien was tempted to fuck her then and there. Jake very much liked that he didn't have a single reason to look away.

Damien must have felt a few sparks over the situation too. He cleared his throat. "We have a lot to talk about."

Jake lowered his head and grinned. For his part, he hoped *talking* wasn't the only activity on their agenda.

CHAPTER 19

SO many feelings bubbled up in Mia—nerves, excitement, love —that she could hardly sort them out. When Damien preceded her and Jake into his bedroom, she assumed rational discussion would be delayed. Though she didn't mind that, it turned out not to be the case.

Damien's bed platform had a drawer on its side that she hadn't noticed before. He leaned down to open it and pulled out a large paper sheet. Mia shivered. She recognized what it was.

"I'm sorry," Damien said, catching her reaction. "I don't mean to bring up bad memories, but I'd like to ask you about this. It's been preying on my mind."

"Okay," she said. If she were him, she guessed she'd have questions.

He spread the copy she'd made for Raeburn on his bed and sat down beside it. "You understood what I designed, didn't you?"

Jake's head jerked back. "If she did, I wish she'd clue me in."

"I *thought* I did," Mia said. "It popped into my mind while I was taped to the chair. My memory works like that sometimes. I don't know where the knowledge comes from, because the clues add themselves together in my subconscious."

"And?" Jake prompted, his eyebrows raised humorously.

"I don't know what Damien calls this, but I think it's part of a quantum/not-quantum computer, a hybrid system for running navigation software with encryption that can't be cracked. That's what the quantum part does. Because of the observer effect and the Schrodinger's Cat whatsis. The minute someone tries to hack the encryption—observing it, you could say—the 1's and 0's stop being an indefinite quantum blur. Suddenly they're 1's *or* 0's,

242

which screws up the data string that's being spied on, making it useless to the spy and probably triggering a warning."

She looked at Damien, who rubbed his jaw in bemusement. "That's the general idea. I'm working on making the quantum side do extra calculations, but that's not germane to this."

"It's for missiles," Jake guessed. "And drones. So enemy agents can't hijack them."

"People can still be hacked," Damien said. "But not the program. My question is how did you come up with the substitutions you introduced? They almost would have worked."

Mia could only shrug. "They're probably bits and pieces of things I read in magazines or saw on science shows. I tried to tell my subconscious what I needed and prayed it would deliver."

"Why would you do that?" Damien asked softly. "Raeburn was threatening you. You knew he was serious. Why not give him what he asked?"

"Because he couldn't be trusted with something that important. And because it seemed like he'd kill me once he got it anyway. I figured trying to fool him was worth a shot."

She'd have thought this was obvious, but Damien shook his head. "You say that as if anyone would have done the same, as if anyone but you would have had the strength of mind."

"I knew Jake and Curtis would come for me. It was only you showing up that was a surprise."

Damien laughed and she wondered if she shouldn't have added the last bit.

"I surprised myself," he said. "Though maybe I shouldn't have. Part of me must have known you were worth enduring Sawyer's mockery of my combat skills."

"You did all right," Jake said. "And if it makes you feel better, he covets your spy drone."

Damien rubbed the lines his grin formed around his mouth. "It's ridiculous how much I love the pair of you right now."

Mia's heart thumped at that. "If I say *I love you* back, will you assume I've gone bonkers?"

Jake's long fingers caressed her nape. "I thought we established you being in love with me safeguards your sanity."

"You think you're being cute," Damien said. "But I'll thank you not to let her fall out of it."

"That's the plan," Jake agreed. "At least if it's up to me."

Damien hesitated a moment before continuing. "Zoe

Raeburn seems to be rational. I saw her in the course of trying to hammer out a deal with Uncle Sam. Maybe you were right about why I've been afraid to allow people close to me." He shifted his gaze to Mia. "I want to change that. I want to let you in."

Mia went to him and took his hands. She was a bit dismayed by his humility. "You're not a beggar. We're all afraid to trust sometimes. While I'd really like you to let us in, please don't forget Jake and I fell in love with you as you are, eccentricities and all."

"Exactly," Jake said. "Make changes if they feel right to you. We love the weirdo you already."

For once, Mia had been the diplomatic one. Damien smiled anyway, bringing her left knuckles and then her right to his mouth to kiss.

His eyes took on a heat that made her insides melt.

"If I'm not a beggar," he said, his voice deeper than before. "Perhaps Jake would be kind enough to remove your adorable mini-dress. It's been a long time since I was inside a woman. I'm really looking forward to changing that with you."

Mia shivered and went wet.

"That would be my pleasure," Jake responded.

A moment later, he was a tall heat behind her, his dexterous fingers sliding the dress's zipper down. She was very glad she had on nice underwear. Damien's slow smile when she stood in nothing but the electric blue bra and panties was wonderfully wolfish.

He was still sitting on the bed. With quick absentminded motions, he rolled up the plan and stowed it in the drawer again. Despite the copy being flawed—and the fun they were about to have—Mia absolutely *knew* Jake was planning to move the schematic to a more secure location at the first opportunity.

Because she trusted him to take care of it, she let her worry float away.

Damien leaned forward to kiss her navel, his fingers skating over the slippery satin that stretched across her rear. The whispery touch was exciting. Her pussy heated more, her arousal running out to dampen the panel. Damien slid both thumbs forward, feathering their pads up and down the tip of her clitoris where the cloth covered it. Every nerve inside her clit shot sparks. When she gushed again, he rubbed his face across her pubis and let out a growling noise.

"This is my favorite perfume in the world," he said.

That was pleasant to feel and hear, but a second later, Mia twitched. Jake had just worked the back of her bra free. He drew the garment off her arms and stepped right up to her.

He replaced the silky cups' support with his hard warm hands. The situation was too delicious. As Jake squeezed her breasts and pulled out her nipples, Mia squirmed between the men's caresses.

"That gets you, doesn't it?" Jake murmured in her ear. "Both of us hard up and touching you."

He *was* hard up. The ridge of his big erection nudged her back unmistakably.

Damien stood without warning, increasing her sense of being sandwiched between powerful male bodies. Needing to steady herself, she set her hands on his ribs. His dress shirt was warm and smooth, and she couldn't resist rubbing it. Damien tipped her face up toward him. As if she were precious, his touch traced her jaw and throat. His hazel gaze seemed to bore into hers.

"We could take you together," he said softly. "Me in front. Jake behind. He'd make you enjoy it. He certainly made me."

Tropical heat flashed through her. Jake's hands tightened on her breasts, so she guessed he liked the idea too.

"That's what you want?" she asked breathlessly.

Damien's eyes crinkled. "It's what I've been fantasizing about ever since he did it to me."

That robbed her of the power to speak. Damien's grin intensified. He pulled her dampened panties down her legs.

She stepped out of them and then held her breath as Damien began unbuttoning his shirt. Why was watching a man do that so damn sexy? Belt unbuckling was good too. And trouser unzipping. And toeing off fancy loafers before shucking the aforementioned.

He sat on the bed to pull off his socks. Ridiculously, she liked watching that as well. His legs were so nice with their solid muscles and dark gold hair. He stood up and skinned his briefs down them. His chest and shoulders invited her gaze to run over them, but she couldn't quite resist the distraction of his hard-on. It was yummy—thick and flushed and pulsing with eagerness. She hoped it and everything else she liked about his body would

245

soon be hers to appreciate.

Without realizing she'd done it, Mia curled both hands together and pressed them to her mouth.

Damien laughed at her reaction. "Thank you. That's very flattering. Jake?"

When she turned to glance at him, she got a start. Jake was naked too, his lean, ripped darkness a lovely contrast to Damien's light.

"Oh boy," she said. "If you two were any sexier, I'd have a heart attack."

"Please don't," Jake said. "We prefer you healthy and squirming."

"Especially squirming." Damien offered her his hand so she could climb onto the low bed. His confidence seemed to have returned full force. "Kneel in the center of the mattress with your thighs spread apart—unless Jake would like to recommend another arrangement?"

"That should work," Jake said agreeably. "Do you have supplies in this table's drawer?"

"I do," Damien said. "Feel free to make use of anything you find."

The men were teasing her with their politeness. "You must think you're both the boss of me now."

If her voice hadn't broken huskily, she'd have had a better chance of passing this off as a complaint. Jake smiled at her with hooded eyes. Somehow he managed to convey love *and* knowingness with the look.

"You're the boss of us," he said, "even when we're bossing you."

Her breath caught inside her throat. He meant this. They wanted to please her.

"It's true," Damien said, his eyes as warm and affectionate as Jake's. "You're the magic ingredient."

"You're a science guy," she protested. "You don't believe in magic."

"When I see you naked in my bed, I do."

Let go, she thought. *Let go and enjoy this.*

"I love you," she said. "I want to give myself to both of you."

"I believe we can arrange than," Jake said.

He swung onto the bed behind her. His palms molded to her

shoulders and then dragged down her arms. He whispered kisses up her nape, nuzzling her hair aside. Nerves tingled everywhere his lips and fingers brushed.

Finally, he slid his hands to hers. "I'm going to hold you for Damien while he slides into you."

Mia's lashes had drifted closed. When she lifted them, the spellbound expression on Damien's face told her something she'd already suspected.

He was always going to like watching.

She smiled and held out her arm to him.

He shook himself from his daze and moved onto the bed in front of her. "Sorry. You two make quite the picture."

Mia skimmed her hands up his muscular chest. "No need to apologize. Jake and I get off on you playing voyeur."

Damien took her face in his hands and kissed her. Being kissed was different from kissing him. He let out his hunger slowly, deepening the kiss, hardening it, gradually catching her against him with his arms. Jake shifted closer too, his hands sliding up and down the places Damien left bare. When Damien broke free of kissing her to kiss Jake, the ache inside her tightened impossibly.

The men's cocks pressed her naked body, hot and urgent and just short of grinding her. Damien wasn't holding back. The sound of the men kissing was very intimate, but she couldn't feel overlooked. She was too intertwined in what was happening. Their strength seemed to buffet her, their greater heat and weight causing her to feel simultaneously thrilled and safe. As Jake's body jostled her from behind, his hand found and cupped her mound. He slid one finger between her folds and into her pussy, using his thumb to polish her swollen clit.

Considering they'd spent the last two weeks having lots of sex, he was expert at fondling her. Sharp sensations shot deep inside her. She couldn't hold back a groan. Damien switched to kissing her for a last long probe.

"Pass me a condom," he gasped as he ended it.

Jake handed him a packet he'd already torn open. While Damien cursed and struggled to cover his throbbing length, Mia kneaded his nice firm thighs with all her fingers.

"That's not making this easier," Damien pointed out.

"I can't not touch you," she justified, her fingers trailing upward to his tight testicles.

As her touch made contact with the delicate skin, he sucked in a breath. Jake released her pussy.

"She's wet as hell," Jake said, which brought a stinging blush to her cheeks. "That badass cock of yours should have no trouble entering."

Damien smiled. He was covered at last, despite her unhelpful help, so his fingers moved to confirm Jake's claim. They stroked her slick folds apart before smoothing around her hips to take hold of her bottom. A shift of his knees and a hitch of her weight upward brought the tip of his apparently badass cock to the precise target they all wanted him to hit.

Damien's hazel eyes locked on hers like a laser beam.

She thought he'd speak, but he just pressed forward. His thigh muscles bunched as his pulsing thickness forged into her, spreading her creaming walls inch by inch. God, he felt good going in. Her neck arched back, the grip she had on him slipping. Jake braced her from behind, steadying her for the long intrusion. She couldn't fall. Her body was caught between two opposing walls.

Damien's grip on her ass tightened. He'd reached his limit inside of her.

"God," he breathed. "I almost forgot what that was like."

When Mia kissed his shoulder, she couldn't resist mouthing it. The muscles in his back rolled as her hands roved its hot contours. Damien's skin shivered like a horse, his pelvis pressing inward a fraction more.

"Please keep doing that," he said. "That feels incredible."

She wasn't about to stop, not even when she felt Jake's generously lubed middle finger slide into her rear passage. Her throat made a noise she didn't expect it to. Jake was rubbing her. Nerves she hadn't known could feel sexy buzzed with waves of hot pleasure. Jake worked in a second finger and she couldn't help gasping. The pressure felt amazing—and not at all painful. Wasn't this supposed to be difficult? But maybe Jake *was* unusually skillful.

"Good?" he asked, his lips against the opposite ear from Damien.

"Yes," she said unsteadily. She was experiencing so many pleasurable sensations her body couldn't to decide which direction to squirm in.

"Good," Jake said in a different, approving tone. He pulled

his fingers free. She heard lube squirt and then his palms rubbing it over his condom.

Damien also heard Jake preparing and the sound spurred him to action. Her excitement went ballistic as he pulled her cheeks apart for the other man. Jake's covered cock nudged her, causing his breathing to turn ragged. With the men to either side of her, they were panting in stereo.

"Don't start thrusting yet," Jake instructed Damien. "I want to make sure she can take both of us."

Damien seemed to like this prospect as much as her. His cock twitched vigorously inside her.

"Do it," she burst out. "I'm going to explode."

"Right," Jake said. "Doing it."

He sounded like he was about to laugh. Since he kept his promise, she couldn't mind. His hands massaged her hips, holding her for the gentle surges that got him in her by increments. The pressure was strange but not uncomfortable. She liked the sense that she was being claimed twice over by men she cared deeply for. When Jake was finally right up against her, something clicked in her hindbrain. Her body went warm all over and her breath rushed out. Her arousal remained coiled inside her, longing to be satisfied, but suddenly every other muscle she had relaxed. It was an extraordinary feeling. Her cheek fell forward to Damien's shoulder, her arms loosening on his back.

"I wondered what it would take to make that happen," Jake said.

"What would make what happen?" she slurred throatily.

Damien trailed the backs of his fingers along her side. "He means you've surrendered completely."

"Yes," Jake agreed. "I guess it takes two big men to master one little girl like you."

That was silly. She'd already given her heart to them. She smiled and dragged her lips across Damien's skin.

"Don't care," she said. "Keep making love to me."

Jake had his own directions. "Now we alternate," he said to Damien. "One of us going into her at a time. Slow and easy is the trick."

It shouldn't have given her a charge to know he'd done this before. It did, though, and so did the moment both men began moving. One throbbing cock pushed in while the other was pulling out. Her body rolled with enjoyment, her spine as flexible as taffy. Her pleasure was sweeter than any candy. She moaned with it, her hold on Damien tightening.

"Stay relaxed," Jake warned.

"Am," she hummed, undulating into Damien's next thrust.

"Christ," he breathed, his fingernails digging in.

She loved the thought that this was hitting him extra hard because it had been so long for him. She was drunk with bliss and power. Jake and Damien's hands were all over her, their bodies pushing and receding. Men were such hard creatures, especially men like these.

"Oh yes," she moaned when Jake caught her clit between two fingers.

He rubbed the hood up and down like he was wanking it.

She came, the kick of ecstasy taking her by surprise. Jake mouthed the crook of her neck as Damien pushed her breast up to suck its tip. She went over harder, her involuntary spasms squeezing her around the men.

Neither could miss this reaction. Damien cursed at the clutch of her pussy around his shaft. He pushed in a little harder, his cock thicker than before.

"Shit," he breathed, obviously trying to rein in his urge to thrust more forcefully.

"Go," Jake said, his own voice harsh with excitement. "I'll hold back."

He held himself just inside her, the flare of his pulsing crown stretching her where her clustered nerves felt it most. Damien went in more strongly and made a longing sound.

"Mia," he groaned.

"Yes," she urged, and he let his lust off its leash.

She held him as—finally—he thrust unreservedly up and into her. Her left hand tangled in his hair while her other roamed his back greedily. He was so damn *built*. She wished she had ten hands to praise his body, but thankfully she had Jake. He was touching Damien as well: his waist, his ass, urging him to do what he'd been craving so badly for so long.

This drove Damien even wilder. He cried out incoherently, his pumping so ardent Mia's need rose in sympathy. She was going to come again. She gasped, and tensed, and then Jake slid slowly into her again.

Both men were in her then, both filling her impossibly.

The extra pressure was too much for Damien. Mia felt his cock jerk and pulse a second before her orgasm swallowed her like a tidal wave.

Jake grunted, his teeth suddenly clamping her shoulder. The heat in her ass increased, and she knew he'd shot off too.

Damien was the first to regain a bit of breath. He used it to pant out a phrase that would have made a nun swat him. The massive climax had taken them all to church.

"Amen," Jake responded wholeheartedly.

◆

Once their legs were steady enough to carry them, they cleaned up in Damien's shower. Mia needed girl-type privacy, so she was the last to return to the sleeping area. Both men were in bed already. Jake appeared very much at home. He lay back on a couple pillows with his hands stacked behind his head, his leanly muscled body on display. Damien faced him on his side. Mia thought she might have interrupted a conversation.

It pleased her that the men were comfortable with each other . . . and that they'd left space for her between them. Damien patted the spot invitingly.

"Fine," she said. "But no sprawling all over me with your big man limbs. What if I need to turn over?"

"We'll let you," Damien said. "I believe Jake and I are both light sleepers."

"You, on the other hand," Jake teased, "could sleep through an earthquake."

Mia clambered into her appointed space where her own stack of pillows awaited. Apparently, Damien had a large supply. They were nice and firm, and the smooth white sheets felt gorgeous on her arms and legs. Would she and Jake be sleeping over often? Would Damien let them add a chair or two? Maybe they'd get used to his place the way it was.

The questions tumbled through her head as she found a comfortable hollow for her cheek on Damien's shoulder. He stroked her hair as Jake rolled toward her in a loose spoon. Mia tugged some more of the sheet up her. She sighed with pleasure as Damien ordered the bedside lamp to shut off.

"All right?" he asked.

"Perfect," she assured him. Her hand rested on his chest, over his slowly beating heart. Damien covered it with his palm.

After a moment, he cleared his throat. "I want to say I understand why you prefer working for Curtis. He's obviously a good friend to both of you."

Mia's eyes opened. Because that didn't seem quite enough attention to give his statement, she wriggled onto her elbow and looked at him. "Curtis *is* a good friend. And working at Discreet can be interesting."

"Yes. Both of you were overqualified for the duties I assigned you."

"Damien," Jake said from behind her. "When people confess they love you that generally means they're interested in spending time with you. You don't have to employ us too."

"I know that." The sheets rustled as Damien moved. "We could draw up another contract."

"No," Jake said.

"No?" Mia and Damien responded almost in unison.

"You're trying to control everything," Jake explained patiently. "To nail it down and get a guarantee. I'm not saying we can't play games like we did when we had a contract. I'm saying I think we need to be regular for a while. To negotiate like ordinary people do."

"So . . . no pre-set rules," Damien said.

"We could let them develop organically, as we get to know each other more."

Damien thought about this before nodding in acceptance. Since he wasn't so tense anymore, Mia lay down again. Jake rubbed the bend of her waist reassuringly. Suddenly, she found herself grinning. Jake had handled that really well. Maybe he was a magic ingredient too. Maybe they all were.

"You said 'organically,'" she teased. "You're like a relationship guru."

"Sheesh," Jake said. "You two aren't the only ones who know words."

"Certainly not," Damien agreed. Mia felt his heart rate pick up slightly beneath her hand. She knew he was about to broach a topic he cared about. "Perhaps I should mention the floor beneath this one is empty. It *could* be arranged to better suit your tastes. If it isn't premature to bring that up."

Jake shifted an inch closer behind her. "That's a reasonable thing to consider, going forward."

Mia snickered. "'Going forward.' Now you sound like him."

She circled Damien's pectoral with two fingertips. "That's a very nice offer. We might need a little time to think about it, but I suspect we'll be tempted."

"We will," Jake said. "And thank you."

"I *want* you around," Damien said. "I missed that even when I was angry."

"Me too," Mia said.

"All right," Jake sighed. "Me three."

His arm reached across her to stroke Damien's chest. He touched him differently than she did—more firmly, using his thumb to trace Damien's breastbone. The stroke was kind. She suspected it was meant to soothe Damien's worries in ways his words might not have. Jake was willing to commit, but he preferred actions over promises.

His ease fascinated her. Suddenly, she wanted to learn everything Jake knew about pleasing men. He'd like training her, she thought. As an added bonus, Damien probably wouldn't mind being her teaching tool.

Whatever Damien was thinking amused him too. She saw him smile even in the dark. Possibly not realizing what he was stirring up in his companions, Jake yawned and relaxed some more.

I could sleep, Mia thought. *At least for a while.*

Damien wasn't as ready to drop off. He rubbed Jake's hand and then her own. "Do you really think we have a chance to work? You know, as a threesome."

"I hope so," Mia said. "I like this a lot. Being with both of you makes me . . ."

"Happy?" Damien suggested as if he were himself.

"Yes. I'm brimming over with happy." Warm right down to her toes, she gently elbowed the sleepy man behind her. "What do your instincts tell you about our chances?"

"Mm. My instincts say the world is brighter with the pair of you in it—and that I'm damn lucky to have fallen in with you. Also, these are excellent pillows. I think I need some for my place. Just in case we have sleepovers there."

"And our chances?" Mia prompted, amused by his joking tone.

"Oh those." She didn't need a light to imagine Jake smirking. "Fortunately, my gut says our chances are excellent."

#

ABOUT THE AUTHOR

EMMA Holly is the award winning, *USA Today* bestselling author of more than thirty romantic books, featuring shapeshifters, demons, faeries and just plain extraordinary human folks. She loves the hot stuff, both to read and to write!

If you'd like to discover what else she's written, please visit her website at http://www.emmaholly.com.

Emma runs monthly contests and sends out newsletters that often include coupons for ebooks. To receive them, go to her contest page.

Thanks so much for reading this book. If you enjoyed it, please consider leaving a review. That kind of support is very helpful!

the Billionaire Bad Boys Club

USA Today bestseller

EMMA HOLLY

SELF-made billionaires Zane and Trey have been a club of two since they were eighteen. They've done everything together: play football, fall in love, even get smacked around by their dads. The only thing they haven't tried is seducing the same woman. When they set their sights on sexy chef Rebecca, these bad boys just might have met their match!

"This book is a mesmerizing, beautiful and oh-my-gods-hot work of art!"—**BittenByLove** 5-hearts review

available in ebook and print

A collection of three full-length paranormal romances: *Hidden Talents, Hidden Depths* and *Hidden Crimes*. Whether they involve irresistible werewolf cops, sexy wereseal kings or sassy firefighting tigresses, these adventures turn up the heat!

"The perfect package of supes, romance, mystery and HEA!"—
Paperback Dolls on *Hidden Talents*

"You will fall head over heels [with] the amazingly sensuous and intensely graphic world . . . One of the best erotic romances I have ever read."—**BittenByLove** on *Hidden Depths*

"If you are looking for suspense, passion and a touch of the paranormal, don't look any farther than *Hidden Crimes*."—
Joyfully Reviewed

available in ebook and print

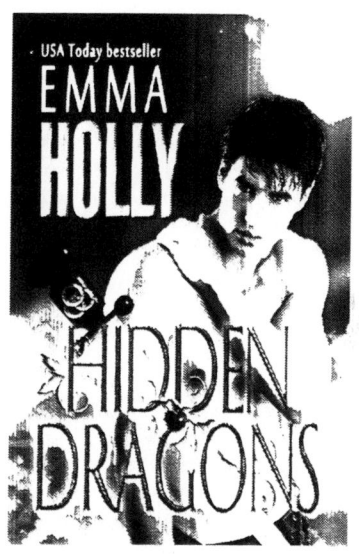

DO you believe in dragons? Werewolf cop Rick Lupone would say no . . . until a dying faerie tells him the fate of his city depends on him. If he can't protect a mysterious woman in peril, everything may be lost. The only discovery more shocking is that the woman he's meant to save is his high school crush, Cass Maycee.

Half fae Cass didn't earn her Snow White nickname by chance. All her life, her refusal to abuse fae glamour kept men like Rick at arm's length. Now something new is waking up inside her, a secret heritage her pureblood father kept her in the dark about. Letting it out might kill her, but keeping it hidden is no longer an option. The dragons' ancient enemies are moving. If they find the prize before Rick and Cass, the supe-friendly city of Resurrection just might go up in flames.

"[*Hidden Dragons*] kept me completely enthralled . . . sexy & erotic"—**Platinum Reviews**

available in ebook and print

USA Today bestseller
EMMA
HOLLY

"I have fallen in love with Emma Holly's *Hidden* series and all its characters."
Joyfully Reviewed

HIDDEN
PASSIONS

SEXY fireman Chris Savoy has been closeted all his life. He's a weretiger in Resurrection, and no shifters are more macho than that city's. Due to a terrible tragedy in his past, Chris resigned himself to hiding what he is—a resolve that's threatened the night he lays eyes on cute gay werecop Tony Lupone.

Tony might be a wolf, but he wakes longings Chris finds difficult to deny. When a threat to the city throws these heroes together, not giving in seems impossible. Following their hearts, however, means risking everything . . .

"I've visited Emma Holly's magical fantasy city of Resurrection, New York, before and have enjoyed the other *Hidden* stories that take place there. They're all very imaginative and compelling, and absolutely scorching hot. *Hidden Passions* continues in that vein, with characters that are sympathetic and likeable, and storylines that keep me returning for more."—joysann, **Publisher's Weekly Blog**

available in ebook and print

ELYSE Solomon hasn't had it easy. She lost her dad and her husband under suspicious circumstances, and her relatives know more than they're admitting about both deaths. Then a mysterious stranger with a briefcase full of cash moves into the basement of her New York brownstone. Arcadius is gorgeous, exquisitely polite, and sophisticated, but nothing about him adds up—that is, until Elyse discovers her sexy tenant is a genie desperate to save his people from a deadly curse. With so much heartache behind her, can Elyse find the courage to help the man who might be her true soul mate?

"FANTASTIC! [T]his may be the best thing she has written to date . . . the first in an epic tale of romantic fantasy."—**In My Humble Opinion** blogspot.com

"One of my absolute favorite authors! . . . Mystery with some awesome romance!!! And an ending that has you begging for more!"
—**Chelle's Book Report**

available in ebook and print

What if the man you loved had a double?

THAT'S the challenge Elyse faces when a flying carpet lands her and her new djinn lover in the glorious city he calls home. Cade's people need help recovering from a curse, but this isn't the only problem they'll have to fix. Cade's trip to Elyse's world created a duplicate of himself, a not-quite carbon copy who firmly believes *he's* Cade's superior.

Arcadius has no patience for modern women, much less for males foolish enough to love them. If only Elyse's aid weren't necessary to catch a sorcerer who's abducting his city's youth! Being in her company makes him too aware of her attractions.

Elyse expects "Commander" Arcadius to be easy to resist. He's arrogant and a chauvinist—and he doesn't think much of her. Then, bit-by-bit, she sees past his prickly exterior. Arcadius is who Cade used to be before they met. If she fell for one man, there's no guarantee she won't fall for the other . . .

"Emma Holly transports you into a fantastic world of magic, mystery, and erotic delights . . . absolutely wonderful." —D. Antonio, **In My Humble Opinion**

available in ebook and print

Printed in Great Britain
by Amazon.co.uk, Ltd.,
Marston Gate.